D1068981

DROWNING IN HONEY

KATE HATFIELD

DROWNING IN HONEY

ST. MARTIN'S PRESS ❧ NEW YORK

A THOMAS DUNNE BOOK.
An imprint of St. Martin's Press.

Library of Congress Cataloging-in-Publication Data

Hatfield, Kate.
    Drowning in honey / by Kate Hatfield.
        p.   cm.
    "A Thomas Dunne book."
    ISBN 0-312-14590-X
    I. Title.
PR6058.A824D76   1996
823'.914—dc20   96-27969
                                        CIP

First published in Great Britain by Transworld Publishers Ltd

First U.S. Edition: December 1996

10 9 8 7 6 5 4 3 2 1

For my godsons,
Edmund, Peter and Felix

Author's Note

Among the many people who gave me advice and information while I was writing this novel, I should particularly like to thank Dr Estela Welldon of the Portman Clinic.

I should also like to thank Mr James Turner, who kindly read through the court scenes and saved me from making several errors in the rules of evidence and court procedure. Any that remain are there because of the needs of fiction and not because he did not point them out.

DROWNING IN HONEY

Prologue

The lifts were still out of order when Michael got home, and he climbed the graffiti-disfigured concrete stairs up to the twelfth floor, trying to ignore the revolting, ammoniac smell of stale urine from the pools at each turn of the stairs. He did his best to pretend that the ascent was an acting exercise. Knowing that he still moved well, he made himself breathe carefully and take the steps slowly enough to reach his own front door with his heart and lungs steady.

As he put his key in the lock, he felt his neck tighten and his hands began to sweat. He turned the key and pushed the door open.

'And what the hell have you been doing?' his wife demanded before he had even crossed the threshold into the cramped hall. She was standing in the living room doorway, dressed to go out. Her makeup was bold, almost as stagey as it had been in the old days when she still thought of herself as an actress, and her dark hair was teased out into a huge mass that made her brightly coloured face look tiny. She was wearing gilt earrings that were far too long for her neck. He hated the vulgarity of it all.

'I bloody told you I had to go out at seven.'

'I was working on the audition stuff,' Michael said, no longer looking at her. 'I'm here now. Where are the children?'

'In bed for Christ's sake! Where d'you think?'

'Have they eaten?'

'What's that got to do with you?'

Michael turned away and pulled off his wet jacket. He took it into the bathroom and draped it carefully over the hot-water tank. That felt tepid, which at least suggested that Penelope had given the kids baths for once. Michael leaned forward until his forehead lay on the barely warm pipe that led out of the top of the ill-lagged copper cylinder.

'I'm off,' Penelope said from the narrow hall. Michael emerged from the bathroom. He said nothing, just nodded. She glared at him and then shrugged and walked out.

When she had gone, banging the door loudly enough to wake the children, Michael unlaced his wet shoes and picked a newspaper out of the overflowing wastepaper basket, planning to crumple it up and stick it in the toes to keep their shape as the leather dried. He had to shake the paper hard to get rid of the cigarette butts, orange peel and crumbs that clung to it. When his shoes were as well protected as he could make them, he took them to the airing cupboard.

Back in the living room, he looked at the dirt and untidiness in disgust, shrugged and tiptoed to the door of the little second bedroom, where his children slept. The boys in their bunks were fast asleep, the nightlight flickering on their calm faces. Relieved, Michael turned to the single bed that stood against the other wall.

'Hello,' he said quietly to his eight-year-old daughter, feeling adequate for the first time that evening.

'Hello, Daddy,' whispered Marianna, brushing her fair hair off her small face and smiling at him. The whites of her eyes gleamed in the half light. 'Has she gone?'

'Yes.'

She held out her arms. As the duvet fell away from her shoulders he saw that she was wearing her old Magic

Roundabout pyjamas. They were her favourites, so well worn that in places the material was nearly transparent. He picked her out of her bed, wrapped her torn red dressing gown round her shoulders, bent down for the book that had dropped to the floor and carried her out into the living room.

There she wriggled out of his arms, buttoned up her dressing gown and set about tidying the room. As she carefully carried the big round overflowing ashtray into the kitchen he almost wept. Shame, pity and exasperation curdled in his mind, making him even queasier than usual.

'Don't worry, Daddy,' she said softly, almost maternally, as she came back. 'We'll get it tidy in no time. Come on, you do the mugs and plates and I'll plump the cushions.'

Obediently he went round the room collecting all the dirty crockery and crisp packets. The narrow galley kitchen was in an even worse state than the living room, but he could not tackle it then. He scrubbed out two mugs, having at them with a bleach-soaked scourer until they were white again, rinsed them scrupulously and made coffee in one, hot blackcurrant in the other.

When he went back into the living room, Marianna was curled up at one end of the sofa. She patted the space beside her. Michael looked around the room. It was no cleaner, but it was a great deal tidier. Sighing, he sat down beside her and rubbed her small, fair head.

'How are you, old girl?'

'I'm all right. Did you learn your part?'

'Yes, I know it now.'

'Good. D'you want me to test you? I can read really well now. I could do it.'

'I know you could, Marianna,' he said, feeling tears threatening him again, 'but I don't want to say it so often that I get stale.'

'No,' she said seriously. 'I hadn't thought of that. You'll need to be fresh tomorrow. I'm sure you'll get it. I'm sure you will.'

'Are you? That's nice. Now, where's your book?'

'It's here, but you look much too tired to read now. Shall I make you some supper? I can cook toasted cheese or scrabbled eggs.'

Smiling at her touching mishearing of 'scrambled', he shook his head.

'I'll have something later. Where did we get to in *The Secret Garden*?'

'Ben Weatherstaff's just told Miss Mary about the robin. He's quite a nice man really, isn't he?'

'Yes, he is. Drink your Ribena before it gets cold.'

'Even though he seems so cross all the time.'

'That's right. And he likes her, you see. It can sometimes be quite difficult to understand that cross people are very nice inside,' said Michael, glad of the opportunity to give his daughter a minute amount of security and then immediately guilty at the thought that it was probably false.

'Don't frown, Daddy,' she said gently. 'You'll give yourself lines and that will never do. It's page twenty-four.'

'OK,' he said, obedient once more. He looked at her over the top of the book as he spoke each sentence, trying to read as well as Martin Jarvis, wondering whether he might be able to get work on radio or possibly even reading for children's audiotapes. He was not sure his agent had ever tried either of those. He must ask. With part of his mind on his pathetic career, part on the voices and characters of the people he was reading about, Michael used the rest to think about his daughter.

Penelope must have curbed her temper and her vicious tongue that evening, for Marianna was relatively calm.

All too often when he came home she was white and trembling. If there were any way he could have protected her, he would have done it. He loved her beyond expression and he longed for her to be happy and safe. In his worst moments he thought that neither of them could ever hope for that.

'What's the matter, Daddy? You've stopped reading.'

'Sorry. I was just thinking about Ben Weatherstaff,' he said, lying as he tried to fend off the thought of what would happen if he failed to get the part. He had had no work for the whole year and it was already the 4th of December. There would be no money for Christmas presents, and Penelope would make the most of that.

Marianna was looking at him with an odd expression on her face. He made himself smile and saw her features relax. That made it possible to ignore his manifold worries and start reading again.

Half an hour later he put her back to bed and at her request sat on the floor beside her while she went to sleep. When he heard her breathing slow and deepen, he pushed himself up off the floor. Looking at her once more before he left her bedside, he saw that her eyes were opening again. She brushed the hair back from her face with both hands.

'What is it?' he asked quietly so as not to wake the boys. 'Did you have a bad dream? Are you afraid?'

'No, I'm never frightened by the bees.'

'What?' he said, completely at a loss.

Marianna rolled her head sideways on the pillow and smiled at him. 'The bee lady says they're not like wasps. Bees only sting people who threaten their hives.'

'Really?'

'Yes. Didn't you know that, Daddy? Bees die when they sting people so they only do it if they have to. Their stings are barbed like arrows, and so they get stuck. Bees can't just take their stings out; they have to tear their whole body away from the sting and so they die. The bee lady said so. Isn't it sad?'

He stroked the hair away from her forehead and bent to kiss it.

'You've been dreaming, Marianna. It's all right. There are no bees here and no ladies either. You go on back to sleep.'

'The bee lady's nice.'

'Is she? I'm glad of that. Shut your eyes again.'

'You won't go, will you?'

'No. I won't go. Don't worry about that. I'll always be here.'

He waited until she fell asleep again and then forced himself back into the horrible kitchen. Deciding that he could not face the scene Penelope would make if he did any cleaning, he averted his eyes from the mess, opened a tin of Whiskas for the two cats, who were whining, washed his hands and made himself a cheese sandwich.

At ten he turned on the black-and-white television to watch an episode of a detective series made by the director for whom he was to audition the next day. He carefully analysed the actors' performances so that he could learn about any idiosyncratic preferences the director might have. When it was over Michael realized that he had no idea what had actually happened to the detective, still less whether he himself had enjoyed the show.

He washed up his plate, had a tepid bath, ironed his shirt for the next day, hung it up where the cats could not get at it and took a quick-acting sleeping pill so that he could at least get some rest before his wife's return.

She reached the flat at half past one and woke him ten minutes later, shoving at his shoulder as she got into bed. He could smell the smoke in her hair and the drink on her breath. Pretending he had not woken, he pushed his breathing lower and forced it into regularity. She was not fooled.

'Come on, Michael, for God's sake! Stop faking. You're as bad as a frigid woman who can't come and is too stupid to admit it. You're pathetic.'

'I'm tired, Penelope,' he said as calmly as possible. 'And I've an important audition tomorrow. If I get the part it'll make life a lot less hellish for all of us. Let me sleep.'

'You're always tired. You're useless, you know, utterly useless. God knows why I didn't see it till it was too bloody late.'

Michael lay back on his pillows, his eyes open as he knew she required, and his mind entirely detached. He heard but did not absorb the words she used to describe him, his failings, her disillusion and her anger. There was no need to listen, after all; he knew all the words. When she paused, he rolled over on to his side, away from her and pulled his pillow round his head. She kicked him, but he was not certain that it was deliberate. Their bed was so mean, barely four foot wide, that it was possible she had just been turning over.

'For Christ's sake, don't bloody ignore me when I'm talking to you,' she shouted, kicking him again and pulling the pillow away from his head.

So it was deliberate, he thought, but he did not move.

'Are you so pathetic you can't even face me now?'

'You'll wake the children.'

'I don't give a fuck whether I wake them or not. They haven't a hope anyway, poor little beggars, with such a pathetic creep for a father. You're a failure, Michael, as a man, as an actor, as a father . . .'

No, I'm not, he said to himself. I'm a good father at least. It's you who cause all the trouble and make Marianna so bloody miserable.

'If you had any guts at all we wouldn't be in this mess.'

Michael felt her muscles tensing for another kick and lay waiting for it. She was yelling at him by then, but he stopped his ears to the sound. He was damned if he was going to give her the satisfaction of a reaction. As he felt her sharp toenails grind into the soft skin at the back of his knee, he wondered how much more he was going to be able to take.

Chapter 1

'Oh yes it is,' said the middle-aged woman in the red coat. 'It's love does that to people. You can tell with even very young children who've always been loved. They get that shiny look and never lose it. Ever.'

Her bored husband shifted the blue overnight cases to a more comfortable position against his legs and sighed, thinking: I wouldn't mind having a go; she looks pretty succulent to me.

They had seen her emerging from the untidy crowd of arrivals as they moved towards their boarding gate. Her hair was blonde and thick, plaited from high on her head to just below the base of her neck. She was dressed unfashionably but comfortably in loose black trousers and polo-necked sweater under an open jacket of honey-coloured suede.

Her well-defined face might have looked austere, even forbidding, if it had not been for the warmth of her grey eyes under the thick fringe. With her square shoulders and her slenderness, she looked like an athlete, and she moved like one too. She was tall and would have stood out in any crowd, but in the mixture of exhausted, irritated, nervous, impatient people in the airport she was as dominant as a lighthouse in a storm.

Enjoying the springiness of the rubber conveyor belt beneath her feet, Melissa Wraxall moved quickly along the glass-walled corridor, oblivious of the attention she was attracting. She was on her way home after a successful week in Paris and she was happy.

The moving walkway ended and she strode across the polished floor to the beginning of the next one, offering to help a tired-looking woman struggling with cumbersome nappy bags and collapsing toys as she tried to persuade two exuberant toddlers to hold her skirts instead of running off to explore more interesting possibilities. Together the two women managed not to lose either child before they reached the baggage hall. There Melissa found the woman a trolley and they parted with friendly smiles.

Her own battered, squashy, brown leather luggage appeared on the rollers of the carousel just as she reached it, which seemed a good omen for her return to everyday life, and she grabbed the handle as it jerked past her. The bag was not heavy. Over the six years since she had set up her own small company, she had learned how to husband her energy for the things that mattered. She set off through the EC customs channel to the outside world and her car.

The pleasure of her week alone among strangers in a beautiful place was still with her, and she was determined not to let it drain away too soon. She had some anxieties, but there seemed no point even thinking about them until there was something she could usefully do. The whole of February had been horribly cold, and rather difficult, but the winter was virtually over and everything would get better once the days grew longer and warmer. It always did.

Even the heavy rain did not spoil her mood. The car park smelled of wet tarmac and petrol, but the car did not let her down, starting as soon as she turned the key. Before she had been on the motorway twenty minutes the rain stopped, and she drove westwards into the sun, enjoying the dramatic black clouds almost as much as the lavishness of light in the gaps.

Blue signs announcing the junctions seemed to follow

each other more quickly than usual and Melissa was wryly amused to notice that her foot was resting much more lightly than usual on the accelerator. She pressed down more firmly, knowing that she could not give way to such childishness for long. The turning for Bath brought her cloud of anxiety closer and even wry amusement seemed preferable as it descended, shutting out the light of pleasure that she had brought back from Paris.

She began to feel peculiar, uncomfortable and slightly detached from the world, as the car started to roll down the steep hill outside the city. Telling herself that the odd feeling and slight dazzle in her eyes came from nothing more than staring into the sun as she drove, Melissa changed gear and felt the engine holding back as the car ground steeply downwards through Swainswick.

It was not until the first single spot of light in her right eye began to spread into a constantly flickering curved line of pennant shapes that she admitted the existence of the migraine. Even then she hoped that she might make it home before the worst symptoms took hold. But as she pulled up at a red traffic light near the sports ground, she knew that she would have to find a safe stopping place and wait.

At the next corner she turned on her right indicator, concentrating on the oncoming traffic. As soon as she was certain that there were no bicycles or motorcycles hidden in the dazzle, she turned right and stopped outside a tall house in which one of her friends had the garden flat.

Trying to ignore what was happening to her eyes, Melissa manoeuvred her car into the parking space. She forgot to lock the doors and stumbled across the wide pavement. With her balance going, she had to hold on to the railings as she climbed down the steps to the basement door and then it took a while before she could see where the bell was. Eventually she found and pressed it, closing her eyes as she leaned against the wall.

'Lissa!' said a worried-sounding voice.

Melissa opened her eyes and tried to focus on her friend.

'Hello, Cecily.'

'My god, how . . . ? What's the matter?'

'Nothing too awful. Just a migraine, but it's making me half-blind. Not safe to drive. Can I borrow your sofa till it goes off? Won't be too long.'

'Yes, of course, you can. You poor old thing. Come on in and lie down.'

Cecily Wells put an arm around her taller friend and urged her into the sitting room. Melissa let herself sink down on to the immense sofa, thought about moving one of the innumerable cushions, which was digging into her back, and heard Cecily say, 'Do you want anything?'

'Nothing. Won't be long. 'S only ever half an hour.'

'All right. I'll leave you to it, but shout if you want me.'

Cecily switched off all the lights as she left the room.

Feeling as though she might roll off the sofa at any moment, Melissa set her teeth and waited for the flashing lights in her eyes to stop. It would probably happen quite quickly. All she had to do was wait. But the waiting was horrible.

Forty minutes later she opened her eyes again, ran her tongue over her dry lips and found a handkerchief to wipe her forehead. When she swung her long legs over the edge of the sofa and sat up, she discovered that her balance was fine and she could see properly again. She looked at her surroundings in pleasure.

The room was typical of Cecily. Big, colourful and untidy, it was full of odd, interesting things. The huge dark-red velvet sofa was heaped with multi-coloured, multi-textured cushions from all over the world. Some, from Rajasthan, had little round mirrors sewn into the embroidery; others were covered with fine, if frayed, antique silk from Lyons. There was American patchwork, old English tapestry, brocade from China, and even some hand-printed black and red cotton she had been given by an artist friend.

A similarly eclectic mixture of pictures hung on the white walls, and Cecily's collection of oriental jars and vases was ranged in the big empty fireplace. There was a vibrant kilim on the polished wooden floor, and a Calder mobile she had inherited from an uncle hung from the ceiling halfway down the long room. Heaps of books teetered on every available surface as well as filling the shelves in recesses on either side of the chimney breast. Nothing matched, and everything had a story behind it. Cecily had told Melissa some of them, but there was plenty she still had to learn.

'Cecily?' she called.

'I'm in the kitchen. Are you OK?'

Melissa made her way out into a dark passage that led to the red-and-white kitchen, which in turn opened out into the garden. Cecily came to the doorway of the kitchen and held out her arms. Melissa hugged her.

'Thank you. That was a bit of a lifesaver.'

'Are you really all right now, sweetie?'

'Sure. Sorry to make so much fuss. You look wonderful.' Melissa pulled back so that she could look at the long, multi-coloured Bolivian tunic that Cecily was wearing over her black leggings.

'If I do, it's a miracle. I'm feeling fat and grubby and rather hating myself at the moment, actually.'

Although she was considerably plumper than Melissa and about four inches shorter, no-one else would have called Cecily fat and, apart from the red ink on her fingers and on the front of her long light-brown hair, she did not look at all dirty. In fact, thought Melissa, apart from the shadows under her hazel eyes and a hint of strain in them, she looked much as usual: not only attractive, and very sexy, but interesting as well.

Before Melissa could tell her so, Cecily said quickly, 'You probably need some tea. I'll put the kettle on. Is it very stuffy in here? I haven't been out today.' She turned away to open the french windows and shivered. 'No, perhaps not. Sorry about the fug. I really detest March. It seems so beastly treacherous, boiling one minute and then like this the next.'

'Do you?' said Melissa, wondering what was bothering Cecily. She seemed to be surprisingly ill-at-ease. 'I think I'm just so glad that spring is on the way at last that I don't really mind it.'

Cecily had retreated to the sink and was filling the kettle. 'Tea? Or would you rather have a drink? I've got some red wine open. It could count as really late lunch rather than early drinks time if you're bothered.'

'I'd better not.' Melissa looked at her watch. 'In fact I shouldn't really have tea either. I ought to get home. Martin's due back in about an hour and a half, and I'd like to deal with the post and talk to Bel before he gets home.'

Cecily looked over her shoulder for a moment, frowning, but all she said was, 'Haven't you been back yet?'

'No. The bloody migraine struck me down almost outside your door. You are an angel to have taken me in – and your sofa is about the most comfortable thing I've ever collapsed on to.'

'I'm glad,' said Cecily. She was busying herself with a teapot and a packet of China tea leaves. 'Do stay and have a cup with me. I'm sure you oughtn't to drive until you're certain everything's all right. The kettle won't be long. Could you bear to get the milk? I'm afraid it's still on the doorstep.'

Melissa went to collect the two pints from the front door. As she came back, she began to understand the source of Cecily's tension and said apologetically, 'I must have disturbed your writing. I'm sorry. I didn't think about it when I rang your bell. How's the book going?'

'Ugh!'

'Like that, is it?' Melissa sat down in one of the white painted basket chairs at the pine table and smiled as she settled into the familiar routine of listening to Cecily's troubles.

They had met nearly five years earlier at a concert during the Bath Festival and liked each other enough to make the effort to become friends. Since then each had become part of the necessary underpinning of the other's life.

'What's the problem?'

'It's gone sticky on me. I can't work out exactly why. It's probably just the stage I've got to. Usually when I'm about halfway through I start wondering why I ever wanted to be a writer in the first place. It's a mad, horrible job and just at the moment, I think I'd rather do anything else – absolutely anything else. Scrub floors even.'

Melissa smiled. It had been clear to her for some time that, depressing though Cecily found some stages of each book, there was no other work that would have satisfied her as well.

'No wonder you said you didn't like yourself much. Is it the plot or the characters giving you gip?'

Cecily sighed and ran her inky fingers through her hair again. 'I suppose it's the plot. I do find this business of planting clues tricky. And I get in such a muddle. If only one's detective were allowed a brilliant flash of intuition, it would make life so much easier.'

The kettle boiled and she filled the teapot.

'Can't you have that? Thanks,' said Melissa a moment later as Cecily handed her a tall bone-china mug of weak China tea. She added a splash of milk from one of the bottles on the table. 'I'm sure I read something

the other day that suggested most real murder investi-
gations turn on somebody's hunch or lucky guess, or just
a coincidence.'

'That may be fine for real life.' Cecily laughed and
looked much more like her usual self. 'But unfortunately
you can't take such liberties in fiction.'

'Pity. What's the book called?'

'At the moment, *Death Comes Quietly*. I don't know
if anyone's used it already. Probably. Someone usually
has nicked all my best titles before I've even thought
of them. I suppose I'll have to trawl through *Books in
Print* at the library to make sure.'

'God, you sound depressed.'

'I am a bit. Lissa?'

Melissa, who had just burned her mouth on the tea,
swallowed and looked up.

'Yes?'

'Oh, nothing.' Cecily laughed again, but she did not
sound particularly happy. 'As I say, I rather hate myself
at the moment.'

'It's probably just the book. I shouldn't worry about
it too much or you won't be able to write at all.' Melissa
cautiously drank a little more tea, waiting. Cecily said
nothing. Still trying to help, Melissa eventually said,
'Now I come to think of it, didn't you leave a message
on the answering machine just before I went to Paris?
I am sorry, Cecily, I forgot. My whole brain goes a
bit weird after these migraines. You wanted to tell me
something, didn't you?'

'Did I?' Cecily looked embarrassed and fiddled with
the lid of a terracotta pot of Provençal herbs that stood
at the end of the pine table. 'I don't remember that. I
expect I just wanted to moan about chapter thirteen,
which is unfair when you've got plenty of your own
problems.'

'No I haven't.'

24

'Lissa, this is one place where you don't have to pretend. You've told me enough to know that I . . . You ought to know that you can talk to me.'

Melissa smiled and drank some more tea. 'It's not really pretence,' she said at last. 'It's a way of keeping it under control. If I start talking about it all the time, it might take me over and sort of exaggerate itself. After all, it's a temporary problem, and minor in comparison with the things everyone else has to deal with.'

Cecily watched her friend as she spoke and then put the lid back on the pot of herbs with a decisive snap. 'I know you want me just to agree and ignore it all, but I can't. Lissa, I care about you too much. Don't you think that your body might be trying to tell you something? Don't you think these awful migraines are a signal that there's something really wrong?'

'No,' said Melissa, laughing. 'It's much more likely to be something in my diet. You know, oranges or something; or cheese. I had some on the aeroplane. I expect that's what did it. Don't look so upset, Cecily. The migraines are vile while they're on, but they hardly last any time at all and I've only ever had about six.'

'But they're getting more frequent, aren't they? Don't you think it might have something to do with Martin?'

'No.' Melissa heard the irritation in her voice and quickly smiled again. 'Sorry if that sounded sharp. It wasn't meant to. I should never have moaned about him to you in the first place. It was horribly disloyal of me.'

Cecily frowned and rubbed an itch in the corner of her right eye, smearing ink there too.

'I wish you'd let go a bit. It's quite safe. You know I care about him as well.'

'I know you do, but even so, I don't like airing our difficulties. Martin is being a bit tricky at the moment, and it's a blessed relief whenever he's out of the house playing squash or whatever else he does, but it'll only get better if I can be patient enough to ignore it. If I let myself whinge about it to you whenever we meet, I may not be able to keep quiet when I get back home. The worst thing in the world would be to start having at him as he has at me.'

'Are you sure?'

'Positive. We have been happy together and there's no reason why we can't be again, provided that I don't lose my temper and say things that I can never take back. I don't know what it is that's been eating him these last few months, but he'll get over it, if I can just hang on.'

'Is it really only months?' asked Cecily, getting up to refill their mugs.

Melissa sighed. 'It's only in the last few months that it's got really bad.'

'In what way bad?' Cecily asked with her back to Melissa.

'There's just been more of it all: more criticism of me, more bloody-mindedness, and more vituperation about my mother.'

'What?' Cecily turned as she spoke and brought the mugs back to the table. She looked surprised.

'Didn't I tell you that? It's the bit I find most difficult to understand. I know I see more of her than most women do of their mothers, but he never used to mind and he never used to say things like—' Melissa broke off and drank some tea.

Cecily watched her. 'What does he say about her?'

'Oh, silly things. I ought not to pay any attention, but it's been a bit like water on a stone recently, and it's begun to get me down. He thinks she's possessive, tyrannical, selfish; that it's she who makes me not want children; that sort of thing. Rubbish in fact. There's no-one more generous and sensible and kind than she is, and she'd love grandchildren if I could see my way to having some. If only Martin would ever agree to see

26

her, he'd realize that he's invented the monster he hates so much and we'd be well on the way to getting back what we had together.'

'I *am* sorry,' said Cecily, reaching across the table to stroke her hand.

Melissa smiled and stood up. 'I'd better be off. He doesn't much like it if I'm working when he gets back, and I must see what's been going on in the office over the last week.'

Bending down to kiss Cecily's cheek as they stood by the front door, she said, 'Don't look so worried. I'm absolutely fine and Martin will be all right again. You're a real friend to listen, but don't take it too seriously. It's probably not half as bad as I've been making out. I'll ring you.'

'We could have lunch. There's a nice little restaurant I've just discovered, cheap enough not to terrify me while I wait for the spring royalty statements to arrive.'

'I don't think you need worry too much. Heathrow was stuffed with your books and there were some of the translations at Charles de Gaulle, too. You won't starve – and the new book will get better. It always does.'

'I suppose so.' Cecily unlocked the front door and waited there while Melissa climbed the steep stone steps up to street level. 'Bye, Lissa. Take care now. Don't let him get you down too much.'

Melissa waved as she got back into the car, wondering whether it was really only the book that was making Cecily feel so low. She decided to drop off a pot of her mother's honey the next time she was passing. Honey could never be more than a palliative but it was often cheering. Her headache was already getting better as she drove across Bath to the Circus.

Chapter 2

Turning into the perfect circle of eighteenth-century stone houses, Melissa forgot Cecily's troubles, and most of her own, in the usual surge of gratitude to her father. She could hardly remember him and had learned not to upset her mother by asking questions. Almost the only fact she had on which to hang her mental image of him was that he had been prescient enough to buy a dilapidated house in the Circus in the days when Bath was out of fashion and surprisingly cheap.

The house was to have been an investment for his declining years, but he had died before he was even middle-aged. Melissa was six then and she had known nothing of his purchase until she had inherited the house on her twenty-first birthday. She was still touched to think that her mother had made so much effort to keep it as a surprise.

The Circus had been black in those days, like much of the rest of the city, and the house itself divided into many small flats and bedsitters. Melissa had been told that she would be unable to get possession of any of them until the tenants chose to leave, but as soon as she saw the house she had been determined to live in it all. Even then, before she knew anything about restoring houses, she had been aware that it would absorb a vast amount of money.

Her history degree did not seem to have fitted her for any well-paying job and so she had become a trainee in a large firm of accountants in Bristol, renting a flat there with three friends. She had quite enjoyed the precision of accountancy and passed her exams with ease, but she had quickly come to dislike being subordinate to other people and she had always detested living in Bristol. As soon as the first of her tenants had moved out of the house in the Circus, she had taken over his ground-floor flat and commuted to work every day.

Since then she had spent much of her money and most of her free time removing all traces of the shabby alterations that had been made in the past, stripping and scrubbing and dismantling the thin partition walls that had been clumsily used to divide the graceful rooms. As other tenants had left, perhaps disturbed by the noise and mess, Melissa had added their flats to her own growing space, until she had regained control of the whole house.

When she had first been married, Martin had joined in the work with enthusiasm, but that had gradually waned, and he had started to spend more and more time out of the house with friends from work.

Melissa had been disappointed, but she had not resented his lack of help. She had been brought up to disapprove of resentment. Besides, she had often told herself, the house was hers and there was no reason why Martin should help her with it.

Each room regained, cleaned and restored to its original shape had been like a gift to her dead father. Every painful, back-breaking, arm-aching minute of picking out generations of distemper from the cornices with a darning needle had been a moment of communication with him. Each altercation with the builders she had had to employ for the structural work had been bearable because the house had been his.

Martin had complained that her hair was always full of plaster dust or paint speckles and that she had ruined her hands with the solvents she had to use, but there was no doubt that he liked living in the house once she managed to recreate some of its original grandeur. He had never said so to Melissa herself, but she had heard him boasting of it to friends and clients and had been glad.

She had owned very little furniture when she first moved in. For two years her only bookshelves had been planks stacked on bricks, and she had used large floor cushions instead of chairs. But gradually, once she had qualified and started to earn a reasonable salary, she had begun to acquire bits and pieces at sales around the West Country and further afield, until the house had started to look as it should. Only the top floor was still empty, its walls simply whitewashed and its floorboards scrubbed and waiting.

She had learned a lot as she searched through books about eighteenth-century architecture, furniture, decoration and painting to make certain that she was getting her restoration right, and she had become much more absorbed in it than in the audits of her paid work. Gradually she had come to think it mad to waste so much time in the office, and she had eventually let herself admit that she hated her job.

Six years before her successful Paris trip she had left Coward & Bowlby to set up a tiny company to commission and sell reproductions of the kind of scarce, terrifyingly expensive antiques she wanted for her own house and could never afford. Travelling about the country in search of craftsmen who could produce work of the quality she wanted; combing museums all over Europe and America for the ideal originals to copy, and negotiating royalties with their owners; designing catalogues, finding customers, and arranging loans with the bank had been much more to her taste than the endless bashing and ticking of Coward & Bowlby's audits, let alone the internal politics that took up almost as much of the employees' time.

She sat on in her car, thinking about those years and hoping that her father would have been pleased with what she was doing. His choice of house suggested that he would have shared at least some of her pleasure in the work, and she wished he could have seen what she had achieved.

Ever since the stone had been cleaned, the Circus had looked pale gold and wonderful. The mixture of curves and straight lines had always appealed to Melissa, and the ordered severity of the columns and perfectly proportioned windows had a kind of discipline that made her feel comfortable.

Only the previous day one of her best French customers had taken her to a restaurant in the Place des Vosges and she had felt the same ease and pleasure there. Although the houses were quite different in age, style and even colour, the reassuring formality and urbane beauty of the Parisian square had immediately made her feel at home.

Eventually the thought of all the work she ought to be doing got her moving. As she was locking the car she noticed Martin's big dark-red Audi parked a little further along the pavement. Frowning, she looked at her watch, afraid that she had spent longer than she realized with Cecily. But the watch told her it was still not quite half past five. Martin never left his office in Bristol until well after that.

Puzzled, Melissa let herself into the house, calling his name. After a moment she heard him answer and then saw him standing at the top of the stairs.

'What's happened? Are you ill?' she said, struck by the pallor of his face. His short brown hair was tousled, too, as though he had been running his hands through it, and he had loosened his tie so that the knot hung four inches below his unbuttoned shirt collar. He looked slumped, his big shoulders drooping forwards and his whole tall body somehow collapsed into itself.

'There you are at last,' he said, sounding as though he had something in his mouth. 'Was your flight late?'

'No. Traffic was a bit thick. Martin, what is it?'

'I've been sacked,' he said abruptly and turned away, tripping on the edge of the stairs. 'As of this morning. Told to clear my desk and go.'

Melissa put her bags down on the stone floor and followed him, biting her upper lip as she tried to think what words she could possibly use to express her real, immediate sympathy without annoying him. Over the past few months that had been frighteningly easy to do and she wanted him to feel her sympathy and use it.

Walking slowly up the stairs after him, she felt vaguely comforted by the thought that his short temper and his sulkiness could have been caused by fear of losing his job. It was unlikely that the employees of any organization would be unaware of management's plans to make redundancies, and Martin, who had always enjoyed the politics at work, would have been among the first to notice the warning signs. If it had been fear that had been making him so difficult, she might be able to let herself relax.

Melissa went into the drawing room and saw Martin sitting in one of the deep chairs, a glass of what looked like gin and tonic in his hand. His long legs were stretched out in front of him. The formality of his dark-blue suit and expensive shirt only exaggerated his look of disintegration. Melissa tried a smile.

'How horrible for you!' she said. 'I am sorry, Martin.'

He grunted, not looking at her, and drank.

'They've managed to stave off making anyone redundant all this time,' Melissa went on, trying to keep everything impersonal. 'It seems horribly unfair that they should have done it now, just when the recession's ending.'

Martin breathed deeply and stared at the floor. Melissa wondered if she had been clumsy and thought it better not to say anything else until he gave her some clues to his mood.

'If you believe that, you'll believe anything.'

She could feel her lips tightening, but she said nothing.

'But it wasn't the recession at all,' he went on, swirling the floating lemon round and round in his glass. 'It was that bloody cow. She's always loathed me because she knows I know more about the job than her. They only made her the SPIC because she's female and they're beginning to be criticized because they've got so few women partners.'

Melissa, who had heard a great deal about the unreasonableness of the Section Partner in Charge of Martin's department over the previous months, did not comment. She had never met the woman and so could not judge whether his rage was justified or not. Part of her had always suspected disloyally that it might have been a bit exaggerated.

She noticed the number of damp rings on the small table beside Martin and realized that he must have been drinking for some time. She felt sorry for him. His job had given him almost everything he valued: status, excitement, friends, rewards and excuses. Anything that he had not wanted to do – or not done very well – could be ignored on the grounds that it interfered with his work. Walking past his chair, she touched his hair casually, hoping that he would accept the caress as a gesture of comfort, but he jerked his head away, scowling.

'Well, it won't be difficult for someone with your qualifications and experience to get another job,' she said, retreating, 'and—'

'Are you so blinkered by your own provincialism that you really don't know how many professionals are out of work at the moment?' he asked unpleasantly.

'I know there are lots, Martin,' she said, as usual doing her best to ignore his irritability. 'But you have plenty to offer. And in the meantime, I could use some help here.'

He lifted his head briefly. Thinking that she could see some pleasure in his bloodshot eyes, she ventured a little further.

'The figures are all in a bit of a mess, and the end of the financial year is coming up next month. If it wouldn't bore you horribly, I'd love it if you could come and sort us out – just while you're looking for something else, I mean – and do the annual accounts. We need the professional touch. I've let things slide a bit.'

The last statement was a lie, but Melissa would have lied a hundred times to give Martin back his self-respect.

He looked at her again and the warmth in his eyes seemed clearer. When he held out his hand, she was quick to take it.

'Lissa, you . . . Well, thanks anyway.'

'I meant it. It's self-interest. I need you.'

Martin let her hand go and put his glass down on the marked table beside him. She longed to wipe up the damaging smears, but she managed to ignore them and stopped herself asking for the details of his redundancy settlement and how long he would be able to keep the car. As she was trying to think of something useful to say, he stood up.

'I'll get out of these clothes and have a bath, I think.' He squinted at his watch. 'And some lunch. I've been drowning my sorrows, you know.'

'Have you? Well, it's hardly surprising. We can talk about it all later – if that would help.'

He grimaced and shook his head.

'OK, whatever. While you're bathing, I think I might go and see what Annabel's got for me downstairs in the office . . . if that's all right with you?'

'Fine.'

As soon as he had gone up to run his bath, Melissa went downstairs to the big, light basement where she had her offices. Her secretary, a pointy-faced, highly intelligent redhead of twenty-three, greeted her with a smile, a cup of tea and an immense pile of letters.

'I heard you arrive, Lissa,' she said, 'and thought it wouldn't be too long before we saw you.'

'How are the chaps?'

'OK, I think. George had to go early today, but James is still in the studio if you want a word.'

'I'll pop in and say hello before I deal with those.' Melissa pointed to the letters Annabel had laid on her desk. 'If you're pining to get off, don't wait. Just leave them in a heap.'

'Are you sure? I am going out tonight, and so . . .'

'You'll need plenty of time to get ready. You go on home. I'll see you in the morning. Thanks for holding the fort.'

'I liked it. Don't worry too much about the mail. It's not nearly as awful as it looks. Some of it's just junk, but I thought you ought to see it before I chuck it out. You'll find personal letters on the top, orders next, enquiries below them, complaints after that . . .'

'Not too many of them, I hope.'

'No. None. I was teasing. Really the only hassle is that John Box is having trouble finding the right kind of mother of pearl for those little Victorian chairs and wants some help. Oh, and they've summoned you to jury service. That's the bunch of lilac stuff at the bottom.'

'Hell!' Melissa knew that she was letting out some of the anger she had not allowed herself to spill over Martin. 'What does this government think it's doing? There aren't many of us still managing to make small businesses work. Why can't they use people who haven't got jobs at the moment?'

Annabel merely smiled before sneaking a quick look at her watch.

Melissa nodded. 'You get off. See you tomorrow.'

Two hours later, when she had talked to her designer and sorted out his problems, and then dealt with all the immediate work that had accumulated during her absence, Melissa telephoned her mother.

'Abigail Hansford,' came the clear voice Melissa loved. She sank back more comfortably into her chair and swung her feet up on to the desk.

'Hello. Me, safely back from Paris.'

'How was it?'

'As always – glorious to look at and be in, and pretty useful too.'

'Good. You can tell me all about it on Saturday. Unless you've had a better offer?'

'That would be impossible,' said Melissa, laughing. 'You know perfectly well it makes me twitchy to miss our Saturdays. Even Paris was no compensation last weekend.'

'Don't exaggerate, darling.'

'Actually I'm not. How are you?'

'Not bad at all. Longing for the spring to start properly. I'm never really happy until I see young bees on nursery flights, however well the colonies seem to have got through the winter. But you mustn't let me bore you with the bees. Joan always says I'm a nightmare at this time of year.'

'How is she?' asked Melissa, hoping that she had achieved the right tone of affectionate interest. In fact she found her mother's closest friend difficult to like and tended to become defensive whenever Joan's name was mentioned.

'Not too bad. Stoical as always. Heavens! It's nearly eight. Hadn't you better go and get Martin's supper ready?'

'Yes, I suppose I better had.' Melissa did not realize how disheartened she sounded until her mother asked:

'What's up, Melissa?'

'I came back to find that Coward & Bowlby have thrown him out; made him redundant, I mean, which is pretty good hell for him, as you can imagine.'

'And for you too, I suspect. I am sorry.'

'It's not so bad for me. After all, I know what heaven it is to be free of the place. I hope he'll come to feel that too, in the end. And I'm sure it won't be long until he gets another job.'

'You sound remarkably optimistic.'

'Well, there's no point imagining the worst when it may not happen,' said Melissa, trying to believe that it would not. 'Of course, I can't tell poor Martin while he's feeling so ghastly, but I think it may turn out to be not quite the disaster it looks at the moment.'

'Really?'

'Yes, I think so. I've . . . I haven't said much before, but things have been a bit sticky between us recently and he's been awfully . . .' She laughed. 'I don't think I can have handled him as well as I should.'

'I did wonder if something was wrong. You've seemed pretty tense for a while now. Joan's been worried about you, too.'

'Has she?' said Melissa as lightly as she could. It had often annoyed her that Joan took such a close interest in the state of other people's lives and emotions. 'I'd hoped it didn't show. Anyway we've got a chance now to put it all right again. Martin's going to come and work for me while he looks for another job.'

Melissa paused, thinking that if it did work out and they got back some of the happiness they had lost she might even think about getting pregnant as he had always wanted. Abigail said nothing.

'It could be the making of us both,' Melissa said, hoping that she was not being absurdly optimistic. 'And it'll be pretty useful actually, too. I've been summoned to do jury service, so I'll be out of the office for two whole weeks. Coming on top of the French trip that could have been tricky, but as it is I'll have Martin to keep an eye on things for me.'

'I hope it all works out all right.'

'You sound a bit doubtful, but I'm sure it will. But, look, I ought to go now. He must have got out of the bath ages ago, and I don't want him sitting up there thinking that I'm ignoring him in his hour of need.'

'No. That would be awful. It was lovely of you to ring. I'm glad Paris went well, and I suspect you'll enjoy your jury service. I did.'

'Did you? That's encouraging. I'll see you. 'Bye.'

Chapter 3

Just over two weeks later, dressed in a plain midnight-blue suit and a paler blue shirt, Melissa drove herself to Bristol for the first day of her stint in court. She found the Old Guildhall, where the courts were in session, without much difficulty, but all the car parks in the area were full. When she had driven twice round the block, increasingly irritated because she was afraid of being late, she gave up and followed a series of brown signs to a tourist information centre, hoping that there might be space outside that. Before she found the centre, she discovered a car park in the old railyards by the river and left her car there.

Walking back across the small swing bridge to the main part of the town, Melissa forgot about being late and stopped for a moment, leaning on the cream-painted iron parapet, surrounded by the cries of wheeling seagulls and the smells of the old port. She could not have identified any of them individually, but they combined into a wonderfully exotic scent that fired her sluggish imagination.

It gave her a sudden vision of worlds to conquer and space in which to be free. The few tired-looking boats tied up along the edges of the Avon seemed to be paradoxically full of power and possibility. They made her feel as though she had hobbled herself with a ball and chain around her feet.

Melissa shook her head to try to force some sense back into her addling brain and decided that it must be

Martin's worsening moods that were making her so full of idiotic fantasies. She was not hobbled and she had no need of freedom from anything but his difficulties. That would come in due course when he found another proper job. Quite a lot of her energy over the past fortnight had been taken up believing that that would happen.

Pushing herself away from the iron side of the bridge, she walked briskly up into the hill to the Guildhall. Inside the old grey building she found a man in a black suit sitting at one small table in the hall and a uniformed security officer at another.

'Jury, miss?' asked the first and when she nodded he directed her upstairs to the jury assembly room.

Having given her name to the usher in charge there, she looked around the long room. It had white walls and was simply furnished with a row of modern black chairs around the walls. The only decoration was provided by brightly painted heads of medieval-looking figures fixed to the ends of some of the black beams in the arched ceiling. They looked incongruous hanging there, disembodied, above the modern furniture and the big orange automatic drinks machine that hissed and rumbled as one of the waiting jurors pushed the buttons that would provide him with a paper cup of ersatz coffee.

Most of the black seats were already occupied, but there was an empty one just beyond the vending machine. Melissa took it, sitting next to a dark-haired man wearing grey flannel trousers and a corduroy jacket. He was reading an unjacketed hardback book and looked completely absorbed, which seemed rather a pity. From what she could see, Melissa thought he had quite an interesting face.

She put her briefcase on the floor beside her, shook out her newspaper and looked at the rest of her fellow jurors over the top of it. Some of them were reading their own papers. Several, mainly older women tightly buttoned into thick overcoats, were doing crosswords in fat paperbacked books. One thin, intense-looking woman with short, artfully ragged, dark-brown hair and very long amber earrings, had a briefcase balanced on her knees as a desk and was typing very fast on a notebook computer. Melissa thought that she looked interesting, too.

Beside her, a much older woman was slowly but efficiently knitting what looked like a most complicated sweater of many colours. A few people were staring vacantly at the wall opposite them, apparently neither interested nor impatient. Their faces were grey and their dull eyes without hope. Melissa shuddered.

Looking at the mainly depressing collection of people, she thought that the waiting room must be rather like an unemployment office and felt certain for the first time since her return from Paris that she had been right to invent a temporary job for Martin.

One of the ushers appeared in the doorway and there was an expectant rustle as the potential jurors noticed him and shut their books and magazines. He was followed by a security officer, who was pushing a large television into the room.

With the others Melissa watched a short video that explained her rights and obligations as a juror. When it was over, the usher took a bundle of cards from a box fixed to the wall and slowly shuffled through them calling out names. The man next to Melissa stood as the usher called 'Adam Blake'.

When he saw her looking at him, his thin, lined face broke into a charming, regretful smile. He shut his book and stuffed it into the distended pocket of his sagging corduroy jacket.

Melissa waited, but her name was not called. A little disappointed, she went back to her newspaper. When she had finished it, she picked up her own briefcase and took out the notes she was writing for her new catalogue. Before she had done more than re-read what was already there, she felt a movement at her side and she looked up to see that the man called Adam Blake had returned.

'What happened?' she asked as she noticed him looking at her as though wondering whether to say something.

'Oh, the prosecution didn't like my face or something. I was stood down.'

His voice was deep and as pleasant as his intelligent, slightly sallow face. When he was not smiling, his dark eyes and the deep lines at either side of his mouth made him look forbidding, but when his lips relaxed and his eyes lit up, he seemed eminently approachable. Melissa, who always enjoyed talking to strangers, smiled back.

'How frustrating for you!' she said warmly. 'But at least you got that far. I haven't even been called yet. By the way, my name's Melissa Wraxall.'

'Adam Blake.' He held out his hand. As they shook hands, he looked as though he were searching for a way of continuing their conversation and eventually added: 'I have always been thankful that Adam's a name impossible to shorten. I've known some real horrors perpetrated on other people, but the worst I ever suffered was Blakey. Did you get lumbered with Melly?'

'As in *Gone with the Wind*?' said Melissa. 'She was Melanie, wasn't she? A few schoolfriends tried it, but I think most of them realized that it was a ludicrous nickname for me. Wasn't that Melly full of sweet, holy resignation?'

'And you're not?' He was watching her face, his own alight with pleasure.

'Certainly not! If I'd been her, I think I'd have whopped Scarlett over the head with a poker the first time she started sidling up to Ashley. Wicked, selfish, tarty little minx that she was.' Melissa heard her voice sharpening distinctly, and she saw that Adam Blake was looking surprised. She smiled again, adding more calmly, 'No. Miz Melly's character is about as different from mine as it's possible to be.'

'That's probably a good thing,' he said, sitting down beside her. 'Am I interrupting your work?' He pointed to her briefcase.

Melissa shook her head. 'That was just an antidote to possible boredom. I'd much rather talk.' She remembered his heavy-looking book. 'Unless you've got too much to do?'

'Certainly not. It's rare to find an English person so ready to chat. I've usually found it very hard to get past people's barriers in this country.'

'Oh, I've got plenty of those,' said Melissa, surprised at her own frankness. 'It's just that they don't often operate with strangers.'

'How curious! Why not?'

'I'm not sure.' Remembering her tiny encounter with the beleaguered mother at Heathrow, Melissa went on more slowly: 'I think perhaps it's because with a stranger you can have a moment of pure friendliness that's never going to be spoiled by anything that might happen later.'

Adam was about to answer when the usher reappeared with a new pack of cards. The first name to be called was hers. She stood up.

'My turn. Perhaps I'll see you later.'

Adam Blake smiled again and nodded slightly. 'I hope so.'

Turning back at the door, she saw that he had already taken the book out of his pocket and was reading again. With the rest of the jury panel, she followed the usher downstairs to court four.

Melissa was not stood down as Mr Blake had been, and she spent the rest of the day in court, listening to the case against a young man accused of 'twocing' – taking a car without consent.

After the jury had been released, Melissa shook hands with some of the others outside the court and was glad to hear from the usher that they were free to go for the day. She left the building and hurried through the rain towards the river and the car park.

When she got home, she went straight down to the offices and found Annabel straightening a pile of letters on her desk.

'Hello, Lissa, how was it?' she said, turning at the sound of Melissa's step.

'Not so bad. Any disasters here?'

'No. It's been fairly quiet. And that shipment to America has arrived at last. They faxed this afternoon. All is well and it cleared customs without any trouble.'

'Thank goodness.' Melissa saw Annabel looking at her watch. 'Are you in a tearing hurry?'

'Heavens no! It's just these new timesheets. Having to account for every fifteen minutes is making me completely neurotic.'

'Timesheets?' Melissa was so surprised that the question was out before her mind had caught up with what must have happened.

'Yes, Martin's got us all doing them. He said they had to be up and running by the time you finished jurying.'

'Ah,' said Melissa, hoping that she was sounding judicious instead of murderously angry, 'he must have misunderstood something I said to him. Scrap the timesheets. We don't need them.'

'Good.' Annabel's relief was tinged with sympathy. Melissa pretended not to notice it.

'I'll run through these letters and then have a word with him,' she said. 'Don't say anything to the other two until I've done that, will you, Bel?'

'OK. Let me know if you want to do any letters tonight. I've still got some of the old filing to finish so I won't be going for an hour or more.'

'Thanks. I can see you're being your usual starry self.'

When Annabel had gone, Melissa propped her elbows on the desk and leaned her chin on her clasped hands, trying to decide how best to deal with Martin. She could not help thinking that if she had been in his place she would have done everything she could to fit in with his ways of working, instead of trying to change them. He seemed to feel no gratitude to her for saving him from the dole queue, and she was occasionally tempted to think that he actually resented her for it.

Hard though it was for her to accept, she was being slowly forced to admit that he might be deliberately going out of his way to make things difficult for her. It had been only two weeks so far, and yet he had caused an astonishing amount of trouble already. Smiling in an attempt to relax her face, she walked down the passage to the little filing room she had converted into an office for him.

'Hello, Martin.'

'Hi, Lissa. How'd it go?'

'Not so bad. A bit of a waste of time, but it had moments of interest. How are things here?'

'Slack, I'm afraid. I caught Bel taking the opportunity of your absence to sneak over two hours at lunchtime.'

Melissa sat down in the spare chair and opened her mouth. Before she could speak, Martin went on, 'But you needn't worry, I've got all three of them doing timesheets now, so we can exert proper control. It'll all be all right once they get used to a bit of real discipline. And the information will help you cost the products as well. Some of your pricing is a bit haywire, you know.'

Melissa took a deep breath.

'Martin, I know that this all seems very casual to you, but it's a way of working that I've arrived at through trial and error, and it's the best way for this sort of business.' She smiled at him. 'Bel and the boys know that I don't mind if they take long lunches provided they're prepared to work extra hours when there's a crisis. They're not junior trainees at Coward & Bowlby. They know perfectly well that they're part of the business and that it's in their interests as much as mine to make sure that it works.'

'You're too trusting, Lissa. They won't respect you unless you toughen up.'

'I don't want them to respect me. I—'

'Well, you should. It's no wonder they take advantage.'

'What I was going on to say is that I want them to feel relaxed and appreciated and interested enough to work at their best. It's a different method from yours, but it works. I've told Bel to cancel the timesheets. Please, dear Martin, don't upset the applecart.'

'Fine,' he said, making it clear that he was extremely angry. 'And while we're on unpleasant subjects, you really are going to have to control your entertaining costs. I see from the accounts that you've taken that young glassblower out to three extravagant restaurants in the past six months. He hasn't done any work for you yet and the goblets he's quoted for are ludicrously expensive.'

Melissa closed her eyes for a second and bit back the comments she wanted to make.

'Yes, they are going to be very expensive,' she said at last, hearing the deliberate patience in her voice, 'but we are also going to make a large profit on them; not enough to justify all those lunches, perhaps, but they will pay off in the future. Again, it's a way of working that I've established over the years. Please don't try to change things that don't need changing.' She smiled again, as cheerfully as she could. 'After all, Martin, if it ain't broke, don't fix it.'

He got up and came to stand close to her chair. He seemed enormous as he loomed over her. She was surprised to find herself a little nervous.

46

'You really shouldn't be so afraid of change. I'm here now. I've seen enough change management in the last few years to know exactly what you need. I'll see to it all.'

'I've got to go and make a telephone call,' she said, getting up and pushing him out of her way. 'I'd quite forgotten but it's frightfully urgent.'

Back in her own office, with the door shut, she leaned against the wall silently cursing. It was quite clear that Martin needed to regain some of the self-respect that Coward & Bowlby had taken from him, but she was afraid that she might not be able to bear the way he had chosen to do it.

Chapter 4

The next morning Melissa drove away from the Circus without regret. Jury service, which had seemed a terrible nuisance on the day she received the summons, was proving to be a bit of a boon. If it did nothing else, it would keep her and Martin blessedly apart for much of the next two weeks. Once she was free of the town, she drove far too fast, hoping that speed would help her get rid of all the thoughts that had kept her awake for most of the previous night.

It did not. As she reached the outskirts of Bristol she told herself she had been just as stupid and feckless as the young man she had been trying the previous day.

There seemed to be no sign of either Adam Blake or the intelligent-looking woman with the computer when Melissa reached the jury assembly room and so she sat down near the vending machine and opened the day's newspaper at once. Skipping the news, she turned to the more appealing bits in the middle and settled down to an article about the rights and wrongs of a new campaign to change the divorce laws. She looked up, hoping to be picked for a trial, as one of the women ushers came in and shuffled the first pack of cards.

'John Dent,' she called.

A nondescript man, rather smaller and thinner than average, got up from a chair close to Melissa's and walked across to stand beside the usher. Looking embarrassed, he pulled the buttoned cuffs of his clean white shirt down below the sleeves of his jacket and pretended to be very interested in something on the floor.

'Adam Blake.' Melissa smiled as she saw him standing up at the far end of the room. He made his way to the usher, nodding to Melissa as he caught her eye.

'Nathaniel Turner.'

A young black man wearing much-pocketed khaki trousers and a loose black sweatshirt with the hood hanging down his back got up and sauntered easily to the small group by the door.

'Melissa Wraxall.'

Delighted to have been called, she folded her newspaper and put it in her briefcase before joining the others.

'Now we really will get to know each other,' said Adam quietly. 'How very nice!'

'Isn't it?' she agreed as a woman answered to the name of Margaret Crosscombe. Having put her knitting into a big canvas and leather-look shopping bag, she pushed herself up from her chair with obvious pain and set off across the room to join the rest. She looked about sixty and must have been suffering from arthritis.

'John Brown.'

No-one answered. The usher looked down at the card at the top of the pile and said it again, more loudly. With nearly everyone else in the room, Melissa looked along the rows of chairs. Eventually a worried-looking man with a wispy beard put up his hand.

'Mr Brown?' repeated the usher, sounding tired.

'Yeah.'

'Come along, then. Thank you.'

As he wiped his hands on his trousers and stood up, she had already taken the next card and called out: 'David Davis.'

A tall, broad-shouldered man with a shock of white hair stood up and was followed by summons for Richard Smith, Mark Graham, Jane Bartlett, Araminta Collins,

Rachel Cohen, Ethel Rogers, Diana Jenkins and Susan Beere.

The last was the woman with the computer. Melissa watched them all as they made their way across the room, some looking pleased, others blank, and most self-conscious. Of them all Richard Smith stood out for his quite extraordinary fatness. He seemed to be hung about with flesh that swayed as he walked, as though it did not really belong to him. Melissa felt sorry for him and then wondered why she thought she had the right to feel any such thing. He was probably perfectly happy.

Araminta Collins was black and conspicuously well-dressed. She was the only one who smiled at the jurors already assembled by the door as though she were pleased to be joining them.

'Come along,' said the usher, leading the way down the stairs to the courts. There was something about her manner that made Melisssa at least suspect that they were heading for something more serious than a trial for 'taking without consent'.

Having led them down the stairs and stopped outside the double doors to court number one, the usher launched into the familiar explanation that only twelve of them would actually be selected to serve on the jury and that when she took them into the court they should assemble on the benches to the right of the door. As their names were called, they were to move to the jury box on the judge's right and take the first available seat. Those whose names were not called should wait until each juror was sworn in. Then if any objections were raised that juror would stand down and another would be selected from the remaining four. Any who were not called would then leave the court.

'Do you understand?' she asked.

Several people nodded, but Araminta Collins smiled

and said confidently, 'Yes. That's quite clear. Thank you.'

'Good,' said the usher. 'Then in a moment we'll go in.' She looked through the wired glass panel in the door and then pushed it open to let the jurors through.

Melissa stopped for a second as she crossed the threshold, immediately struck by the atmosphere in the court. There was tension, but there was excitement too. Everyone in the big, crowded room looked alert. None of the waiting lawyers looked at all like the lackadaisical pair who had appeared in the 'twocing' case she had tried the day before. Even the black-robed ushers, who must have watched innumerable trials of all sorts, seemed affected and kept catching each others' eyes, smiling as though in anticipation of what was to follow. The press benches were full and none of the journalists looked at all bored.

Sitting down on the bench to the right of the door as she had been instructed, Melissa looked across the court to a row of police officers who were sitting behind a long table with several sinister tagged plastic bags on it. Even the police seemed tense.

Only the judge appeared unmoved as he sat in his archaic robes, more like a figurehead than a man, under the flaunting lion and unicorn crest, and no-one could have told what he was feeling.

Melissa looked along the row of jurors and saw that some of the others had felt the powerful atmosphere too. She waited for something to happen that might explain why everyone was so wired.

Charles Harcombe QC, who was to act for the prosecution, pushed a finger between his Adam's apple and the starched white collar at the neck of his gown, easing the tightness. Catching the judge's eye, he nodded slightly and then looked towards his opponent, Gina Mayford. Knowing that she had taken silk only the previous year and was still struggling to match the income she had been making for several years as a successful junior, Charles admired her apparent calm.

Despite her confidence, he knew that he had the better evidence for once, which was lucky. Having lost his last two cases, he needed a big win, and this trial was clearly going to be well publicized. There were more journalists than usual in Bristol, and several of them were from important newspapers.

Picking the gold hunter out of his waistcoat pocket, Charles was relieved to see that he could not have much longer to wait. He knew that as soon as he was on his feet and talking his experience would carry him through. It was the waiting he always disliked.

The judge looked up and nodded to the clerk. He shuffled the pack of small beige cards the usher had given him and called out the names of the first twelve jurors: Adam Blake, Susan Beere, Melissa Wraxall, Araminta Collins, Nathaniel Turner, John Brown, John Dent, David Davis, Margaret Crosscombe, Ethel Rogers, Richard Smith and Diana Jenkins.

One by one they went to the jury box. Some of them were obviously uncomfortable, and stumbled or blushed as they walked the length of the court; others were interested and apparently at ease. A few were clearly excited by the tension they could sense.

Both the senior barristers watched them carefully, trying to assess their intelligence, possible prejudices and likely sympathies as they sat down in the double row of blue leather seats on the judge's right.

Charles Harcombe was immediately wary of one woman, who looked to him to be an archetypal lefty feminist with her thinness, her short straight hair, dangling amber earrings, unpainted face and long droopy skirt. Her mouth was bitter and her greenish eyes seemed cold. She was bound to cause trouble in the jury room, Charles thought, even though she would probably sympathize with many of his arguments.

He was also bothered by the tall, broad-shouldered, sixtyish man, whose name was Davis. He looked like a tough, unreconstructed member of the old Labour party, possibly even a union official. In Charles's opinion he would probably have far too many sympathies with the defendant and be bossy enough to do his damnedest to force the weaker members of the jury to side with him.

On the whole the women looked more prepossessing than the men for once. There were two who were particularly well-dressed, both wearing well-cut suits. One was black with what he knew was called 'big hair', and the other white with a thick blond French plait. They shared the same air of confidence and intelligence and would probably be useful, Charles thought. There was one more who seemed all right. Much older than the other two, she was a homely body with a slow, arthritic walk, a big shopping bag and well-permed grey hair, but something about her suggested a common sense and an endurance that he welcomed.

Of the remaining two women, one was neither here nor there, a tidy, inconspicuous middle-aged black woman who answered to the name of Ethel Rogers. The other, Diana Jenkins, might present another kind of problem. She looked horribly suggestible and smiled nervously at anyone who caught her eye. Charles knew her type all too well; they liked to agree with everyone and were terrified of argument. Not much use in a jury room, he thought.

Of the men, he immediately despised one for his wobbly fatness and another for his acne, his weedy beard and fearful, shifting eyes, but he quite liked the look of the fit-looking, slim black man. He would be unpredictable, of course. If he had ever had any dealings with the police himself, he would probably mistrust the prosecution on principle. On the other hand he might well take against the defendant's arrogant manner and superlative good looks, which had worried Charles all along.

None of the thoughts or doubts showed in his face. To the jurors, most of whose names he had not even registered, the spectators, and even the judge, he looked perfectly confident in his impressively shabby wig and long black gown. The gold pocket watch, double chin and unfashionable stoutness seemed appropriate in court, however absurd they would have looked in the world outside.

Gina Mayford had her back to him, still watching the jurors as they settled into their seats. She had decided long ago that it was impossible to guess from any juror's appearance how he or she would vote when it came to the verdict, but she could never help trying. Some of her cases had ended in verdicts so perverse that she had longed to cross-examine the jurors to find out how they had persuaded themselves into such bizarre decisions.

This one is going to be tricky, she told herself for the umpteenth time, but then what case isn't?

When all the jurors had been seated, the clerk turned to the dock and said loudly: 'Michael Beechen, the names that you are about to hear called are the names of the jurors who are to try you. If therefore you wish to object to them or to any of them, you must do so as they come to the book to be sworn, and before they are sworn, and your objection shall be heard. Do you understand?'

Michael, who had been doing his best to think of the trial as a performance so that it would seem less appalling, bowed. Knowing that the jury were the most important part of his audience, he had been watching them as closely as either of the barristers.

Years earlier he had been taught that anything he said

on a stage would sound more convincing if he concentrated on a single member of the audience instead of the whole mass. As soon as the jurors had been selected, he had started to search the men's faces for the one he would talk to when it was his turn to testify. Rejecting the fat one and the thin, wispily bearded one at once, he had looked from the young black man to three older white men and started to panic. Two of them seemed to have nothing in common with him at all. If he had met them in the world outside the big white courtroom, he would probably have done his best to avoid them. The third was different, a thin, dark-haired man with a lined face and intense dark eyes. He looked impressively intelligent and self-disciplined, but so austere that he almost frightened Michael.

Eventually he had turned reluctantly to the women and after some thought selected the tall blonde in the stunning navy suit. She looked quite severe, too, but as she sat down she smiled at her neighbour and suddenly seemed much more human. Michael liked her height, her elegance and her obvious self-control. Just about his own age, she seemed to be the sort of person who would not let herself be ruled by emotive propaganda. He thought that she might be able to discount any speechifying from the prosecution and concentrate on what had really happened and why.

The clerk turned to face the jury and explained to them that they must each stand and swear the oath that was printed on the cards in front of them. When the spotty, bearded man stumbled over the words, blushing and stammering, the usher took the plastic-covered card from him and read the simple words for him to repeat.

Charles Harcombe muttered internally: I knew it. An illiterate fool. Well, with luck he'll just keep quiet in the jury room and let the others get on with it.

Watching the juror wiping his hands on the front of

his trousers and pulling at his inadequate beard, Gina Mayford felt for his fear and humiliation. Despite having watched the same scene repeated hundreds of times before, everyone in court was staring at him contemptuously as he tried to repeat the words in the right order.

When the last of the jurors had been sworn, the clerk said to them all: 'Michael Beechen is charged on an indictment containing a single count of murder . . .'

Some of the jurors gasped and stared at the dock. Reminding himself that at least his training had taught him how to be looked at, Michael smiled faintly and stared at the brightly coloured and gilded crest above the judge's head.

'. . . the particulars being that on the evening of the fifth of December 1992 he stabbed Penelope Beechen. To this indictment he has pleaded not guilty. It is your charge, having heard the evidence, to say whether he be guilty or not.'

Once the clerk had stopped speaking, the judge directed the remaining members of the jury panel to leave the court. When they had gone he leaned slightly forward to say, 'Yes, Mr Harcombe.'

The barrister heaved himself to his feet and twitched the sides of his gown so that they hung more elegantly at either side of his rounded waistcoat.

'Members of the jury,' he said, addressing them slowly and kindly, so that the stupid and the illiterate would be able to understand, 'together with Mr Miles Joseph I represent the Crown in this case. My learned friends Miss Georgina Mayford and Mr Richard Copeman are appearing for the defence.'

He paused to give them time to look at Gina Mayford and her junior. She pretended not to notice, continuing to read one of the papers in front of her.

'The defendant, Michael Beechen, has been accused

of murdering his wife, Penelope, by stabbing her several times through the throat and chest.'

He looked up at the jury box and smiled. The well-dressed black woman crossed her legs and leaned back in her seat, looking as though she were attending a board meeting rather than a trial. One of the other women looked worried, but most of the rest were impassive or disapproving. As Charles had suspected, the lefty feminist was already bristling. Somehow he would have to play on her sympathies for the dead woman and stop her hating him because he was an example of the patriarchy she probably loathed.

It was intelligent of the defence to have briefed a woman, Charles thought as he continued with his opening speech. He had said most of it so often before that he could unreel the words without even thinking about them.

'The charge of murder, members of the jury, is a most serious one and it is your duty to listen to the evidence so that you can make up your minds as to the facts of the case. His lordship will explain to you the points of law on which the case depends, but it is for you and you alone to judge the facts. It is my duty to prove to you beyond reasonable doubt that Michael Beechen intended to do his wife serious bodily harm and that he killed her. If, when you have heard the evidence, you are not convinced by it so that you are sure, then you must acquit him. If you are satisfied that he acted in lawful self-defence then you must acquit him. If, on the other hand, you are satisfied that even if he killed her intentionally he was provoked in the way his lordship will explain to you then you must convict him of manslaughter.'

Charles went on to describe the evidence he planned to bring before them, slightly underplaying the significance of it all in case any of his witnesses let him down.

'As you will hear,' he went on, 'this is a most distressing case and I trust that you won't let your natural feelings of repugnance and sympathy at what you will hear affect your judgment of the facts. They, and they alone, must form the basis of your verdict.'

Michael knew that he had been right to pick the blonde juror, whose name he remembered was Melissa Wraxall, as soon he saw her making short notes on the pad in front of her. She was obviously taking her job seriously. Several other jurors followed her example, which seemed to be a good sign, too. If she had leadership qualities as well as the common sense and warmth he had already divined in her, all would be well.

'On the night in question,' Charles went on, beginning to get to the interesting part of his opening, 'the defendant, Michael Beechen, arrived home after a long day at the television studios where he had been auditioning for a part in a future series. He was tired and short-tempered after taking the bus home to Bristol through dreadful weather and heavy traffic, and he had failed to get the part. He reached the flat where he lived with his wife and their three children shortly after half past eight in the evening, expecting the children to be in bed.'

Charles Harcombe looked at the jury from under his jutting dark eyebrows, challenging them to put themselves into the position of such a man on such a night. Behind him Michael watched them, too, and saw that Melissa Wraxall was staring at him. He had not meant to arouse her interest in him as a man until he came to give his own evidence, but the opportunity was too good to waste. He looked gravely back at her, willing her to understand him.

Michael thought he saw horror in her intelligent grey eyes just before the lids concealed them from him. He comforted himself with the knowledge that her expression would change once he was allowed to tell her what had really happened, and he knew that he just had to keep his head until then and not let her dislike affect him. The prosecution's job was to paint him as a monster. He had to remember that. He and Gina Mayford would get a chance to put the record straight in due course.

As prosecuting counsel continued his speech, Michael gazed at the lion and unicorn and silently recited nursery rhymes to keep his memories of Penelope in check and his face expressionless.

'The children were not in bed, members of the jury,' Charles Harcombe was saying calmly. 'Marianna, the eldest, was reading to her two brothers on a sofa in the living room. The detritus of the day lay all around them on the floor: toys, discarded clothing, a mug half-filled with cold tea with cigarette butts floating in it. The room looked unbelievably untidy to a man who, you will hear, needed cleanliness and order in his life.'

Michael could not help checking on his juror again, and he thought he saw a faint softening of her antagonism. He had known as soon as he took in the well-pressed look of her expensive, simple clothes that she cared as much as he did for cleanliness and order.

'When he went into the kitchen to remonstrate with his wife, he found her smoking and reading a magazine. There was a tumbler half-full of sherry beside her but no sign of any cooked meal. The sink was full of unwashed dishes. Remains of food, both raw and cooked, lay about on the worktops. In one corner their two cats were eating the trimmings and giblets of a defrosting chicken. They were not in a dish of any kind but simply lying on the worktop. The cats were sitting there, amid the food and the dirty crockery, licking up the raw meat and blood.'

Charles Harcombe privately criticized himself for having stressed the squalor that had been described to him so vividly by the investigating police officers as he saw the revulsion in the eyes of several jurors.

'As I have said,' he went on, showing no sign of regret and working out how to salvage his position as he talked, 'Beechen is a fastidious man and it is likely that he was as revolted by the sight as many right-thinking people would have been. But he did not lose his temper and hit his wife then, which might have been understandable if not excusable.'

The lefty feminist scowled as she twisted one of her long amber earrings with her left hand.

'On the contrary, he was enough in command of himself to collect food for the children's supper and eventually put them to bed. When he had tucked the two boys up in their bunk beds, he read his daughter a bedtime story. He then kissed all three children, switched off the main light but put on a low-voltage lamp that they usually had because the younger boy was scared of the dark, and left them.'

Several of the women jurors smiled warmly as they heard that, but Michael was not looking at them and so he did not see their warmth fade. He was unaware that his slight, detached smile made him look not only contemptuous but also bored by what was being said about him.

'We do not know precisely what happened next, but about ten minutes later the defendant telephoned his wife's doctor to announce that there had been an accident,' said Charles Harcombe. 'She enquired as to the nature of the accident and when he had told her a little, she drove to the flat at once. There she found her patient lying on the kitchen floor with seven stab wounds in her body. Seven, members of the jury.'

Once more Charles paused to allow the enormity of what he had said to sink into the slowest jurors' brains. When he decided that they had had enough time, he went on, 'There was blood all over Penelope's body, over a four-inch kitchen knife . . . and over the clothes, face and hands of her husband.'

Gina Mayford watched the jurors look towards the dock again. The austere-looking man's severe face was surprisingly full of pity but there was anger or distress on several others'.

'Having ascertained that there was nothing she could do to help Mrs Beechen, the doctor telephoned the police and waited with the defendant until two officers came. They took the defendant to the police station, where he was questioned by senior officers. He made no confession and gave no explanation for what had happened, and he was later charged.'

Charles Harcombe waited until the judge had reached the end of the notes he was writing. When he was ready, he looked up and nodded.

'I call Dr Jane Newbridge,' said Charles, swinging the full sleeves of his gown and psyching himself up for the piece of theatre that he was about to star in and direct.

Michael watched his wife's doctor climb the steps to the witness box and knew that she detested him. A woman of about forty, she was wearing a plain, inexpensive beige tweed suit over a thin brown sweater. Once she had sworn to tell the truth, she waited, looking quite composed, for the examination to begin. As she described what she had seen and heard, Michael could not fault her accuracy or the dispassionate tone she used.

When the prosecution's questions were over, Gina Mayford got to her feet.

'Dr Newbridge, were you Penelope Beechen's general practitioner?' she asked in a voice that was quieter and less histrionic than her opponent's. She looked much younger than he, too, and a great deal less arrogant.

'That's right,' said the doctor with a smile. 'I had treated her for almost four years.'

'Treated her for what?'

'For anything that brought her to the surgery, that is anything from an infection to the birth of her youngest child.'

'Could you be more specific?' asked Gina.

'Apart from the pregnancy, she came for the sort of minor ailments of which we see a great deal.'

'Such as?' The barrister frowned slightly, as though she were trying to understand something that had been clumsily expressed. The doctor smiled again and began to look both bored and patronizing. Several jurors decided not to like her.

'The odd heavy cold, which she called 'flu; thrush or cystitis; diarrhoea sometimes; piles. The kind of thing many mothers of her age suffer.'

'Did she ever complain to you of anything else?'

Michael was impressed to hear nothing in Gina's voice to suggest how important that question was to them. He waited, hoping that the doctor was going to abide by her oath.

'Yes, she told me she suffered from premenstrual tension. There were times when she took oil of evening primrose or vitamin B6 for it.'

'And did either of them work?'

'That's a difficult question to answer. It's a subject on which doctors differ.'

'No doubt,' said Gina with a half smile, 'but did they work in this case?'

'I don't think so. Not completely or perhaps she might have gone on taking them.'

'I see. And what are the symptoms of the syndrome?'

The doctor sighed but she pulled herself together to give a list that was familiar enough to all the women in court, although some of the men in the jury box looked puzzled and others disgusted.

'Shortness of temper,' said the doctor abruptly, 'some

62

fluid retention, a craving for sweet and salty foods, a feeling of despair sometimes, great tiredness, headaches.'

'And anything else?' Gina's voice was still calm and apparently disinterested.

'Anger sometimes.' There was some reluctance in the doctor's voice as she produced those two words.

'I see. And were you also Michael Beechen's doctor?'

'No,' said Dr Newbridge more happily, 'although I did see the children from time to time for inoculations and so on.'

'What condition was he in when you arrived at the flat that night?'

'Distressed.'

'I'm sure he was. After all, his wife was dead.' Gina allowed a little asperity to sharpen her voice. 'I actually meant: what was his physical condition?'

'I did not examine him. He was bloodstained, as I have said.'

'You did not notice if there were any other marks on him?'

'I did not examine him,' said the doctor with barely suppressed impatience. 'It was not my job, but I could see that there were marks on his face and scratches on his hand and arm, as though his wife had tried to defend herself.'

'Might there have been other marks that you did not see?'

'There might,' said the doctor curtly. She seemed to resent the questions.

'Thank you. What did the kitchen smell of when you were examining the body?'

'Goodness!' said the doctor, clearly taken aback. 'Blood obviously. It's a sweetish, heavy smell when present in those quantities. And excrement, too. When death has occurred so violently, there is sometimes involuntary voiding of the bowels.'

63

'Could you distinguish any smells that were not from the body?'

'Not as far as I can remember.'

'Thank you. Will you wait there? My learned friend may have something more to ask you.' Gina bowed to Charles, who stood up and rearranged his gown with another flourish.

'Dr Newbridge, you testified to Mrs Beechen's minor illnesses. What, if any, part would stress have played in the onset of such illnesses?'

'There again doctors differ,' she said, seeming more at ease. 'In my experience stress certainly lowers the body's resistance to infection in many cases, and in Mrs Beechen's particular case there is no doubt that stress was a causative factor.'

'Have you any evidence as to the cause of the stress itself?'

'Yes. Living in a small flat with three children and little money is in itself cause for stress and, from what I could see during my few domiciliary visits, her relations with her husband were not easy.'

'Not easy in what way?'

'He gave her a lot of orders, even when she was ill, and very little sympathy. In fact he behaved very coldly to her, as though they had nothing to do with each other apart from negotiations about the housework. She exhibited more signs of stress in his presence than when she visited the surgery with her children.'

Susan Beere wrote a note on the pad in front of her and then sat up with a ramrod back. The young black man slumped even lower in his chair. The superbly moulded muscles in his chest were clear through his sweatshirt. He let his chin sink into his chest and he closed his eyes.

'Thank you, doctor, you may step down.'

Jane Newbridge left the witness box and several jurors shuffled in their seats as though they were relaxing in the knowledge that there had been nothing in the evidence that was at all difficult to understand.

The next witness was a police officer, who testified that he had been called to the flat by Dr Newbridge and that he had found the deceased lying on the kitchen floor with blood all over her and a vegetable knife with a black handle and a triangular blade on the floor beside her. The exhibits officer, sitting with the police at the table exactly opposite the jury box, produced a tagged plastic bag.

'Is this the knife?' asked Charles Harcombe. When the police officer had confirmed that it was, the plastic bundle was passed to the jury while the barrister continued his questions about the state of the flat. The jurors passed the light package from hand to hand and looked at it conscientiously but in some embarrassment, as though they were not sure what they were supposed to notice.

To many of them it seemed a remarkably small knife to have killed anyone. It looked very ordinary, the kind that could be found in many kitchens in Great Britain.

The police officer described the squalor of the Beechens' kitchen and the position of the body and what he had seen of the bloodstains on the floor, walls and cupboards. When it was her turn to speak, Georgina Mayford asked him only one question.

'Of what did the kitchen smell?'

The officer looked as surprised as the doctor had been, and several of the journalists at the back of the court exchanged glances. One or two even whispered together. The judge looked up from his notes and frowned at them. Silence fell.

Michael wondered how anyone who had been in his kitchen that night could have forgotten any grisly detail. All of them were continually in his mind, as vivid and horrible as they had been at the time.

After a moment, the constable asked if he could refresh his memory from the notes he had made at the time.

Having been given permission and read them, he said slowly: 'It's a long time ago. I didn't note anything down. There were food smells and dirt, as far as I can remember. Blood, too, of course.'

'Anything else?'

'Cigarettes,' he said, suddenly sounding pleased. He smiled. 'There was the smell of smoke and I think one of them must have burnt something. There was definitely a smell of burning. I looked round, but there wasn't anything alight when I got there. Someone must have put it out.'

'Thank you,' said Gina Mayford quietly.

Charles Harcombe got to his feet as she sat down and told the judge that his next witness was the scene-of-crime officer who had examined the flat and that his evidence would take some time.

'Ah,' said the judge, looking at the clock over the main door to the court. 'In that case, I will rise for the short adjournment. Members of the jury, will you please be ready to return here at a quarter past two. I must warn you not to talk about this case to anyone who is not also a member of the jury.'

Everyone stood up, the judge retreated through the door behind his elevated throne and, looking a little uncertain, the jurors at the ends of the two rows of seats shuffled out of the box, through the jury room and out into the passage beyond.

Chapter 5

While the judge sat down to succulent roast lamb, Michael was taken down the chilling stairs from the dock to the cells beneath the courts. Locked into a small barred room, he was given a tray with food and a mug of tea. He did his best to eat, but the mouthful of meat and vegetables seemed to grow larger as he chewed and it stuck in his throat when he tried to swallow. Pushing the plate away from him, he drained the tepid tea and gave up.

As a child he had learned that one of the first symptoms of carsickness was a feeling of great distance from the other people in the car. Their voices would sound as though they came from miles away, and their preoccupations became incomprehensible. If it had not been for the knowledge of the sickness to follow, the sensation would have been wholly pleasant. He tried to recreate it in the comfortless cell in the basement of the Old Guildhall in Bristol.

He was not successful. He could build protective spaces between himself and most people but the bond with Marianna was too strong. All her feelings of terror, shame and desperate unhappiness came through the space he pulled around himself. He ached to protect her, but there was nothing he could do except worry.

It was better, he told himself, that the children were with his sister rather than any of Penelope's relations, who would probably poison their minds against him. But Jane had never had children of her own. She might not understand how much care and patience Marianna needed.

The boys bothered him less; they were much more resilient and would survive most things, even unhappiness. But Marianna might not. So few people understood that her apparent maturity and surprising domestic competence merely concealed a terror of conflict and criticism. Michael knew all too well that his daughter would do and say anything to avoid making people angry with her. Jane, with all her toughness, her efficiency, her detachment and her entirely adult circle of friends, probably would not be able to understand that.

'He's a cool cuss, isn't he?'

Michael looked up and saw two prison officers watching him. He turned his chair so that they could see only his back and waited with what little stoicism he could muster for the start of the afternoon's torment.

While he sweated out the lunch adjournment, the jury divided into groups. Some of the jurors left the Old Guildhall quickly, without even talking to any of the others. Melissa, who had been sitting between Susan Beere and Araminta Collins, asked if they would lunch with her and, when they agreed, suggested inviting Adam to join them. The four of them walked round the corner to a coffee shop, which also offered hot food.

Melissa liked Araminta Collins, who invited them all to call her Minty, finding her funny as well as sensible and thoroughly well informed about the difficulties of carrying a small business through the recession. It turned out that she had a company manufacturing children's clothes, which she marketed by mail order. Melissa, as always worried about finding suitable presents for her godchildren, asked how she could get hold of a catalogue.

'I'll bring one in tomorrow,' said Minty with a quick smile. 'Isn't it amazing how the oddest things turn into marketing opportunities?'

They both laughed and were surprised when Susan Beere criticized them for not taking their duty as jurors seriously enough.

'I'm not sure we've heard enough yet to be able to think about the trial constructively,' said Adam. 'If we start speculating about our verdict already, on the basis of only the prosecution's opening speech and a couple of witnesses, we'll be more likely to make a mess of it than otherwise.'

'How sensible!' said Melissa, just as Susan was saying irritably:

'You sound like a negotiator or a conciliator or something.' She hitched up the droopy neck of her ochre-coloured sweater, which was slipping over one thin shoulder. 'Are you?'

'No. I teach at the university,' he said with some amusement, 'and whatever negotiating skills I might possess can have come only from trying to persuade my lazier students to write their essays on time. And you, what do you do?'

'I'm a freelance journalist.'

As Adam asked her about her work, he set off a lecture about the prejudices women face whenever they come up against the legal system. Listening to his interjections, Melissa decided that her first impression of him the previous day had been remarkably accurate. Despite his formidable aura of intelligence, he had a lively sense of humour.

Since almost everything he disagreed with in Susan's lecture had also annoyed Melissa, she felt· pleasantly supported and joined in with an argument she would usually have avoided. Minty contributed some trenchant comments, too, and as it became clear that all of them had strong and rational points to make, Susan began to lose some of her prickly aggression.

Some of the other customers looked at them curiously

as they left the restaurant, obviously wondering what could have brought such an unlikely quartet together, but they were interested enough in what they were discussing not to notice. As they walked back to the Old Guildhall, Minty and Susan went ahead. Adam smiled at Melissa and apologized for talking too much.

'You didn't,' she said at once. 'Not a word too much. You said most of the things I wanted to – and much more articulately than I would have done. I'd probably have got angry, too, and that always makes one sound stupid in an argument.'

'It does, doesn't it?' said Adam warmly. 'I used to be afraid of anger – both in other people and in myself – until I understood what a handicap it is. Then it lost its power to scare.'

'D'you know,' said Melissa, watching him with a gleaming smile in her eyes, 'I can't actually imagine your being frightened of anything.'

'Well, that just goes to show how deceptive appearances can be,' he said, laughing. 'Here we are. You first.'

Melissa edged her way into the row of blue leather seats and sat down between Minty and Adam.

A few minutes later Charles Harcombe took his witness, the scene-of-crime officer who had examined the Beechens' kitchen, through a description of what she had found there on the night of the murder. During the officer's testimony, photographs of the murder scene were passed from the exhibits table to the jury.

Watching the effect of the glossy coloured prints on the various jurors, Charles wondered yet again why the defence had allowed them to be shown. He looked at Gina Mayford, but she was apparently untroubled. He began to worry about what he might have missed. There must be something to make her so calm.

He knew what the thrust of her case would be, because

he had been properly notified that she was going to call an expert in domestic violence. But he could not see how even an explanation of the private torments of a man in a violent marriage would persuade the jury that Beechen was not guilty of murder. However unhappy he had been, he had killed the woman, and however provoking she had been, and most men would have found her intolerable, he had not hit out at once but waited to kill her until the children were in bed.

Because of that self-possession, no defence of provocation was going to work in such a brutal killing, and to Charles's eyes the photographs were proof of just how brutal it had been.

They showed Penelope's body lying, face upwards, on a black-and-white checked vinyl floor with the small black-handled knife beside her. There was blood all over the handle as well as the short blade. It looked dark, brownish red and clotted. Her dyed-black hair looked untidy as it lay spread out around her head. She had been wearing jeans when she died and a low-cut T-shirt, which had once been white.

There were horizontal splashes of blood on the edge of the stained worktops and the cupboard doors, where they were mixed with vertical drips, thinner and browner, of what must have been tea or coffee and something thick and yellow that looked like dried egg yolk. There was blood on the floor, some in long, radiating splashes, more pooled near the body. And there were bloody smears on the floor, the cupboards, the untidy worktops, and the sides of a tall, overflowing, lidless rubbish bin. She had obviously not died quickly.

Her legs were twisted one under the other and the arms flung out at either side. Once she had ceased to move, the blood had spread across her front, soaking through the thin knitted cotton and puddling between her breasts before it dried into the thick, brownish mass that the photographs showed. Her round face was contorted, either by anger or some spasm that dying had forced through her body.

When Melissa had passed the photographs on to her neighbour, she raised her eyes to look towards the dock. Charles Harcombe noticed the tightness of her mouth and the anger in her eyes and knew that he had been right to assume she would be on his side.

Michael was carefully not looking at her. He could imagine what the photographs were like and he knew that she was sensitive enough to be completely sickened by them.

As they were passed from hand to hand, the scene-of-crime officer continued to explain what she had seen. In a warm, slow West Country voice she described the exact position of all the bloodstains on the kitchen floor, walls, cupboards and ceiling, testifying that their shape proved that Penelope Beechen had been standing with her back to the window when she was first stabbed and that her assailant, who must have been at least five inches taller than she and righthanded, had been standing in front of her at the time.

After the photographs, the evidence of Michael's fingerprints on the knife came as an anticlimax. The testimony became yet more damning but increasingly dull, centring on hairs and fibres that had been found in the kitchen, on Michael, and on his wife's body.

Once again Gina Mayford asked whether the witness had noticed any smells in the kitchen. She too said that there had been a smell of burning.

'Did you find anything to explain that smell?'

'Yes,' said the witness. Having checked her worksheet, she added: 'There was one saucepan on the hob, which had boiled dry. There was the residue of burned rice and water at the bottom. And more of the same around the gas burner of the cooker, where the rice had boiled over.'

'What kind of saucepan was it?'

'Heavy gauge aluminium, approximately ten inches in diameter, with a heat-proof plastic handle.'

'I see,' said Georgina Mayford. 'Did you examine the underside of the saucepan?'

'No,' said the officer, looking very slightly concerned. Charles frowned.

'Thank you. Would you wait there? My learned friend may have something to ask you.'

Charles half rose and told the judge he had nothing more. The scene-of-crime officer was allowed to leave the witness box just after four-thirty. Having listened to her evidence all afternoon, the judge adjourned the trial for the night, reminding the jurors again that they were not to discuss the case with anyone.

Melissa, hating the way the defendant had kept staring at her, blundered out of the court. She was surprised to find that rain was pouring down on the street outside.

'Can I offer you half my umbrella?' asked Adam Blake from just behind her.

Melissa turned to smile at him, shaking her head. 'It's all right,' she said, relieved to find that her voice was working normally. 'I've got a car just down the road. Where are you heading? Would you like a lift?'

'No, but thank you very much. I live in Bath. There's a bus in fifteen minutes. I'll see you in the morning.'

'I'm going to Bath, too,' said Melissa. 'Do let me give you a lift. Come on, or we'll both be soaked.'

Without waiting for formal capitulation, she led the way to the multi-storey car park where she had left her large Rover that morning. Adam followed her. She was walking so fast that she kept treading in deep puddles that splashed dirty rainwater up the back of her legs.

'Are you all right?' he asked as they turned into the concrete building out of the rain and waited for the lift.

'Who could be, after those photographs?' she said, still

73

feeling sick at the thought of them. 'It's horrible. He must have done it, and yet he looks so normal. Almost attractive and slightly familiar, too. I detest the thought that I might actually have met a man who could do that to a woman he was married to – or to anyone, come to that.'

'He was an actor. You've probably just seen him on television,' said Adam, putting his arm across the open doors of the lift to prevent them closing on her. 'You obviously don't read the tabloids. There was quite a lot about the case last December.'

'Was there? I'm ashamed to say I often don't even look at the news bits of the paper. What did they say?'

'Oh, a fair amount about his early glamorous success and the difficulty of making a living from acting and the pains of being a was-kid. There were photographs, too, which made them look a most unlikely couple.'

'In what way?'

'Well, as you saw today, he's a tall, healthy, good-looking sort of bloke, and conventionally well dressed, but she was quite different.' Adam shivered suddenly. 'It sounds like an appalling marriage, doesn't it? I wonder why she put up with it for so long.'

'I'm sure Susan could explain a battered wife's motives better than I,' said Melissa a little maliciously, 'but perhaps she stayed because of the children, or because of poverty, or . . .' She hesitated and then added more soberly, 'Or perhaps she simply felt that it was up to her to make things right between them. Women tend to do that, I think. And then, of course, a lot of marriages go a bit sour for a while but improve later on. I'm sure they often do improve. She could have been gritting her teeth and waiting for that.'

Adam turned so that he could watch her face as she drove. Melissa glanced at him for a second and thought suddenly that his students must find him enormously attractive, despite the thinness of his tired face and the first few grey strands in his dark hair. He smiled at her and she felt herself smiling back. The car swerved slightly and she took a tighter grip on the steering wheel, staring straight through the windscreen again.

'I suppose that's possible, but . . .'

'Are you married?' she asked when Adam did not finish his sentence.

'Me? No. I took rather a scunner to the whole idea of it after one attempt went wrong.'

'What happened?' Belatedly realizing how tactless she had been, Melissa quickly added, 'Sorry, you probably don't want to talk about it.'

'Oh, I don't mind these days. It was quite a long time ago. I used to be a priest, Catholic. I left the church, but I was saved from marriage at the eleventh hour by a woman who was a great deal more sensible than I gave her credit for at the time.'

'That sounds a bit confused.'

'Does it? Perhaps I'm still defensive about it. I left the church to marry her, and no doubt flung over her all my miseries and thwarted longing for human love, and must have frightened the poor girl out of her wits. Luckily, she was strong enough to get out while she had the chance, thus saving us both from years of unhappiness – or worse. Recently I've come to feel positively grateful to her.'

'How impressive to be so charitable!' said Melissa. 'I'd have been hurt and furious.'

'Perhaps, but look at it this way: instead of domestic angst, I have a thoroughly easy life, absolutely free, subject to no-one and answerable to no-one.' Adam laughed. 'I have no horrible marital rows, resentful silences, brooding sulks or miserable misunderstandings. A lot of my married friends seem to have to put up with all that most of the time.'

'Perhaps I ought to envy you,' said Melissa casually.

The lights changed and she took her foot off the brake.

Driving along the wet road with the sodden black trees dripping on to the banks at either side, she had a sudden, vivid memory of the first of her rows with Martin. She had hardly ever thought of it since, but the details came back to her as clearly as though it had happened the previous week. With them came feelings, shockingly intense.

One winter soon after they were married, she and Martin had been staying with friends in London. The house was exactly opposite a T-junction at the bottom of a small hill. Black ice covered all the roads, and snow was still falling as they arrived.

When Martin parked his beloved car outside the house, Melissa suggested that he move it further along the street in case another driver should skid down the icy hill and crash into it. Even nine years later she could feel the shock she got when he ignored her advice without a word of explanation.

Later that night, asleep in the spare room that overlooked the road, they had been woken by the most tremendous crash. Martin had got out of bed and stood by the window, pulling up his pyjama trousers with one hand as he moved the curtain aside with the other. When he said nothing as he glared down into the icy street, Melissa joined him, shivering in the unheated darkness. A few slow, fat snowflakes were falling past the orange-coloured streetlight. They looked gentle, peaceful. Following them down to the ground, Melissa saw what had happened. The car, symbol of Martin's power and success, had been buckled almost in half by a van that had skidded down the hill.

A moment later, ripping his dressing gown off the hook on the back of the door, Martin swore at Melissa as if the whole incident were her fault. She fumbled her way downstairs to find the telephone to call an ambulance for the van driver while Martin cursed and wrestled with the complicated locks of the front door.

Never once during the subsequent discussions with their hosts, the ambulance driver and the police did Martin acknowledge that following his wife's advice would have saved the car, his face, and a great deal of trouble; and he never referred to the incident again. It became quite clear to her that, subconsciously or not, he did believe that she had caused the accident by suggesting it might happen.

Adam sat in silence, watching her. When Melissa said nothing, he said, 'Do you? Envy the freedom, I mean?'

'Only sometimes,' she said, pushing the memory down again. With an effort, she added: 'I suspect most married people have moments of regretting their lost liberty, perhaps forgetting that had a high price, too.'

'The grass always being greener on the other side of the fence? Yes, probably. And, of course, it never is when you get there.'

Melissa turned impulsively to smile at him again and then hastily looked back at the wet road. 'You're wonderfully encouraging,' she said. 'Do many people try to confess to you still?'

'Certainly not. Why?'

'The temptation is almost overmastering. Something about you seems to invite it – and to promise understanding, if not forgiveness. Dear me, this has all got rather deep for such a new acquaintance. Perhaps we ought to talk about the weather, or nicknames.'

Adam laughed properly then, sounding thoroughly amused. When he spoke his deep, slightly husky voice was transformed.

'We've already done both of those. I've no intention of prying into your life; still less inviting confidences to which I've no right. But as you say, we've gone a long way already. Will you tell me something?'

'If I can,' she said warily.

'Why are you called Melissa?'

She laughed, too, with a warm sound that made him smile. 'Oh, because my mother's a fanatical beekeeper. "Melissa" is the Greek for bee, you know.'

'Yes, I do know. My subject is Classics. Were you teased for it as a child?'

'Not much. I used to deliver long lectures to any taunters about its derivation and about beekeeping, and they soon learned to leave me alone through sheer boredom. Now, here we are in Bath. Where would you like to be dropped?'

'Wherever is convenient to you,' he said. 'There's no need for you to get involved in another one-way system if you don't have to.'

'Then how about where the A4 joins Queen Square?'

'That sounds perfect. You've been very kind to save me from the bus.'

'I've enjoyed it,' Melissa said truthfully, feeling more lighthearted than she had since Paris. 'Look, I'll be passing the bottom of the square at half-past eight tomorrow morning. If you're there, I'll give you a lift. Up to you.'

She drew up on the double yellow lines, putting on her hazard warning lights.

'Then I'll see you tomorrow, Melissa. Thank you.' Adam held out his hand. She took it and enjoyed the warm, dry firmness of his grip. He let her go, backed out of the door and slammed it shut.

Waving at him through the rain-streaked window, Melissa drove up the steep hill to the Circus and Martin.

Even before she looked at her letters or spoke to her secretary, Melissa put her head round the door of her husband's office and smiled at him.

'Did you get a more interesting trial today?' he asked as he saw her.

78

'A bit. How were things here?'

'Not too bad.' He frowned. 'You've certainly added to the extraordinary devotion in which your staff hold you by countermanding my timesheet orders.'

Melissa, who had hoped that the whole argument could have been forgotten, heard the fury in his voice. She sat down and tried to explain again in a way that he might be able to accept. Martin was well in control of himself, but his brown eyes looked hot and his mouth was pinched.

'Martin, in a tiny business like this, things like timesheets produce nothing but unnecessary friction. We don't charge our customers by fractions of hours spent on their business, as an accountant would. The cost of Bel and the boys is part of the general overhead.'

'I know that perfectly well,' he said through his teeth, 'since I've been checking your books, but it's not the point. You've got to show the staff who's boss, Lissa, if you're to get anywhere.'

Melissa sighed and wished that she had had a cup of tea before tackling him. She had managed to disguise the extent of her fury so far, but it seemed to be getting more difficult with every day that passed.

'Darling,' she said, trying not to sound angry, 'don't let's argue about it again, please.'

Martin looked down at his spreadsheets and then back at his wife. His shoulders were tight with suppressed anger and his hands were trembling.

'I really don't appreciate this continual belittling,' he said. 'I have a lot to offer your potty little business, but you're too damned stubborn to use it. I am not a nine-pounds-an-hour bookkeeper, you know. Coward & Bowlby charged my time out at two hundred and fifty pounds an hour.'

'Yes, I know they did,' she said, but he paid no attention.

'That's what my expertise is worth. You bloody well

ought to be thankful you're getting it for almost nothing, instead of ignoring everything I say and humiliating me in front of your staff day after day.'

Melissa put her head in her hands. There was so much loathing in his voice that for the moment she could not answer. She thought of telling him that she had never intended to humiliate him and had indeed done all she could to protect him from the scorn and dislike of Bel and the two designers.

She was also tempted to tell him that she had noticed the malicious little things he had been doing. On his first day he had mislaid an important order, which might easily have been a mistake, but since then he had paid cheques into the wrong account, failed to pass on urgent telephone messages, and refused to pay bills to which Melissa had asked him to give priority.

None of the things he had done had actually caused any financial loss but several of them might have, and he had been building up a lot of bad feeling in the office as well as causing trouble with at least one important client. Like all small businesses, hers was badly stretched. The loss of any major client could be disastrous.

'I wish you wouldn't take it like that,' she said at last. 'We both know that your working here is only a temporary measure to tide you over until you get another job at your own level. In the circumstances, don't you think it would be absurd to fall out over the way I run the business?'

Martin scowled and opened his mouth. Melissa suddenly realized that she could not bear another lecture on her shortcomings, lack of ambition, failure to appreciate him and whatever else he had dreamed up during the day. She stood up, put the grey tweed-covered chair tidily against the wall and left his office without another word.

As she hung her jacket on the back of the chair in her own room and settled down to go through the day's letters and the notes Annabel had put on her desk, Melissa decided that her headache was bad enough for some paracetamol.

It seemed absurd that she had not foreseen the effect of inviting Martin into her business. Her optimistic fantasies of getting back the pleasure they had once taken in each other had clearly been ludicrous. She felt stupid and unhappy and desperately worried.

Trying to put Martin and his troubles aside, she started to work. Almost at once she was interrupted and looked up to see Bel in the doorway.

'Did you see the telephone message from Dick Walston?'

'No, who's he?' asked Melissa.

'An American decorator. We haven't ever dealt with him before, but the Delaherbes recommended us and he'd like to come and talk to you about some things he wants. It's all rather urgent because he's leaving England again the day after tomorrow.'

'Then why didn't he get in touch before?' demanded Melissa irritably. 'Sorry, Bel. I know you don't know any more than I do.'

'I do actually. He was pretty frank. He told me that he'd been sure he'd find plenty of original antiques, what with all the Lloyd's names having to sell up and things, but there's been a lot less available than he assumed. He's falling back on us *faute de mieux*. He said that he'd sent a fax last Friday but that was a fib. There hasn't been one. I've looked in the basket and all round the machine in case it dropped on the floor like in that film.'

'Well, I suppose we'd better have him to dinner here tomorrow night before he leaves the country,' said Melissa, wondering about the fax and whether Martin had taken it. 'If he's really going to buy from us, we can't afford to stand on ceremony or complain about being second best. And with the jurying I can't get up to London. Have you got a number for him?'

'Of course,' said Annabel, amused, pushing up the sleeves of her acid green sweater. 'Have I ever forgotten to take a number from a potential customer?'

'Never. Never. I take it back.' Melissa smiled. 'Will you ring him, explain why I'm not doing it myself, and ask him whether he can cope with dinner at eight tomorrow? You've got the train times, haven't you?'

'Yes. I'll tell him I can meet him and bring him here. Any letters?'

'Not yet. I'll leave a heap on top of your typewriter for tomorrow morning. Thanks.'

Annabel left the room, to reappear ten minutes later with the news that the American would be on the 6.15 train from London and had sounded pleased to be invited to the house.

'It usually helps to make a sale,' said Melissa, thinking about what she would cook. She pushed her fingers through her fringe. 'If I leave you a shopping list tomorrow, can you do a Waitrose run for me?'

'Of course. I'll cook, too, if you like. I did last time, after all.'

'Thanks, but I think I can manage. Will . . . ? No, never mind. I must have a word with Martin.'

Melissa went back to his small white-walled room to tell him about the American, adding in yet another attempt to placate him, 'I hope you don't mind, but it just is the easiest way of dealing with new customers. He can see the stuff that we use upstairs, come down here if there's any actual business to be done, and get everything settled in one visit.'

'I'm all for it,' said Martin, looking round from the dark-green metal filing cabinet, where he was riffling through some old PAYE records. He seemed to have buried his rage. 'It'll be cheaper than the restaurants

82

you patronize. Who else shall we have to balance him? We ought to have four.'

'I was going to ask you about that. What about Bel? She's been so helpful recently I'd like to include her a bit more in the social side of the business. Get her used to dealing with customers so that when the wretched recession really does end and we can expand a bit she can be promoted.' Silently, she added: and if you could see her out of the office, you might be able to appreciate that she is a human being and treat her better.

'That sounds fair enough,' he said, shutting the filing drawer with a bang and returning to his oak desk, 'but I've seen too much of her over the past fortnight. I really don't want her at my dinner table.'

'All right,' said Melissa equably, keeping to herself the reminder that the dinner table, and indeed the house, belonged to her. 'Then who? What about Cecily? She fits in with everyone and she's always good value. And we know her well enough to ask her at the last minute.'

Martin smiled and reached for the telephone. He looked almost like the man she had loved and married.

'You do have some good ideas. I'll give you that. Would you like me to ring her?'

'Oh, I would, Martin. Thanks.'

Pleased to have got something right for once, Melissa went back to work in her own room. At the back of her mind was a faint sensation of pleasure that she eventually traced to the knowledge that she would see Adam Blake again the following day.

Chapter 6

He was waiting outside the Francis Hotel the following morning. The rain had stopped and Bath was looking its best in the clear sunlight. The stone of the buildings looked like clotted cream where the sun caught it and elsewhere glowed softly gold against a crisp blue sky. Melissa stopped her car, pushed the fringe away from her forehead, and smiled as she leaned across to open the passenger door.

'I did wonder whether you'd come,' Adam said.

'You needn't have. I enjoyed your company yesterday far too much to waste the opportunity of having a bit more of it.'

'How nice!' He got in beside her and sat in silence as she drove extremely fast towards Bristol. Aware that what she was doing was reasonably safe even if it was illegal, he managed not to cling to the door handle or even to his own hands. Eventually he asked in a mild voice, 'Are you always so impatient?'

'What?' she said vaguely. 'No. Sorry. I wasn't thinking. It's just so nice to get away, and I did think that if we reached Bristol soon enough we might have time for some breakfast. I was in much too much of a rage this morning to eat anything.' She eased her foot off the accelerator a little.

'We're in much the same boat then,' said Adam, breathing more easily. 'Not that I was angry, but I'd run out of milk, bread and butter, so there wasn't much I could have except black coffee. I seem to be an incorrigibly bad housekeeper, despite years of practice.'

'You don't sound too worried about it,' Melissa said, admiring his admission of incompetence. It was completely different from Martin's habit of blaming someone else for every mistake he ever made, however trivial.

Adam laughed. 'I'm not. I worry about all sorts of things but not my lack of domestic skills. After all they affect no-one but me. Are we going to talk about the weather this morning, or are you going to let me help?'

Surprised, she looked at him, frowned and looked away again. After a moment, she said, 'I'm not sure that I need any help, although it's charming of you to want to try.'

'Charming is a pretty revolting word in that context,' Adam said dispassionately. 'Quite a put-down. Did I sound that intrusive?'

'No,' said Melissa at once, liking the easy way he had put his protest. Because of that she had to tell him a little. 'No, you didn't. It's just that I don't see why you think I should need any help.'

'Ah. Perhaps I've got it all wrong,' he said slowly, watching her out of the corner of his eye. 'I just got a very strong impression yesterday that you're having a bad time at the moment. I wondered if I could do anything to assist. Lend a sympathetic ear. That sort of thing. Nothing heavy.'

Melissa drove in silence, surprised that what she thought had been well concealed should have been so obvious to a virtual stranger. Because she liked him, and because he had asked no personal questions, she did not want to spurn his offer of sympathy.

'I've never got into the habit of telling my troubles to other people,' she said at last, making a silent apology to Cecily, who had listened so patiently and so often. 'Things are a little sticky at home just now, but I don't

85

think there's anything anyone else can do about it. It's a fairly common story, after all. I married a man I thought I loved, who thought he loved me. For a while we had an extremely good life together. Then we had patches when it became less good, and at the moment it's virtually intolerable.' After a moment she shook her head and added, 'I can't actually think why I'm telling you this.'

'It may be a common story, but none the less painful, I suspect.' His voice was neither critical nor sentimental, just factual and surprisingly gentle.

'It's chiefly my fault at the moment,' she said when she could speak again, 'because when he was made redundant a couple of weeks ago, I invited him to work for me as a stopgap – so that he didn't have to sit about brooding – and it's beginning to look as though that was the worst thing I could have done for both of us.'

She stopped talking and bit her lip. Adam watched her profile and wondered how to reach her.

'It doesn't sound too heinous a crime,' he said eventually. 'Pretty sensible really if you had a job in your gift.'

Melissa drove into the car park, found a space on the second floor, parked, pulled up the handbrake with a firm movement, and turned to face him.

'No, not heinous; just completely idiotic. It's been clear to me for some time that the way Martin makes himself feel better after he's made a mistake, failed at something or been beaten at a game or for a job, is to put me down. I ought to have had the wits to see that a major humiliation like being thrown out of a job he loved would lead to trouble. To bring it on myself at work as well as in the evenings was plain stupid. I was silly and sentimental enough to think he might be grateful for my saving him from the dole, and that that would make him easier to be with. Mad.'

'It sounds generous rather than mad to me,' said Adam as he got out of the car. Leaning on the roof and looking at her as she activated the central locking system, he added, 'Doesn't he see that his only alternative would be signing on once the redundancy pay's gone?'

'He doesn't seem to look at things in quite that practical way,' said Melissa drily. 'Let's have breakfast and talk about something else.'

'Fine.' Adam took her arm and walked close beside her out of the car park. 'You can tell me about beekeeping. I've always longed to have some hives and I read everything I can on the subject.'

'Are you taking the mickey,' Melissa demanded, 'because of what I said yesterday about my schooldays?'

'Don't be so prickly,' he said severely. 'Of course I'm not taking the mickey. I am really interested. If you like you can come and have a drink with me tonight and see the evidence in my bookshelves.'

Her face broke into a smile.

'You can't imagine what you've let yourself in for,' she said. 'I'm hard to stop once I get going on the subject of bees. My mother's a great expert and I've learned a lot from her. It's a fascinating subject.'

'Good,' said Adam, enjoying her enthusiasm as much as the prospect of the lecture. 'Come on.'

Three-quarters of an hour later, they walked into the Old Guildhall, having enjoyed themselves and eaten an enormous breakfast of bacon and eggs, coffee and croissants. As they reached the doors of court number One, Adam stopped.

'Thank you,' he said. 'When we have to listen to all the horrors this morning, I'll remember that: the bees and you, I mean. You can't imagine what you've done for me today.'

Melissa smiled and shook her head. 'In that case we ought to breakfast together every day. You've smoothed me out and defused all my rage. I'm almost back to thinking this is just a blip and that things will get better with Martin in due course. Thank you.'

'Well, I'm definitely on for a daily breakfast if you are,' Adam said lightly. 'We'd better go in. Morning, Susan.'

'Good morning,' said Susan Beere politely as they walked in through the double doors.

The three of them sat down and waited for the rest of the jurors. Eventually everyone was assembled and the door behind the bench opened. The court rose and the judge appeared to bows and a great shuffling and coughing from all around the big white room.

The prosecution called their first witness of the morning, and Marianna Beechen walked towards the witness box. Dwarfed by the size of the room, and looking very vulnerable in the crowd of dark-clothed adults, she climbed into the box. She was hardly tall enough to see over the edge. A chair was provided for her.

Michael had not seen her dress before, and assumed that it had been chosen by his sister. It looked much more expensive than any of the second-hand clothes and rejects that Penelope had picked up from jumble sales and charity shops. Made of smooth jade-green wool, the dress had a wide yoke decorated with two large, flat, pearl buttons. Marianna's fine fair hair had been newly washed and it gleamed in the light that hung over the witness box. She looked pretty as well as fragile.

Watching her, Michael felt as though his insides were being slowly eaten by some malignant creature with large, blunt, tearing teeth. He longed to be able to reassure her, since he could not save her from what was to come, but as usual there was nothing he could do.

He had protested against her appearance in court, but there had been nothing his lawyers could do either. She was the only witness to what had happened, even though she had not actually been in the kitchen that night.

Her coming ordeal was just one more horror piled

on all the others that tormented Michael, as was the fact that Gina felt that Marianna's appearance would be essential to his case. If the prosecution had not called her, Gina had told him, she would have had to do so, whatever he felt about it.

Gazing at the brightly gilded crest opposite the dock, Michael wished that he could pray. He hoped that the lawyers would remember that Marianna was only eight years old and temper their vicious, manipulative questioning.

Charles Harcombe took off his wig and smiled at Marianna.

'Is your name Marianna Beechen?'

'Yes,' she whispered, shutting her eyes and pushing back her flyaway blond hair with both hands. It was a clumsy gesture. Her hands looked pudgy yet very flat as she pressed them against her forehead. She opened her blue eyes again and let her hands fall to her sides.

Charles smiled, but Marianna did not respond, looking at him instead with an expression that made even some of the journalists shiver. Her eyes were afraid and yet somehow accepting, like the eyes of a child who has always been bullied and expects nothing better.

'Marianna,' said the barrister, 'do you remember the night when your mother died?'

'Yes.' The clumsy hands pushed the blond hair away from her face again and then picked at one of the pearl buttons.

'Can you tell us what happened?'

She nodded and put her hands in her lap.

'Mummy was in the kitchen,' she said quietly but distinctly. Her voice was well articulated and without any kind of regional accent. Michael was proud of that. He had worked hard to achieve it. For a second he let himself look at her again. She was staring at Charles Harcombe.

'The boys were hungry but she didn't want them to

have any supper yet. So I read to them.' Marianna half turned so that she could look at the judge out of the corner of her eyes. There was some doubt in her voice as she added even more quietly: 'It was *Thomas the Tank Engine.*'

'It's a good story that,' said Charles Harcombe, raising a tiny smile from his witness. 'Did you enjoy it?'

'Yes.'

'What happened then?'

'Daddy came home.'

'What did he do?'

'He asked me why the boys weren't in bed. It was after their bedtime, but I couldn't put them to bed if they didn't have any supper, and she wouldn't let me get them supper. I told him.'

'And then?'

The fine hair was pushed away again and the beautifully shaped lips, which were the most adult feature of her small face, quivered.

'He went into the kitchen and they shouted a bit and then he came back with cereal for us all and we ate it and then he put us to bed.' Marianna's voice dropped again. 'I wasn't very hungry.'

'And then?'

'He read me a chapter from *The Secret Garden,*' she said more loudly, but she still did not look at her father.

'A whole chapter? Didn't that take a long time?'

'Yes. But he often reads me a whole chapter.' She smiled a little and looked round, nearly as far as the dock. 'He likes it, too.'

'Was there anyone else in the flat then?'

'No,' said the child, looking surprised.

'Did anyone else come in at all that evening?'

'No.'

'I see. And what happened then, after your father finished reading to you?' asked Charles Harcombe.

No-one in the jury box had moved. Throughout the previous day at least one of the twelve had usually been coughing or re-crossing legs or writing notes or scratching. Now they all sat still, as though any movement might distract the child.

'I tried to go to sleep.'

'Did you manage?'

'Not really.' Marianna hung her head. Her voice was only just audible as she added: 'They were shouting and banging and then it was quiet and then the lady came.'

'Which lady?'

'The lady doctor.'

'Did you see your mother?'

'No. The lady said I was to look after the boys and she'd look after her and Daddy.'

'Are you ever afraid of your father?'

There was a tense pause until the child managed to answer.

'Sometimes,' Marianna said very quietly.

'Why is that?' There was no emotion in the barrister's voice. He seemed to be working hard to avoid suggesting what he wanted the child to tell him.

'Because he got cross with Mummy.'

'Why?'

'When she's untidy.'

'What did he do then?'

Marianna did not answer.

'Did he ever hit her, Marianna?'

The child looked up. There was obvious surprise on her face.

'Can you tell me in words, Marianna?' said Charles Harcombe patiently. 'Did your father ever hit your mother?'

'No,' she said in a voice that was positively robust in contrast to its earlier tentativeness.

'Thank you. You've been very helpful. My friend,

Miss Mayford here, is going to ask you some questions now. Do you feel all right?'

'Yes, thank you.' She turned her frighteningly accepting eyes towards defence counsel and once more waited, her hands out of sight of the jury.

Georgina Mayford smiled as she, too, took off her wig and stood up. Without it, she looked much more alive, not nearly as forbidding as she had seemed earlier, and even attractive. The child seemed to feel the warmth, and her watchfulness relaxed a little.

'Marianna, did you ever try to tidy up the flat?'

The child nodded and pushed her hair away from her face. 'Sometimes, but she didn't like it when I did.'

'Who didn't like it, Marianna?'

'My mother.'

'Why didn't she like it?' Georgina Mayford sounded merely interested, as though there was no criticism of anyone implicit in her question.

'I don't know,' said the child, looking bewildered. Georgina Mayford smiled again with reassuring friendliness.

'Why did you tidy up if she didn't want you to?'

Marianna pushed at her forehead again, although her hair had stayed well back from her eyes for once. Michael, who had seen her make the same gesture since babyhood whenever she was afraid, closed his eyes.

'Why, Marianna?'

The child whispered something that none of the jurors could hear. Georgina Mayford gently asked her to speak louder.

'So that she wouldn't be cross with Daddy,' said Marianna just audibly.

'But wouldn't he be cross with her if the flat wasn't tidy?'

'Yes.'

'Marianna?' Miss Mayford's voice was immensely kind, but neither patronizing nor sentimental. 'Why did you mind more about your mother being cross than your father?'

The child looked puzzled and she pushed her hair away again. Her eyebrows were nearly joined together over her nose as she frowned.

'Did you mind more about your mother's crossness than your father's?' asked Georgina, obviously searching for the explanation behind what the child had said.

She nodded, but she did not say anything.

'What happened when your mother was cross?'

The child's head drooped and she whispered something.

'Marianna, can you tell me a little bit louder? I couldn't hear.'

'She hit him,' came the whisper, slightly louder.

There was a ripple along the jury box as people sat up straighter. Michael opened his eyes and looked at Melissa, willing her to believe and understand. She refused to look at him, apparently mesmerized by Marianna's face. Michael's lips tightened and then relaxed again as he remembered that he still had time to convince her himself.

Several of the journalists smiled in satisfaction as they were given a nice new angle for their stories.

'Your mother hit your father?'

'Just only when she was cross,' Marianna explained earnestly.

'Did she ever hit you?'

'No.'

'Or the boys?'

'Not like that.'

'What happened when she was cross with you?'

Two big tears slid down the child's pale cheeks. She did nothing about them.

'Did she hit you?' asked Georgina Mayford again, sounding very gentle.

The blond head was slowly shaken. Marianna seemed to be studying her hands.

'What did she do?'

The child raised her head and looked at the barrister, who smiled again.

'She shouted and she said things.'

'What kind of things?'

There was a long silence.

'I can't remember,' whispered the child, looking away.

Melissa, sitting in fascinated horror, knew beyond all doubt that the last answer was a lie, and she clenched her fists, driving her nails into the palm of each hand. She realized that she was afraid the barrister might try to push Marianna into telling the truth.

'What was it like when she hit your father?' Georgina Mayford asked instead in her patient, tender voice.

Charles Harcombe hoped that his face showed none of his irritation. It was perfectly obvious what Gina Mayford was trying to do and it was absurd.

'It hurt him,' said Marianna slowly, still looking down at something below the edge of the witness box. Then she looked up again. 'Sometimes he had to get the doctor.'

'Which doctor?'

'I don't know,' she said and for the first time her voice broke. She pulled a handkerchief from her sleeve and blew her nose. 'I'm sorry. I don't know. Don't be cross. I'm sorry.'

'No-one here will be cross. Do you know what "knocked out" means?'

'Yes.' Marianna screwed the handkerchief into a ball and stuffed it back in the sleeve of her dress.

'Did that ever happen when your mother hit your father?'

'Sometimes.'

94

'Did anyone get the doctor then?'

The child shook her head slowly from side to side.

'Why not, Marianna?'

'She wouldn't let me.' The child's voice was only just audible.

'Just a few more questions now: can you remember what sort of smells there were in the flat that evening?'

Marianna thought for a while and then said much more easily, 'Burning. Something was burning in the kitchen.'

'Before your father came home or after?'

'All the time.'

'Thank you. Now this is nearly the last question: did you stay in bed all the time they were banging and shouting?'

The child looked across the court towards Georgina Mayford, then towards the judge and finally to her left. She did not seem to be looking at her father as he sat in the dock with his handsome head bowed, but at someone in the benches behind him.

'Marianna, you must tell the truth. Did you stay in bed?'

'No,' she whispered, staring in appalling fear at her questioner.

'Did you go into the kitchen at all?'

'No,' she said a bit more confidently.

'What did you hear, Marianna?'

The child bit her lips and blinked and shook her head. Georgina Mayford waited, saying nothing. Charles Harcombe was looking at his notes. Everyone else in the court seemed to be staring at the witness box.

'Marianna?' Georgina Mayford's voice was gentle but its tone made it quite clear that the child could not be allowed to keep silent.

'He said, "Don't hit me",' Marianna said at last.

There was a ripple of relaxation in at least half the

court. Charles Harcombe seemed to frown. Several of the jurors re-crossed their legs. One or two even shrugged. It did not seem at all surprising that a woman facing a knife would hit out at her attacker.

'Could you hear anything else?'

'Yes; he told her that she shouldn't be so dirty. The kitchen was disgusting. She was a bad mother. She should have given us our supper. She should have put us to bed. He said she was a bad mother.'

It was as though a plug had been removed, letting the words pour out of Marianna. Her face was very white and her lips were trembling, but her voice was much louder and firmer than it had been at the beginning of her testimony. 'She was a bad mother. She was.'

Adam Blake shivered suddenly. His face looked as though he were in pain.

'I see,' said the barrister. 'Thank you. You've been very brave and helpful, Marianna. Did he say anything after that?'

'Yes. Lots of times he said "Don't hit me".'

'And your mother: could you hear anything she said while he was saying that?'

Marianna shook her head and then whispered, 'I couldn't hear. He just said "Don't hit me".'

'All right, Marianna. Thank you. Now Mr Harcombe may have some more questions to ask.'

The child looked at the other barrister. There was still no sign of protest in her, only fear and acceptance.

'Marianna, did your mother ever hit you or the boys?'

'Not like that,' she said again.

'And your father, did he ever hit you?'

'Sometimes he slapped us if we'd been naughty.'

Michael frowned. He could not remember ever having spanked Marianna. The boys, yes; sometimes it was the only way to stop them wreaking havoc on the flat or each other, but not Marianna. He had never hit her.

'What sort of things were naughty?'

Marianna looked surprised.

'If we spilled something or broke it,' she said readily. 'If we were cheeky or didn't do what we were told. Or if we made too much noise.'

'Where would he slap you?'

'Sometimes on our faces. Sometimes on our hands or our, you know, our bottoms.' Once more she looked sideways at the judge. He was writing a note and did not see her nervous glance.

'With his hand or with something else?' asked the barrister in a matter-of-fact voice.

'With his hand.'

'Did it hurt?'

'A bit.'

Michael was appalled. He had never hit her and he could not imagine what she was doing. She must be identifying with her brothers, which would be typical of her sensitivity to other people, but it was hellishly dangerous. He could see that the jury were getting completely the wrong impression of him.

'Did it ever leave a bruise or make you bleed?'

'No.'

'Never?'

'No.'

'On the night that you heard them in the kitchen, Marianna, before your father started saying "don't hit me", did your mother answer any of those things he said to her about being dirty?'

Marianna nodded.

'What did she say?' he asked, sounding casual.

'She shouted at him.'

'What were the words? Can you remember them?'

Again she nodded and seemed to pull herself together. Her voice was stronger, almost angry, when she eventually spoke.

'She said that it was all very well for him to say she was dirty but she said he was just as bad. She said she had to wash his filthy underpants every week. That's what she said. She did.'

Michael looked at the crest over the judge's head. Every muscle in his body was taut and his head felt as though it were burning from inside his skull. He hated both barristers for putting Marianna through such an appalling ordeal. He hated her for telling the huge roomful of strangers what she had overheard. And most of all he hated Penelope for what she had done.

The jurors noticed that his detached, arrogant half-smile was gone. There was a whitish line around his mouth, as though he was having to work hard to keep silent.

'Thank you, Marianna,' said Charles Harcombe gently. 'That's all. You can go home now.' He waited until she had climbed down from the witness box and then put his wig back on, straightening it with both hands.

The jurors watched as Marianna walked towards the back of the court and put her hand into that of a tall fair-haired woman in her late thirties. She looked enough like Michael Beechen for several of the jurors to assume that she was related to him, but her strong face was plainer than his. She did not smile as she took his daughter's hand, but she looked quite kind as she led the exhausted child out of the courtroom.

Melissa, feeling sick, rummaged in the bag at her feet for a sugarless peppermint. She could not look at anyone else on the jury and, as the clean mint taste cleared her mouth, she concentrated on the lawyers.

Georgina Mayford was listening to something her junior counsel was whispering over her shoulder and apparently paying no attention to anyone else in court. She did not even look up as Harcombe called his next witness, a Mrs Jane Cawleigh.

'Mrs Cawleigh,' he said when she had taken the oath and identified herself, 'will you tell the court how you came to know Michael and Penelope Beechen?'

'Yes, we were all at drama school together.'

'That would be how long ago?'

'We left,' she said, frowning, 'let me see. We left ten years ago this summer.'

'Have you kept up with the Beechens since then?'

'Yes. We all live in Bristol now and I saw quite a lot of them, particularly after my children were born.'

The simple give-and-take of unemotional voices was a relief after Marianna's evidence and nearly everyone in court relaxed visibly. Only Michael stayed tense. He did not trust Jane Cawleigh. There had been too many times when he had gone home to the flat to find her and Penelope psyching each other up with complaints about him.

'Can you describe what you saw of the relationship between Mr and Mrs Beechen?'

'It was lovely at the beginning,' said the witness at once, not looking at the dock. 'They seemed really to love each other at the stage when the rest of us were just discovering sex.'

Yes, thought Michael, that was true. I'm surprised she's prepared to admit it, or that she even noticed it.

'It was different with Michael and Penelope,' Mrs Cawleigh continued. 'They were sort of shiny with love.'

Some of the more sophisticated jurors were watching her in surprise as they remembered that she was testifying for the prosecution; others were smiling sympathetically.

Michael knew that she was just softening them up. He looked at his particular juror and was glad to see that her expression was reserved. A woman like Melissa Wraxall would be much too sensible to be manipulated by Jane Cawleigh.

99

'What happened after the beginning?' asked Charles Harcombe.

'It all seemed to change after Marianna was born. Michael started to change, as though he'd discovered that he disliked all sorts of things about Penelope that he hadn't noticed before or that hadn't bothered him in the beginning.'

'What things?'

'Oh, like her relaxed attitude to housekeeping and her informal warmth. She was a terrifically warm person, and he seemed to despise that. And of course he started to display very strong views on the duties of a wife and mother.'

Michael stared at her, wondering whether she really believed what she was saying or whether she hated him so much that she was twisting reality out of revenge.

'Could you explain to the court what you mean by that?' said Charles Harcombe.

'He criticized her all the time, correcting whatever she did for the child and always wanting her to do more to clean and tidy the flat or prepare food. He was cold and . . . Olympian. He hated—'

'I am afraid you may not give evidence to the state of the defendant's mind,' said Harcombe, sounding genuinely regretful. 'How did Penelope Beechen react when he criticized her?'

Mrs Cawleigh smiled and looked pleased. 'When he got particularly unreasonable, she would just tell him to do whatever it was himself. She was no doormat.'

'And did he do things about the house?'

'Sometimes.'

Sometimes, thought Michael angrily. Nothing ever got done unless I did it. You know that perfectly well. Your best friend – my wife – was a slut, a vicious, filthy slut. And you know that, too.

'Thank you. Will you please wait there for my learned friend?'

Gina Mayford got to her feet and smiled politely at the witness, taking time to pick up her notes before she spoke.

'When you visited Penelope Beechen with your children, what was the condition of the flat?' she said at last, looking up at the witness box with a pleasantly enquiring expression.

'It was untidy,' said the witness after a pause.

'And the children?'

'I don't understand.'

'I'm sorry. In what condition were her children?'

'Perfectly normal for their age. They made a lot of noise and spilled their food over their clothes and ran about.'

'Was there any difference in their behaviour when their father was in the flat?'

'Not noticeably. He always tried to make them quieter.'

'Did he ever do anything with them to amuse or educate them in any way?'

'He read to them and played with them. Sometimes he took them out for a walk.'

'And did Mrs Beechen do the same?'

'Not at the same time.'

'Did she do it at other times?'

'Yes, sometimes.' Mrs Cawleigh looked uncomfortable and Michael waited for Georgina Mayford to ask more about what Penelope had ever done for his children, but she did not. He looked at the back of her wig with its silly little tail and willed her to push Jane further. He had given Gina Mayford enough information about the way Jane egged Penelope on to some of her wilder excesses of hatred. The jury ought to be told about it all.

'It sounds from what you're saying as though he was the more caring parent. Is that true?'

'He may have done more for the children in practical ways, but the only warmth they had was from Penelope.'

Michael was so surprised that he forgot about being on show and performing for the audience. His face looked absolutely blank and his mouth even dropped open a little way until he remembered where he was. He shut it then in a hurry.

'You told my learned friend that Penelope Beechen had a relaxed attitude to housekeeping. What did you mean by that?' asked Georgina Mayford, apparently unmoved.

'She never felt the need to impress people with conventional domesticity and never minded if the flat was untidy.'

'Was it merely untidy?'

'That would depend on your personal taste and obsessions. It was certainly untidy, but then any room of that size that has to contain three young children soon becomes untidy.'

'How clean was it?'

Michael was glad to see that Jane had at last begun to look uncomfortable.

'Put it another way, Mrs Cawleigh. Would you have wanted to bring up your children in that flat?'

The witness flushed and bit her lower lip. 'It all depends on what the children are used to. Mine are accustomed to a rather different way of life,' she said after a pause.

'I see. Yes, I quite see. Now, you have said that Michael Beechen gave his wife orders.'

'Yes, that's right.' The witness sounded happier, more assured. 'He behaved as though she was his servant.'

Georgina Mayford raised her thick, neatly shaped eyebrows. 'You have also said that his wife refused to accept his criticisms or his orders. If so, how could he be said to have treated her like a servant?'

That's better, thought Michael. She's doing her job at last.

'He treated her like that,' said Mrs Cawleigh defensively. 'She just refused to accept the treatment.'

'Thank you. Did he ever strike her that you saw?'

'Only once.'

'And did she ever hit him?'

Jane Cawleigh looked at the barrister who was standing in front of her and said with immense deliberation, 'I never saw her do anything violent to him. Ever.'

Once again Michael was so surprised that he looked directly at his accuser. He hoped that his much-derided acting skills were adequate to express the ferocious contempt he felt for her. Eventually she looked at him and he was pleased to see her flush and look away.

Georgina Mayford, who was watching her carefully, said, 'I would like to ask you again whether you ever saw Penelope Beechen strike her husband, and I must remind you that you are on oath.'

'I never saw anything like that,' said the witness deliberately. 'Never.'

'I see,' said Gina, raising her eyebrows again. 'Please wait there.'

Charles Harcombe asked the witness about the occasion on which she had seen Michael Beechen hit his wife.

'We were all on holiday together, at the beach. Their younger son wandered off and got lost. Not surprisingly, Penelope was terrified. Connor was only two at the time, and she'd heard just as many horror stories about abductions and paedophile rings as all the rest of us. She was crying and desperate. Michael told her she was making an exhibition of herself and he hit her across the face.'

'Thank you, Mrs Cawleigh.'

The witness was allowed to go. Michael Beechen watched her all the way from the witness box to the double doors that led out of the court. She stumbled once and blushed again. He looked pointedly at Melissa to make sure that she had noticed.

Chapter 7

Once again Melissa spent the lunch recess with Adam, Minty Collins and Susan Beere. Minty was looking even more magnificent than the previous day in a wonderful grass-green suit. Her big gold earrings, swept-back black hair, rich black skin and bright brown eyes made her look twice as alive as the rest of them.

Beside her Susan Beere seemed washed out and almost bedraggled in a loose round-necked olive-green sweater and the same long printed woollen skirt she had been wearing the previous day. Even the rectangular chiffon scarf she had looped loosely around her neck did not help, despite the rich autumnal colours of the material.

'That was vile,' said Minty as she studied the menu. 'Of all the things in the world I hate, the worst is watching a child being tormented.'

'How I agree!' said Adam.

'In that case, you've seen nothing,' said Susan bitterly. 'Marianna Beechen was positively cosseted compared to thousands of children – and grown women - in this country today.'

Melissa, who was increasingly upset by Michael Beechen's horribly obvious concentration on her, thought that Minty's breezy common sense was exactly what they all needed after the morning in court. Susan's bitterness might be justifiable, but it did not seem very helpful at that moment.

Melissa smiled at Minty, but she also said, 'Mrs Cawleigh's evidence did make me furious. I know it's the prosecution's job to make us hate Beechen and sympathize with his wife, but the defence didn't challenge the evidence that her life was ghastly.'

'I'm relieved,' said Susan, twisting her long earring round and round between her fingers until Melissa feared for the earlobe. 'You never seem at all troubled by any of the evidence. I was beginning to think that you shared the men's view that Penelope Beechen was a slut who deserved everything she got.'

'Not all the men in court think that,' said Adam, at the same time as Melissa was saying, 'How extraordinary! I've been seething ever since the trial began.'

'Well it hasn't shown. In fact you've been making me quite angry sometimes,' said Susan Beere frankly, 'as you sit there looking so superior and unmoved, while I'm having to fight to stop myself leaping to my feet to join in. I detest having to sit in silence while all that sexist nonsense is being aired all over again.'

'I'm sure,' said Minty with a wicked smile. Susan's tight, pale face relaxed slightly and Melissa blessed Minty's brave sense of humour.

'All right, I know I talk too much,' Susan said, looking much more human, 'and too bossily, but it's so frustrating to watch this case. It's quite clear what was going on in the Beechens' marriage, but you could tell from this morning's questions that the defence are going to twist it, and all the prosecution did was fiddle about asking unnecessary questions. I could have done a much better job.'

Melissa shivered, reluctant to be plunged back into the Beechens' marriage before she had to be. She would much rather have discussed the perils of owning your own business with Minty Collins if she could not repeat the cheerful, easy pleasure of her breakfast with Adam.

'What do you mean about the Beechens' marriage?'

he asked, making Susan look irritably at him across the table.

'Just that Michael Beechen was a familiar type of loser. He wasn't very good at his job and so he had to be cock-of-the-walk at home. He failed to get the part he was auditioning for that day, and so he came home needing all the ego-boosting he couldn't get from his work. He had to feel like an achiever somewhere, and home was the only place where he wasn't shown up by more successful people.'

'Can't you understand that?' said Minty, sounding more conciliatory than Susan. 'We all need somewhere we don't have to fight for approval.'

'I can understand the need, all right,' said Susan angrily. 'It's the means he used that I can't bear. He was obviously a domestic tyrant who bullied his wife to make himself feel better.'

Melissa looked at her with interest. She had described precisely the kind of man that Martin seemed to be. Catching sight of Adam's sympathetic expression, Melissa glanced down at the menu in her hands.

'Look at what happened on the night he killed her,' said Susan, apparently unaware of the sudden tension. 'The first thing he did was criticize his wife to their eight-year-old daughter – there's loyalty for you. Then he marched into the kitchen, where his stressed-out wife was putting her feet up for a minute, and laid into her verbally. Then he overrode all the arrangements she'd made for the children's evening and put them to bed, feeling better than his wife by spoiling – and therefore being adored by – his children. Then he went back and started beating his wife up.'

The other three were sitting in silence watching her as she spoke. Then Minty shook her head.

'You can't be sure of any of that. I'm sure you've known people like that. We've probably all seen them or at least read about them. But you haven't any proof that this Beechen was one.' She waved at one of the waitresses. 'It's too easy to look at a stranger with a few characteristics that are familiar from someone you know well and think the two people are the same all through. They can't be.'

Melissa made a mental note to keep her anger with Martin well away from her analysis of the evidence against Michael Beechen. It would be dreadful to decide he was guilty simply because his behaviour reminded her of her own husband's, or even because his continual staring at her made her feel so threatened.

'You may be right.' Susan's mouth looked thin and her eyes were as bitter as her voice.

'I'm going to have some cold meat,' said Adam to the waitress and then added to the others: 'We haven't all that much time left.'

All three women ordered salad. When it came Susan sat twisting a lettuce leaf round and round her fork. Her eyes were hard, but she did not speak. The other three made polite conversation as they ate and tried to draw her into it. The only time she spoke again was when Minty said something about the defence of provocation. Susan shook her head, making her long silver-and-amber earrings swing madly under her cropped hair.

'I don't think that they can use that. Beechen scuppered his chances by taking such a long time to kill her. That's why the prosecution have made such a meal of proving how long he spent putting the children to bed. If he'd hit out when he first saw the state of the kitchen, he'd probably have got away with it. The judge would have let him off with a suspended sentence. To most men of that class and generation wives simply exist to tidy up after them, and they probably would think that anyone who lets her kitchen descend into that kind of filth deserves to be killed.'

'Steady on,' said Adam, looking not at Susan but at a piece of rare cold beef on his fork. 'We haven't yet heard anything of the defence case. We can't assume that he killed her, let alone second-guess what his defence might have been, or the judge's reaction.'

'That's fair, Sue,' said Araminta when she had swallowed the last piece of tomato from her plate. 'You must admit it's fair.'

'Yes, I suppose it is. Thank you so much, Adam, for setting me right.' She laid down her fork without having eaten anything. 'I must go. I have some shopping to do. See you all later. Minty, can I pay you back for my share later?'

Minty nodded and ordered coffee.

Back in the jury box fifteen minutes later, they listened to evidence from the forensic pathologist who had performed the autopsy on Penelope's body. He described the cuts all over her neck and upper body.

'Were they simple stab wounds?' asked Charles Harcombe as colour photographs of the body were passed from the exhibits officer to the judge.

'No,' said the pathologist. 'As you can see, my lord, one of the wounds above the left breast is wider and more ragged than any of the others. In that case the knife was twisted back and forth before it was withdrawn.'

'Would that have been before or after death?'

'It's impossible to say. Some of the wounds may have been inflicted post mortem.'

The judge looked down at the photographs that had been passed to him from the exhibits table. After a few moments he signalled to an usher, who passed them to the jury. Unlike the original pictures of the body in the kitchen, the new batch had obviously been taken in the mortuary.

They did not show the entire body, which made it

easier for the jurors to feel dispassionately interested in what they saw. There were two slashes across the corpse's neck. The lips of each wound had spread apart, as raw steak does when it is cut with a very sharp knife, and then hardened in the air. There was another, more ragged cut just above the collar bone, and several more about the breasts, including the one the pathologist had described. Two patches of blackening bruises disfigured the right arm.

As the photographs were passed back to the exhibits table, the pathologist was led on to describe the victim's stomach contents and the quantity of alcohol she had drunk. When the prosecution had finished with him, Georgina Mayford's junior rose to conduct the cross-examination. The young barrister did not challenge any of the evidence that had been given so far. Instead he asked whether the pathologist would consider the wounds to have been the result of a 'frenzied' attack.

'It is impossible to judge the state of mind of some-one committing this kind of assault,' said the witness carefully.

'But you would presumably not judge such an assailant to be calm and collected?'

'No indeed.'

'I would be right, would I not, in saying that there were far more wounds than necessary to kill?'

'Certainly,' said the expert, showing some surprise.

'And that very few of the cuts are deep enough to cause any real damage, despite the copious bleeding that they caused?'

'That's perfectly true.' The pathologist smiled. 'But one deep wound in the heart is quite enough.'

'Yes indeed,' said the barrister with a hint of malice in his voice. 'And were either of us Horace Rumpole we could quote the relevant speech of Mercutio from

Romeo and Juliet. Were there any marks on the body of previous violent assaults?'

'Not that I could see.'

'No bruising, burning, scratching? No sexual violence? Anything of that sort at all?'

'No. The only bruising that I found was that on her right arm. It was consistent with the defendant's having gripped her just below the elbow with his left hand.'

'From the photographs,' said the barrister, looking down at his set, 'there seem to be two distinct groups of bruises.' He looked up again at his witness. 'How would you account for that?'

'They suggest that the assailant's grip shifted or that the victim managed to pull away and was then caught once more.'

'And were there any cuts on her arms and hands?'

'None.'

'Didn't that surprise you?' asked the barrister.

The expert was silent for a moment and then nodded.

'Yes. It is usual in stabbing cases where there are multiple wounds to find some cuts on the arms and hands, but it is not inevitable. The victim of a stabbing may try to defend herself by shielding her face and body with her arms, but there are other ways.'

'But you were surprised that Penelope Beechen had not used her arms to defend herself?'

'Slightly.'

'Thank you, doctor.'

As the young barrister sat down, the pathologist looked at Charles Harcombe, who was rising to his feet once more.

'Did you find any evidence to suggest that Penelope Beechen had tried to defend herself?'

'Yes,' said the pathologist. 'We took scrapings from

under her fingernails and found traces of human skin. The quantity was too small for identification, but the defendant had scratches on his left arm, which could have been caused by the victim.'

'Thank you. You may step down.'

After the remaining formal evidence of arrest and interview had been given, Charles Harcombe looked at the judge. 'That completes the evidence for the prosecution, my lord.'

The judge looked at the clock. 'I see that it is nearly four o'clock. I shall adjourn the case until half past ten tomorrow morning.'

Adam followed Melissa out of the court and round to the multi-storey car park automatically without even being offered a lift. As they were walking through the slight drizzle, he said abruptly, as though it really mattered to him, 'Do you think that there are any happy marriages at all?'

'Who can possibly tell?' said Melissa, sounding depressed. 'There must be, but I can't for the moment think of any, and listening to all that makes it seem unlikely. Why?'

'Oh, I suppose that despite my doubts I've always had a sneaking hope that one day I'll discover that it is possible for a human being to love and not damage another person,' said Adam. His voice held a suggestion of despair, which was quite different from his usual cynical humour.

Melissa saw that he was staring straight ahead, but it was unlikely that he could see anything. His eyes were blank.

'Come on,' she said gently, leading the way into the lift at the entrance to the car park and trying not to inhale the various revolting smells that rose from the floor. She pressed the button for the second level.

'It is depressing, though, isn't it?' he said.

'Yes, like a glimpse into an abyss one thought was merely a rut in the ground.'

'Can you explain that a bit?' Adam had begun to look interested instead of blank or despairing. Melissa forgot that she had already regretted confiding in him and tried to explain what she meant.

'What Susan said about Beechen at lunch today made him sound a little like my husband, and yet, however difficult Martin is, he could never in a million years be violent like that. The difficulties we're in at the moment are like a little divot in a lawn compared to the vast chasm that the Beechens had, which makes me realize what an absurd fuss I've been making.'

She paused and then made herself sound lightly amused as she went on. 'But even so, it's pretty tricky not to feel as angry with poor old Martin as I do with Michael Beechen - and vice versa. Although they're not the same at all.'

'No, I don't suppose they are,' said Adam.

Melissa smiled at him and he reached out to touch her hand just before the lift doors opened. A moment later, they emerged into the less offensive, dimly lit, petrol-smelling gloom of the car park. A small Peugeot, driven far too fast, squealed as its owner saw them and braked far too late. Melissa grabbed Adam's hand and pulled him into the safety of a large concrete pillar. The small car stopped a foot beyond the spot where they had been standing, skidding sideways in a patch of leaked oil. Melissa, still gripping Adam's wrist, leaned against the cold concrete, and closed her eyes.

We might be dead by now, she thought, as she felt the after-effects of shock pulsing through her body. Well, at least that would have solved all the problems.

The driver of the Peugeot wound down his window to hurl a filthy insult at them and then sped off. With the roar of his over-revving engine in her ears, and the pungency of the exhaust fumes catching at her throat, Melissa lay against the pillar. The concrete felt very hard, and rather scratchy, against her head. She opened her eyes.

Adam's face was very close to hers. She smiled slightly and was glad when he leaned forward until his lips were touching her forehead.

'Are you all right?' he murmured. The sensation of his lips moving against her skin made her shiver.

'I don't know,' she said, not moving. She felt his weight leaning on her a little more heavily.

His lips moved slowly down her face until they reached hers, clinging and soft like very fine suede. She felt herself sigh and her eyes closed again. Adam put his hands behind her head to protect it from the concrete as he kissed her. She let her hands slide up his back to touch his neck.

Only the sound of the lift doors opening again made them stop. Breathing hard, Adam pulled away from her. He looked at her with an intensity that was almost frightening. Then his face relaxed. After a moment he got his breathing under control, too, and said absurdly: 'That wasn't cricket, was it? I'm so sorry, Melissa.'

Straightening up, she felt completely unreal, and bathed in a kind of easy delight that was new to her. 'Don't worry about it. It took two,' she said, finding that her voice was surprisingly normal and that she could smile. 'The after-effects of shock, I suspect.'

'Probably,' he said and then shook his head, still watching her. 'No it wasn't. I've been wanting to do that all day. You . . . But I didn't mean to take advantage of you at a weak moment. I'm sorry.'

At that Melissa laughed. Feeling more certain of herself and her defences, she took his arm and led him to her car. 'That's a wonderfully Victorian expression, dear Adam,' she said. 'You didn't take advantage. I'm a grown-up, too, you know. Neither of us should have done it. We both did. I loved it. It can't be the prelude to anything else, but don't let's pretend.'

'No, all right,' he said. Then he smiled brilliantly. 'I loved it too. If I promise to behave, will you come and have that drink with me tonight?'

'What drink?' she said, unlocking the car.

'We talked about it this morning when I was trying to persuade you of my real interest in bees.'

'I thought you were joking,' she said. 'Alas, I can't tonight. In fact I ought not to have been dallying here with you at all. I've got an American client coming to dinner and I need to hurry.'

'Perhaps another evening?' said Adam, wondering how fast she was going to drive if she was worried about the time. He would not have sacrificed her presence for safety, but he would have quite liked to have both.

'Perhaps. Thank you.'

Chapter 8

Melissa ran into the house when she had parked the car, flung her coat over a chair in the hall and went straight to the kitchen. The flowers and food she had asked Annabel to buy were neatly laid out on the big scrubbed table, the white wine was already in the fridge and the red standing beside the corkscrew and a simple, charming eighteenth-century decanter engraved with vine leaves.

Checking the time, she decanted the wine, washed her hands and prepared the food with all the neat efficiency she could muster, trying not to think about the things Martin might do to sabotage any deal she might make with the American, or about the forbidden bliss of lying back being kissed by Adam Blake. That had to be buried and forgotten.

As soon as the honey-glazed duck breasts were safely in the oven and the lemon slices that would provide their garnish slowly caramelizing on the hob, the floating island pudding in the fridge and the first course of grilled vegetables laid out on plates, Melissa picked up the flowers and hurried to prepare the dining-room.

The whole point of inviting potential clients to the house was to attract them to her taste so that they would buy furniture and accessories from her. It was vital that the room looked as good as possible. By the time she had finished the table, she was quite pleased.

Pale yellowish candles of her mother's natural beeswax added their pungent, interesting scent to the sweet-smelling mixture of imported red roses and black grapes that she had arranged as a centrepiece. The mixture of white and silver, gold and rich red against the glowing mahogany pleased her, and she thought that the crimson damask walls and pale-honey-gold blinds made an excellent background to it all.

Fleeing upstairs to change at ten to eight and planning to deal with the drawing room when she was dressed, Melissa wrenched her ankle as she slipped just outside her bedroom. She rubbed the joint, wincing, and hobbled on into the bathroom. There was no time for a bath, but she had a quick shower. Starting to dress before she was properly dry, she had to keep stopping to rub water drops off her back or legs. She ruined one pair of tights by pulling them up too savagely and broke a nail as it snagged in the torn crotch. She tried to slow down, telling herself that Annabel would be bringing the American to the house and could give him a drink. Even if she herself were late Martin would be unlikely to do anything really destructive with Annabel as a witness.

As Melissa was slapping on a little eye make-up and lipstick, she saw that wisps of hair were escaping from her plait. With unusual clumsiness she unpicked it all, brushed it vigorously and then plaited it up again.

Reaching the drawing room only a few minutes after eight, breathless, she looked round it to see whether there was anything she needed to do. The yellow, white and pale-blue room was looking all right, she thought. A fire was burning in the stone fireplace, the rug in front of it was straight and unwrinkled, and all the antique needlework cushions had been plumped up on the yellow sofas. There were no books or magazines lying around on the tables.

Martin was sitting in one of the yellow-and-white-striped chairs, with his feet up on a stool, reading the newspaper.

'You look a bit flushed,' he said, looking up.

'I've been rushing about,' said Melissa. 'It was very good of you to tidy up in here for me. I'm really grateful, Martin.'

'Nothing to do with me. Annabel skived off this afternoon after she'd done your shopping and so it must have been her.'

'She is wonderful,' said Melissa. 'I couldn't do without her. I'll just nip down and get the flowers.'

She was carrying a large white vase of mixed narcissi and early pale-blue irises into the room just as Annabel brought Dick Walston to the door. Melissa put her vase down on the little satinwood table to the left of the fireplace and turned back to greet her potential client with as much grace as she could muster.

He was quite as tall as Martin and more distinguished-looking, with thick greying hair and a good forehead. Dressed with the utmost conservatism, he looked almost ambassadorial, but his smile had an engaging twist to it that suggested he might be less conventional than he seemed.

Ignoring Martin's unspoken protests, Melissa asked Annabel to stay for a drink and, once he had poured out a glass of white wine for each of them, discreetly collected another glass for Cecily.

She arrived fifteen minutes later, looking as spectacular as Melissa had expected and much more cheerful than the last time they had met. Annabel took the opportunity of her arrival to slip inconspicuously away.

Dick Walston's eyes brightened at the sight of Cecily as she stood looking at him, and his smile twisted even more. Melissa smiled in private relief, thinking that the evening would probably turn out all right after all.

At thirty-nine, Cecily was well past the usual age for dazzling men, and yet Melissa had never entertained her without seeing the male guests succumb to her charm.

They expanded in her company, and relaxed, and even the dullest managed to raise a laugh.

That evening she was wearing a full but floppy skirt of dark-red silk, which looked as though she had dug it out of her grandmother's dressing-up box, and a short black beaded jacket that was hooked tightly over her breasts. The jacket was not cut particularly low, but it looked as though it might have been, and there was something about her gleaming, loosely piled brown hair that suggested that not only it but also the jacket might collapse. She had managed to wash out all the inkstains.

Melissa kissed her and Cecily put both arms up round her neck in return.

'It is sweet of you to ask me here and feed me,' she said, beaming as though she had not been offered a square meal for weeks.

'We couldn't do without you, as you very well know. Now, come and meet Dick Walston. Dick, this is an old friend of ours, Cecily Wells. She writes the most exciting – and bloody – murder stories. You might not think it to look at her, but she's a real spine-chiller.'

'Glad to meet you, Ms Wells,' drawled the American. 'I've not read your books. Are they published in the States?'

'Oh, yes. And I've got a lovely lot of hugely generous fans there. I go over for the Bouchercon every year and they positively swarm round me wanting autographs and things.' She shuddered as though in the grip of overwhelming ecstasy. 'I really do adore being in the States.'

Remembering her depression over the current book, Melissa could only admire Cecily's technique. Her out-pouring ought to have sounded corny and gushing and generally silly, and yet for some reason it did not. She was merely presenting herself, as usual, as a woman who loved everything that life offered and would probably manage to find fun even on a municipal rubbish tip.

'That's rare,' said the American. 'Most of the British people I've met dislike the States, even when they pretend not to.'

'I like it a lot, except when I'm in Manhattan,' said Melissa politely. 'There I have to say that I have all kinds of negative thoughts and long for the peace of Bath – or even Boston.'

'Manhattan's not so different from London these days,' protested Martin, who had not in fact been to New York for eight years or more.

'No,' agreed Melissa hypocritically, 'but that's why we live in Bath.'

'Ever since I read *Northanger Abbey* as a boy, I've wanted to see Bath. Has it been much modernized and spoiled?' Dick addressed his question to Cecily, but it was Martin who answered.

'There are the major changes brought by cars, but otherwise I'd have said it was pretty much the same as it was in Jane Austen's day, apart from the more downmarket tourists, and the Crusties, of course. You get the same feeling of being overlooked all the time and gossiped about.'

There was a short uncomfortable silence broken by Cecily's saying cosily, 'Oh, come on, Martin. At least Lissa doesn't drag you to the Pump Room every day to be shown off and made to recite polite inanities to people you hate. That's my impression of old Bath – although I must admit it's taken more from Georgette Heyer than Jane Austen.'

'Cecily, you'll be giving Dick a very peculiar idea of your brains if you go on like that. You ought to know, Dick, that she does have a master's in Eng. Lit. from Vassar,' said Melissa cheerfully.

'Does she now?' he said, pushing his elegant spectacles closer to his eyes. 'Why an American school?'

'Let's dine,' said Martin, interrupting. 'Lissa, it's all ready, isn't it?'

'Yes, of course. Will you take Dick and Cecily into the dining room, while I collect the food?'

'Sure.'

They were sitting opposite each other discussing the American university system and Martin was pouring claret into their glasses as Melissa brought in the cold grilled vegetables. When she had handed them round and sat in her own chair at the foot of the table, she smiled as brilliantly as possible at Dick Walston and began her sales talk.

'You don't mind if we do business over dinner?' he said at once, obviously surprised.

Realizing that she must have sounded too pushy, Melissa did her best to recover her position.

'Oh, no. I know that you haven't got very long. Annabel said you're flying back tomorrow. That's why you and I are sitting next to each other,' she said with an attempt at the easy frankness that had served her best in the past. 'Those two are old friends. They can keep each other amused while you tell me what you want.'

'OK,' he said and started to list the objects he needed for a small, very expensive hotel near Boston, in Milton. 'It's a wonderful old house,' he finished up, 'and I want to give it some of that English country house feel with little gracenotes to make it look as though the family has just moved out. I want a knife box on an old chest, and pretty wine tables amongst the glass coffee tables, with a Canterbury or two to hold the magazines.'

'I see exactly what you mean,' said Melissa with almost genuine enthusiasm. 'And I'm sure we can help. After we've eaten I'll take you round the house and show you the sort of things we make. OK?'

'That'd be great,' he said.

Melissa smiled and started to ask about the houses

he had decorated in the States, wishing that she could be back in Carwardines, or even the driving seat of her car, talking to Adam. The effort of keeping her mind on her job was surprisingly tiring and it was a relief to be able to take the dirty plates down to the kitchen at the end of each course.

When she came back with the pudding, the conversation sounded fast and funny, led as always by Cecily. Melissa relaxed and let her mind play about with the things she and Adam had discussed. She was disappointed when, as soon as there was a gap in Cecily's story, Dick Walston turned back to be polite to her.

'I do think this is the loveliest house,' he said. 'Martin, you must be proud of your wife.'

Melissa stiffened and noticed that Cecily, too, was looking wary. They carefully did not look at each other until Martin said, sounding almost normal: 'I am, very proud. It's good of you to say so, Dick.'

Then Cecily winked at her friend, so quickly that neither of the men could have seen it, and said, 'I think she's brilliant. And utterly amazing to keep going through all this awful recession. Everyone else I know has been struggling like mad while Lissa seems to sail on through as though there were no difficulties at all.'

'It's partly the people I deal with, Cecily,' said Melissa quickly. 'And partly luck. I really have been enormously lucky.'

'That always helps,' said Dick Walston. He ate some of the floating island pudding. 'This is good. What's your line of work, Martin?'

'Oh, I'm just an accountant,' he said in a tone that made Melissa anxious. His eyes were quite unfocused and he was holding his head in a way that always worried her. She wished that she had been able to intercept the American and warn him about Martin's state of mind and sensitivities. She could not think of anything to say that would not make his humiliation worse and her subsequent punishment more severe.

'I've been meaning to ask you something for simply ages, Martin,' said Cecily seductively. 'My own account-ant has been really extraordinary recently. He's been waging a hideous war against me when he does the annual accounts. He says that I can't charge the business for the clothes I had to buy for my last promotional tour of the States.'

'He's quite right,' said Martin at once, smiling at Cecily's indignation and looking more natural. His eyes were sharpening again into their normal state. 'The Mallalieu case makes that incontrovertible. Clothes that you could wear at other times, even if you don't, are not chargeable as a business expense.'

'But it's outrageous,' said Cecily, as though she were dealing with some subject of cosmic importance, albeit with amusement somewhere in the background. 'When I'm at home I wear things like this. I'd never have bought those stiff suits and tidy shirts for myself.'

'Too bad, I'm afraid, my darling girl,' he said with such a warm-sounding laugh in his voice that Melissa almost got up to kiss Cecily again.

Melissa had to hold on to her gratitude until the end of the evening, by which time she and Dick had been down to the offices to go through the photographs and drawings of all Melissa's latest acquisitions and plans. Then she hugged Cecily and whispered, 'You are a dream of a friend, you know. You've turned Martin from being a grumpy bear into a human being. I don't know what I'd have done without you tonight. I wish you lived with us.'

'So long as you're pleased, angel,' said Cecily, patting her tall friend on the cheek. 'I enjoyed myself a lot.'

'Good. You didn't bring the car, did you?'

'That sounds very censorious. Do I seem so drunk that you don't think I can drive?'

Melissa looked down at her, noticed the twinkling smile, and nodded. 'Frankly, yes.'

'Quite right, darling, but you needn't worry. I came in a taxi.'

'Well, I'm sure Martin will drive you home. He's going to drop Dick off at the station for the last London train. Martin?'

'Of course. We'd better set off if we're to get you to the train on time.'

The American shook hands with Melissa. 'I'm very impressed with what I've seen, Lissa,' he said, smiling. 'I'll comb through your catalogue and fax you for quotes as soon as our plans are further advanced. OK?'

'Sure,' she said, still trying to summon up the warmth and confidence she knew that she needed to keep the business going. The thought of what might happen if she could not began to loom ahead of her. She smiled widely and, she hoped, convincingly. 'I've enjoyed meeting you, Dick. When you're next over here, you should come in daylight and we can show you Bath. It's a town like no other anywhere.'

'But don't come in the summer or at Christmas or you won't be able to see anything. A wet Sunday in February is the best time to see Bath's buildings unencumbered. Eh, Lissa?'

'I suppose that's right, Martin,' she said, relieved that he seemed cheerful again. 'Although the stone looks much better in sunlight. Come anyway, Dick, whenever you're back in England.'

'That'd be great. Well goodbye, and thank you again.'

Melissa waved them off, glad that Cecily would be there to stop Martin trying to upset the American and spoil the deal, and then she shut the door and set about clearing the dining room. Martin had always tended to get angry with her if she tried to wash up herself, demanding to know why she paid a daily cleaner if she wanted to do her own menial work. But the plates were valuable and the cleaner refused to believe that detergent would rub off the gold leaf. She was liable to scrub at them with anything she could find in the sink cupboard. Besides, Melissa liked her beautiful possessions and even washing them up could be a pleasure.

All the plates and glasses were not only washed and dried but also put away before Martin got back and Melissa had even started to clean the mahogany table. When she heard his car drawing up, she took her cloths and polish quickly back to the kitchen, stripped off her apron and sprinted up the backstairs so that he found her undressing beside a half-full bath when he reached the bedroom floor.

'I think it went rather well, don't you?' she called through the communicating door to their bedroom as she took off the rest of her clothes and got into the bath. 'You were absolutely right to ask Cecily. She really does lift these dinners and they could get a bit lugubrious without her. I hope Walston sends a big enough order to make it all worth while.'

'She's always been good value,' he said. 'Although her clothes! I do think she might make a bit more effort. That skirt this evening; I wouldn't polish a floor with it.'

You wouldn't polish a floor with anything, said Melissa to herself, even if the wood were dull and cracking and you had nothing else to do with your time. Aloud she said, 'I thought she looked stunning. And did you notice that Dick was breathing in time with the rise and fall of her breasts?'

'No.'

'Oh, yes. When I was handing the floating island pudding I noticed. He was quite clumsy spooning up the meringues and I looked to see why. He was absolutely riveted to her front.' She squeezed a spongeful of warm water down her back. 'I'm not surprised. It was looking particularly magnificent this evening. There is that about her clothes, Martin; their shabbiness does make her seem extra specially radiant herself.'

'Perhaps. Are you going to be long?'

'No. But if you're planning to take over this bath, why not have a hotter one all to yourself in the spare bathroom?'

'Might as well save on fuel costs to make up for your extravagant entertaining habits,' said Martin. 'I don't mind sharing your water so long as you haven't put any of that stinking oil in it.'

'Certainly not.' Melissa got out of the bath and wrapped herself in a big warm towel. There seemed no point in saying that she could easily afford all the entertaining she did for the business, let alone enough gas to heat a second bathful of water. 'It's quite pure. A little soap contamination, but nothing else.'

'Great. I won't be long. Don't go to sleep.'

She paused in the doorway as he said that, its meaning unmistakable. Lying back in bed, waiting for him, she tried to feel eager or even resigned. It did not work and by the time he appeared by the bed she was anything but receptive. In the old days she would have told him so, kissed him and gone to sleep, but that no longer seemed possible. He was too unhappy for her to risk adding to his distress. She managed to smile and held out her arms.

Martin subsided into them and without a word started to kiss her neck. Kiss seemed a rather gentle word, she thought a moment later, for what he was doing. When she put her hands on either side of his face to push him gently away, he grabbed them and forced them up above her head against the pillows. He stared down at her with what looked terrifyingly like hatred. Pinning both her wrists down with one hand, he pushed himself inside her with the other, hurting her.

'Martin, wait.'

126

'Shut up,' he said furiously before starting to bite her shoulder as he stabbed at her.

'Martin, don't. Please stop it. Martin, it's horrible. Martin.'

'Shut up, shut up, shut up, shut up,' he said, matching the rhythm of his thrusts.

Giving in, because there was nothing else to do, Melissa closed her eyes and just waited for it to end.

When he was done, Martin lay against her for a few minutes, panting, and then released her hands, pulling away without a word. He rolled on to his back and lay staring at the ceiling.

Melissa could think of nothing whatever to say. She was hurt and angry and, for the first time, really afraid of him. Hoping that he would say something, anything, to prove that he was still the man she had once loved, she waited in silence. But he said nothing. After a while she turned her back, tucked her square chin into the pillow, and tried to sleep.

It was not a successful effort and as soon as she had heard the first snore from Martin, she slid out from under the duvet, wrapped herself in a dressing gown and walked painfully downstairs to the kitchen. Taking a teaspoon from the cutlery drawer she reverted to childhood and helped herself to some of her mother's best heather honey from one of the jars on the shelf by the window. Abigail used to dose her with honey for everything from sore throats to nightmares or even tantrums.

The familiar sweetness helped a bit, but Melissa could not face going back to lie beside Martin so soon, and so she went on down to her office. There, she switched on the electric fan heater, pulled a grey mohair rug round her bare feet and for the next three hours read Cecily's latest published murder story.

Chapter 9

The following morning Melissa waited in bed, pretending to be asleep, until she heard Martin going downstairs for his early morning run. As soon as the front door had banged behind him, she got up, bathed, washed her hair and tried to decide what to wear. She did not feel up to the dark-blue suit. It was not exactly uncomfortable, but it required a certain confidence, which she no longer had.

Her most comfortable black trousers were back from the cleaners and eventually she put them on with a matching polo-necked sweater and a loosely woven crimson jacket. Having bundled her clean hair back into a black scrunchy instead of taking time to arrange it properly, she tried to disguise the deadness of her face with blusher, mascara and lipstick.

When she went down to the kitchen to make a cup of coffee, she saw that Martin had left her a note. Wondering if he had brought himself to apologize, and if he had what she would find to say to him in return, she unfolded the small piece of paper.

Lissa,
Forgot to tell you yesterday, but some of the chaps from the squash club have asked me to have dinner with them tonight.
Martin

Making a pot of coffee automatically, Melissa rehearsed all the old excuses and explanations for the way

Martin behaved, trying to will herself into even liking him. Eventually she admitted that, for the moment at least, she could not do it. She drank half a cupful of coffee far too hot before flinging the rest into the sink and washing out the cup. Martin's mug lay unwashed beside his used teabag, which had leaked thick brown fluid all over the worktop.

He was jogging back into the Circus in his running kit as she edged the car out of its parking space, but he pretended not to have seen her. At that moment it seemed impossible that they would ever be able to retrieve any kind of normal life. Melissa did her best to find something to think positively about as she drove down the hill to Queen Square, but all she could latch on to was the fact that in two days' time she would be seeing her mother.

It was not that she planned to tell Abigail what had happened. Their relationship had never included tricky emotional confidences. But Abigail lived in an atmosphere of calm, kind rationality that seemed enormously attractive just then, and very much safer than anything Melissa had managed to create in her own house.

Adam was waiting for her on the corner outside the hotel, looking perfectly familiar in his grey flannel trousers and the shabby mole-coloured corduroy jacket he always wore. His smile became astonishingly brilliant when he saw her drawing up beside him.

As he got into the car, he leaned towards Melissa as though he were going to kiss her again. She flinched and he pulled back at once.

'Don't worry,' he said quickly. 'I was only going to kiss your cheek. Everyone does that, even in Bath. It's quite respectable.'

Melissa did not know what to say, torn between wanting to explain everything to him and a feeling that the less she involved him in her life the better it would be for everyone. He frowned and briefly touched her hand.

'Kissing you yesterday was wonderful, like . . . oh, like drowning in honey; but I accepted what you said. I'm not going to do it again. The idea of forcing myself on you fills me with horror. Don't worry about it.'

Melissa looked at him, knowing that he could not have had any idea of what had happened the previous evening and yet comforted. His choice of words seemed to legitimize some of her loathing of what Martin had done.

'What is it?' Adam asked gently.

'Sorry,' said Melissa. 'I must be half asleep. I . . . Ignore me. I'm in a weird mood this morning, Adam. I didn't sleep much. It's probably that.'

'I doubt it,' he said, examining her face. 'But you don't have to tell me anything.'

At that she smiled and nearly told him all of it. Instead she said, 'Is the invitation to a drink still open? I've been stood up for this evening in favour of my husband's fellow squash players, and it would be nice to have a drink with you and see your bee books.'

'I've promised to see some of my students at the university at five,' Adam said, 'but what about dinner somewhere a bit later? I should definitely be back in Bath at, say, eight.'

'That sounds lovely,' said Melissa. 'I know you haven't got a car at the moment. Shall I come and pick you up?'

'Why don't we meet at the restaurant near where I live, and then if I'm held up at least you'll be able to have a drink in the warmth instead of hanging about in your car. Do you know Michele's in Bear Flat?'

'Bear Flat?' said Melissa. 'Are there any restaurants up there?'

'There speaks a woman whose address is in the Circus,' said Adam. Seeing her surprise, he added, 'I looked you up in the telephone book. Yes, there are places to eat in Bear Flat, and Michele's is a treat. You'll see.'

'I stand corrected,' said Melissa with enough dramatic emphasis to let them both laugh and pretend to forget everything else.

That morning in court Georgina Mayford started to put Michael Beechen's defence before the jury. It was not the defence she would have chosen to run but it was the one he had insisted was the truth. She had had no option but to accept his instructions.

Unlike her adversary, she did not play with her gown, smoothing the edges down over her chest and flinging the generously cut sleeves back and forth as though to emphasize her legal status and authority. Instead she stood very still, with her ringless hands resting lightly on the bench in front of her.

Some of the jurors and several of the journalists felt sorry for her. The judge, who had watched her work before, did not. He knew that she was an excellent advocate and he waited with carefully hidden interest to see how she would conduct the defence.

'Members of the jury,' she began, her pleasant voice neither cajoling nor hectoring, 'my learned friend has told you that on the night of fifth December last year Penelope Beechen was killed by one or more of seven stab wounds caused by the four-inch carbon steel vegetable knife that you have already seen. He has told you that all the scientific evidence points to the fact that my client, Michael Beechen, wielded that knife. We do not dispute that. He did.'

There was a movement in the jury benches and Sue Beere muttered to Araminta Collins, 'I told you so.'

Michael Beechen heard the whisper and frowned. He knew that most of the women in the jury were against him, but he thought they ought to have the manners to keep quiet.

Waiting in the cells beneath the court that morning, he had been doing the familiar voice exercises he had learned at drama school and trying to practise the answers he would soon have to give. His voice kept failing him. It would start all right and then grow husky. Pain would grip his throat and his voice would die completely. He knew that if he sounded at all afraid, or if he contradicted himself or showed any signs of guilt, he would fail to convince them of the truth.

He thought that Melissa Wraxall was looking much less cool and elegant than usual, and for the first time he wanted to make her like him as well as believe him. His throat felt tight and raw. He wished that he had some cough sweets to suck and tried to make sure there was enough saliva in his mouth by rubbing his tongue backwards and forwards against his palate.

'What my learned friend has been unable to tell you,' Georgina Mayford was saying, apparently oblivious of the whispers and movements in the jury seats, 'is why Michael Beechen should have stabbed his wife, the mother of his three children, to whom, as all the evidence has shown, he is devoted.

'In the evidence that follows I shall show that for a period of eight years, since their first child was born, he had lived in fear of his wife.'

'Oh, nonsense!' mouthed Sue and wrote a note on the pad in front of her, savagely underlining it.

'That is, members of the jury, fear of the violent, physical attacks Penelope Beechen made on him.' Georgina Mayford moved her shoulders slightly and for once there was audible emotion in her deliberately calm voice as she went on. 'You will learn from him exactly what happened on the night of fifth December, and why he picked up the knife you have all seen. As you have already heard, as soon as he realized how seriously his wife was injured, he telephoned her doctor. The rest of what happened that evening is as my learned friend has described it. At no time during all the subsequent hours of questioning did Michael Beechen admit that he had murdered his wife.'

She paused, coughed to clear her throat, and then went on more loudly, 'That was because he had not killed her unlawfully. He hit out in blind terror of his life. His wife died, but it might easily have been he who was killed, or perhaps one of their children.' Gina gave the court a moment's silence to remember the smallness and vulnerability of the only one of his children they had seen.

'It had been Michael Beechen's nightmare ever since the first attack that his wife would turn on the children and harm them.'

Michael's eyes closed again for a moment as foul memories banished even present anxieties from his mind.

'Until that night, he had put up with his wife's attacks and his own injuries for eight years, never retaliating because of his fear that with his greater strength he might hurt her seriously. But on that one evening, he was so frightened that he did hit out.'

Georgina Mayford's voice was still apparently cool, but there were undertones of anxiety and pleading that made some of the women inclined to believe her.

'Members of the jury, in calling the evidence that you will hear it may at times appear that I am trying to blacken Penelope Beechen's reputation so that in sympathy for her husband you will acquit him.'

She turned to face the jurors fully for the first time, throwing back her head and straightening her shoulders.

'But appearances can often be deceptive,' she said clearly in a voice that rang through the large white-walled court. Beechen straightened his own shoulders and managed to push some of his memories away. 'My purpose in examining the witnesses you will hear is solely to establish the truth of what happened that night. Blaming women sometimes seems like a national sport, and it is one with which no intelligent person should have any truck. We are not here to blame, or indeed to excuse, Penelope Beechen for anything she did during her life.'

That's neat, thought Charles Harcombe sourly as he noticed several of the jurors smiling and nodding. He comforted himself with the knowledge that whatever Gina Mayford might say to them his case really was unassailable.

'She is not on trial,' Gina went on. 'Her husband is. We are here only to establish whether or not he killed her unlawfully. As his lordship will tell you, a killing in lawful self-defence is no offence. Self-defence is lawful when it is necessary to use force to resist an attack or to defend yourself.

'I shall be calling Michael Beechen's doctor and some of the casualty officers who have treated him in the past, and you will hear from them of the severity of the injuries his wife inflicted on him. But first you will hear from Michael Beechen himself.'

The jurors considered Beechen as he left the dock, wondering how a woman the size and weight of his wife could ever have terrorized a man so much larger than herself.

He did not look like a wimp to any of them, even to Susan Beere, who had once commented in print on the hangdog vulnerability that photographs of some members of the embryonic 'men's movement' seemed to display. She had been much criticized for adding that some of them seemed to have 'hit me, hit me' written all over them.

'Is your name Michael Beechen?' asked Georgina Mayford formally when her client had settled himself in the witness box.

'Yes.'

'And is your usual address Flat 49, East Tower, Latchings Estate, Bristol?'

'Yes.'

'Will you please tell the court what happened on the night of fifth December last year?'

Michael breathed carefully, as he had been taught in his student days, and looked at the jurors. He only just managed to resist the temptation to smile at Melissa before he forced himself to think back to the night when Penelope died.

'I arrived home from an audition fairly late,' he told Melissa as though they were alone in a small room together, 'about half past eight, I think. The bus from London took longer than usual because it was raining and there was a lot of traffic. I was quite worried because my wife had been showing the first signs of PMT the previous day, and that always had a bad effect on her.'

Melissa was taken aback to find herself addressed so directly, but she could not help listening.

'Can you describe the effect?' asked Gina Mayford. Michael never looked at her. To Melissa, he answered:

'It made her violently angry.'

'With whom?'

'Almost anyone she had to deal with, but chiefly with me.'

'I see,' said Gina, surprised that her client refused to look at her. It was going to be quite hard to question him as she had planned if he continued to appear so indifferent to her. 'Thank you. Please go on.'

'I hadn't seen her that morning because I'd had to leave the flat before she got the children up. That worried me because when she was suffering from PMT she often snapped viciously at Marianna when she was trying to get the boys ready for school.'

'Who was getting the boys ready for school?'

'Marianna,' he said impatiently, looking at his counsel

for a second. He turned back to Melissa to explain: 'She always did her best to take over the tasks that upset Penelope and that was one of the worst. Marianna worked very hard to keep things together when her mother was out of control. She—'

'Why was getting them ready for school such a problem?'

At his counsel's second unnecessary interruption, Michael Beechen looked angry. Not even his considerable acting skill could disguise it. He thought that despite her legal experience Gina Mayford understood nothing of putting a story over. After a moment's silence, he shrugged and slightly shook his head and looked back at Melissa.

'They'd lose things, you see: a shoe, their reading books, their lunch boxes. All that annoyed Penelope when she was in a state and so Marianna would go round the flat looking for everything that would be needed before her mother could lose her temper.'

'Did you ever try to remonstrate with your wife over her behaviour?'

'Often.' Michael thought he saw some softening of Melissa's intent expression. 'If I was out of work, I'd go round the flat myself tidying up so that things could not get lost. That made her angry. I often had to point out to Penelope that if she didn't reduce the flat to a complete tip, the children would find it easier to keep track of their belongings.'

'What was her reaction to that?' asked Georgina Mayford as calmly as usual. Even her hands were still.

'She usually poured out a diatribe about how tyrannical I am and how I made her slave for me, tidying up all the time,' he said bitterly, wishing that Melissa had not suddenly turned away from him to look at her neighbour. It seemed like deliberate rejection and it hurt. Michael tried to pull himself together.

'And sometimes she hit me. I could never make her understand that it was not for my benefit that I wanted the place clean and tidy but for the children – and for her.'

Georgina Mayford smiled encouragingly at her client, but he did not see it. 'Thank you. Now, on the night when she died, what happened after you returned home from the audition?'

Michael took a moment before he answered. He knew his lines and he knew that he could put them over convincingly as long as Gina Mayford did not interrupt too often. He licked his lips and began to tell Melissa what had happened, ignoring everyone else in court. Her head was still averted from him, but he knew that she could hear him. Other people had cut themselves off from him before. He hoped he would be able to put up with it until he could make her listen to him properly. In the end she would listen; he was sure of that.

'I got back and the flat was in its usual chaos. None of the children were in bed and there was no sign of Penelope. I asked Marianna how she'd been and she said "Not too bad", but she was white and trembly. I realized that Penelope had been having at her. Marianna also told me that they'd had no supper.'

Michael pinched the bridge of his nose between finger and thumb as a sudden headache bit into his forehead. When he took his hand away from his face he saw that Melissa had turned back and that she was looking at him again.

'I went into the kitchen, where Penelope was sitting smoking and reading a magazine. There was a tumbler half-full of sherry beside her. There was food all over the worktops, and the cats, and no sign of supper being cooked. I got some bowls of cereal ready for the children and took it out to them.'

'Did you say anything to your wife?'

137

'Yes. I told her what I was doing.'

'Did she answer?'

Michael took another deep breath before carefully exhaling again. He reminded himself of Marianna and what Penelope had made her suffer. That gave him the strength to go on to say what had to be said.

'She told me to please myself,' he said carefully, 'that all I was fit for was waiting on little children; that if I'd been any good as an actor I'd have been infinitely more successful by then, and we wouldn't have to live in a pokey little two-bedroomed flat twelve floors from the ground, and she wouldn't be bored out of her skull.

'She also said that she had no need to ask whether I'd got the part, because she knew I'd fail again. I'd always fail.'

His carefully modulated voice began to sound ragged and he cursed himself until he saw Melissa looking encouragingly at him. Perhaps showing a little weakness had been no bad thing. Concentrating on her, he got ready to plough on.

'Did you answer her?' asked his lawyer.

'There seemed no point,' he said, shrugging his shoulders. He had his voice under control again. 'She knew the realities of trying to make a living from acting as well as I did. She knew that if I could have got more or better paid work I would have done. I left her and went to feed the children and put them to bed.'

Most of the jurors wished that they did not have to listen to the full account of what had happened to Penelope Beechen, but some were excited. Melissa just hoped that Michael would stop looking at her as though there were some kind of connection between them.

'And what did you do then?' asked Georgina Mayford deliberately. There was just a hint of stoicism in the way she was standing that suggested she, too, might dislike the story.

'I read to Marianna and tried to reassure her – she knew what was probably coming as well as I did – lit the boys' nightlight, turned off the main light and shut the door. Marianna didn't like it shut, but I knew Penelope was likely to start yelling at me and I wanted to shield the children as much as possible. I went back to the kitchen and Penelope started in on me at once.'

'Can you explain to the court what you mean?'

Not to the court, thought Michael, but to Melissa Wraxall. Any woman who looked as she did would have detested Penelope.

'She shouted that I had ruined her life, that she'd always been a better actor than me, that if I hadn't interfered she'd have had a much more successful career than mine. That I was useless. All the usual things.'

There was a contemptuous sniff from someone on the jury benches.

'What did you say?' Georgina Mayford had begun to sound more intense, less professionally at peace with herself than before.

'Nothing. There was no point. I noticed a smell of burning, and I lifted the lid of the pan on the cooker. When I saw that it had boiled dry I remonstrated with Penelope as patiently as I could and turned off the gas. The pan was of very high quality. It had been a wedding present from my mother, along with most of the decent things in the flat, and it had been completely spoiled. We had no money to waste throwing away good saucepans.'

Several inhabitants of the public benches at the back of the court looked disappointed. Beechen's words were so formal, so dull, that it sounded as though their drama was going to be watered down.

'Before I knew what was happening, Penelope had seized the pan. She yelled at me that it was her kitchen

139

and that if she wanted to boil saucepans dry she bloody well would and that I had no business interfering with her. She screamed that she hated me. I could see that she was going to hit me with the pan. Usually, she took care not to mark my face, but this time the pan was coming straight at my eyes. It was nearly red hot.'

He paused and looked helplessly towards the jury box, trying to make Melissa understand the terror he had felt as Penelope's hatred was revealed in all its monstrous violence.

'She told me she wanted to burn me so that my face would be spoiled. I could feel the heat of the pan on my skin from two feet away. I dodged and so she only caught my hand instead of my face.

'I whipped my hand away and caught hold of her wrist. She seemed to be even more out of control than usual and I—' He caught his breath, lowered his head for a moment, and then made himself look up again and go on. 'I was terrified. She was yelling and swearing and I simply couldn't hold her. She told me she was going to kill me.'

'Did she actually use those precise words?'

'Yes. She said life would be much easier if I was dead and so she was going to kill me,' he said drearily, dragging out each syllable.

'What did you do?'

'I grabbed her right arm with my left hand,' he said, holding out his arm as though demonstrating his grip to the jury, 'and held the hot pan away from us both. She was clawing at my left hand with her nails and trying to prise my fingers apart. The nails were chipped and torn as usual and they scratched me. The scratches have all healed now. I reached out for something to use as a kind of shield. I kept dropping things. They slid away from me on the worktops. I couldn't find anything. She was shrieking and yelling at me and hitting me and scratching. I kept her right arm as far away from both of us as I could and felt around with my right hand for something, anything, to help.' His voice, which had been rising towards hysteria, dropped once more. 'And I picked up the knife.'

As the jurors watched, they saw his face whitening. Once more there was absolute silence in the court as there had been when his daughter was giving evidence. He had everyone waiting to hear what he had to say next.

'What happened then?' asked his barrister. Michael took a sip of water from the glass in front of him.

'I told her to drop the pan and to control herself,' he said more calmly. 'She wouldn't. She just went on yelling and hitting and scratching me. My left arm was getting tired and aching as I held the weight of the pan in her hand as high above her head as I could. I moved my right hand. I never meant to kill her.' He stopped and looked helplessly at Melissa.

'It sounds stupid,' he went on, shaking his head. 'But I never did want her dead. All I wanted was to make her stop hitting me.'

'How many times did you stab her?'

'They say it was seven. I can't remember. All I can remember is being desperate to stop her. At first it was just putting the point of the knife against her skin as I told her to stop hitting and scratching me. And she wouldn't stop. She didn't seem even to notice the knife. I had to push it in a bit futher to make her notice. I had to, to make her stop. I had to. The blood started to pour out. But even that didn't stop her. Eventually, I . . .' For a moment he seemed unable to go on and simply stared at Melissa, willing her to understand. He caught sight of a slight movement to her left and looked across to see one of the other women jurors frowning at him, her face coldly incredulous.

'I just don't remember anything else until I realized she

was lying there on the floor absolutely still and that there was blood all over the kitchen and both of us,' Michael said, turning his gaze back to Melissa. 'It felt sticky between my fingers and almost gritty under my nails. I was terrified the children would have been woken and would come and see. Luckily the telephone's in the kitchen and so I rang for the doctor straightaway and just waited.'

'Did you not go to see how the children were? Whether they had been upset by the noise?' asked Georgina Mayford, sounding surprised.

Michael's face creased as he frowned and shook his head.

'No.'

'Why not?'

'Because I knew that I ought not to wash or clear up the kitchen or anything before the authorities got there, but I couldn't go into the children with their mother's blood all over me. How could I? I just waited until the doctor came.'

'I see. Yes. Thank you,' said Gina Mayford as her client took a handkerchief from his pocket and wiped his hands over and over again. He even pushed it under his fingernails, picking at them.

'Lady Macbeth,' hissed Susan Beere under her breath.

Gina waited until Beechen put the handkerchief back in his trouser pocket.

'Mr Beechen, can you go back a little further in time and tell the court why you stayed with your wife when she treated you so violently?'

She did not look at her client as she asked that question. There was a pause.

'I loved my wife,' Michael said at last with a faint quiver in his voice. 'During most of every month she was the woman I had fallen in love with. Sometimes, when she was normal, she would even apologize for the bad times and ask me to help her. I tried but nothing worked.'

'What happened when she was not normal?'

'Sometimes she would just pick quarrels about silly things or tell me how I had failed her. At others she would hit me, sometimes just with her fists but more often with any weapon she could lay her hands on.'

'Can you give us an example of the weapons?'

'Yes. Sometimes she would use screwdrivers or the hammer we kept in the kitchen for repairs. Occasionally she used knives or other things from the kitchen; once she pressed the hot iron into the small of my back.'

Melissa winced and noticed that several of the jurors were looking horrified.

'Did you seek treatment for any of the injuries?'

'Yes. I sometimes went to my GP and sometimes to hospital casualty.'

'Where did you go with the burn on your back?'

'To my GP.'

'Did you do anything else?'

'Yes. I went to the police – not my local station – to ask if there was anything they could do, and then to the Family Information Service for advice about what sort of protection I might be able to get.'

'When your wife attacked you, did you ever hit back?' asked Georgina Mayford.

'No. I was afraid that I might hurt her. Whenever I saw her coming at me with a weapon I would try to get it away from her. But sometimes she hit me from behind when I was not expecting it, and that's when I used to get hurt.'

'How could you love her when she did such things to you?'

'I don't know, but I did love her.'

'Was your love the only reason why you continued to try to make the marriage work?'

'No,' said Michael at once, knowing that the one thing that was completely safe to reveal was his anxiety for

143

Marianna. 'There were the children, too. The thought of leaving them alone with her was horrible. You see, if she hadn't got me to beat up, perhaps she would have gone after them. I couldn't risk it. At least being bigger and stronger than Penelope I had a chance of defending myself.'

'Thank you, Mr Beechen,' said Georgina Mayford, looking at him once more. 'Would you just wait there?'

The judge, having looked at the clock on the wall and then at his own watch decided to adjourn the trial until two o'clock.

Chapter 10

'Lunch?' suggested Adam to Melissa as soon as they had reached the passage beyond the jury room.

'D'you know, I really don't think I could eat anything after that. I feel much more like a brisk walk. I've got a bit of a headache. Would you mind?'

'Not at all. I take it that you want to walk on your own?'

'Yes,' she said, relieved that he had understood her so easily.

'I'll see you later then. Be careful.'

Surprised by the instruction, Melissa nodded and watched him walk towards the usual restaurant with Sue and Minty. She herself set off for the river, where she thought the air would be fresher and she might be able to breathe more comfortably. Before she had walked more than a hundred yards, she saw a telephone box. Reluctant, and yet persuaded by an impulse she did not understand, she decided that she had to re-establish contact with Martin. It might be easier to do that by telephone than face to face.

'What's the matter, Lissa?' he asked impatiently as soon as Bel had put the call through to him.

'Nothing's the matter. I just wanted to find out if you're all right.'

'Of course I am. What the hell are you doing now? Checking up on me to make sure I'm here and working for my derisory wages?'

'Oh, Martin, of course I'm not.' Melissa closed her

eyes and leaned forwards against the glass wall of the telephone box. It felt very cold on her forehead. Trying to explain, she added: 'I've just been listening to accounts of horrible domestic brutality in the trial I'm doing—'

'Oh, I see. This is a subtle way of punishing me for last night, is it?'

'Far from it,' she said, stung into more frankness than she had planned. 'But, since you've raised the subject, perhaps it's a way of asking for an explanation. If I could understand then I might not mind quite so much.'

'Must you try and analyse everything? I was a bit clumsy last night. There are different ways of making love, you know. It happens like that sometimes. Sorry. Is that what you wanted? To make me grovel?'

'I've obviously interrupted you at a bad moment,' Melissa said, doing her best to avoid sounding as angry as he.

For her the words 'a bit clumsy' did not begin to describe his deliberate, punitive roughness. She could hardly bear to remember the early days when they had touched each other with care and tenderness, minding whether the other was happy and enjoying what was happening.

Melissa straightened up and noticed that she had left a patch of slightly sticky sweat on the glass wall. Taking out a paper handkerchief, she wiped the glass, saying: 'I'll go now and leave you in peace. See you when I get back this afternoon.'

'Bye.'

Melissa put down the receiver and waited until the machine spat back her phonecard. Then she walked through the town to the river. There was an empty bench overlooking the boats and she sat down, huddled in her overcoat, and stared at the rusty sides of what she thought must be a tug. The air was a little less stale, but the whole lifeless scene in front of her was depressing.

Everything seemed to be grey, black or brown, and there was decay wherever she looked. A group of seagulls shrieked as they flung themselves in concentric circles across the dark-grey sky, and traffic thundered somewhere behind her, but she heard none of it.

Adam found her sitting hunched on the red-painted bench at half past one. He sat down beside her and, without looking at her, said: 'I don't want to disturb you if you want to be on your own, but if there's anything I can do, will you tell me?'

She looked at him at once and he saw that her eyelashes were damp. Apparently unembarrassed, she rubbed them with her handkerchief and murmured something about the biting wind. He saw with pity that she was completely unaware that she had smudged mascara all round her eyes.

'I just needed to get away,' she said at last. 'It's very hard not to draw parallels between what we've had to listen to and . . .'

'I can't imagine there being anything in your life that is at all similar to anything we've heard about in that court,' said Adam at once. 'Melissa, the woman we've heard about this morning was obviously disturbed.'

'We don't know that yet,' she said, trying to be sensible and look at both sides of the question. 'All we've heard is that she hurt her husband, or so he claims. There's been no proof. I suppose she could have been a psychopath. On the other hand, so could he and the things she did to him merely attempts to defend herself, if she did them at all. We don't know. I don't see how we can ever know with the sort of evidence we're being offered. That's the problem.' Melissa breathed deeply and then coughed as the cold air reached too far down her throat.

Adam put his hand on her knee. She could feel the coldness even through the material of her trousers. Staring forwards again, she put her own gloved hand on top of his naked one.

'Oh, this trial! How I detest it!'

'So do I,' said Adam, 'although without it you and I would never have met, and I'm coming to think that that would have been a real deprivation.' He paused and then added firmly, 'You can't think how I admire you, Melissa.'

'That's kind,' she said mechanically, staring straight ahead, 'but I don't see how you can. As far as I can see, all I've done since we met is moan at you about what a mess I'm making of my married life, persuaded you into kissing me, and then told you ungratefully that we must never do it again.'

Adam smiled and shook his head. Melissa waited, wishing that she had not said anything.

'On the other hand,' he said, striving for easy cheerfulness, 'you are extraordinarily good company.' He stood up. 'Come on, or we'll be late and that'll be very embarrassing.'

Melissa let him pull her to her feet. A little sunlight found its way through a gap in the clouds and she suddenly saw that she was not surrounded by depressing ugliness after all. The rusty ships and brown water were part of a picture that also included plump, wetly gleaming cobblestones and black trees whose budding branches reached upwards to spread elegantly against the thick sky. There were smooth bollards and well-painted red doors to add colour to the grey and brown and black. Looked at whole, it was an attractive scene. Only some of the individual components were ugly.

Turning to Adam, she saw the deep lines that had been drawn on his face by pain or stoicism, the thick, slightly greying hair, the worried eyes, the determined chin and the gentle, generous mouth. It was a face of contradictions, but it added up to the man who had surprisingly become a friend. It was a good face and trustworthy. She smiled. The anxiety drained out of his dark eyes, and they lit up as he smiled back.

'Better?'

'Much.' Melissa pulled up the sleeve of her heavy coat so that she could see her watch. 'You're right. We ought to be getting back.'

'And we must pick you up a sandwich as we go. Otherwise you'll start fainting.'

'Yes, Nanny.'

'Oh, come on! I'm not that bad. I just think you ought to eat something.'

He bought her a cheese sandwich, which she ate as they walked back to the Old Guildhall. Melissa felt absurdly uncomfortable to be eating in the street, but by the time she had finished the limp bread and dull cheese, she admitted to herself that she had been hungry.

Back in court, Charles got to his feet and rearranged his gown, hoping that his face showed every bit of the anger he felt. Usually he had to hide his real emotions in court and simulate others, but this time it would be a positive advantage for the jury – and the defendant – to know precisely how sceptical he was and how disgusted with the story he had heard that morning.

'Mr Beechen,' he said slowly and offensively, 'I put it to you that what you told the court before the short adjournment was an ingenious and well-constructed tissue of lies, in which there is not one single scintilla of truth.'

'No,' said Michael simply. He did not sound angry, merely tired. Something about his acceptance of the insult reminded many of the jurors of his daughter.

'Is it not in fact the case that, having lost patience

with your wife, whose behaviour was clearly difficult, unpleasant and possibly even dangerous to the children, you decided to kill her?'

'No.'

'Mr Beechen, which newspapers and journals do you take?' Charles had dropped his accusatory manner and spoke as though making simple conversation with a stranger.

'None,' said Michael with a puzzled smile. 'We couldn't afford luxuries like newspapers. The only one that was ever delivered to the flat was the local free sheet.'

'Do you expect the court to believe that you never read a newspaper?'

'Certainly not. When I was not working I went every morning to the library after I'd taken the children to school. I would read *The Times*, and the *Independent*, all the theatrical journals, and general weeklies such as the *Spectator*.'

'Then you will be aware of the spate of articles that followed a report to the House of Commons on the subject of male victims of domestic violence last year.'

Michael saw at once what the barrister was trying to do and almost flung up his hands in despair. 'Yes,' he said, glad to see that Melissa did not seem to like the prosecution any more than he did.

'What effect did those articles have on you?'

'They made it possible for me to tell my doctor some of the truth about what Penelope had been doing to me when I went to him last November after she had burned my back with the iron. Until then I had thought that I was the only man it ever happened to and I did not think anyone would believe me.'

'Are you sure that the articles did not simply suggest to you a way out of your difficult marriage? Did you not in fact plan to kill your wife and begin to set up your defence with that visit to your doctor?'

'Certainly not.' The haughtiness was back in Michael's voice.

'What exactly did you tell the doctor when you went to see him about your injury?'

Michael hesitated and then looked across at the jury box with resignation.

'At first I told him what I always told him, that it was the result of an accident, that I'd tripped and brought the iron down on top of me.'

'Why at first?'

'Because he did not believe me. So then I told him that Penelope had done it, but I couldn't bear him to know it all and so I told him it was an accident, that it was she who had tripped, while she was holding the iron, and that it hit me. Only when he told me that the burn mark on my back could not have been made like that did I tell him what had really happened.'

'And what exactly was that?'

'My wife had hit me with the iron.'

'So you have said, but what were the circumstances?'

Michael shrugged. 'She was ironing the children's school uniforms while they played with Connor's Lego, and—'

'I thought that you said your wife was a bad housekeeper?'

'Usually yes.' Michael tried to hold on to his irritation because he knew it would put Melissa against him – he knew she hated overt anger just as much as he and Marianna did – but it was hard. 'But on that evening she was ironing their school uniforms. I arrived back from a meeting at my agent's and she started to lay into me.'

'Could you explain what you mean by "lay into"?'

'Yes, it was the usual diatribe about the little money I earned and about my various failings.'

'Will you tell the court what failings your wife accused you of having?'

'My failure to become a successful actor,' said Michael sharply. God forbid that he should have to tell this pompous, punitive, fat man all the rest of it.

'But you used failings in the plural. What else?'

Michael gripped his lips together, feeling outraged.

'Mr Beechen,' said the judge quietly, 'you must answer.'

'I suppose my failure as a husband,' he said reluctantly after a long, damaging pause.

'Your sexual failure, you mean?' There was a remarkably offensive edge to Charles Harcombe's voice.

Knowing that the barrister was probably deliberately trying to goad him into losing his temper and so showing him to be a man capable of irrational violence, Michael desperately tried to hang on to his self-control.

Georgina Mayford got to her feet in one quick movement, distracting the court's attention from her client.

'My lord, my learned friend is hectoring the witness here.'

'M'lord,' said Charles Harcombe tightly, 'I am merely struggling to persuade the witness to explain fully what his wife's accusations were in order to give the court a full picture of the real relationship between them instead of the one-sided impression that we have been given so far.'

'The question is relevant. Mr Beechen, you must answer it,' said the judge.

'Very well. Yes, my wife did consider me a sexual failure. But it is hard to imagine a man who could—'

'Thank you, Mr Beechen. So, your wife attacked you verbally, criticizing your sexual prowess, your ability in your profession and your earning power. That must have made you extremely angry.'

'Yes, it did.' Michael just about had his feelings

152

under control again, but he knew he could not take much more. The humiliation of having Penelope's taunts repeated to all the prurient spectators in court appalled him.

'What did you do?' asked Harcombe unpleasantly.

'Nothing.'

'Nothing? Your wife has just insulted you in terms that would make most men furiously angry, in front of your own children, and you did nothing? Do you really expect the court to believe that?'

'I turned away and said that I was going to have a bath.'

'Was that not in itself a fairly aggressive reaction?'

For once Michael felt almost amused. He shook his smooth fair head.

'I'd have thought it the least aggressive thing I could have done,' he said. 'If I had criticized her, which I could easily have done, that would have simply escalated the aggression and frightened the children.'

'Perhaps your wife did not see it like that. What did she do?'

'She said, "Don't turn your back on me, damn you," and the next thing I knew, she had put the iron full in the small of my back. I felt the pressure of something but not its heat until it had burned through my sweater and my shirt. Before I could do anything about it, or even move, it was through my vest and on to my skin.' He looked towards the jury box and half smiled. 'As you can imagine, I moved then, very fast.'

There was a short pause, as though Charles Harcombe were trying to imagine anyone not noticing a hot iron in the small of the back until it had burned through to his flesh.

'What was it you said that your wife had been ironing?' he asked, sounding puzzled.

'The children's school shirts.'

'And what are they made of?' Charles sounded curious, almost as though he had never heard of a child's school shirt before.

'I have really no idea.'

'Most children's school shirts these days are made of man-made fibres, sometimes mixed with cotton. A coolish iron has to be used, does it not?'

'I have no idea.'

'Really? You never ironed any of your children's clothes, then?' said Charles Harcombe quietly.

Michael saw the trap at last, and he took a while to answer. Eventually he said, 'No. I ironed my own shirts, because my wife refused to do them, but I never ironed any of the children's clothes. I always have cotton shirts, which, as you may know, need a very hot iron.'

'I see. What did you do to help in the flat when you were not earning?' Once again Charles Harcombe had managed to make an apparently innocuous question sound offensive.

'Whatever needed doing that my wife would allow.' Michael permitted himself the suggestion of a snap. Then he softened it by trying to explain. 'Although she was not at all houseproud, she was angry in defence of what she saw as her territory. I sometimes managed to tidy up while she was distracted, cleaned when I could, took the children out for fresh air whenever possible, read to them, fed them, bathed them, and put them to bed as often as not. When they were ill, I sat up with them.'

'But you never ironed their clothes. Why not?'

There was another pause.

'I don't know. It never arose.'

'And yet the condition of their clothes offended you, didn't it?'

'Sometimes.'

'What did you do then?'

'If we were going somewhere where it mattered that

they should be clean and tidy, I would change their clothes.'

'And do what with the soiled ones?' Charles Harcombe managed to sound merely interested and no longer critical or arrogant.

'Put them in the laundry basket in the bathroom,' said Michael at once, wondering where the questions were going.

'For your wife to wash and iron, I see. And what kind of place would it be where it mattered how your children were dressed?'

'Anywhere we might meet people we knew.'

'Can you give me an example?'

'Yes. If we were going to visit my mother for example. It matters to her that her grandchildren should be clean and tidy and clean.'

Melissa noticed the repetition of the word 'clean' and wondered about it.

'Did you ever raise your hand to your wife?' asked Charles Harcombe, apparently uninterested in the unusual emphasis.

'No. I never hit her.'

'Really? Will you tell the court what happened on the day of your daughter's sixth birthday when you and your family went with the Cawleigh family to the seaside?'

For a moment Michael's old loathing of Jane Cawleigh was all he could think about, but then he pushed it away from him and remembered Melissa's sympathy. He looked at her.

'I did not hit her. I slapped her when she became completely hysterical after our son wandered off,' he said quite calmly. 'She thought he was lost and she was screaming and yelling and terrifying the other children. I slapped her face to shock her out of the hysteria. It was not hard and it was not a proper blow. It was a simple open-handed slap.'

'Crying was a pretty natural reaction, was it not, to the disappearance of a two-year-old child at the seaside, where he might have wandered into the sea and been drowned or been abducted?'

'No, it was not, and it was not simply crying. She was out of control.'

Melissa found she could no longer look anywhere near Michael Beechen as he talked to her across the crowded court. She began to imagine a woman, a noisy, untidy, emotional, unhappy kind of woman, faced with the cold, superior, perhaps deliberately uncomprehending anger of which Beechen seemed capable. His determination to have his flat tidied and his children neatly dressed began to seem less reasonable than it had at first.

With a chill seeping into her mind, Melissa decided that the scene over the ironing board might look quite different from the point of view of such a woman, a woman who was perhaps thinking as she raised the iron: 'Listen to me, and answer what I'm saying. It matters. If you won't answer, I'll make you. You must hear what I'm saying. I need an answer.' Her verbal cruelty might have been meant to have the same effect.

'I see,' said Charles Harcombe. 'Now, there were other times when she made you very angry, weren't there?'

'Yes.'

'By doing what?'

'We've been over this.' Michael felt exhausted and could see no point in being put through the whole sorry business yet again.

'Nevertheless, please tell the court the sorts of things your wife, Penelope, did that made you angry.'

'Her refusal to keep the flat in a state that would have made her, my, and the children's lives a great deal easier. Her violence. Her taunts. And her terrorizing of the children. They all made me angry.'

156

'Her taunts. Yes, you have mentioned them. Did you always respond by turning away from her when she criticized you?'

'Usually. In the very early days I sometimes used to try to defend myself, but it never made any difference and I had given up trying to communicate with her when she was out of control.'

'What form would your attempts at defence take?'

'I would explain why I had had to do certain things she had disliked or been unable to do what she wanted.'

'Or perhaps why you wanted her to do things she did not consider important?'

'Sometimes.'

'I see.' Charles Harcombe absentmindedly took his gold hunter out of his waistcoat pocket and swung it to and fro on its chain. With his portly figure, his heavy gold watch chain, yellowing wig and long gown, he looked like a caricature of the kind of barrister who has never experienced any of the privations or difficulties discussed in the courts or even breathed the same air as any juror, let alone a defendant. Michael hated him.

'What things did you do that she disliked?'

'Oh dear. We've been through this too.'

The judge frowned. 'You must answer the questions put to you, Mr Beechen,' he said with courteous firmness. 'Your counsel will object if there is anything inappropriate asked of you.'

Michael bent his head momentarily in what he hoped was a graceful gesture of apology and continued: 'Cleaning the flat when she wanted it to be a mess; not . . . having sex with her when she wanted it; being around in the flat when she wanted me to be out and working; not getting parts she thought I ought to have got. I suppose,' he said, pausing and looking down at the floor of the witness box so that no-one could see his eyes, 'what it boiled down to was not being the kind of man she thought I was when she married me.'

'I see.' Charles Harcombe sounded faintly disappointed. He put away his watch. 'And was she the woman you thought you had married?'

'Part of the time,' said Michael, thinking: that's none of your business and completely irrelevant.

'I see. Were your acting jobs increasing or decreasing during the years of your marriage?'

'I'm not sure.' The constant shift in the direction of the questions was upsetting and Michael found his concentration lapsing. He was going to make a fool of himself if he wasn't careful, but how could he keep his mind on the questions when the man was deliberately trying to rile and confuse him? 'About the same, I think, but they tend to go in bunches in any case. You get a run of offers and then nothing again for months.'

'Did your wife's taunts make it more difficult for you to obtain work?'

'Yes, I think they did,' Michael said after taking a moment to think about the proposition. 'Going for an audition with her criticisms ringing in my ears was not conducive to confidence or relaxation.'

'So you blamed her for your lack of professional success, did you?'

There was another short pause while Michael looked towards his counsel for help. She kept her face discreetly and professionally blank as she looked down at her notes.

'Not completely,' he said, 'but she certainly did not help.'

'I see. Did you get the part for which you had auditioned on the day your wife died?'

'No.'

'Thank you. So your wife sometimes seemed quite different from the woman you thought you married. Her poor housekeeping made you very angry. She taunted you with your sexual failure and your inadequate earning capacity. She was unpleasant to your children. And she hit you and burned you. You believed that if you were to divorce her, your children would be at risk. You finally killed your wife by stabbing her to death. And yet you expect the court to believe that you did not intend her to die when you picked up the knife and drove it through her skin and into her flesh, all four inches of it, right up to the hilt?'

'Yes,' said Michael tiredly. 'I do.'

Harcombe left a significant pause before he said, 'I see. Well, perhaps you would wait there. My learned friend may have something more to ask you.'

Georgina Mayford got to her feet and, apparently ignoring the jury, the judge and everyone in the court except for Michael Beechen, asked him quietly, 'What was Penelope's reaction to that slap on the beach?'

Michael delved into his memory. He was breathing more quickly, and shallowly, than usual.

'It stopped the hysteria,' he said at last. 'She kind of sobbed once – not crying, just adjusting her breathing. And then, once she was properly calm, we both went to look for Connor and found him in no time, which we couldn't have done while she was still hysterical.'

'Did she ever speak to you about the slap?'

'No. I don't think she ever mentioned it.'

'I see. You told my learned friend that your wife terrorized your children. You have also stated that she never physically hurt them. What form did her terrorizing take?'

'She was desperately critical always and screamed at Marianna over trivial faults. All the children were afraid of her, but it was worst for Marianna, partly because she was the eldest, I think. She was petrified of her mother's anger. That is why I couldn't bear the thought of leaving, because they'd have had no protection then.'

'Yes, I see. Thank you, Mr Beechen, you may step down.'

Michael left the witness box and walked as gracefully as possible across the floor of the court to the dock, where his two warders waited for him. He was exhausted but it seemed important to move well and give the unsympathetic jurors no clue to his weakness. One of the warders opened the door of the dock and he stepped in with as much pride as he could gather round himself, not touching the sides of the wooden enclosure even when he climbed the three steps.

The judge adjourned the trial until half past ten the following morning.

Chapter 11

Melissa got home soon after five that afternoon and went straight down to her office, where she was greeted by the sight of her secretary sitting in the visitor's chair, sobbing. At the sound of the door, Annabel bit her lip in a useless attempt to stop crying and stood up. Melissa dropped her bag on the desk at once and went to put both arms round Annabel. They stood there in silence, Melissa just holding on to the younger woman until her sobs calmed.

'What's up, Bel?'

'Sorry.' Annabel sniffed and took a handful of paper tissues from a box in the top drawer of the desk. When she had blown her nose and wiped her eyes, she dropped the tissues into the wastepaper basket, saying: 'I didn't mean to do that. I know you hate it.'

'Don't worry about that. What's happened to upset you so?'

'Oh, I just had a bit of a run-in with Martin, and he . . .' Bel's green eyes filled with tears again. Forgetting the box of tissues, she pulled her shirt out of her skirt and mopped her eyes with the hem. Melissa could not help smiling at the unselfconscious gesture.

'He said that if I can't pull myself together and concentrate on my work, I'll have to find another job. Oh, Melissa, I—'

'Sit here, Bel, and listen to me,' said Melissa, holding on to her anger with difficulty. 'There is absolutely no question of your having to find another job. None. I need you here.' She saw that Annabel was not convinced, and tried again.

'Martin's in a great state at the moment what with not being able to find another job of his own. It's no excuse for being beastly to you, but I hope you'll try to understand and put up with it. It won't go on for ever, Bel. Honestly.'

Annabel looked up, sniffing again.

'I would hate to lose you,' said Melissa with great clarity. 'You know I rely on the work you do. Your job is safe as long as the company exists.'

'Good. Sorry.' Annabel flung the used tissues into the wastepaper basket. 'I shouldn't have taken him so seriously, but you see he seems so powerful. It never occurred to me that . . .'

'I know. But it's over now. If he's still here, I'll talk to him now. If not, then when he gets back after his squash-players' dinner. Have you got a headache? You look as though you have. There's some Nurofen in the drawer or paracetamol upstairs.'

'He is still here. And I'm fine now. The headache'll go off soon and I don't like taking pills.'

'Good for you. Now, any disasters today? Anything I need to deal with before I tackle him?'

'No disasters, but there are some quite important letters and messages.' Bel sniffed and took another tissue.

'All right. Fetch them and we'll run through them before I do anything else.'

When the urgent decisions had been made and holding action taken to postpone various others, Melissa sent her secretary home. Both the designers had already left and she was alone again with her husband. Furious, but still just in control, she sat back at her desk and tried to think how best to tackle him. In a way talking to him might be easier now that she had Annabel's distress to discuss.

Melissa walked up and down her office, trying to work herself back into what she had once seen described as 'gracious wifeliness', suppressing her memories of the night before, and reminding herself that the things Martin did and the difficulties he caused probably came as much from insensitivity and his own distress as from deliberate malice. He had always been clumsy with people and he still had a small boy's need to blame someone else for his own mistakes.

He had taken a terrible blow to his pride when he was made redundant, and that was probably still making him aggressive. Melissa knew that she must not match his anger. That could only make things worse. She wanted to make sure that he did not take out his miseries on Annabel again, but it had to be done in such a way that it did not lead to an unmendable quarrel.

When Melissa was sure that she had controlled her fury enough to be able to talk calmly, she tidied her hair, put on some more lipstick, and walked down the corridor to Martin's office.

He glanced up as she came in, raising his eyebrows. She thought he looked pleased with himself and felt her own anger dangerously close to the surface.

'Martin, what did you say to upset Annabel so much?'

He shrugged carelessly.

'Very little,' he said. 'I merely reminded her that she is paid an unnecessarily generous salary and ought to work a bit harder to earn it. I pointed out that there are plenty of better qualified people out there who would do her job better than she does and more conscientiously for less money.'

'Didn't you realize that she'd think you were threatening her with the sack?' Melissa tried to speak calmly, as though she were merely asking an ordinary question.

'Trust you to be melodramatic about it. Annabel knew perfectly well what I meant.'

'Actually, she didn't, Martin,' said Melissa, disliking the injustice of his accusation. There was very little she hated more than dramatic scenes, and she was beginning to think that he positively enjoyed them. 'I found her sobbing her heart out in my office when I got back. Look, don't you think sometimes you could just try to imagine how other people feel?'

'Hah!' His short burst of completely humourless and contemptuous laughter made it necessary for Melissa to take a tough grip on her temper again. She forced herself to smile at him.

'That's pretty rich coming from you,' he said, ignoring the smile. 'You never even bother to think what it's like for me being humiliated in this bloody depressing grey basement day after day.'

Melissa took hold of the back of the chair in front of her, trying to stop herself pouring out all the furious words that were in her mind.

'The only thing that humiliates you here is the way you wade in and cause aggro,' she said, doing her best to sound ordinary and to forget everything that had happened the previous night. 'If you could just be yourself and stop pretending to be all-powerful – just let things ride for a bit – all would be well.'

He scowled and said nothing.

'Oh, Martin,' she said in despair, 'life would be so much easier if you could just not try to impose your will on everyone else. We all know that you won't be working here for ever. Can't you leave well alone until then?'

Martin pushed back his chair and stood up. He seemed immensely powerful as he put both hands on the edge of his desk and leaned towards her. She could see the enlarged pores on either side of his nose and the few short black hairs that poked out of his nostrils.

'But it isn't well enough, Melissa. Look here, if you'd only grasp the opportunity I'm giving you, you'd be able to raise what's little more than a hobby into something that might actually make money one day. Real money. You'd be able to sell out and clear a handsome profit.'

'But I don't want to sell.' Hearing her voice rising, Melissa stopped talking, waited a moment and then started again. 'I like doing what I do.'

'You're too easily satisfied, Lissa.' He smiled at her with a deliberate, patronizing kindliness that made her want to spit. 'You ought to raise your sights. I can help you to make something useful out of this business while I'm here, just as I once helped you to pass your accountancy exams – and persuaded Coward & Bowlby to keep you when they were having to weed out all the other less than satisfactory trainees. But you'll have to agree to do things my way or you'll fail again.'

Gripping her hands so tightly on the chairback that her knuckles began to look like uncooked chicken's feet about to poke up through her skin, Melissa ignored his insults and reminded herself that she had never failed an exam in her life. It did not matter if Martin rewrote the history of her years in accountancy. It really did not matter. The only thing that mattered was not losing her temper and telling him precisely how she felt.

'Listen to me, Martin. I like my business as it is. It has survived the recession. It makes a good enough living. I don't want more. I don't want the kind of world you thrive on. As you know, I hated it. That's why I left Coward & Bowlby in the first place.'

Melissa breathed carefully, wondering how to make him listen properly to what she was saying without taking his head and banging it against the wall. Appalled at herself, she pushed the thought away and made her voice sound calm. 'Please try to understand. Can't you?'

Martin laughed in her face. For a second it occurred to Melissa that he might be trying to provoke her into losing her temper.

'What I understand is exactly what that American writer Camille Paglia means about women and grass huts,' he said with theatrical contempt.

Melissa, feeling the tension setting up pains all over her head, deliberately relaxed her gritted teeth, unpicked her fingers from the chair one by one and flexed the aching joints.

'For a man who rarely reads anything except thrillers, it's surprising that you've come across her work.'

'There you go again. Sneering at me the whole time.'

'But I wasn't sneering.' Melissa was genuinely astonished at that accusation. She did not want to get sidetracked away from the things she had to say and so she did not bother to explain that it was the idea of Martin's choosing to read Paglia's books – or even knowing of their existence – that surprised her.

'There is a difference between a grass hut and a hundred-storey skyscraper,' she went on, trying to make him understand. 'I don't want either. I want something in between, and it's something that I have found and achieved here. Please, Martin, can't you let me have that at least?'

'There are only two things holding you back from genuine achievement. One is that you can't bear the thought of owing me anything. And the other is that you're terrified of being more successful than your bloody mother.'

The new accusations were so wild that most of Melissa's anger retreated and she even smiled as she walked round the chair and sat down on it.

'Oh, Martin, don't be a clot.'

It seemed impossible to get him to see that she was not motivated by the same things that drove him. Melissa did not measure herself by the distance she could put between her achievements and other people's. She did not find satisfaction in proving that other people were weaker, less successful, poorer, less fit, or any of the other things that made Martin feel good about himself.

'Christ, how you despise me!' All the fury that she had been at such pains to conceal seemed to have infected him. He made no effort to disguise it. He was still standing up and glaring at her. She put her hands to her eyes to rub away the itch that suddenly plagued them, forgetting that she had made up her eyes again before the afternoon session in court. Lights began to flash in her right eye.

'No, I don't despise you,' she said, looking down at her blackened fingertips and hoping that the migraine would be short-lived. She lifted her head and faced him, willing herself to feel gentle, placatory. 'Far from it. I just wish that for the time you're working here you could simply fit in and not rock the boat. When you're on your feet again you can build up whatever sort of skyscraper business you approve of for yourself. But just let me keep mine as it is. Please, Martin?'

'I can't think why you ever asked me to come and work for you,' he said sullenly, shuffling some of the paper on his desk.

'I did it to give you a breathing space,' she said with difficulty, 'and because I thought we might get back some of the happiness we used to have if we were physically nearer each other for more of the time. I never thought it would turn out as badly as this. I'm sorry.'

The lights in her eye were flashing more insistently and she began to feel her sense of balance going. She could no longer read the labels on the backs of Martin's dark-green box files and she knew that she would have to lie down in the dark soon, but she could not bear the thought of telling him what was happening to her.

167

He turned away, saying with ferocious sarcasm, 'You really know how to make a man feel good about himself, don't you, Lissa? It's always been one of your specialities, that.'

Stung by his tone and by his apparently deliberate provocation, she said sharply before she could stop herself, 'You've been trying to punish me ever since I got back from Paris, but it's not my fault that you were made redundant.'

'It's not mine either.' His voice snapped like a Chinese firecracker, but there was a kind of satisfaction in his hard smile. 'Although I know perfectly well that you think it is.'

'No, I don't,' she said tiredly. She knew that however often she repeated that he would never believe it.

'I must go or I'll be late. Don't wait up for me.'

'I won't,' said Melissa, thinking gratefully of her bed.

When Martin had had plenty of time to change and get out of the house, she followed him upstairs to their bedroom, shut the grey-and-white striped curtains, removed the linen and lace coverlet from the bed, switched off the light, and lay down until the migraine had finished with her.

It was not until she had been sick, washed out her mouth, slept a little and woken up with her eyes working normally again that she remembered she was supposed to be meeting Adam Blake for dinner in Bear Flat, of all extraordinary places. Tired and aching, but aware that she would feel better if she left the house for a while, Melissa got up and saw that she still had half an hour before she was supposed to meet him.

Driving down through Bath fifteen minutes later, she castigated herself for handling Martin so badly. It was hard not to react to his apparently deliberate taunts, but she felt that she ought to have been able to do it. She still could not understand why things had gone so wrong between them or why he was not prepared to try to put them right. Looking back, trying to see when their relationship had begun to turn bad so that she could work out why it had happened, she wondered whether it could have been her obsession with the rescue of the house that had started the damage.

Martin could justifiably have resented the house, she thought, both for the time she had had to spend on the actual work and for the amount of emotional energy it had absorbed. Looking back, she could see that she had lavished on it a lot of the care he would have liked devoted to children. But he had never said anything about resenting the house, and he was rarely slow to tell her what he did not like about her and the things she did. Besides, it had not been until she had actually left Coward & Bowlby that he had become so irritable and difficult and by then she had been working on the house for years.

He had started to carp at her almost as soon as she had left, complaining about her business methods, her looks, the way she spent her time and her money, whittling away at the confidence that provided her mental foundations. Sometimes it had seemed as though only her friendship with Cecily – and her mother – had kept her going. Melissa had resisted Martin's destructiveness for as long as possible, making all sorts of silent excuses for his bad temper, but in the aftermath of a debilitating migraine none of them seemed good enough any longer.

She reached Bear Flat, a windy suburb on the south side of Bath, ten minutes later, found the restaurant Adam had chosen, and parked the car a few yards away. The wind seemed much more violent than any that penetrated the Circus and she pulled her overcoat more tightly around her body, wondering why Adam had decided to live in such a cold, depressing place when he could presumably have had a flat conveniently near his work in Bristol.

Pushing open the glass door of the little restaurant, Melissa smiled. The hot, crowded room looked as though it had been unchanged since the 1960s. There were red-and-white checked tablecloths and candles stuck in Chianti bottles. Highly polished copper saucepans hung on the whitewashed walls and there was even a garish painting of the Bay of Naples opposite the bar on which a huge, gleaming espresso machine hissed.

Looking round the simple room in appreciation, she saw Adam standing by a table at the far end. He waved.

'Hello,' she said when she reached him. He kissed her cheek.

'You're freezing,' he said. 'Come and sit down. There's a radiator just behind the table. Did you have to park miles away?'

'No. Hardly a step, but the wind is icy. Have you been here ages?'

'Only about five minutes.' He watched her as she took off her coat and draped it over the back of the chair. 'You're ill, aren't you? Melissa, you shouldn't have come. What's the matter?'

'No, I'm not ill,' she said. 'I had a migraine earlier and they do leave me looking a bit washed out, but I'm fine now. Really.' She smiled at him. 'May I have some of that wine?'

He lifted a carafe full of purple wine and started to pour.

'Wouldn't you rather have white, or something else? Doesn't red wine trigger migraines?'

'I don't think so. Not mine anyway. They don't seem to be affected by cheese or chocolate either. I don't know what sets them off. I'd love some.'

He poured it out and then gave her a menu, saying, 'The best things are usually the *risotto ai funghi* and the *saltimbocca*, but you might prefer something else.'

'That sounds lovely. I'll follow your advice.'

Adam waved at a large waiter, whose dark curls hung down to the open collar of his blue shirt. He was wearing a red-and-white checked tablecloth as an apron over his jeans.

'What's it to be then, Adam?' he asked with no trace of an Italian accent.

'The usual please, Michele, if your mother's cooking today.'

'She is. Mushroom risotto and veal and sage. Coming right up.'

When he had hurried away, Melissa said, 'You two seem to be friends.'

'We are. I eat here quite a lot and I've become fond of the whole family.'

'It's a real find. I've never noticed it before as I drove through Bear Flat, but I wish I had: it makes me feel astonishingly young again.'

'Me too, but you can't have been of restaurant age when places like this were commonplace.'

Melissa laughed. 'My mother was most enlightened and was taking me to restaurants from the age of . . . oh, I don't know. Yes, I do though. I've never thought of it before. I was six. It must have been just after my father died. I don't think we ever went out to eat before that. How odd!'

Adam looked as though he were choosing his words carefully before he spoke. 'I hadn't realized that you'd lost your father so young,' he said at last. 'That must have been tough. Do you remember him well?'

'Hardly at all,' said Melissa honestly. 'Not even what he looked like. I've often wanted to know more, but my mother's always hated talking about him, even though she used to make herself answer any questions I asked when I was a child – before I realized how much it upset her.'

'That must have been tough, too.'

'Not really. It would probably have been worse – for me – if I'd been a bit older when he died and actually known him, if you see what I mean. But it's been awful for her. She must have loved him so much. There's never been anyone else in her life in all those years. She has the most tremendous guts as well as astonishing benevolence. You can't think how I admire her.'

Adam's smile transformed his face, making Melissa think of the way a heavy wave breaks over a dark rock, spilling down the sides and washing the whole thing in light.

'That's rare.' Seeing that she looked puzzled, he added: 'To find a woman who is prepared to admit that her mother means a lot to her.'

'I don't have any difficulty doing that. She's wonderful.' Melissa sighed and then smiled. 'I know what you mean, though. It's almost a rite of passage for women these days to start moaning about their mothers. I don't know whether it's just that mine is such a star or . . . maybe my father's death made us closer than most families. I don't know.'

'Perhaps it was that,' Adam said, watching her over the rim of his glass.

'Well, whatever it was, I couldn't do without her. She's not only one of my best friends, but also my prop and stay. We . . . oh, well, you don't want to hear all that.'

Still smiling brilliantly, Adam raised his glass, 'To your mother.'

'To my mother,' answered Melissa, smiling back at him before she drank. She settled herself more comfortably, leaning back against the cushioned banquette. 'This evening is improving by the minute.'

'I'm glad. You're beginning to look better too, less pinched and grey. Melissa, you puzzle me.'

'Do I? Why?'

'Oh, because.'

'You can't do that to me,' she said lightly. 'It's not cricket.'

He laughed at her borrowing of his phrase. 'I wasn't going to stop there. I was just having a pause for thought. You puzzle me because you seem so tough and sure of yourself, and so cool in all that elegance, and then suddenly it's as though a shutter is whisked open in your eyes and one sees a quite different person looking out. That's not a chat-up line, by the way,' he added, seeing her frown.

'I didn't think it was. I was just trying to imagine what you thought you saw.' Melissa drank some wine.

Adam sat watching her and was about to speak when Michele returned and planted two plates piled with soft, fragrant rice, studded with huge pieces of *porcini* in front of them.

'Ah, that smells wonderful,' Adam said.

Michele was back a moment later with a large hunk of parmesan and a grater to scatter the mounds of risotto with cheese.

'There. I hope you enjoy it. You need feeding up, Adam. You're starting to look gaunt. It won't do.'

'Nonsense. But we will enjoy it. Dig in, Melissa. It's best straight away.'

She obeyed, and let the large soft grains ooze their delectable taste across her palate. The richness of the mushroom-flavoured rice and the sharp strength of the cheese combined into a serious sensual pleasure. Neither of them said anything more until their plates were empty.

'I could happily stop there,' said Melissa. 'It was wonderful. Now tell me what you meant.'

'All right. I may have got this completely wrong – after all, I hardly know you – but behind the confidence, the clothes, and all that common sense there seems to be someone much more vulnerable, and much warmer.'

'Isn't that true of everyone?' said Melissa, obliquely admitting that he was right.

'I don't know. It may be. But there's more and this is where you may be angry with me. Perhaps I shouldn't say it.'

'Only you can judge that.' There was enough frost in her voice to stop him, but he persevered.

'When we met,' he said slowly, 'I felt as though I already knew you well. It was – is – the most extraordinary feeling and it makes me want to say all sorts of things to you that one doesn't normally say to an acquaintance of a few days – just as one doesn't normally kiss them as we did yesterday. I'm sorry if it makes me seem impertinent.'

'It doesn't,' she said honestly, 'and to be frank, I do know what you're talking about. It's not a one-sided feeling. But it has to be resisted, Adam. It really does. I long to be able to let this extraordinary friendship rip and see where it takes us, but I'm not in a position to do any such thing. I regret it – bitterly – but it's a fact, I'm afraid.'

'Even though we can both feel it?' he said mildly enough.

Melissa leaned back against the velvet-covered banquette and closed her eyes. She felt exposed and at risk, but there was something about him that made her reluctant to pour the verbal equivalent of boiling oil over him, which she had done once or twice before when men she knew had propositioned her.

'Yes.'

Michele arrived to take away their risotto plates and a few minutes later substituted the *saltimbocca*. Melissa was relieved to see that the meat was thinly beaten and that there was not too much of it. Her nostrils caught the smell of the sage. Its dusty bitterness was backed by a rich sweetness in the wine-flavoured sauce.

'Tell me, Melissa,' said Adam suddenly, 'what's your happiest childhood memory?'

'Goodness!' she said, surprised but relieved that he had changed the subject. 'I'm not sure. There were so many. I had a very happy childhood. What about you?'

'So-so,' he said.

'No. I meant what was your happiest memory?'

'Oh, that's easy.' Adam's savagely lined face softened in the candlelight. If Melissa had been of a sentimental turn of mind she would have thought he was seeing his memories replayed in the dancing blue and yellow flame.

'It was a picnic. I must have been about seven or eight, I suppose. As a family we weren't great picnickers, but someone had come to stay – I can't remember who – and to entertain them we took sandwiches up into the hills.'

'What made it so good?' asked Melissa when he stopped talking.

'Oh, so many things: the colours of the day – it was one of those bright summer days after rain when everything looks clearer than usual, washed in some way; the food was good; my mother cheerful. She didn't look at her watch once in the whole day, and normally she did it all the time as though she was endlessly waiting for the next thing to happen, hoping it would be better than the last and always being disappointed.'

Seeing Melissa's face, Adam quickly added, 'And we children had a glorious time paddling in the stream. It was one of those tumbling, hurried mountain streams, you know, with boulders and lots of noise, and we messed about in it for hours. I can still remember feeling the coldness of the water through my boots. They weren't leaking or anything, but the rubber grew colder and colder and you could feel it on your skin, just as you could feel the bubbling, rushingness of the water. Oh, it was lovely!'

'It sounds fun,' said Melissa, relaxing as she enjoyed the thought of the austere, sympathetic man at her side as a damp, messy small boy.

'It was. I felt like a child, which was rarish.'

'I'm not sure I understand.'

'Don't you? I'm glad of that.' Adam drank and then stared up at the smoke-stained ceiling. He looked at her again and she thought that his face looked stripped of its defences.

Aware that he had let her into something important, Melissa forgave him for his invasion of her well-guarded self, but she could not think what to say next. She was not used to such intimacy with anyone except Cecily. After a while, with an effort, Adam said, 'Can you really not think of any parallel occasion out of your happy childhood?'

'Oh, I'm sure I could,' she said. 'But there was no single incident like yours. In fact the only childhood memory that really sticks with me is a bad one; presumably because there were so few of those.'

'Tell me about it.'

Reluctantly she started to describe a Christmas holiday, when she was four. Her parents had taken her to stay with relations. There had been a lot of other children there and a vast tree with piles of presents heaped up under it.

'It looked incredibly exciting,' she said, talking more fluently once she was properly launched into the story. 'I suppose because it was all on such a big scale for an only child like me. On the day itself the older children handed out the presents, and more and more were put in front of me. There was one that seemed particularly enticing and I started unwrapping that first. I got the gold paper and the ribbons off and found that it was a box, a pretty box, covered in flowery cotton with that wiggly red braid round the lid. Rick-rack it's called, I think. I was absolutely certain that there was something wonderful inside the box and so I pushed at the bright brass hook.'

Her palms began to sweat as she remembered the sensation of pushing the sharp hook back with clumsy, pudgy fingers and she shivered. Taking a grip on herself, she finished the story.

'The lid flipped back and a jack-in-the-box leaped out, shrieking. You know the way they do?'

'Yes,' said Adam, ignoring his food.

'It had a cruel face – white with very red lips – and I was terrified. I tried to push it back but the spring was so strong that each time I tried to shut the lid the damn thing kept leaping out again and screeching. The assembled relations couldn't understand why I was in such a state and some of them started to laugh.'

'It must have been horrible,' said Adam taking her more seriously than she had expected.

'It was, actually. And the worst bit was wondering why my aunt, who had always seemed so nice, should have played such an unkind trick. Of course she hadn't meant to, but that's what it felt like. And they all seemed to be in it together, you see.' Melissa's voice was rising as though she were still the frightened child of the story. 'In the end they were all laughing as I struggled to get it back in. Only my mother understood and tried to make them see. She pushed the jack back for me and shut the lid. But they went on laughing.'

'You poor thing. Perhaps it was that episode that makes it so hard for you to believe your own feelings are justified,' Adam said before he could stop himself. As he saw her face, he knew he had made a mistake, but he could not unmake it.

Melissa took up her knife and fork and neatly cut

off a piece of veal. She smiled politely, but she said nothing.

Adam ate a mouthful of meat and then, trying to make her understand that he was not going to force her into any revelation she did not want to make, said slowly: 'Don't you always try to find reasons to make light of what you're feeling to prove that you're perfectly all right really?' At the sight of her face he added quickly: 'That's not meant to be a criticism.'

'I don't understand what all this is about,' she said, sounding almost angry, 'and I'd much rather not talk about it. Can't you tell me about more of your past or something?'

'Whatever you like,' he said at once. 'I didn't mean to trespass.'

Melissa nodded and finished her veal in silence while Adam told her about the years he had spent in Rome as a young priest, describing the older, simpler parts of the city he had found, where he could forget the grandeur of the baroque buildings and the astonishing worldly power of the church to which he had signed over his life. It had all seemed quite overpowering after his Nonconformist upbringing in Wales, he told her.

Melissa thought of asking him what had made him make such an extraordinary change in his life, and what had then forced him halfway back, but she thought that they had had more than enough intimacies for one evening. She let him talk almost uninterrupted.

'Would you like some pudding?' he said later, 'Or coffee?'

'Some coffee would be nice.' Melissa still felt stiff, and annoyed with herself for being so. It seemed a poor return for his friendship.

'We could have it here or at my house, which is just round the corner. That's not a chat-up line either,' he added with a glinting smile.

Her face, which had been closed in, relaxed as she smiled. She looked years younger.

'Thank you,' she said. 'I would love to have coffee with you in your house, Adam.'

They split the bill without fuss and walked to his house, a small blackened Edwardian cottage with a bay window in a row of fifty others that looked exactly the same. He switched on a harsh light in the white-painted hall and opened a door.

'You go on in, light the fire – it's already laid – and I'll make us some coffee.'

Melissa walked alone into his room and found a surprising simplicity. Plain speedwell blue curtains made of thick cotton covered the bay window. The same material covered two saggy old armchairs. A scrubbed and limed oak table stood in one of the alcoves beside the chimney breast, piled with books and papers and lit by a black Anglepoise lamp. In the other recess were white-painted adjustable shelves crammed with books and journals. The floor was covered with rush matting and the only picture was a perspex clipframed poster of a Picasso madonna and child.

The mother looked very young and very thin, her peachy dress falling away from one sharp shoulder to reveal her small breast. Her dark hair was twisted into a loose knot on the top of her head, which was bowed over the child with a tenderness that was almost unbearable.

It touched Melissa that a man of Adam's age and apparent cynicism should have chosen such under-graduate kind of surroundings. But in a way they suited him. He was the least arrogant or pretentious man she had ever met. A small wood fire had been laid in the black grate and obediently she lit it, pumping the bellows until she began to feel a little warmth.

179

'Here we are. Milk, or do you take it black?'

She turned and saw him carrying a tray.

'Black, please. Adam, I do like this room.'

'Do you really? It's absurdly underfurnished, but I haven't got round to doing anything about it. It's mine and I love the peace of it, and that seems to be enough.'

'Yes, I can understand that,' said Melissa, thinking of the cluttering emotions that filled her own big, richly decorated rooms.

They sat over the fire, drinking coffee and talking with an ease that surprised her after the constraint that had fallen on them in the restaurant. Eventually, with considerable reluctance, she put her empty mug down on the tray and said that she ought to leave. Adam stood up at once and went to fetch her coat.

She followed him out into the hall and let him help her on with it.

'Adam, I have really enjoyed this evening. Thank you.'

'Good,' he said with his hands on the collar of her black coat. He turned it up so that it framed her face and held it there, his fingers just brushing her skin. 'I was afraid I'd spoiled it.'

Melissa shook her head. She did not pull away and he stood there with his hands at either side of her face, exercising all of his powerful self-discipline.

'No. It's hard to—' She broke off, looked exasperated, and then tried again. 'I just wanted you to know that what you said earlier got to me rather. Um. I don't really understand what's going on, but I want you to know . . . Oh damn it all, why are words so difficult? Look, you said you liked bees.'

'Yes,' he said, looking mystified and rather worried. He took his hands away.

'I always go to my mother's on Saturdays for lunch. My husband never comes. He plays squash with his friends and goes to the pub. It's a kind of day off for both of us, has been for years. Would you like to come with me and see the bees and all her stuff? She runs courses and things for aspiring beekeepers and could tell you far more than I did.'

'I'd love it,' he said, his face breaking once more into a smile. 'But I don't want to force myself on you – or on her.'

'You're not.'

Chapter 12

'Dr Patley, will you tell the court how you first came to know Michael Beechen?' said Gina Mayford when her first witness had sworn to tell the truth at half past ten on Friday morning.

'Certainly. He has been my patient for the past four years.'

'Has he consulted you frequently?'

'No. He came once with a broken arm, once with a bad burn on his back, and three times, I think, with cuts that needed stitching.'

'Do you know for certain what caused the injuries?'

'Not the cuts nor the broken arm. They could have been the result of accidents or even mugging. Unfortunately people do get mugged in Bristol sometimes. But the cause of the burn was obvious. It was in the shape of an iron. Someone had undoubtedly held a hot iron in the small of his back.'

'What action did you take?'

'I dressed the burn and gave him a prescription for painkillers.'

'Did you take any action to find out who had burned him or to prevent a recurrence of such a wound?'

'I asked him who had done it and advised him to call the police if it should ever happen again.'

'Did you yourself inform anyone else of what had happened?'

'No.'

'Why not?'

'Social Services are short of time, staff and money,' said the doctor firmly. He sounded regretful but not ashamed. 'There are too many more urgent problems than those of an educated man of six-foot-two who may or may not be being deliberately hurt. Unlike children at risk, the elderly, or the mentally infirm, he could defend himself if he had to.'

'As he did in the end,' said Georgina Mayford. The implication was obvious.

The doctor did not flinch, but the judge said with the utmost severity, 'That is comment, Miss Mayford. You will have the chance to make a speech at the end of the evidence.'

'I beg your lordship's pardon,' said Georgina, apparently unabashed. She turned to face the witness again, saying: 'Thank you, doctor. Will you please wait there?'

Charles Harcombe smiled to himself as he got to his feet, confident of being able to handle a witness like Patley.

'When you first saw the defendant in your surgery,' he said pleasantly, reminding the jury of what Michael had said about his visits to the doctor, 'what did he tell you about his injuries?'

'That they were the result of a mugging.'

'Were the injuries consistent with that story?'

'Yes. As I said, people do get mugged in Bristol.' The doctor had clearly not had much experience in court for he spoke irritably. His tone suggested that if his manners had not been so good, he might well have added: Weren't you listening, Cloth-ears?

'What did he tell you when he came to the surgery last November to have his burned back treated?' Charles's voice was still easy.

'At first he told me that the burn was the result of his falling against the iron, then that his wife had accidentally hit him with it,' said the doctor with heavy patience, 'and finally that she had done it deliberately.'

'Could the burn have been caused accidentally?'

'I do not think so. An accidental blow with an iron would have left a less precise mark on his skin. The edges of the one I saw were completely unblurred and it was undoubtedly the result of an iron having been placed flat against his back and not moved until it was withdrawn. It must have been deliberate.'

'Did you ask him why he had lied to you?'

'I did not put the question in such pejorative terms,' said the doctor irritably. 'But I told him that I knew the burn must have been caused deliberately and I asked again about the earlier injuries, of which I had details in front of me. He admitted that they, too, had been caused by his wife.'

Michael moved his hands involuntarily, gripping his knees. He hoped that the jurors had not noticed the movement. His memories had to be kept well below the surface. He decided that it would be best if he thought about something else entirely while all the other witnesses were speaking. *The Secret Garden* might help. He decided to rehearse the whole plot in his mind while he waited, and perhaps think about Marianna's delight in the moment when the heroine first cleared the weeds from around the flowers in the neglected garden.

'If we accept for the moment that the defendant's injuries were deliberately caused, have you any direct evidence of who inflicted them?' asked Charles.

'No,' said the doctor.

Charles Harcombe bowed to the judge and said to the witness, 'I have no more questions.'

Since Georgina had no more questions either, Dr Patley was allowed to go. He was followed into the witness box by three other doctors, who had all worked in the accident and emergency department of local hospitals and testified to the occasions on which they had stitched

Michael Beechen's wounds and once set his broken right arm. Georgina Mayford allowed her junior to question them, and he elicited all the details of the injuries and the treatment they had required.

Michael was grateful to the last of the doctors, who spoke well and really did give the court some idea of what it must have felt like to have had two deep screwdriver cuts driven into your back. At the time Michael had been terrified that his kidneys had been damaged, but the X-rays had eventually reassured him.

After the last doctor had left the stand, the judge adjourned the trial until quarter past two and the jurors were sent out of the court into the unreal bustle of the city. Melissa stood in the cold drizzle, waiting for Adam. He came, almost last, talking to Mrs Crosscombe.

'How are you?' said Melissa when they reached her. 'Horrible, isn't it?'

'Yes, I think it is,' answered Mrs Crosscombe, taking a transparent pleated plastic hat out of her shopping bag and shaking it open. 'I hate this weather, too.' She pulled the bag-like hat over her permed grey hair and tied the short tapes into a bow under her chin.

'The damp gets into one's bones, doesn't it?' agreed Adam warmly. 'We're off to find something to eat. Can we persuade you to join us?'

To Melissa's relief, Mrs Crosscombe said that she had shopping to do, and left them.

'Let's not go to Cawardine's today,' Melissa said, 'I saw a whole lot of the others going in there. Let's go somewhere else, where we don't have to talk about the case.'

'Yes, of course,' said Adam at once. 'Are you all right?'

Melissa shivered again and turned up the big collar of her coat.

'Not really. That man keeps staring at me as though he knows me and thinks I must be on his side. It's . . .'

She took a deep breath, smiled as dazzlingly as she could and added: 'It gives me the willies a bit, actually.'

That afternoon the defence called another doctor, an expert in domestic violence, who said that his name was George Abel-Fowler and that he was leading a research project into the subject.

Georgina Mayford led him through his qualifications and publications to establish his credentials with the court and then asked him to describe his findings about the development of violence within a marriage. After he had given an account that was familiar enough to everyone who read any reasonably serious newspapers, she asked him how many of the victims were male.

'Research suggests that one in six couples will experience some form of domestic violence,' said the expert dispassionately, 'and that it is possible that up to half of the victims are male. Indeed evidence from hospital accident and emergency departments supports the view that slightly more male victims than female require hospital treatment.'

When she had given the jury long enough to grasp the importance of the figures, Gina Mayford asked the expert witness why such men did not retaliate.

'To begin with, in most cases, their early training forbids them to hit a woman,' said Dr Abel-Fowler. 'There is also considerable denial and optimism.'

'Could you explain that to the court?'

'Over and over again men who have joined in my research study have explained how they would tell themselves that "she didn't really mean it"; that the assault was a unique incident that could never be repeated. By the time the victims are prepared to admit that the assaults are real and that they are unlikely to stop, the pattern is usually established and the husband is unable either to extricate himself or to retaliate.

'Why is that?'

'Men are usually deeply humiliated by the experience of assault by their wives, and the physical battery is likely to be accompanied by verbal aggression. The victims are often taunted about their potency, their masculinity, their work and so on. Under such assault, their self-esteem reaches rock bottom and they begin to feel that they don't deserve any better. It becomes extremely difficult to break out of such a destructive relationship.'

Michael looked at the witness box and wondered how his life would have turned out if he had known about Dr Abel-Fowler and his work. Bitterness made his face look and feel very cold indeed.

'Do the husbands in some psychological way benefit from the relationships?' asked Georgina Mayford.

Susan Beere wrote herself another furious note.

'No,' said the doctor at once, sounding angry. 'Of course they do not. No more than a woman suffering such assaults benefits.'

'Thank you, doctor. Would you wait there so that my learned friend can ask you some questions?'

As the witness waited for Charles Harcombe to begin to attempt to salvage the suddenly faltering prosecution case, people in court began to fidget. It was clear that the doctor's expert evidence had made more than one of them extremely uncomfortable. When nothing happened Dr Abel-Fowler turned his head slightly so that he could look at Charles Harcombe, who was shuffling his papers on the bench before him. Eventually he pulled his notes into some kind of order and looked towards the witness box, but he still did not rise.

'Mr Harcombe?' said the judge, surprising everyone. 'Have you no questions for this witness?'

'I'm sorry, my lord,' said Charles Harcombe as he got to his feet. He seemed heavier than usual, almost clumsy. 'Yes, I have some questions.'

The judge looked very obviously at the clock and then slightly shook his head. It was already half-past three and he usually rose at four.

'Dr Abel-Fowler,' said Charles slowly, quite pleased with the effect he had created. 'Can you explain why more male victims of domestic violence require hospital treatment?'

'Yes. Men tend to use their hands when they are battering their wives, whereas women with their smaller body weight and lesser physical strength are more likely to use a weapon, such as a household implement or sports equipment, for example a baseball bat.' The doctor's voice had lost all its anger and its colour. It sounded almost like a recording.

'I see. Might it not also be partly because women are more accustomed to putting up with things? Haven't we all read of – and indeed met with – incidents in which men make considerably more fuss than women over wounds and illnesses?' Charles smiled confidingly, as though he were admitting to making an unnecessary fuss over a headache or two himself.

'I should have thought that the evidence for that was at most circumstantial,' said Dr Abel-Fowler stiffly. 'I think that women suffering the kind of wounds I have seen in some battered husbands would certainly seek medical treatment. Broken limbs and large burns and knife cuts or screwdriver wounds all require treatment.'

'Have you ever come across in your own work, or in the published results of other people's work, a man who himself hits his wife after suffering assaults by her?'

There was a short pause.

'In my own experience battered husbands may eventually retaliate in the way that battered wives do.'

'That's not what I asked,' said Charles. 'To put it more clearly: is there any evidence of a man who hits his wife simultaneously suffering her assaults? In other words, if he is violent independently of her, is there any possibility of his suffering in the way you have described?'

'I should have thought it unlikely. If he is capable of hitting her at all, then he is unlikely to become a victim of regular beating. The relationship would certainly be violent, but it would not be one-sided violence.'

'Thank you,' said Charles with a wider smile and even the suggestion of a bow towards his opponent's witness. 'Now, you have told my learned friend that men who are beaten by their wives gain no benefit – psychological benefit – from the relationship.'

'Yes,' said the psychiatrist, sounding sharper than when he was producing facts and statistics.

'My learned friend's choice of the word "benefit" wouldn't have been mine.'

Georgina Mayford looked up from her notes with an expression of surprise.

'What I should like to ask you now is whether such men participate in the relationship in any way?' Charles watched his witness with an expression of innocent interest.

'Of course they participate in the relationship,' said the doctor, sounding thoroughly irritable. 'They are part of it. But if you are asking me whether they are to blame for it then the answer is no. No more than battered wives are to blame.'

'But if they are part of the violent relationship, as you have testified, they must bear some responsibility for it, must they not?'

'It is possible to be part of something and not be responsible for it. The victim of a road accident, for example, is part of the accident, but not responsible for it,' said the expert coldly.

'Invariably?' Charles tried to sound casual and slightly mocking. When his witness did not answer, he went on: 'I believe that statistics show that a considerable percentage of pedestrians who are killed on the road are found to be well over the safe alcohol limit for driving. Doesn't that suggest that those victims might bear some responsibility for what happened to them?'

'Possibly.' The doctor was clearly both reluctant to answer the question and angry that it had been asked. 'But there are plenty of accidents in which only the drivers are drunk. Besides, my use of a road accident was purely for illustrative purposes.'

'Oh, I know it was. As a psychiatrist, are you familiar with the term "passive aggression"?'

'Naturally.'

'Would you explain to the jury what it means? In laymen's terms, if possible.'

The doctor smiled tightly. ' "Passive aggressive" is a description given to behaviour that is designed to anger or otherwise distress another person without any overtly aggressive words or actions being used.'

'In still more laymen's terms,' said Charles, turning to smile at the jury himself and finding many of them looking at him with more sympathy than usual, 'it sounds like what used to be called "dumb insolence" when I was at school. Would you agree, Dr Abel-Fowler?'

'I suppose that dumb insolence could come under the general rubric of passive aggression, yes.'

'Very well. Suppose an unhappy woman is trying to make her husband acknowledge the pain and difficulty in which she is living.'

There was a pause, during which the doctor in the witness box stood looking politely expectant. When Charles said nothing, the doctor nodded. 'Very well. I am supposing that.'

'Excellent. And suppose further that she bursts out with a complaint about him, possibly exaggerated or unjustified, and he says nothing, simply turns away and leaves her with her anger unresolved. Could that, too, come under the rubric of passive aggression?'

'I suppose it could, but without more data and a fuller understanding of the relationship it is not possible to say categorically.'

'But it *could* be termed "passive aggressive"?'

'Yes it could.'

Most of the jurors knew exactly what the questions were phrased to achieve, but Jack Brown was completely lost. Bored yet anxious, he looked sideways at David Davis, who had taken him to the pub every day for lunch, and saw that he was looking angry.

'And would you say that such unobvious aggression could be as destructive of a relationship as the more overt kind? Shouting, hitting, that kind of thing?' asked Charles.

'It's impossible to make a generalization like that,' said the doctor, his own anger overlain with something else, some much more personal emotion. 'In some relationships, it might be true,' he went on. 'But in others not. You could not say, for example, that a man who beats his wife so badly that he puts her in hospital is less damaging than a man who will not engage with his wife when she tries to play games.'

'What kind of games have you in mind?'

'Nothing specific,' said the doctor sharply. 'The kind of emotional games people do play with each other.'

'I am interested in your use of the word "games". My concerns have nothing whatever to do with games.' Charles stressed the last word, making it sound as though the doctor had been discussing tiddlywinks or at the most noughts and crosses. 'I have been talking about a difficult marriage, in which a man who disapproves of his wife's habits and character criticizes them and tries to change them, and then refuses to answer any of her complaints about his coercive behaviour. Is it beyond the bounds of possibility that she might strike out and hit him in order to make him confront her and the problems of her life?'

'It is not beyond the bounds of possibility,' said the doctor reluctantly.

Mrs Crosscombe, who had been blowing her nose, put the handkerchief away in the sleeve of her pink cardigan and nodded energetically.

'Excellent. We're getting somewhere at last,' said Charles. 'What might make such a man finally engage with his wife and confront her?'

'Very many things,' said the doctor, sounding more at ease.

'Could you give us some examples?'

'The triggering emotion could be extreme fear for himself or for someone else; a particular humiliation that reflected something in his childhood; perhaps merely reaching the end of his tether, being too tired simply to find the endurance to continue.'

'I don't understand.' Charles had stopped playing with his watch or his papers. He was standing as still as Georgina Mayford usually did. Even his voice sounded less fruity and confident. 'I thought you were telling us about a man who is passively aggressive towards his wife, yet you sound as though you are describing a martyr, a victim so pliant that he will suffer anything his wife does to him and endure it as though there were some merit in that.'

The doctor merely frowned.

'Thank you, Dr Abel-Fowler, you've been very helpful,' said Charles Harcombe after another significant pause. 'Please wait there for my learned friend's re-examination.'

'Miss Mayford,' said the judge before she could move, 'how long is your re-examination likely to take?'

'Very little time indeed, m'lord,' she said, smiling at him with a nicely judged mixture of confidence and pleading.

'Very well.'

She stood up. 'In your experience, doctor,' she said, 'have you come across people who are violently aggressive without provocation?'

'Yes, indeed I have.' The doctor's confidence suddenly seemed to have been restored.

'And what might the cause of such aggression be?'

'Many things. Unresolved childhood trauma, for example, or simply an inability to control violent impulses.'

'Thank you. Now, you told my learned friend that in a violent marriage, it would be unlikely for a man who could hit his wife to become her victim. Could you categorically state that one single incident of a husband slapping his wife out of hysteria would make him incapable of suffering domestic violence in the way the men of your study have suffered it?'

'Certainly not. No-one could categorically state that.'

'Thank you, Dr Abel-Fowler. M'lord, I have nothing further.'

'Then I shall adjourn until half past ten on Monday morning.'

Chapter 13

Three-quarters of an hour later, Melissa let herself into her house and went down to her office, praying that Martin would not come storming in with a complaint or a challenge of some sort. She needed some time to absorb the shock of the afternoon's evidence.

The first person to open the door was Annabel, her face alight with pleasure.

'What is it, Bel?' asked Melissa, so relieved to see her looking happy again that she did not mind the interruption.

'The first consignment of the new glass has arrived,' Annabel said with excitement making her voice sound like a triumphant peal. 'Oh, and Dick Walston has faxed through a request for a quote on a lovely big list of things for the hotel job he's doing. I'm getting some preliminary figures together for you now. We ought to be able to clear a healthy profit.'

'Glass?' Melissa felt as though she were trying to grip something spongy through a fog. The news about Dick Walston registered somewhere in her brain but she could not concentrate on it just then.

'Yes. Come on, Lissa, what's the matter? You know, the ones Giles was going to copy from the background to that stunning portrait you found.'

'Oh those ones.' Melissa felt the first renewed stirrings of interest in her work. 'Yes, of course. Where are they?'

'The chaps have got the case in the studio. We've been hanging on until you got here. We didn't think it would be fair to do more than look at the packing note without you.'

'You are good eggs,' said Melissa, striving for the right tone of amused commendation. 'Martin in? He ought to be here for the ceremonial unwrapping.'

'No actually,' said Annabel looking self-conscious. 'I think he's out somewhere.'

'Oh, dear! Has he been upsetting you again?'

Annabel blushed even more vividly, but she simply shook her head.

'Well, that's all right then. Let's be having it.'

Together they went to the studio, where a wooden packing case two feet by three stood on the grey haircord carpet. The two young designers, who reduced Melissa's sketches, photographs and measurements of the objects she had chosen to technical drawings for the craftsmen to work from, looked up at the sound of their voices.

'Goody! Lissa, you can't imagine what superhuman self-control we've been exercising as we stare at it,' said James. 'Shall I do the honours?'

'Would you?'

He took a short crowbar and carefully inserted the end under one of the nailed-down boards on top of the case. There was a satisfactory tearing sound as the nails were wrenched out of the white, splintery wood. It was repeated three times before he could pull off the whole top. Then Melissa knelt down in front of the case and gingerly pulled away handfuls of straw. Beneath that were yellow and white polystyrene chips and, as she cleared them away, she saw the neat row of thirteen paper-wrapped cylinders. Twelve were for the client; the thirteenth for her records.

Hardly breathing, Melissa wiped the palms of her hands down her trousers, and knelt down to pick up one of the packages. Pulling away the coarse paper, tearing it twice, she revealed the ten-inch-high goblet.

She set it down on the flat part of James's drawing table, where the glass caught the light from his halogen lamp. There was no cutting or engraving on the goblet and yet it glistened. Light seemed to hang on the smoothness of the glass like a layer of some unctuous shining substance.

Melissa looked at the goblet, quite satisfied, and thought of the day she had discussed her plans with the young glass blower who had made it. He had taken her into the glass house where his two assistants were at work and she had watched, entranced, as they heated blobs of glass, twirled and swung them, blowing them and twisting them into shape. The hot, sticky-looking yellow material at the end of the pipe had lengthened and bellied out and turned transparent as she watched. A deft turn of the glassblower's wrists, a tap here and there from his assistant, and another bowl was ready.

'It is the most miraculous stuff,' she said, breathing out fully as she absorbed the perfection of her latest acquisition. Objects seemed much safer to her than people. Objects had no wild or difficult emotions.

'Glass?' said James, watching her with amused affection, which she did not see. 'Yes, marvellous. Too expensive, too fragile, but marvellous.'

'James, I'm beginning to think that you're the perfect businessman,' she said, smiling up at him. 'Not sentimental like me. Nothing that looks as simple and perfect and *light* as that could ever be too expensive. Good. Bel, will you take that one up to the drawing room cabinet for me? Thanks. George, could you or James nail the case up again and organize delivery to the client?'

'Of course.'

'Good. I'll go and work on a suitably triumphant letter to him, and—'

'And a bill,' came Martin's voice from the doorway. Melissa turned and saw that he was teasing, for once, instead of hectoring. 'A fat one, I hope, Lissa, given the number of expensive lunches you fed to your young glassblower. Is that the product at last?'

'Yes,' she said, smiling in a friendly way as Annabel replaced the glass beside James's drawing board. 'Isn't it stunning?'

'Pretty nice,' Martin agreed, lounging over to the table where the drawing board stood. 'But I'm not sure it's worthy of quite the fuss you're making. Kneeling to it like that!'

Laughing, he reached out and picked the glass up, examining it against the light and then turning it upside down so that he could feel the foot.

'He's left a bit of roughness here,' he said. 'Considering what you've had to pay for it, I think that's a bit rich. Couldn't you knock a bit off the price, Lissa?'

Melissa deliberately ignored the contempt she could feel from her subordinates because there was no reason why Martin should know anything about glassblowing. She smiled and hoped that he would not find her explanation patronizing.

'That used to be the mark of hand-blown glass in the eighteenth century and even later, Martin. It can be smoothed off, but people – buyers of that sort of glass – often like to know that it's real, so even now-adays some blowers like Giles tend to leave a slight unevenness.'

'Ah, I see,' he said, staring at her as he put the glass down. He misjudged the edge of the table. Melissa could see what was going to happen as soon as his fingers relaxed, but she could not reach the glass in time or even speak. She opened her mouth as the goblet fell towards the floor. It hit the edge of the packing case and smashed into a glistening cascade of useless, dangerous splinters.

'God, I'm sorry, Lissa,' said Martin, sounding all

197

too casual in the ringing emptiness. 'Annabel, fetch a dustpan and brush, will you?'

Melissa could feel the blood draining out of her face. A muscle leaped and fluttered in her left eyelid and she had to put up a finger to hold it down. She stared at the pile of sharp-edged glass fragments, knowing what the edges of any one of them could do to someone's skin, almost seeing the photographs of Penelope Beechen's body, and left the room without a word.

'You look awful,' said Martin from the doorway of her office a few minutes later.

'How very encouraging!'

'Don't take it like that. It was meant to be sympathetic,' said Martin, sounding hurt. That made Melissa look up and stare at him, slowly shaking her head from side to side.

'I've said I'm sorry about your bloody glass, Lissa, but it's only money. You could get it back off the insurance, if you wanted. It was an accident.'

Was it? thought Melissa. Aloud she said: 'Martin, will you tell me something?'

'What?'

'Why did you want to marry me in the first place?'

He stiffened and looked less pleased with himself. 'Why on earth are you asking me that now of all times?'

Melissa shrugged. Her first fury at what she believed to be his deliberate smashing of the glass had receded, but the other feelings it had aroused were more difficult to suppress.

'There's nothing special about now,' she said carefully, trying to find a way to say the unsayable, 'except that this trial I have to listen to every day has opened a few locked doors in my mind and I'm prepared to admit some things I've kept behind them until now.' She was appalled to feel heat and dampness seeping into her eyes and blinked.

'Like what?' Martin asked coolly, leaning against the door jamb with his left foot crossed over his right. His hands were stuck in the pockets of his trousers, his jacket hanging open. He looked negligent, unworried, superior. She realized sadly that he was enjoying the sight of her white face and wet eyes.

'That you don't like me very much,' Melissa said with difficulty.

Her husband merely straightened up and took his hands out of his pockets. His lips tightened in disapproval. 'Lissa, don't go on like this. Don't you think I've got enough on my plate without you rootling about in our lives as though you were a chicken on a dungheap? It's difficult waiting for the headhunters to get back to me about jobs; and it's hellishly frustrating working here in this potty little company of yours. But, as you've kindly pointed out, it is not my business – in any sense of the word. I'm prepared to stick with it for another week or two until I find a proper job.'

Melissa suppressed her immediate reaction, which would have been to say: That's big of you!

'But you're not happy, are you?' she said aloud, trying as always to remember that he was a human being who felt hurt as she did and who could not really want to be as difficult as he seemed.

'Who would be, in my situation?' He glared at her and then looked away, saying with a despairing resignation that shocked her: 'Anyway, what's happiness got to do with anything?'

'I don't know,' she said with more gentleness than she had felt for some time. 'Martin, it's a horrible situation for us both.'

'My dear girl, don't get hysterical. And don't go complaining about me to your bloody mother tomorrow.'

'I never do,' she said, her gentler feelings beginning to die, 'as you very well know.'

He looked at her and, for a moment, she thought that she saw behind his mask of anger the man she had once believed she knew, vulnerable, reachable, in need. Trying to forget all the things that had gone wrong between them, she smiled and spoke directly to that man:

'Look, why don't you come with me tomorrow? It's ages since you've seen her, and if you had a chance to talk you'd realize that she's fond of you, that she's not some kind of witch, and that she doesn't do anything to harm you and me.'

'We've been through this so often, Lissa,' he said as the mask slipped back over what she thought she had seen in his face. 'You know perfectly well that I hate it there. Anyway it's not safe for me to be anywhere near her wretched bees.'

'But it's still only the third week of March. The bees aren't flying in any great numbers yet. You'd be in the house all the time. There's not the remotest chance of your getting stung. Please come.'

'Certainly not. In any case, I've got a squash game booked.' He turned away.

'All right,' she said, remembering belatedly that she had already invited Adam to go with her. 'I'll bring you back a pot of her best honey instead.'

At that Martin turned in the doorway. His reddening face looked tight, and angrier than she had ever seen it. There was no sign of any vulnerability or friendliness at all.

'What on earth is the matter now?' For once Melissa allowed her full impatience to come out in her voice. Then she moderated it. 'I was only trying to be friendly.'

'I hate honey,' he said through his teeth.

'You've never said that before,' she said, astonished. 'I thought you liked it. Why have you never told me something as easy to deal with as that? I keep trying to find out what you really feel and think so that I don't make everything worse for you, and you won't even tell me you don't like honey. How can you expect me ever to get anything right?'

She propped her head in her hands, feeling deathly tired and wondering why she went on and on trying to keep something alive between them, when he apparently did everything he could to kill it. She felt as though she could hear the noise of the breaking glass again.

'You ought to have seen that I detest it,' he burst out. 'It ought to be obvious enough. There are times when I feel as though I'm drowning in it in this bloody house. Everything is honey-coloured – your hair and your skin and most of your clothes. All the food you cook tastes of it. Sometimes it makes me feel physically sick as well as revoltingly sticky to hear you talk about your mother and her bees and their honey. There are days when I have to stand under the shower and scrub myself clean.'

He left, banging the door shut behind him. Melissa sat at her desk, trying not to shiver. Difficulties there had often been with Martin during the past months, but he had never sounded so vicious – or so desperate. She knew that she ought to do something to help him back to normality, but she could not imagine what. Whenever she tried to be kind he slapped her down and whenever anything went right for her, he tried to destroy it. She was sure that behind his unkindness there was misery, real, aching misery, but he would not let her near it. There seemed to be no way of reaching him, let alone saying – or doing – anything useful.

The door of his office slammed at the end of the long basement corridor. Ten minutes later, when she had learned to breathe again, made a cup of tea and drunk it, Melissa followed him. On the way to his room, she noticed that the door to Annabel's office was tactfully shut.

'Martin?'

'What?' He looked up from some papers on his desk, glaring. He, too, was breathing faster than usual.

Melissa shut the door behind her and leaned against it, both her hands still clasped around the knob. Its hard coldness seemed comforting. She took a deep breath.

'What exactly did that little speech of yours mean just now?'

'For Christ's sake, Melissa! Can't you leave me alone for a single minute? It means that I dislike honey. Why must you women always dig around for ulterior motives and hidden meanings?'

'I don't,' she said at once, which was mainly true. 'But you sounded so violent then that I can't believe it was just to do with honey. I wish to God you'd tell me what you're really after.'

'All right, if you must have it: honey seems to stand for everything your mother does to us. As you know perfectly well, I can't bear the fact that you're so tied up with her. It's not natural. You should have children of your own. Even in her bloody beehives the new queen leads a swarm away from the old hive to start a new colony.'

Melissa achieved a smile. 'You've been doing your homework,' she said, managing to sound quite friendly again. Keeping civil seemed tremendously important, with all the difficult feelings surging just beneath the surface of her mind.

'Anyone who'd had to live with you for as long as I have would have picked up that much,' said Martin in a voice which showed that he could not care less about civility.

After a moment's silence, Melissa said hopelessly, 'I wish that I could understand you, Martin. I really try, but I can't any more. When you talk like that you sound as though you detest me. It all comes back to the same thing. We must sort it out. It's mad to go on hurting each other like this.'

Martin glowered at the papers on his desk. Melissa waited. Eventually he looked at her again.

'What is it that you are trying to tell me?' she asked when he still did not speak. He held his head with his hands clamped at either side of his forehead and stared at her. She saw that he was shaking with effort.

'You don't even listen, do you?' he shouted. 'All right, I'll tell you again. I detest the taste, smell, look and feel of your mother's honey. I wish you'd finally cut the umbilical cord. I loathe everything about this house. The smallness . . . the provincialness of your business irks me beyond belief. Your staff drive me up the wall. I can't wait to get out of here, back into the world, and do some work. There. Satisfied?' He swallowed. His hands dropped back into his lap. In a quite different voice he said: 'Oh, by the way, I'm going up to London on Monday to see another firm of headhunters.'

'I see. Thank you, Martin,' Melissa said and let herself out of his office. It seemed quite impossible even to contemplate work and so she went upstairs to her bedroom, took two paracetamol and thought about telephoning Adam.

With some difficulty she resisted the temptation and rang up Cecily instead. They talked mostly about her writing, which was beginning to go better, and what it was like doing jury service. Melissa tried to explain why the trial, which Cecily had been following in the local newspaper, was upsetting her so much, but since she could not bring herself to mention Martin's name her explanation was not very clear.

Chapter 14

'Sorry I'm a bit late,' said Melissa at a quarter past twelve the next day as Adam came to the front door of his house. She was wearing dark-blue trousers, a big soft jersey, and another pair of her comfortable flat shoes. 'I hope you didn't think I wasn't coming?'

'No,' he answered, looking down at his tweed suit, 'but I think I've put on the wrong clothes. Shall I change?'

'Why not, if you'd be more comfortable? My mother's a very informal woman. She never expects suits and ties. I should have told you.'

He laughed, told her he would not be more than five minutes and ran up the small staircase, moving like a man much younger than his lined face had always made him seem.

'It's really good to see you, you know,' she said when he returned wearing baggy brown corduroy trousers and a checked shirt under a supple tweed jacket. He locked the front door behind them, wondering why she seemed so tense.

'Are you sure I'm not in the way?' he asked. 'I feel a bit like a gatecrasher.'

'You're not. I know my mother will like you, and I rather suspect you'll take to her, too.'

'Tell me about her, Melissa. I'm nervous, you know.'

'You needn't be,' she said, as she unlocked the car doors. Her voice was gentle and for a moment her face relaxed. 'She doesn't frighten anyone. Everyone likes her except Martin, and there are reasons for that which may have nothing to do with her, I think. Physically . . . Well, she and I are said to look very alike. I find it hard to describe her. She's almost my best friend, I suppose, apart from Cecily Wells.'

'The crime writer?'

'Yes. We've known each other for years. She's terrific, too. You'd really like her. Have you ever read any of her books?'

As she spoke, Melissa realized with a small shock that she did not want Adam ever to meet Cecily. She pushed the thought away.

'I've read some,' he said, without giving any clue to his reaction to them. 'It's good to see you looking more cheerful.'

'I always enjoy my Saturday jaunts,' said Melissa, relieved to be able to admit it. For the first time she let herself acknowledge just how much she hated having to disguise the pleasure she took in her visits to her mother's house.

Adam looked sideways at Melissa, wondering what her wretched husband had said or done to her that morning. Adam had no idea of what the man even looked like, let alone how he behaved, and yet he hated him.

As they left the last houses on the edge of Bath, Melissa's face began to lose its tightness. Watching her, Adam noticed when each set of muscles let go: first in her neck, then her forehead and finally around her mouth. At last she looked almost as free as she had done when she was leaning against the hard concrete pillar in the Bristol car park, smiling at him and wanting him.

'Here we are,' she said, taking a sharp turn to the left just after they crossed the Kennet and Avon Canal. 'It's not long now. I ought to have asked you, Adam, are you allergic to anything that my mother might have cooked for lunch?'

'No. I tend not to like things like bone marrow, but

it's an emotional reaction, not a physical one. I can eat anything really.'

'It won't be any sort of offal. I suspect it'll be a joint. She likes to cook conventional English food. And pudding will be something to do with honey because she's always experimenting for her latest cookery book.'

'Your mother writes as well, then? Heavens, she sounds alarming!'

'Don't be absurd. You'll realize how idiotic your fears are as soon as you meet her.'

'I hope so,' said Adam gloomily. 'Melissa, don't laugh at me like that. I'm not in the habit of going about with glamorous women like you, let alone meeting their mothers. It makes me nervous.'

'Adam! It really needn't. There's nothing glamorous about either of us.'

He laughed and thought of describing just what the sight of her had done to him when they first met.

'She started writing before she had the shop or museum, in the winter when the bees don't need so much attention,' Melissa explained. 'The first book was about setting up the apiary and she's gone on writing every winter since then. Occasionally she produces technical stuff for other beekeepers, but usually it's more general books or recipes. A few years ago she wrote a lovely children's story about life in a beehive. It was quite successful.'

'I'd like to read it,' said Adam. 'I still have a strong yen for a certain sort of children's book.'

Melissa half turned so that she could smile at him again. It seemed unlikely that a man who read the kind of dry, scholarly works he habitually carried with him should choose to read children's stories of any kind.

'What about sequels?' he asked before she could find out more.

'She says she doesn't want to repeat herself just for the

sake it of it and that there's nothing more to tell children about a beehive. I think it's a pity, but I see what she means. The last thing she could bear would be to turn bees into anthropomorphic characters in some fictional series,' said Melissa, noticing how a patch of sunlight gleaming through the clouds was reflected in a patch of rainwater just ahead of her car.

The puddle looked like a pool of molten metal, richly yellow and gleaming. As the tyres splashed through it the light caught the droplets and made them shine in the air before they collapsed.

'Her publishers keep nagging her to do another one and promising lots of money, but she keeps refusing. Money beyond her immediate needs has never particularly interested my mother.'

The narrow road twisted and turned between high banks, made even taller by the trees that grew out of the top. The thickening cloud let through just enough sun to glisten on the damp ivy leaves and illuminate the pale-yellow primroses.

Melissa braked and turned into an almost concealed road to the right, which was even smaller than the one they had been on. The hill was so steep that they seemed to be creeping, almost head first, down into the wooded valley.

'Sorry about this. I hope it's not making you feel sick.'

'I like it. What a spectacular house!'

'Nice, isn't it?' said Melissa, making a U-turn at the junction of three roads and stopping with the car pointing back the way they had come.

'I wanted you to see the front properly before we drive in,' she went on. 'Inside the gates all you see is the side of the house and the outbuildings. This is the best bit.'

'You mean this is where your mother lives?' said

Adam, sounding amused. No wonder she was not interested in money beyond her immediate needs, he thought, with a house like that.

Built of the same honey-coloured stone as Bath itself, the house stood behind a low wall, square and elegant with a deep cornice and a grey-slate mansard roof. Each of the three main storeys had seven perfectly proportioned windows and there was a pair of dormers in the roof beneath two tall chimneys. It was a beautiful house, but large for a single person, thought Adam as he clung to his common sense, and to his determined rejection of anything that smacked of the kind of ostentation he had come to detest during his years in Rome.

'I could take you in through the main door,' said Melissa, waving at the simple iron gates that hung between two urn-topped pedestals, 'except that we never use it.'

She re-started the engine and drove a hundred yards or so back up the road, to turn sharply right in between the back gates of the house. Adam saw a smooth lawn divided by an avenue of pollarded lime trees, well-kept borders, a greenhouse or two, a dovecote and a mass of what had obviously once been stables. Rising behind the house was the hill, studded with groups of white beehives.

'Your mother must be very fit,' he said, looking up at the precipitous steps between the hives.

'She is.' Melissa laughed. 'You'll see after lunch if she takes you to see the bees. I'm always breathless before we're halfway to the top, but she positively dances up the hill. When she started keeping bees she was afraid that the steepness of it would force wind up into the hives, but something about the angle of the hills and the direction of the valley means they're protected from anything except a hurricane. And the last one of those bypassed this whole area.'

She parked neatly beside a red Nissan Micra, which was splattered with mud. 'I see Joan Radborn's here.

She's a very old friend of my mother's. I hope you'll like her.'

Aware of a faint hardness in Melissa's voice, Adam was intrigued. He followed her out of the car. Before they reached the house the back door opened and a woman emerged. From where Adam was standing, she looked almost exactly like Melissa, but with no fringe and shorter hair.

She stood on the step with her arms open. Adam watched Melissa walk forwards and lean into her mother's embrace. The two tall women clung together for long enough to make Adam hesitate.

'It is good to see you, darling.' Abigail kissed her daughter and reached one hand out past her. 'You must be Adam Blake,' she called out, smiling.

He walked towards them both, dazzled by the sight of the two of them together.

'Good morning, Mrs Hansford,' he said, taking her outstretched hand.

Standing close to her, he could see that her skin was much more lined than her daughter's and her hair less brightly blonde, but the elegant shape of their faces was the same. They both had well-defined cheekbones and long necks, as well as the steady grey eyes and emphatic dark brows and lashes that he had already decided were what transformed Melissa's face from simple prettiness into something much more striking.

'It is so good of you to let me come here.'

'It's a pleasure.' Abigail led the way to the drawing room, and for a moment Adam stood beside her in silence as he looked around the big, beautiful, easy room.

Its walls were painted a creamy yellow colour that was only a little paler than the stone of the house itself and the whole room seemed full of light. The clouds must have parted just then, for the sun poured in through the three long windows at the front of the house.

Light fell on rubbed ivy green velvet and old wood, on the cracked leather seat of a battered brass club fender, on the very English landscape paintings and on masses of yellow, white and blue spring flowers, piles of books and old porcelain bowls of pot pourri. Nothing smacked of either grandeur or display. All the furniture was obviously there to be used, and it looked comfortable and slightly shabby.

Adam's breathing deepened and slowed, and Melissa could see that the room was having its usual effect. She could never be quite sure whether it was the look of it, the mixed scents of woodsmoke, books and flowers, or simply something to do with her mother's character, but Melissa had never seen a stranger enter the room without letting some tension go. It struck her that the atmosphere had something of the same ease and peace of Adam's very different room.

'Melissa, will you pour yourself and Adam something to drink?' said Abigail, leading him across to a wing chair that stood at the left of the fire. As they walked round it, Adam saw a grey-haired woman sitting there. She looked considerably older than his hostess.

'This is Joan Radborn. Joan, Melissa's friend Adam Blake.'

The woman in the chair gestured to a pair of sticks that lay on the floor beside her.

'Will you forgive my not getting up, Mr Blake?' she said in a resonant voice that was surprisingly deep for such a delicate-looking woman. Her fine-boned face was as lined as his own and her blue eyes were deep-set and watchful.

'But of course,' he said, shaking her hand. 'I'd be horrified if you tried.'

'Sit there, Adam,' said Abigail, pointing to a small sofa near Joan's chair. 'I must check on lunch.'

'I'm sorry we were late,' said Melissa from the drinks tray.

'Couldn't matter less.'

'What would you like to drink, Adam?' Melissa asked as her mother left the room.

'A glass of wine perhaps?'

'Sure. Joan, can I refill your sherry glass?'

'No, I'm fine, thank you. Driving back down these lanes is not something I'd like to do under the influence of alcohol.'

'I'm sure it's not,' said Adam. 'Driving isn't a problem for you then?'

Melissa looked across at them, surprised by his directness. Joan did not seem to mind it.

'No. It's my back rather than my legs,' she answered just as frankly. 'The sticks are just for balance, but getting up and down is always tricky. How are you liking Bath? Abigail told me you're a relatively new resident.'

'It's very pleasant,' he said non-committally, reverting to a stranger's politeness. 'I prefer it to Bristol, where I lodged for my first few years at the university. For some reason that seemed infinitely depressing.'

'Abigail always thought that about Bath.'

'I know,' said Melissa, coming back to hand Adam his glass of wine and interrupting them. 'It's something I've never understood. This house is heaven, of course, and it's where I grew up, but I like Bath better. I'm not sure why. Perhaps it's the formlessness of the country that gets me down. And even if it sounds revoltingly precious, I do love having Georgian architecture all round me.'

'You're very lucky to live in the middle of it.'

As Adam spoke Melissa noticed that Joan was looking at him with the kind of intense scrutiny she must have applied to her patients in the days before she retired.

Melissa felt suddenly protective. She knew just what sort of conclusions Joan was tempted to draw about people from the slightest evidence.

'I know I am,' Melissa said, looking away from the doctor, 'and even luckier to have inherited it. The house belonged to my father.'

'You mean you have the whole thing, not just a flat?' Adam sounded horrified. 'In the Circus?'

'Yes.' Melissa tried not to feel defensive. 'I told you: I know I'm lucky.'

'No wonder you were so surprised by my living in Bear Flat,' he said with a glimmer of slightly grim amusement. 'I never thought I'd meet anyone . . .'

'You must come and look at it soon and tell me what you think,' said Melissa, not wanting to hear another diatribe about how immoral it was for a childless couple to live in a house big enough for four families. She had heard it all before from all kinds of people, and she hated the thought of listening to criticism from Adam. 'It's still not entirely furnished. That's been happening floor by floor as and when I can afford it,' she said.

'Well, that's a relief at least.' He and Joan were laughing as Abigail reappeared in the doorway.

'Lunch is ready,' she said.

Joan Radborn reached for her sticks.

'Can I help?' asked Adam.

She shook her head, smiling. 'Only by going on ahead and not watching me.'

Abigail smiled at her friend from the doorway and then turned away.

When Adam reached the door he noticed a framed drawing, which hung near it. He stopped at once. 'That is superb.'

Abigail turned back and nodded. 'Yes, isn't it? Most drawings of teenage girls are moony and romantic, but that one looks as though Melissa's just climbed a mountain or is marching her way through strong waves. She was fifteen at the time.'

Adam looked at the drawing with his head on one side. He checked the original and then returned to the portrait. 'I see what you mean: she is looking out, isn't she? There's nothing introverted or dreamy there at all.'

'That's what I've always thought,' said Abigal warmly. 'I love it that she's never succumbed to that awful business of measuring every thing, idea and person against her own emotions. And the drawing seems to sum that up for me.'

Adam glanced back at Joan and was interested to see a kind of stubborn doubt in her expression. She caught his eye and smiled. He nodded as though he not only understood what she meant but also agreed with it.

'And thank you both very much,' Melissa was saying, laughing and unaware of the silent communication that was being carried out behind her. 'I am here, you know, listening to all this.'

Her mother laughed too, and put an arm casually around her shoulders. 'I know you are, darling, but I can never resist it when new people see in you all the things I particularly value. Come on, Adam; the lamb will be getting cold.'

Obediently he followed them into the formal, glaucous-walled dining room, longing for the time when he would be at home and at ease in the big, beautiful house. When he caught himself fantasizing about belonging there, he savagely told himself to grow up. He would never have any right to more than casual friendship with Melissa. Already he knew he was lucky to have that.

At first it had been Melissa's cool, blonde slenderness and her remarkable face that had appealed to him, but once she had let him see a little way past her defences he had become involved with her in a way that both surprised and exhilarated him. And then he had kissed her, and seen in her response something he had never experienced in all his attempts to love and be loved: an immediate, quite free, giving of some part of herself. She had never let her guard drop so far again, but he could not forget what he had seen, and it made him feel protective as well as everything else.

Abigail stood at the head of the formally laid table and waved Adam to a chair on her right. Melissa automatically took the place opposite him, leaving the foot of the table for Joan. She appeared only a few minutes later, walking with some difficulty, but hardly leaning on the sticks at all. Her face showed signs of concentration rather than pain.

Abigail was carving a leg of lamb at the mahogany sideboard, where an old-fashioned silver-plated hotplate supported dishes of vegetables and silver gravy boats. Having filled one plate, she carried it to Joan, saying over her shoulder, 'Adam, do go and help yourself.'

Later, when they were all eating and no-one had started to talk, she said, 'Melissa said you're interested in bees, Adam.'

'Very much.' He grinned across the table at Melissa, reminding her of their shared breakfast in Bristol. 'Unfortunately I have no space to keep them myself.'

'Oh, you should try. You can fit a hive or two in most town gardens and they're incredibly rewarding, quite apart from the honey they provide. But if you're really interested, I think this afternoon's going to be warm enough to do the last of my external checks. If there are any signs of queen failure or mice or non-laying or anything, I'll be opening the hive. Would that interest you at all?'

'Yes it would, if you don't mind a stranger there. And if the bees won't. I thought they hated unknown people among the hives.'

'Only if they're unaccustomed to comings and goings

and frightened. I make sure there are always people working among my hives all year round so that the bees learn that people aren't threatening. With so many visitors I need to keep the colonies as sweet as possible.'

'I can imagine. The insurance costs must be horrific.'

'Not too bad in fact. Luckily we've never had any bad accidents with the public; one or two stings, of course, that's inevitable, but the sufferers were very sensible. I'll kit you up with white overalls so that they don't think you're a bear,' Abigail went on, leaning towards him and sniffing frankly. 'And it doesn't smell as though you're wearing aftershave, which is one of their pet hates.'

'No,' he said, flushing slightly, which amused Melissa. 'I never do.'

'Quite right, too. They're pretty torpid at the moment anyway. Melissa, you've finished. D'you want any more?'

She got up to help herself to some more vegetables as Adam asked something about the long, intricate dances bees perform to direct other workers from the hive to the best source of nectar. Returning to her place, Melissa turned to Joan. 'They're well away. I thought they'd get on,' she said quietly.

Joan nodded slowly, looking down the polished table towards Adam, whose attention was riveted to what Abigail was saying about the gloriousness of a hot summer's day when the air is full of the sound of the bees and the scent of nectar as they fan their wings above it to evaporate the water and turn it into ripe honey.

'Yes,' said Joan, adding even more quietly, 'she could do him a lot of good.'

'What do you mean?'

Joan turned to Melissa, her faded blue eyes sharpening. 'I just thought he looks as though he needs Abigail's simplicity and serenity,' she said. 'He's wounded, Melissa. You'll have to be very careful.'

'I don't know what you mean,' she said, hearing

real criticism in Joan's voice. 'Don't you want some redcurrant jelly?'

'Thank you,' answered the doctor peaceably. 'How have you been? I haven't seen you for weeks.'

'Oh, not too bad,' said Melissa, smiling politely. 'You know, just life and all that. And you? How's the directory of drugs coming along?'

'That's not too bad either. But it's exhausting work. Entering all the data on to the computer, I mean, not actually compiling them. I find that really interesting – if sometimes frightening.'

'Ever since you told me what you were doing I've been wary of taking any medicines at all,' said Melissa. 'Occasionally I succumb to headache pills, but that's all.'

'I don't think you should worry too much about analgesics if you're taking nothing else and avoiding alcohol. It's the more powerful stuff, particularly the psychotropic drugs, that can be so tricky if they're combined with other chemicals.'

'I'm sure,' said Melissa, once more finding her mother's best friend more difficult to talk to than nearly anyone else. She thought of asking Joan about her recurring migraines, but then remembered what various doctor friends had said about hating being consulted on social occasions.

Joan nodded and watched Abigail talking in a clear voice at the head of the table.

'And so,' she was saying, 'the workers in a hive do sometimes reject a new queen if she's too arrogant, which is why one tends to starve her first and/or wet her so that she is humble enough not to worry them. You'll see how it's done later in the year when you come back.'

'Isn't it extraordinary?' said Adam, turning to Melissa. 'It must be terribly hard not to attribute emotions and human reasoning to the bees when you're so close to them. I'd be tempted all the time.'

'Oh, I am,' said Abigail with a mocking smile that seemed to be directed at herself as much as anyone else. 'But I find them so much more sensible than most humans that I usually manage to keep the two separate in my mind.'

Adam laughed with a freedom Melissa had never yet seen in him. After a moment he looked at her mother more seriously.

'I can understand exactly why they appeal to you,' he said, 'but there are some pretty sinister aspects to them, don't you think?'

Abigail raised her eyebrows and turned her head slowly from side to side. 'No, I don't think so.'

'Oh, come on,' he said robustly. 'Think of their ruthless expulsion of bees that have lost their usefulness; the imprisonment of the queen; the ripping out of the male genitals after mating; the murder of the drones when they're no longer needed; all that sort of thing.'

Abigail sat in silence, the interest and pleasure cooling out of her face.

'I grant you that the organization of a beehive is marvellous, much more sensible than anything humans achieve,' Adam said, noticing her withdrawal, 'but I think a bit of human inefficiency is worth paying for a little more tolerance of weakness – not to speak of actual thought, let alone verbal communication, without which . . . Sorry, that's all come out rather muddled, but I expect you know what I mean.'

'Of course I do. And you're right,' said Abigail, reaching across to refill his wineglass. 'Put in those terms there's no comparison. But, as you say, a hive is so marvellous that it's hard not to admire it more than the usual human muddle and useless destruction. At least the bees destroy only to ensure the colony's survival. It just seems so much more rational than the vicious way humans behave, positively enjoying the harm they cause.'

'All humans?' asked Joan from the foot of the table. There was an indescribably affectionate sound in her voice and her eyes glittered. 'Or just adults?'

'You're right, too, Joan, and of course it's only some of the adults,' said Abigail, smiling. She turned her head back towards Adam to explain. 'Joan's always teasing me for finding children so much more rational than their parents.'

His face tightened into a frown. 'I don't know any children well enough to judge – unless you count undergraduates as children?'

'Certainly not. Judging by the ones who are brought here, the rationality stops at about six. Until then they are absolutely direct in their questions and responses. They don't hide their fears or twist their needs.'

'They must be very secure children, then, the ones who come here,' he said slowly. 'From my memories I'd have said that a great many hide their fears.'

'Not from Abigail,' said Joan cheerfully from the other end of the table. 'They trust her, and they seem to love the facts she gives them, too. That's why schools bring their pupils here and parents are so keen on her holiday courses. They come from miles around.'

'I can imagine Marianna hiding her fears,' said Melissa suddenly, remembering the child in the witness box. 'Adam and I are both on the jury of the most hideous case. Have you read about it, either of you?' She looked from her mother to Joan Radborn, turning her head as though she were a spectator at a tennis match. 'The killing of a woman called Penelope Beechen by her husband.'

Abigail got up from the table and began to collect the plates. 'I don't think we ought to talk about it, darling.'

'Technically you're right, I know. The judge did warn us not to discuss the case with anyone who isn't on the jury, but this is a safe house. It can't matter here, surely? Besides, who's to know?'

'I'm afraid it does matter. Marianna Beechen is one of the children who sometimes comes here.' Abigail switched off the hotplate, ignoring the astonished look that Melissa was exchanging with Adam.

'She comes here?'

'Melissa, we mustn't talk about it. Anything I say might influence you, and I don't want to be committing contempt of court or anything – or encouraging you to do so. We must not talk about her.'

'I suppose you're right,' said Melissa after a pause, 'but there are about a million questions I want to ask.'

'That's exactly why she's right,' said Adam with a smile. 'May I help you with the plates, Mrs Hansford?'

'How kind! Could you bring some of the dishes through to the kitchen for me? It's not far. Are they too hot? There's a cloth there.'

When they had gone out, Melissa stopped thinking about the Beechens and the extraordinary coincidence that had brought Marianna to her mother's house and instead took advantage of Adam's absence to say, 'Joan, what did you mean that I had to be careful of Adam?'

Her mother's elderly friend considered for a moment and then shrugged. 'Just that if you encourage someone as lonely and as tightly controlled as that man to let go, the consequences could be hard to contain – and whatever they were, you'd consider them your responsibility, wouldn't you?'

'Probably.'

'That might make it hard for you to be kind. And he needs kindness – among other things – very much indeed.'

Melissa shook her head, frowning.

'I don't understand what you're worrying about,' she said eventually. 'I like him. That's why I brought him here. I knew he and my mother would enjoy each other.'

Joan peered at Melissa over the top of her spectacles. 'You're not that naive, Melissa,' she said. There was criticism in her voice, but concern too. 'You must have seen that he's falling in love with you. And you're tempted to let him, aren't you? It doesn't surprise me at all. He's interesting, clever, sensitive, good-looking, absorbed in you, and sad; how would you of all people be able to resist a man like that?'

'Oh, nonsense!' Melissa pushed her chair back from the table and crossed her long legs. Joan was being not only as intrusive as usual, but absurdly dramatic as well. 'We only met last Monday.'

Joan raised her eyebrows. 'Well, just be careful. Of yourself as well as him. You matter,' she said as Abigail returned, carrying a pale-gold flan on a dark-red plate. Adam followed her with a pile of pudding plates.

'Do I hear you diagnosing and prescribing again, Joan?' asked Abigail from the sideboard.

'It was once my job,' said the doctor with a smile. 'I can't help it. My turn to explain, Adam. Abigail believes with the utmost conviction that no human being has the right to give orders or even advice to another, not even to warn. It is the one subject on which we differ fundamentally.'

Melissa, who knew of her mother's philosophy but not of Joan's objection to it, was about to speak, but Adam opened his mouth first.

'But surely, you warn your visiting schoolchildren of the dangers of bees?' he said to Abigail.

'That, yes. It's a fact, like the rules of jury service. I explain how stings work and why bees sting. Just as I would explain to a child that putting a hand in the fire is dangerous. It's interfering in less practical ways that I so dislike. Once you start doing that, you make yourself responsible for the consequences.'

Her face looked quite cold as she added, 'You can't let that happen. People must be allowed to make their own mistakes, not yours. And you can't be responsible for theirs.'

'But isn't it hard to watch people you care about hurting themselves?' he asked, clearly understanding that he was troubling her and yet determined to put his question.

'Sometimes,' Abigail said frowning. 'But that's just something you have to put up with. If they aren't allowed to make their own discoveries they will hurt worse in the end. Quite apart from the fact that people can't generally hear a warning before they've damaged themselves, I don't think it's fair to impose on them the results of what I've learned.'

Melissa nodded, her huge affection for her mother showing in her eyes, her smile and the whole position of her body and her hands. 'I can bear witness to that, Adam. She's never interfered at all. I've never come across another mother who's been so careful never to crush or constrain her child.'

Abigail bowed her smooth head.

'What a testimonial! Thank you, darling.' As she spoke she was cutting the flan into quarters and sliding each piece on to a plate. 'This is a honey and saffron tart. Is that all right for you all? There's cheese on the sideboard if you'd prefer.'

They all accepted the tart and when they had finished it, and a pot of coffee that Melissa made, her mother suggested that they should show Adam round the bee museum and shop before she took him to see the hives. Joan decided to stay behind in the warmth to read the Saturday newspapers.

Chapter 15

As Abigail pushed open the bottom half of the old stable door, and ushered him into her shop, Adam found himself inside a long, light room lined with polished beech shelves. Some were filled with brightly jacketed books; others with jars of honey, every colour from glossy, rich, dark brown to thick, hardly golden white; and still others with jars of cosmetics, furniture polish, and beeswax candles of all shapes and sizes.

Melissa took down six pots of heather honey from Abigail's out apiary on Dartmoor and carried them to the till, where a young woman wearing a mauve and pink flowered dress with a big lace collar smiled at her and asked how she was.

'I'm fine. And you, Ann?'

'Not so bad,' she said, ringing up the price of the honey on a thoroughly modern till.

'Why did you choose that particular honey, Melissa?' asked Adam, looking at the variety on offer. 'There seem to be a vast number of options.'

'I just like the taste of heather honey best,' she said, 'but you ought to try some of the rarer ones. Ann's probably got tasting jars open.'

'Sure,' said the young woman, sliding off her high stool.

'Try this one, Adam.' Abigail was holding a pot of set honey that was almost white. 'It's ivy: a curious taste, but one I particularly like.'

'Isn't it poisonous?' Adam looked askance at the spoonful he was being offered.

Abigail laughed. 'No. The nectar of ivy flowers doesn't harm the bees and the honey seems to be fine. I don't always collect and bottle it, but I did last year, and I'm quite pleased with the result. The weather was just right and the ivy was covered in flowers.'

Adam licked the white plastic spoon gingerly. 'Mmm,' he murmured when he had swallowed the honey and dropped the spoon into a small bin by the side of the till. 'It's a strange taste, isn't it? A curious mixture of terrific sweetness and something else I can't quite pin down. Do you like it, Melissa?'

She was about to answer when her eye was caught by a man moving erratically in between two groups of beehives half way up the hill. She looked more closely at him.

'Oh, God! It's Martin. What on earth is he doing? He must be mad. What if he's stung?'

Abigail looked at her daughter for an instant and then out of the window. Seeing Martin fall a moment later, she ran to a tall cupboard in the wall. Pulling out a white boiler suit and a pair of white wellingtons, she put them on over her clothes, saying urgently, 'Melissa, get the smoker going. Quick. Ann, ring for an ambulance at once.' She knelt down beside a small fridge and took from it a white cardboard box about three inches long and one wide. Pulling on her veiled helmet she ran towards the hives, tucking the mesh down into the neck of her white bee suit as she went.

'What's going on?' asked Adam, shocked by the urgency he could feel all around him and feeling humiliatingly ignorant.

Melissa, who was taking down from one of the shelves a copper can with a conical lid and what looked like bellows attached to it, said hurriedly, 'If he's stung he may go into anaphylactic shock. I can't explain now. Ann will tell you.'

With shaking hands, Melissa took off the lid of the copper can and put what looked like a roll of old sacking into it. She lit the sacking, put the lid back on the can and then pulled on a white bee suit like the one her mother had been wearing, fumbling with the fastenings and cursing as her fingers failed to work as quickly as she wanted.

'Is the ambulance coming?' she asked Ann, who was replacing the telephone receiver just as Melissa thrust her feet into a pair of short white wellingtons and bent to tuck the trousers into them. She wrenched her broken nail so badly that it ripped again, much further down, making her gasp and thrust the finger into her mouth.

'Yes. It may be twenty minutes or more, but they're on their way.'

'OK. Adam, don't come out. Ann'll tell you.'

She ran out of the building to join her mother, pumping the bellows to check that a cloud of cool smoke poured out of the conical cap of the smoker. As she reached Abigail, Melissa saw that Martin had already been stung many times and was lying on his back on the muddy grass. Bees were crawling all over his scarlet face and he was twitching in pain and terror. His breathing was shockingly laboured. Seeing her coming, he struggled to sit up against Abigail's restraining hands.

'Lie still, Martin. I must put the adrenaline in,' said Abigail through her veil.

'No. Not you. I won't . . . Let Lissa do it.'

'I have done it before,' said Abigail in a calm, deliberate voice. 'Lissa hasn't. She's here, but she's going to smoke the bees so that they get back into the hives. Lie still. It'll make it worse if you thrash about. Don't try to brush them off.'

Melissa was directing puffs of smoke all around Martin and then towards each of the neighbouring hives, and saw that the clouds of angry bees were beginning to lessen.

'Sorry, Martin,' she said as she puffed towards him and saw his breathing worsen. She smelled a powerful, musky aftershave and wondered why he had been stupid enough to drench himself in it before coming to the bee farm. If he had listened to her as often as he had claimed, he would have known the effect aftershave had on bees.

'It's the only safe way to distract them and get them to go. There; they're starting to move off. It's all right. Don't panic.'

'Lissa, you must do it.' Martin's panting voice sounded terrified. Abigail turned to say through her veil, 'Melissa, you'd better. He won't let me. It's agitating him, and it's urgent. I'll take the smoker.'

'I've never injected anyone before,' Melissa said, trying to keep her own panic in check.

'Never mind. I'll tell you how. Come here. Kneel down.'

Melissa applied the smoker's bellows once more, put the whole contraption down on the ground and went to kneel beside her mother. Afraid of being stung herself, she had pulled on heavy gauntlets as she left the safety of the shop. Seeing the delicacy of the short syringe in her mother's hand, Melissa stripped off her gloves and hoped that the smoke would send the remaining bees back into their hives before they decided that she, too, was a threat. She was not allergic to bee venom as far as she knew, but she was well aware of the number of people killed by stings every year.

Abigail gave her the syringe and Martin lay back on the grass, panting and scarlet-faced. Melissa looked at him and saw that he was staring at her as intently as Michael Beechen stared each day in court. Martin's face had swollen so that his eyes were half concealed in lumpy puffs of flesh, but she could see enough to know that he was trying to tell her something. She looked away, trying to ignore the desperation she could feel all around her and the tremors that were wrenching Martin's body.

'How do I do it?' she asked her mother in a voice of superficial confidence.

'Take a thin pinch of skin from his upper arm.' Abigail spoke with extraordinary calm. 'That's right. Now, I've uncapped the syringe. Slide the needle under the skin, shallowly. Good.'

Melissa put the point of the syringe against her husband's flesh and tried to put out of her mind everything she had ever heard over the years about adrenaline and the speed with which it might kill if it were injected accidentally into a vein. Her hands were sweating.

'That's right. Push it in flat just under the skin. Don't dig it into him. Flat. No: flat. Yes. Like that. Well done, Melissa. Just a bit further.'

She pushed on, and glanced once more at her husband's face. He still looked at her, simultaneously dependent, demanding and angry. She felt her clammy hands shaking.

'Now, slowly push down the plunger. Good,' said Abigail. 'That's right. Push it right in. Ah. Excellent.'

'It works as quickly as that,' said Melissa, seeing the fearsome scarlet receding from Martin's face, leaving the bumps of the stings vivid against the new pallor of his puffy skin. He still looked afraid but the gasping breaths were slowing down. His swollen eyelids closed.

'I'm going to give them some more smoke to keep them in the hives. Don't move for a minute or two, Martin. Melissa, take the syringe out gently. Good. Put the plastic top back on and we'll throw it away. You'll be all right now, Martin. We've sent for an ambulance.'

She blew some more smoke at her bees and Melissa

saw that almost all of them had returned to their hives. Moving as smoothly as possible, Abigail took the heavy brown coat from Martin's shoulders and threw it on the ground. His shirt was mainly cream-coloured.

'Ah, good. Now. Can you stand? Melissa and I will help you.'

Together, looking like space workers in their white suits and veiled helmets, they lifted him and helped him walk back into the stable block.

Adam was standing looking out of the biggest mesh-covered window with Ann. Neither spoke as Abigail and Melissa half carried Martin to a chair near the till and helped him to sit down. He looked exhausted, but he raised his head.

'There's no need for an ambulance. I'm all right now,' he said, still panting slightly. His voice was slurred.

'I'm sorry, Martin,' said Abigail firmly, 'but I can't take the responsibility. You must be checked over. It's an appalling shock to the system, as you very well know. Why did you come? Sorry. Don't worry about it now. We can talk later. They'll be here soon.'

'I needed Lissa. I have to talk to her.'

Melissa started to shake and suddenly realized that she was in danger of falling over. Waves of heat rolled over her, leaving her deathly cold in between. She leaned against a bookshelf and, when that did not feel safe enough, she put both her hands behind her and slid down until she was sitting on the floor, knocking down books so that they fell all round her.

Adam looked at the others, realized that they could do nothing to help, and went to Melissa, clearing a space among the fallen books so that he could squat down beside her.

'Hold on,' he said, and his deep voice reached her even through the faintness and the shivering. 'He's all right now. Hold on.'

She unclasped her hands and reached for Adam. He completely ignored her husband and took both her hands, holding them and saying nothing until he heard the sound of an ambulance siren in the distance. He knew then with complete certainty that he could help her if she would only let him. A burst of happiness pushed away all his anxieties.

Once Martin had been strapped into the stretcher and carried out to the waiting ambulance, Abigail looked at her daughter. 'One of us had better go with him. Unless you want to do it, Melissa, I will.'

'Will you? I couldn't . . . Not yet.'

'It's all right. My bees: to a certain extent my responsibility. Stay here with Adam until you feel better and then go and collect pyjamas and things for Martin and take them to the hospital. He's bound to be kept in overnight at least.'

'What on earth was he thinking of?' said Melissa, lurching between anger, guilt and anxiety. 'He knew the danger he'd be in if he were stung. It was only yesterday that he refused to come to the house because of it, and there he was prancing about in the middle of the hives. He must be mad.'

'There'll be time for all that later. I'll wait at the hospital until you get there. Will you explain to Joan what has happened and tell her I'll be back as soon as I can?'

'Yes, of course. I'd forgotten all about her. I'm sorry. I . . .'

'He'll be all right, Melissa,' Abigail said with her usual unassailable confidence. 'Ann, don't forget to order a replacement adrenaline syringe, will you?'

'I'll make a note. Would you like me to collect the smoker and put it out?'

'Oh, yes, would you? Just before you go this evening when the bees have had time to calm right down. Thanks. Sorry, Adam, the peaceful Saturday lunch was a bit spoiled. We'll do it again on a more auspicious day.'

'Thank you. I'll look after Melissa and bring her to the hospital in due course. Don't worry about her.'

'No, all right.'

She stripped off her white boiler suit and left them. Ann asked Melissa whether she would like a cup of tea.

'Yes, please. I'll be OK in a minute. I just . . . came over all peculiar.'

'That's hardly surprising,' said Adam, taking her hands again. 'It was horrible. But he is going to be all right. Your mother said so.'

Ann had disappeared, and so Adam went on: 'What was it all about?'

Melissa sighed and tried to sort the facts out from her swooping emotions. 'That was my husband.'

'I gathered that from Ann.'

'He's allergic to bee stings and liable to go into anaphylactic shock, which is what you saw. Do you know anything about it?'

'Very little,' said Adam, wanting to know, but even more wanting to keep her talking. That seemed important.

'Well, my mother could probably explain better, but as far as I understand it the system reacts to the bee venom by releasing massive amounts of histamine into the body, making bits of it swell hugely. I'm not sure how it works, but if nothing's done, the heart stops beating. He could have died, you see.'

Her voice faltered and then strengthened again as she added: 'The only way of getting the heart to keep pumping strongly enough is to inject adrenaline, which is what we did. That's why my mother keeps it here. Lots of people have no idea that they're allergic because they've never been stung. People who've once had an anaphylactic shock tend to carry an adrenaline syringe with them wherever they go.'

'But not your husband.'

'No. For some reason Martin has always refused.' Melissa's lips tightened as the old exasperation resurfaced. 'He keeps a syringe in the fridge in the Circus, and updates it every few years, but he won't take it with him when he goes out.'

'Here's your tea,' said Ann, coming back with a heavy stoneware mug in her hand. 'I know you don't usually take sugar, but I put some in because it's good for shock.'

Melissa drank, hating the sickliness of the over-sweetened liquid. When she had finished it, she stood up again and asked Adam whether he could drive.

'Yes.'

'Could you bear to get us back to Bath then? The car is insured for anyone I give permission to.'

'All right,' he said, looking out of the shop door at the big, glossy car and thinking of the narrow bumpy roads with some misgiving. 'Come on. Thank you, Ann.'

'It's a pleasure. You'll tell me how Martin is, won't you, Lissa?'

'Sure. You've been very kind. I'll see you next weekend, probably. If not before.' Melissa nodded to her and walked unsteadily to the car. Before she got there she remembered Joan and went to tell her what had happened. Adam insisted on coming with her.

Later, when she was sitting in the passenger seat of her car, securely clipped into her seat belt, she said, 'I can't help thinking about his face.' Her teeth clattered against each other. 'Sorry.'

'Don't worry. He's going to be all right. You're OK, Melissa.' Adam put the key into the ignition and fired the engine, adding lightly, 'It remains to be seen if I can get us safely home in this hideously expensive-feeling barouche of yours.'

Melissa managed to smile and watched him drive with perfect competence back to the Circus.

'Thank you,' she said more calmly when he had parked outside her house. 'D'you want to come in while I forage for Martin's clean pyjamas and razors and things or would you rather not?'

'I'll come if you promise to tell me when I get in your way.'

The first thing Melissa saw in the cool, stone-floored hall was a piece of folded writing paper lying on the table with a torn envelope. She stood still for long enough to make Adam ask her whether there was something the matter. Breathing with extra care, she seemed to gather herself together and went to pick up the letter. Unfolding it, she glanced down for an instant and then looked up, smiling.

'Thank god for that,' she said. 'It's not from Martin.'

'I don't understand.'

'Sorry, Adam.' She sighed deeply. 'For a second I thought that he'd left me a letter, which sent all sorts of mad ideas through my brain. But he hasn't. It's not from him. It's all right. He can't have done it on purpose.'

'What on earth do you mean?'

'I . . . It's just . . . Oh, hell! He knows what bee stings do to him and yet he went and positively invited the bees to sting him. When I saw the letter I suddenly thought he might have been meaning to . . . well, you know.'

Adam came towards her, but he did not touch her.

'Melissa, that's ludicrous. No-one would deliberately bring on himself what's just happened to your husband.'

She thought back over the last three weeks since Martin had been made redundant and the various destructive things he had done, trying to rid her mind of the residual fear that he might have turned that destructiveness on himself.

'No, you're probably right. Sorry, Adam. Perhaps it's the trial that's been making me all melodramatic. What a day for you!'

Melissa put the piece of paper back on the table and then, at last realizing that the writing she had glimpsed was Cecily's, picked it up again and read it.

Martin,

I'm sorry but I can't go on. The thought of Lissa and what we must be doing to her is making me feel too guilty. I know you've always said she wouldn't mind, but I think you're wrong.

Our time together has meant a lot to me, but we have to stop now. We really have to stop. It started out as simple, undangerous fun, but it's got so heavy that it's frightening me. We have to stop before we damage someone. I'm sorry about this afternoon, but I daren't see you until we've sorted this out. Could you bear to telephone before Lissa gets back from her mother's? Please?

C

Adam watched the blood receding from Melissa's face and thought that she might be going to faint.

'What is it?' he asked urgently, reaching out to her.

Melissa thought that she felt nothing at all. She handed Adam the small sheet of paper and went to sit on the bottom stair. The cold of the stone reached quickly and painfully through her trousers, but she did not move. Adam looked up from the letter, his face puzzled.

'I don't understand,' he said. At the sound of his voice the numbness in Melissa's brain started to recede.

'I'm not sure that I do either. Not completely, but some things are beginning to be a bit clearer.'

Adam came to sit beside her on the stair. He did not touch her, but he was so close to her that she could feel the warmth of his body.

'Who is C?' he asked.

Melissa licked her lips and tried to keep her increasingly violent thoughts under some kind of discipline.

'Cecily Wells. I told you she was a friend. It looks as though Martin and she have been having a love affair of some kind.'

Adam saw that her eyes were screwed up and he wondered if she were going to cry. After a moment she managed to go on.

'Looking back over the past few weeks, I can't think why I didn't realize. He's been leaving clues all over the place, sort of trailing the affair in front of me, but I hadn't noticed. At least I don't think I had.' Melissa remembered that Cecily had wanted to tell her something before she went to Paris and then funked it when they were face to face. She could not imagine why she had not understood then.

'Well it obviously explains today's performance,' she said much more coldly. 'I wonder if Martin understood quite what a risk he was running or if he's a fool as well as everything else.'

'Melissa, don't. Don't let it make you hate them. That's . . . Don't let yourself get bitter. It's not worth the damage that would do to you.'

She shrugged, wondering what he expected her to feel.

'He must have put the letter here for me to find,' she said, trying to explain why she was so angry. 'It's hardly the kind of thing you'd leave lying around if you didn't want it read, is it?'

'I don't know,' said Adam, wondering how her discovery was going to affect him.

Melissa covered her face with both hands and he had to strain to hear her.

'How he must hate me!'

Adam pulled her icy hands down from her face and tried to warm them between his own.

'I don't suppose for one minute that he does,' he said reluctantly. 'If he did, he'd have simply left you for this woman, and revelled in deserting you, wouldn't he?'

'Perhaps. God knows. I don't understand him at all any more.' Hearing the sound of panic in her voice, she set about reasserting control. After a few minutes' silence, she took her hands out of Adam's and smiled at him politely. He shivered at the sight of the shutters coming down in her eyes.

'Still, talking isn't going to help, is it? I'd better do something about his pyjamas and so on.' She pulled herself to her feet, trying to think of some way of watering down her feelings. 'And I suppose I ought to ring Cecily. She has probably got a right to know why he isn't going to speak to her.'

Adam watched her, aching for her and unable to think of a single thing he could do to help. 'Are you sure that's wise?' he asked at last.

'Probably not, but I think I'll be able to keep my temper with her.'

'That isn't what I meant. Look, I don't know . . . This may sound silly. But if she really needs to know, would you like me to tell her for you?'

Melissa looked more like herself as she shook her head. 'No. I must do it, but if you can hang on for a bit and perhaps drive me to the hospital, that would be nice. Would you?'

'Yes.'

Melissa showed him into the big, luxurious drawing room and went on upstairs to pack a small suitcase of things that Martin might need. When it was done, she carried the bag down to the hall, picked up the telephone receiver and punched in Cecily's number. After four rings she heard a wary voice saying, 'Hello?'

'Cecily, it's me, Melissa.'

'God, Lissa, you sound tired. Are you all right, sweetie?'

'No. Martin nearly killed himself this afternoon,' she said. As soon as she heard Cecily gasp, Melissa understood too late why she had wanted to speak to her. Trying to minimize the punishment, Melissa went on: 'But he'll be perfectly all right by now, if extremely sore. He's been taken to the hospital. My mother's with him.'

'Lissa,' said Cecily in the most serious voice Melissa had ever heard from her.

'I don't know how much you care for him,' Melissa said, 'but it seems you have some kind of right to know where he is. I'm going there in a minute with clothes and shaving things and so on, but I won't stay long.'

'We must talk, Lissa.'

'Yes, probably, but not, I think, just yet.' Something was buzzing in Melissa's head.

'Lissa.' This time there was a plea in Cecily's voice. 'Help me.'

'God damn it! You were my best friend and you knew—' said Melissa, her voice breaking. Angry tears spurted out of her eyes before she could even think of stopping them. She tried to say something else. Her voice no longer worked. She felt Adam take the telephone receiver from her and replace it on its cradle. Then she felt his arms pulling her against him and his hands holding her head against his shoulder. He said nothing; he just held on to her as thunder crashed through the sky.

Chapter 16

They had put Martin in a little single room at the edge of the men's medical ward and sedated him. When Melissa went to visit him directly after breakfast on Sunday, she found him asleep. Quietly pulling forward a grey plastic chair, she sat down and stared at his disfigured, lumpy face, trying to understand him.

Over and over again she told herself that even if, for some bizarre reason, he had wanted to get himself stung, he could not have meant to kill himself. No-one who lived or worked anywhere near Bristol ever needed to look far for a way to commit suicide. The Clifton suspension bridge had helped hundreds of people into the oblivion they craved. Martin could not have wanted that or he, too, would have jumped. Perhaps the shock of Cecily's rejection had made him forget what the bees could do to him.

Even as she thought about that possibility, Melissa knew that it was not credible. No-one who had ever suffered one anaphylactic shock could forget the risk of another. Whatever Martin had been doing in the middle of the apiary must have been deliberate.

A nurse came in soon after ten and asked Melissa in a breezy voice whether she would like a cup of coffee. She shook her head and whispered her thanks, not wanting to wake Martin out of what might be a healing sleep.

As she sat in the pale-green room, which smelled of disinfectant, misery and recycled air, Melissa made herself consider all the reasons why Martin might have deliberately put himself through all that agony. The only one that made any sort of sense to her was that it could have been an attempt to force her to notice that he had been screwing her best friend.

Melissa hated the word her mind had thrown up, just as she hated the thoughts that were surging up through her long-established defences. Like the jack-in-the-box, they would not stay down. Itching, suddenly, she rubbed the palms of her hands on her trousers.

In the silence of the overheated hospital room, she thought that her proper place would be the witness box of court number one in Bristol under cross-examination about what she had done to her husband. With the memories of Michael Beechen's trial so vivid in her mind, it was not at all hard to conjure up a convincing picture.

Melissa peopled her imaginary version of the big white court with lawyers, spectators, witnesses and a judge. They all had familiar faces. She could smell the leather of the seats and the dampness of some journalist's rain-drenched mackintosh. And she could feel her own resentful fear of the questions.

'Did you know that adrenaline injected directly into a vein can kill, Mrs Wraxall?' asked the voice of the prosecutor in her mind.

'Yes, I knew.'

'At the moment when you were sliding the adrenaline syringe into your husband's arm, what did you feel?'

'I don't remember.'

'I must remind you that you are on oath.' The imaginary voice was sneering and accusatory. Melissa could feel herself flushing in reality.

'I felt an impulse to do as much damage to him as I could,' she confessed in her mind, knowing that she would never be able to make the admission to anyone else. The flush receded as she protested: 'But I suppressed the impulse. I did not harm him. He is still alive.'

'Of course you have harmed him,' said her mental prosecutor. 'Why else is he in the bed in front of you? Why are you sitting there staring at his unconscious face? Can't you see the marks of the stings on him? Can't you imagine how it felt? You drove him to risk the most extraordinarily painful death he could imagine.'

'No, I did not. It was nothing to do with me. He chose to do it to himself.'

'But why did he choose to do it?'

Melissa closed her eyes and leaned forwards until her head was resting on the side of Martin's high bed. She could feel the rough cotton of the cellular blanket against her skin. Her head was aching and she felt unsafe.

'You must answer the question, Mrs Wraxall.'

Was that the judge speaking, she asked herself in an attempt to stop her accusing thoughts, or prosecuting council? Sitting up, forcing herself to look at Martin's distorted face again, she tried to find an answer. Eventually, she said silently, 'Perhaps because I refused to fight with him.'

'Why?'

'Because I hate mindless rows and he never wanted any other sort. I wanted to find out what had gone wrong between us so that I could understand him and show him how to understand me. If we had done that, we could have changed things: we could have stopped hurting each other. But he wouldn't even try. He didn't want to understand; what he wanted was a war he could win. And to do that he needed an enemy to beat. Me. But I wouldn't play.'

'So what did you do?'

'I turned away.' As her lips formed the words, Melissa thought of Michael Beechen turning his back on his wife just before she pressed a hot iron into the small of his back and shuddered.

'Do you love him?'

Do I? she asked herself in her own voice and not the voice of Charles Harcombe or even the judge. Did I ever? Do I even know what love is?

Feeling a hand on her shoulder Melissa jerked round, her face blank with shock and her breathing hard and fast. When she saw a man in a long white coat with a doctor's name-badge on it, she managed to smile.

'Mrs Wraxall?' he said. 'My name is Thomas Edbury. I am the psychiatric registrar. I've already talked to your husband briefly and I'd like to have a word with you, if I may?'

'Why does Martin need a psychiatrist?' Melissa asked, frowning. 'He's suffering from bee stings.'

'When he was brought in yesterday your mother asked to see me and suggested that I might be able to help him.' He smiled and gestured towards the door. 'Could we have a word?'

Melissa nodded and slowly got to her feet, more surprised than she would have admitted to anyone. Abigail had always shown a wariness of psychiatrists that almost amounted to mistrust.

'Would you like to come outside? I don't think your husband will wake for some time, but we could talk more easily somewhere else.'

Melissa obediently got up and followed him out, thinking irrelevantly how well his gleaming white coat suited his dark skin. He led the way to a large drinks machine, very like the one in the jury assembly room at the Old Guildhall in Bristol.

'Coffee?' he said, pushing a coin into a slot in the machine. 'Milk and sugar?'

'Just plain coffee, please,' she answered, waiting for him to accuse her.

A moment later he handed her a cardboard cup, pushed some more money into the machine, waited and then turned to face her with his own cup in his hand.

'We're on our own here for a bit. Let's sit down,' he said. 'Now, tell me how you are.'

'Me? I'm fine. There's nothing the matter with me. I can't imagine why you think there should be.'

Dr Edbury raised his eyebrows, but his smile was quite kind. 'If I'm right about what happened yesterday, your husband has just carried out an enormously aggressive act,' he said calmly. 'It would be surprising if you were unaffected by it.'

Melissa frowned. She waited, saying nothing. Dr Edbury drank some coffee and then went on, without looking at her, 'It must feel like the emotional equivalent of a punch in the face – or worse. Your reactions to it might help me to understand him. Can you tell me why you think he might have done it?'

Melissa shook her head and took a sip of the coffee, making a face as she tasted it. She realized that he could not have seen her gesture and so she said, 'I don't know that he did do it deliberately. It could have been an accident, or at least partly accidental. I mean, he knew that if he were stung he might go into anaphylactic shock, but I don't think he could have expected more than one sting or realized what that much venom could do to him. You see, he doesn't know very much about bees.'

'I don't know anything at all,' said Dr Edbury. 'Tell me about them.'

'I wouldn't know where to start.'

'Try.'

'All right. Look, bees sting to defend their hives. When one of them has stung an intruder all the others smell something called an alarm pheromone, which is part of the venom, and they come whizzing to join in, aiming presumably to sting the intruder to death, whether it's a mouse, a bear or a man. Whatever it is.'

'I see. And your husband did not know that?'

'I don't know. But he might not have. The only other time he's ever been stung was in the garden at my mother's house, hundreds of yards from the hives. He was in bare feet and he trod on the bee. He did go into anaphylactic shock then, and she had to inject him with adrenaline, but he was only stung once.' Melissa shook her head. 'Sorry to be so untechnical about it all.'

Dr Edbury finished his coffee and crushed the cup between his hands before tossing it into an overflowing bin. He said nothing but sat watching her again, his eyebrows raised.

'What?' Melissa said irritably. 'What has that told you? Why are you looking at me like that?'

'Like what?'

'Like a judge.'

'That was unintentional. I have no right or wish to judge you.'

'You obviously think he did do it on purpose and that it's my fault. Why? What did he say to you?'

'Fault doesn't come into it,' said Dr Edbury quickly. 'He has not said much, but it's easy enough to see that he's desperate.'

'I know he is,' said Melissa. She stared down at the floor. She did not want to make excuses for herself, but she could not bear the doctor to think that she was insensitive enough not to have noticed Martin's misery. 'Did he tell you that he's been having a love affair with my best friend?'

'Yes, he did tell me that.' He waited a bit but when she said nothing more, he asked: 'How much do you know about current theories of why people fall in love?'

'Nothing whatever,' said Melissa irritably. She assumed that he was about to start lecturing her on

241

the reasons why males are biologically programmed to impregnate as many females as they can lay their hands on and that therefore no woman had any right to expect fidelity from any man. It was a point of view she had heard several times before and not one with which she could sympathize.

Three young nurses walked quickly past them, their rubber-soled shoes squeaking against the vinyl floor tiles. Melissa got up and walked to the opposite side of the corridor. She leaned against the wall, watching Dr Edbury.

'There are three principal theories, or perhaps four,' he said, ticking them off on his fingers. 'There's the ancient Greek view that the search for love is caused by a longing to discover the lost half of oneself. To make oneself whole.'

'I suppose that makes sense of a sort, although it seems a bit sentimental,' said Melissa, looking down at her feet. She noticed that the leather tassel on one of her loafers was about to become detached and made a mental note to take the shoe to a cobbler as soon as possible.

'There's a more modern version of the same idea,' Dr Edbury went on, apparently untroubled by her refusal to join in his game, 'which holds that it's the search for a person with all the qualities and defects that are the opposite of one's own, a person who can be one's perfect complement.'

Melissa said nothing. There seemed nothing that needed saying. The other shoe seemed to be all right, its tassel still firmly attached. The doctor's little lecture had nothing whatever to do with her or Martin and was giving her no useful advice about how to help him, or herself. It would be much more sensible to think about her shoes.

'And then there's the current psychiatric idea that when we fall in love, we choose a person who can recreate a childhood relationship in which we were unhappy or damaged,' said the doctor calmly, watching her all the time.

She moved a little, but she would not look at him. He could not be sure whether the movement was caused by cramp or some kind of recognition.

'The subconscious hope behind such an apparently perverse choice is that it gives us another chance to get the relationship right and therefore heal the old hurt.'

'Yes?' Melissa knew that Martin had never told her about any damaging childhood relationship, but it was perfectly possible that he might have had one. She looked up with a little less hostility.

'The trouble is, that while the hope is still subconscious we can only recreate the hurt and reinforce the damage.'

'Well, I suppose that's possible. After all, there are lots of men who remarry a new version of the wife they've just divorced. I'd always assumed that was simply to get a younger version, as though the first were like an obsolete car that needed replacing, but your theory makes as much sense, perhaps more. Although Cecily is quite different from me and so I don't think it can apply in this case.'

'And just occasionally,' said Dr Edbury carefully, 'the subconscious plan behind the relationship is punishment: the new beloved becomes an available target for all the old rage.'

Melissa walked back across the corridor to sit down again. 'Now that really might make sense. Martin would never tell me what was making him so angry with me. I thought it was his misery, but I suppose it could have been a hangover of some remembered fury.'

Dr Edbury raised his thick eyebrows and smiled slightly. He did not speak. He waited in silence for a while and then, when Melissa said nothing else, he stood up and pushed his chair neatly against the wall.

'I know you've been having a bad time and that what

your husband has just done has made you angry. Don't be ashamed of that,' he said.

'That may be difficult,' she said, sounding surprised but more receptive, as though his gentleness had made her more vulnerable than his earlier implied criticism.

'He's got a very bad time ahead of him,' said Dr Edbury more briskly. 'He has to learn to come to terms with himself. You can't do that for him, but he might need you to be there and to help.' He looked at her and she thought that she saw compassion in his round brown eyes. Her skin seemed to freeze on to the bones of her face as she took in the significance of his pity.

'Could you be there, Mrs Wraxall?'

Melissa looked down at her feet again, not even seeing the tassels on her shoes. She remembered what Martin had done to her on the night of her dinner for the American client; she thought of the broken glass, and of Martin's affair with Cecily, and his near death. She wondered what he would do next and whether she could bear to go on living with him any longer. Then she remembered him on the ground, panting, with the bees crawling over his face.

With a huge effort, she said, 'If that's what he wanted, I'd have to try, wouldn't I?' She glanced up at the doctor for a moment. 'You would have to be unbelievably cruel to desert someone who's just been through what happened to him yesterday. Yes, I'd have to try.'

Dr Edbury held out his right hand. 'Don't misunderstand me. Don't feel guilty about your anger. And if there's any help I can give you, please let me know.'

Reluctantly Melissa let him take her hand.

'Will you let me know when he's in a fit state to talk?'

Dr Edbury nodded and then pointed down the long, linoleum-floored corridor. 'The lifts are that way. I'll walk you out.'

Melissa set off towards the outside world. He left her beside the row of blank stainless steel doors.

As she walked out into the main hall of the hospital, with its bustle and its little shops and its noise, she came face to face with Cecily. They both stopped, tried to speak and then waited for the other one. Cecily looked as though she had been crying for hours.

'Let's go outside,' said Melissa at last. 'I know it's grisly weather, but it's not actually raining.'

Cecily turned without a word and walked towards the doors that led to a small garden where patients sometimes walked on sunny days. There was a teak bench at the edge of one of the paths and they sat down on that, looking at a flowerbed full of depressing, savagely pruned roses.

'You see, you didn't want him,' said Cecily suddenly, as though they were already halfway through a conversation. 'And you said over and over again whenever we'd all been together that you were pleased with me for making him happy. You even said I turned him from a grumpy bear into a human being after that dinner with the American. You seemed to be giving me permission, Lissa. I thought you knew all about it then, and were relieved. Lissa, I'd never have done it if . . .'

'Irrational, isn't it?' said Melissa, who was still not sure what it was that she did feel. One of the nastiest parts of her mind, which she almost instantly rejected, told her that Cecily would be well punished for what she had done if she actually had to live with Martin for any length of time.

'It's not the affair per se that worries me most, I think,' she said, upset to hear her voice trembling a little. 'It's your participation in Martin's plans to punish me. You're . . .' She broke off, tried to organize her thoughts, failed, and found herself talking without any of the old censorship. 'Weren't we friends, Cecily? Didn't it mean anything to you? It did to me. I cared about you, a lot.'

'Lissa . . .'

'Was it always a sham? Were you laughing at me all the time I was so fond of you? Did you tell Martin all the things I said about him? Did you both laugh at me?'

Melissa was surprised to hear the words that poured out of her; she had not planned to say any of it and was shocked.

'Oh, God! Lissa, don't.' Cecily's tears started to leak down the sides of her reddened swollen nose again. 'You weren't being punished. It wasn't like that. And I've never laughed at you. God forbid! And Martin never said a word about you. Neither of us did. It wasn't that sort of thing at all. You don't understand.'

'What sort of thing do you think it was then?' Melissa thought that she had managed to sound quietly interested, but Cecily flinched and then sighed.

'It was only a way of making him happier – and me less lonely.' Her eyes filled with tears again and she coughed as though to free her breathing. 'As soon as it started to change into something else, I tried to stop it.'

Melissa looked at her, surprised. Cecily had always seemed complete and utterly satisfied with her life. Melissa wondered how Dr Edbury would have summed her up.

Cecily pushed the tangled hair away from her face. 'Sometimes living and working on my own make me feel absolutely cut off from everyone. People like you find that hard to understand, I know. My agent didn't like my ideas for the new book and I was afraid I'd never write another one, and there was Martin absolutely desperate for someone to make him feel good about himself again. I thought that an uncomplicated sexual friendship might do the trick for both of us.' Her voice dropped as she added: 'And for a while it did.'

'How long has it been going on?' asked Melissa, frowning against the various pains that were slicing into her.

'About three months. He came round to the flat one Saturday by chance just before Christmas when the squash match was cancelled and it just sort of happened on the sofa. It wasn't planned, you know. It just happened.'

Melissa remembered her migraine and the way she had lain back on Cecily's sofa.

'That was the only time we talked about you,' Cecily went on earnestly. 'I protested at the beginning and reminded him that you're – that you were my friend. And he said that nothing we did could hurt you since you'd never need to know about it. It wouldn't take anything from you, he said, provided that we kept our emotions under control and didn't start making any what he called "silly plans".'

She mopped her streaming eyes with a crumpled, hardened lump of ink-stained pink lavatory paper from her pocket.

'Honestly, Lissa, I knew that if it wasn't me it would be someone else, and surely better me, who . . . who cares about you, than a predatory stranger who might get all the wrong ideas. It was such a little thing, Lissa. You don't have to be so upset about it. It was trivial in comparison with your marriage. There wasn't any punishment involved.'

Melissa looked at her, trying to understand what had been going on between them all. She wondered whether some of her bitterness might have come from the efforts she had been making to keep her sudden, extraordinary affection for Adam within acceptable limits. The thought that while she had been trying to stick by her marriage and make it work, at some real cost to herself, Martin had been cavorting with Cecily on her sofa was almost too

247

much to be borne.

'Wasn't there? He's always behaved as though it's my fault whenever anything went wrong at work or at home; my fault that he was sacked; and my fault that he wasn't made partner before that. He's come home evening after evening yelling with rage about "feminists" and "you bloody women" because of the partner in charge of his work, who apparently always loathed him.'

'Lissa, don't. Don't say any more. Please.'

'What a perfect way of taking revenge on me! To seduce away my dearest friend; to prove that a woman I care for – and admire – sees in him things that I can't begin to appreciate.'

'Lissa,' said Cecily with difficulty. She blew her nose with a horribly liquid sound and pushed the inadequately absorbent lump of paper tissue back into one of her jacket pockets. 'You can't imagine how sorry I am about it all. What a mess! It started so cheerfully but it's actually been getting glummer and glummer. In fact, I wrote to him yesterday to say that we ought to stop.'

Melissa stared at the rose stumps, not wanting to admit that she had read the letter.

'I've tried so hard to keep our marriage going and do everything – nearly everything – he wants.' Melissa suddenly remembered her own clean handkerchief and took it out of her pocket to offer to Cecily, who accepted it without a word and blew her nose exhaustively.

Melissa got off the bench and walked towards the car park. Leaving Cecily behind her, she tried to think what she ought to do next. Dr Edbury had made it clear that she did not need to sit at Martin's bedside. She wanted to see Adam, but it did not seem fair to go to him while she was in such a state. She drove home and parked the car clumsily. It was so unlike her to squeeze the tyres against the edge of the pavement that she almost wept in frustration. Instead, she reversed the big car carefully until the expensive rubber was at least four inches from the kerb.

When she got out she felt as though her body had been beaten all over with spiked canes. She was surprised to find that she had forgotten to double lock the front door or set the burglar alarm. It was terrifying to think that she might be cracking up. Then she heard her mother's voice and understood.

'Melissa? Is that you, my darling?' Abigail appeared at the top of the stairs. 'I let myself in. I hope you don't mind.'

'I don't mind at all,' said Melissa, dropping her bag on the floor. Abigail came down the stairs and put an arm around her daughter's waist. Melissa let her head fall sideways on to her mother's shoulder. 'Thank God you're here.'

An hour later Melissa went upstairs to wash her face, while her mother made a pot of coffee. Later, Abigail made Melissa sit down at the table, while she put slices of bread into the toaster.

'I don't suppose you've eaten anything today,' she said.

Melissa shook her head. 'No, but I had some revolting coffee out of the hospital machine. Yours will be much better. Good and strong. I need it.'

'You sound as though you're in even direr need of honey.' Abigail took a pot off the shelf and reached into the fridge for some butter. 'How was Martin?'

'Sedated and asleep.' Melissa put her elbows on the table and rubbed her face. 'What a mess! Did you see it coming?'

'Not like this,' said Abigail. 'But I didn't see how you'd be able to go on as you were for much longer.'

'Did you dislike him?' asked Melissa, turning her small yellow-and-white plate on its side. She bowled it up and down in front of her. Abigail recognized a gesture she had not seen for a quarter of a century. She laid a hand on the back of Melissa's head for a moment and then turned away to put the slices of hot toast into a silver rack.

'It wasn't so much that I disliked him,' she said slowly, 'as that he seemed so like your father.'

Melissa stopped playing with her plate and frowned. After a long pause, she said: 'I don't understand. You loved my father.'

To her surprise Abigail flushed.

'I've been thinking about it a lot recently,' she said, pouring coffee into two large cups and adding hot milk. She pushed one towards Melissa. 'Blaming myself and excusing myself and telling myself that it probably wouldn't have made any difference anyway if I'd told you all about it. Don't look so puzzled. I'm trying to explain.'

'About what?'

'He sometimes made loving him pretty difficult.'

'Why? What are you telling me? What happened to him?' Melissa felt dreadfully cold. 'Didn't he die? Did you just throw him out? Divorce him?'

'Oh, no. He died all right,' said Abigail. 'I've never lied to you about him, Melissa. I just didn't tell you the whole truth, that he killed himself.'

'No.' Melissa only whispered her protest but it carried enough horror to make her mother wince. She drank some coffee and tried to explain.

'I probably ought to have told you before, but I couldn't. It would have been far too much for you at the time. You were only six. And then as you grew up, there never seemed to be a moment when I could tell you.'

'I think . . . Even if . . .' Melissa gave up. It seemed impossible to put words to any of the feelings that were swirling around inside her.

'I cannot stand those women who try to make children

take their side in marital rows,' Abigail went on. 'I've seen it often, and I think it's both dangerous and unkind. I was so . . . muddled when he killed himself that I didn't dare let any of my feelings out.' She put the cup carefully down on its saucer. 'I behaved like the bees, I suppose, and waxed over everything I felt about him so that it couldn't damage you. But that may have been a mistake, too.'

'You wouldn't ever talk about him.' Melissa tried to cope with some new feelings, which did not seem to belong to her. 'I sometimes wondered why not, and I told myself it was because he had been so wonderful and you'd loved him so much that you couldn't bear to be made to remember what you'd lost. I seem to have been a fool in several directions at once.'

'I'm sorry.' Abigail reached across the table to touch Melissa's hand. It was hard for her not to snatch it away. 'There were good things about him, lots, just as there are about Martin, but I couldn't help him, and I was afraid that if Martin really did turn out to be like him, you wouldn't be able to either. I suppose in a way I couldn't trust myself to tell you things about our life with your father without letting out some of the anger too.'

'Anger?' said Melissa, frowning as she tried to understand.

'Yes. I'm ashamed of it, but his suicide did make me very angry. There were things we could have done – he could have done – that would have made him less unhappy. He could have taken his pills for one thing, but he wouldn't. They helped him deal with all the things that tormented him. I used to find it really hard to keep my patience sometimes when he stopped. It was asking for trouble. I didn't want you to know that, or to learn to hate him for abandoning you. That's why I never told you.'

'I see,' said Melissa vaguely. Her mind did not seem to

be working at all. It was as though all her mental energy was being spent in containing her feelings. 'So, did you hate him then?'

'Sometimes in my frustration I almost came to hate him. And I felt endlessly guilty, too, as I think he intended. That made me determined never to put myself in the same position with anyone else ever again.'

Melissa stared at the long cracks in the scrubbed table, noticing that some minute crumbs had become wedged between them. Picking at one with her tidily shaped nails, hardly aware of what she was doing, she realized that she wanted to shriek and bang her fists on the table and demand something. She felt powerless, angry and most desperately needy.

'What was he really like, my father?' she asked eventually. 'I think you ought to tell me now. I think you owe me that, at least.'

Abigail gasped. After a while she recovered her equanimity and looked at her daughter as though wondering how much to say. The repeated encouragement and advice she had given her husband in his misery had not saved him. One of her worst fears had always been that her attempts to help might have made him more desperate than he would have been without them. Her twin resolutions never again to tell anyone else what to do and never to talk about what her husband had done had been so powerful for so long that she found it hard to break her silence. Even Joan Radborn knew little of what had actually happened.

'I have to know,' said Melissa urgently. 'I was thinking this morning that I've been lying to Martin for ages, pretending that I cared about him when I didn't; lying to myself; and in a way lying to you by never telling you how ghastly it's been.' She broke off and closed her eyes against the sight of her mother's face.

Biting her lip, Melissa added, 'And now I find that

you've been lying to me, too. We've all been lost in this morass of well-meant deceit. It's . . . I can't see what's real any more. You must help me. I feel as though I'm drowning. You must tell me at last what it's really all been about. You must.'

Hearing the hysteria in her voice, Abigail looked at Melissa again and tried to acknowledge the hurt in her grey eyes. But she could not find any words. Melissa remembered some of the things that Dr Edbury had told her and they took on a new – and horrible – significance.

'Why did you never even warn me? When you saw me with Martin, why didn't you tell me about my father then?'

'What could I have said? "Don't marry that man because he's like your father"? "I think you may find that you won't love a man like that for very long"? Or perhaps, "I know better than you what will suit you"? Would you have been able to accept any of those?'

'I don't know.' Melissa sounded – and felt – defeated. She wanted to say: you're my mother; you should have known what to say and how to save me. But she knew that that was ludicrous. She was an adult, too, responsible for her own actions and her own mistakes.

'And had I any right to say any of them?' said Abigail unhappily. 'What if I'd been wrong about the similarity between them? What if it was just my neurotic memory of your father that made me think Martin was like him? What if it was merely my being possessive of you that made me think it would be a bad marriage for you? What if you'd been more like your father than I realized? You look like me, but it would have been vanity – idiotic too – to assume that that meant you were the same person as I. You have your father's genes in you, too. If you'd been like him, Martin might have been exactly the right husband for you. No-one else could have judged that.'

Melissa dragged the remnants of her self-control around her feelings. She tried to remember what she was really like when she was not half-submerged in horrible emotion, and to talk normally.

'Sorry to be so hysterical,' she said at last. 'It's just hard to take it all in. How did he do it?'

'He hanged himself,' Abigail said, sounding sharper than Melissa had ever heard her. There was a suspicious amount of wetness around her eyes, but the eyes themselves seemed hard. 'I'd been out with you somewhere and found him when we got back. I've always been terrified that you saw, but you never said anything. I couldn't ask. But I've always wanted to know. Did you see?'

Melissa shook her head, then nodded, frowning. 'I don't know. I don't remember.' She thought of the jack-in-the-box, and she thought about all the signs of Martin's affair that she had ignored. 'Perhaps. I don't know anything any more.'

Is that why I feel so responsible for Martin? she asked herself. Did I see my father dead and blame myself for what he did? Was Dr Edbury right? Did I see my father hanging and spend my adult years looking for a man as much like him as possible so that I could cure them both – or punish them? God forbid!

'I've always hoped that you didn't see, and told myself it was quite likely,' Abigail was saying. 'I saw him as soon as I got through the door, hanging from the banisters just in front of me. I turned round and stood between him and you and told you we had to go out to buy something. I can't remember what: bread I think. And I took you to a friend's house and came back and rang the police.'

'Why did he do it? Did he leave a letter?'

'Yes.'

'Have you still got it?'

Abigail shook her head. Melissa did not know whether she could believe the negative and that seemed almost the worst of all.

'What did it say?'

'Not a lot. It seemed to me to be a kind of "you'll be sorry when I'm dead" letter. I burned it in anger, which has made me ashamed often since then.'

'I'm sorry,' said Melissa, recognizing that the pain was still raw for her mother, too, despite the twenty-five years it had had to grow a protective scab.

After a long, uncomfortable silence, Melissa added, 'Now that you know we're in the same boat after all, won't your principles let you give me a bit of advice?'

Abigail got up and walked to the far end of the kitchen, leaning on the edge of the sink, her neat fair head bowed.

'I'm sorry,' said Melissa. Clinging to the positive emotions, trying to ignore the others as well as she could, she added more gently, 'That wasn't meant to sound bitter. Honestly.'

'No. I know. But I feel guilty all the same, which is what I always swore I'd never let myself feel again. No, I haven't any advice. What could I possibly say that you wouldn't already have thought?'

'Put it another way, then. If you were me, what would you do?'

'Oh, that's easy enough.' Abigail came back to smile at her daughter. 'I'd divorce Martin as soon as possible.'

'And?'

'And nothing. I'd carry on as I had been, working and waiting on my own until I myself were certain of who I was and what I needed. But I'm not you.'

'Ah,' said Melissa, detesting the anger she could feel and the betrayals. 'I see.'

'I've learned a lot over the years,' said Abigail with obvious difficulty, 'but I've never been brave enough to test it. My life is organized so that I never need to share control with anyone else. People come and go, but they are always visitors. Even Joan. I have never again ceded any part of my sovereignty. That feels to me like strength: not everyone would agree.'

She picked at the torn, bloody skin on her knuckle, where she must have cut it as she sliced the bread for toast. Melissa had never seen her so out of control.

'Joan definitely thinks it's a weakness. As you and I've often agreed, there are two ways to look at everything.'

Melissa looked down at her own hands, wishing that she and her mother had had their conversation years earlier.

'Don't look so tormented, Melissa,' said Abigail, sounding more like her usual self. 'You will find your way. You just have to grit your teeth until you see it.'

'Yes,' she said, managing to smile again in spite of the earthquake that seemed to be happening inside her mind. 'But it's a bit bleak, isn't it?'

Abigail's face was transformed, the anxiety melting into a familiar affection and gentle amusement. 'Only if you think that love is "woman's whole existence".'

Melissa frowned, realizing that her mother was quoting something but unaware of its source and finding it hard to think about anything except her father, his death and what that had done to them both.

'*Don Juan*.' Abigail still looked amused. 'Lord Byron. "Man's love is of man's life a thing apart. 'Tis woman's whole existence." What an idiocy! What a source of anguish for millions and millions of women!'

'Don't you get lonely?' Melissa was trying to imagine herself living as her mother lived. 'Cecily did, and that's why she joined in Martin's little game.'

'No lonelier than a great many married women – and men – of my acquaintance,' said Abigail. 'But it's only my recipe for a happy life. I'd never dream of trying to impose it on anyone else.'

'No prescriptions?' said Melissa, and at last there was some amusement in the sound again as well as all the rest.

'None. But plenty of honey. Come on, darling. Let's eat some toast and get all these tricky feelings under control.'

After a moment Melissa nodded.

Chapter 17

Michael knew that something had happened to Melissa Wraxall as soon as he saw her edging into her seat in the jury box on Monday morning. She was wearing a suit again, not the navy-blue one of the first two days of his trial, but black with brass buttons and a striped shirt, which ought to have made her look even more sophisticated than usual. Her hair was neatly plaited again, too, instead of in the loose, curling tail she had shown on the days she wore her trousers, and she had made up her face properly. But in spite of all her tidy smartness, she looked damaged, a little as Marianna used to look on the days when Penelope had been upsetting her.

Ever since the trial had got properly under way he had known that there was a bond of some kind between him and Melissa, but until that morning he had not realized quite how strong it was. He waited impatiently through all the usual performance of the judge's arrival for the day's proceedings to begin. There were very few more witnesses to come, and then the awful Charles Harcombe would sum up, then his own counsel, then the judge, and then it would be up to the jury.

'Constable Radstock,' said Gina Mayford to the witness who had just been sworn in, 'would you please tell the court whether you recognize the defendant?'

'Yes, miss,' said the portly police officer, drawing out the vowels in the long, sheeplike accent of his native county. 'He came to the station one night last winter.'

Michael had detested him then, with his fatness and his slowness and his horrible mockery, and he hated him again. It had been an evening of the utmost humiliation.

'Can you remember which night that was?'

'May I consult my notes, my lord?' he asked the judge, man to man.

Given permission, Constable Radstock took his notebook from the breast pocket of his tunic and held it up in one hand so that everyone in court could see it and flicked it open.

'It was the morning of November the seventeenth, my lord.'

'And what had he come to report, Constable Radstock?'

'That his wife had hit him,' said the policeman, his round brown eyes almost disappearing in the deep creases of his smile. 'When I asked him how big she was, he told me she were a little slip of a thing, not five feet four even.'

'What did you do?'

'Well, miss, to be frank, I told him to give 'er one.'

'You seem amused by something.' Georgina Mayford's pleasant voice sounded very cold.

'Well, look at him there. He's a big man and strong too. I've seen some fighters in my time and they've all had those big shoulders and deep pecs they call them nowadays. He could have lifted a woman of five feet four off of her feet with one hand. I told him to go on home and stop wasting my time.'

The constable seemed to feel a frisson of disapproval from some of the people near the witness box, for he added in a less certain voice, 'We'd had a murder that morning already, one death of an old woman living alone of hypothermia, and four break-ins reported. We hadn't the time to go sorting out a nagging wife.'

'Thank you, Constable. Would you just wait there for my learned friend to ask you his questions?'

259

'Constable Radstock,' said Charles Harcombe, smiling so merrily at the witness that he visibly cheered up, 'what did the defendant do when you told him to go on home?'

'Do? He did nothing, sir.'

'Well, did he say anything then?'

'Yes, sir.' PC Radstock looked up at the judge and recited: '"Well I didn't think there was much point", is what he said. I remember it well. It was the first sensible thing he'd said.'

'Thank you. Would you just wait there?'

Georgina Mayford half rose from her seat, saying, 'We have nothing further, my lord.'

'You may step down, Constable,' said the judge smiling politely. The large policeman heaved himself down the steps of the witness box and waddled out of the court.

Georgina Mayford then called a volunteer from the Family Information Service, who testified that Michael Beechen had been to see her, too, on the seventeenth of November the previous year.

'And what advice did he need?'

'He wanted to know whether there was anything that could be done to protect him from his violent wife.'

'What did you tell him?'

'That he had the same rights as a woman at risk of domestic violence, that is: he could go to court to seek an injunction against her; he could leave the marriage and seek asylum in a refuge; or he could get a divorce.'

'Did he ask you anything else?'

'Yes. He asked what his chances were of having his wife evicted from the marital home and retaining custody of their three children. I had to tell him that I thought his chances were pretty slim. He would need some very powerful evidence, preferably of threats or actual damage to the children. He said that his wife had never threatened the children.'

'Did he give you any evidence of her alleged assaults on him?'

'Yes. When I told him that he would have little hope of banning her from their home without some powerful evidence, he stood up, turned his back to me and lifted up his sweater and shirt. He had a white dressing in the small of his back. As I watched, he picked up one corner with his nails and peeled the dressing back.' Her face creased and her voice faltered as she added: 'There was a large burn on his back, exactly the size and shape of an iron.'

Michael's eyes met Melissa's and he knew that she did understand. He nodded and she looked away.

'Did it look like a bad injury?' Georgina Mayford's cool voice suggested that she was discussing nothing more horrible than a sprained ankle. Despite that, the witness looked upset by the question.

'It's very hard to say. After all, I'm not medically trained. Clearly the burn must have been extremely painful, but I can't say any more than that.'

'Did he tell you of any other injuries?'

'Yes. He described a series, which included two broken bones and three cuts that he said had needed stitching. Two had been made by knives and one by a screwdriver.'

'Did he say how the bones had been broken?'

'Yes. He said that on each occasion his wife had hit him with a hammer across the arm.'

Georgina Mayford had nothing more to say, and since prosecuting counsel did not wish to cross-examine the last witness, Georgina thanked her and told her that she could step down. Turning to the judge, she added, 'That concludes the case for the defence, my lord.'

He looked at her over the top of his spectacles, nodded, and then looked at her opponent. 'Mr Harcombe?'

'May it please your lordship,' said Charles with a smile as he got to his feet. The closing speech was the part of any case that he most enjoyed, and this one was going to be a corker. He rather wished that he could look at Beechen while he spoke and watch his handsome, arrogant face shrink into an admission of guilt. But of course he could not. For very good reasons, the dock was positioned behind counsel. He could feel Beechen looking at him and hating him. Despite his long experience, Charles almost minded.

'Members of the jury,' he said, slowly, looking from one to the next, noticing which faces were blank with stupidity and which were still interested, 'you have listened over the past days to some very distressing evidence and it would not be at all surprising if your emotions had become involved. Indeed, it would be surprising if they had not.' He smiled at them and noticed the worried-looking woman smiling back. He had always known that she would be dangerously suggestible.

'On the basis of your own experiences, you may feel partisanship with the victim, Mrs Penelope Beechen, or indeed with her husband, the defendant. But, when you come to decide on your verdict in this case, as his lordship will tell you, you must put aside emotion and partisanship, as you must put aside horror and disgust, and judge the case on the evidence alone. You, and only you, are empowered to decide the facts of this case. The law is a matter for his lordship.

'You have heard that on the night of the fifth of December Michael Beechen came home from his audition, fed his children, put them to bed and then stabbed his wife. My learned friend has not disputed that. Indeed, it is indisputable. Penelope Beechen is dead. You have seen the terrible photographs of her body.

'Her husband, the defendant you see in front of you, killed her. His fingerprints are on the knife. In his evidence he has acknowledged the fact that it was he and only he who used the knife that stabbed his wife to death. It is the prosecution's case, as you have heard, that he did it deliberately, in full possession of his faculties, and intending to cause her serious bodily harm.'

Charles took a moment to rearrange his gown and clear his throat, collecting the wandering attention of some of the more uninvolved jurors. When he saw them looking at him again, he went on:

'You have heard evidence of her poor housekeeping, her demands on her husband for money he did not have, for attention, for sexual congress, for luxuries he could not afford to buy her. You have heard more than one witness, called both by myself and by my learned friend, testify to the very difficult character that Penelope Beechen possessed. You have heard the witness state on oath that he loved her. You may think that it would take a saint to love a woman like Penelope Beechen. And it is quite clear from the evidence you have heard that her husband is no saint. You have heard him tell you himself that he ignored her distress on more than one occasion, and indeed that he once hit her. You will want to ask yourselves, members of the jury, why a man whose wife behaved as Penelope Beechen did would testify that he loved her. It might make you question the value of some of his other statements on oath.'

Trying to keep his face clean of both anger and loathing, Michael stared at the back of the yellowing wig and thought: how I hate you! Have you any idea how real people think and feel? Protected by your money, your job and your power, you can't even begin to imagine what I had to live through.

'My learned friend has brought before you evidence to suggest that Mrs Beechen was not only a difficult and unsatisfactory wife but more than that: that because of her monthly hormonal changes she was a violent woman who so terrorized her husband that for years he put up with serious physical assaults, which left him with broken

263

limbs, burns and knife wounds that required stitching. Clearly he did suffer some injuries, for he had them treated, as you have heard, by casualty officers and by his general practitioner, but we have only his word that they were inflicted by his wife.'

Michael was glad to see that Melissa was writing notes again. She was far too sensible to be taken in by Harcombe's gross twisting of the facts, but there was no denying that he did sound convincing. Her notes would help her to keep her head.

'It is, I submit, highly relevant that he did not tell anyone that his wife was the author of these assaults until last winter, when the first widely available reports were published of what is becoming known as husband battering. Beechen himself admitted to reading some of those reports in the *Spectator*, and *The Times* newspaper. There were also reports he could have heard on the radio.

'Like any normal people, you will have been asking yourselves whether as he read and heard those reports the defendant did not see a way out of his dilemma. He was married to a slut, an unpleasant, critical, difficult, demanding slut, of whom many reasonable men might wish to be rid. And yet he was afraid that if he left her he would lose his children. We have heard evidence to suggest that he is devoted to them, and it is an admirable fact. How could such a man contemplate leaving his children with a woman of the type Penelope Beechen was?'

Charles paused there, smiling at the jury to make them concentrate on his use of the evidence brought by the defence. His dark eyebrows lifted his forehead into anxious lines.

'You can probably imagine, members of the jury, how great the temptation must have been to set up the scenario that has been described in the court. A battered husband, battling to defend himself against an ill-tempered virago! Who could not feel sympathy for him? Who could not acquit him?'

Charles smiled again, enjoying himself increasingly, and he leaned a little further towards the jury.

'And yet, ladies and gentlemen, what reasonable person could truthfully believe such a story? For the defendant is eleven inches taller than his wife was, and three stones heavier. You have heard evidence of his fitness and his skill with his hands. Here was no seven-stone weakling unable to protect himself.

'But when he came to kill his wife, he did not hit out in understandable, if not forgiveable, anger. He carefully made certain that his children were fed, washed and put to bed, and he even read his daughter a story: a whole chapter of *The Secret Garden*, which must have taken him at least half an hour to read aloud. Then he went back into the kitchen where his wife was reading a magazine and stabbed her, expecting this court to believe that that was the only way in which he could defend himself against her. He has claimed that she threatened to kill him with a red-hot saucepan, but there is no evidence to support that claim, except the faint mark of a burn on the defendant's wrist, a burn that could have been caused by all kinds of things, such as brushing against the hot shelf of an oven. And he stabbed her seven times.'

Pausing there, Charles held out his right arm, fist upwards, elbow bent and made a hard, thrusting, stabbing movement and then another and then another until he had pushed his imaginary knife into the air seven times.

'Seven times, members of the jury. What reasonable man could possibly do that with a sharp steel knife and not expect his victim to die? Just imagine the scene that night. Look at the defendant, remember what you have heard about what happened in his kitchen, and ask yourselves what you can believe.'

265

As he sat down, the jurors obediently shifted their gaze to the dock. In contrast to his pale-skinned, dark-haired, jowly accuser, Michael Beechen looked astonishingly healthy. His complexion was good and the whites of his eyes were clear, his carriage was superb, and they could all see the width of his shoulders and the length of his arms. The thought of his being at the mercy of the woman they had seen sprawled, dead, on her kitchen floor described did indeed seem absurd.

Michael knew that they were all looking at him, but, after a quick glance at Melissa to make sure that she was still concentrating, he stared at the crest above the judge's chair, trying to keep his expression calm and confident.

Georgina Mayford got to her feet and for the first time she smiled directly at the jury.

'Members of the jury, you have been very patient through these last days, and you must be facing the final part of your work here with some concern. But you need not be too anxious, for your job is straightforward. You have to decide whether the evidence that the prosecution has brought is enough to prove beyond all reasonable doubt – that is, enough to make you certain – that my client is guilty of unlawful killing.

'The evidence you have heard has been enough to prove beyond all reasonable doubt that Penelope Beechen died from the wounds inflicted by my client.' She shook her head. 'No-one should have any doubt of that at all. Where the prosecution has brought no proof whatsoever is in the matter of his intention or his expectation. His lordship will explain to you the law as it relates to murder and you will learn that Michael Beechen could be guilty of that only if he intended to deprive his wife of her life, or to cause her very serious physical harm.

'As you have heard, when he stabbed her on that dreadful evening, he was acting in self-defence. Members of the jury, you saw the photographs of Penelope

Beechen's body. Such evidence is rarely admitted to murder trials because it is usually thought to be prejudicial. In this case, the defence wanted you to have every possible means of understanding what had actually happened that night, and so the photographic evidence was not excluded.

'You will have seen from those very upsetting pictures just how superficial most of the stab wounds were. Because of that you will be able to believe my client's explanation of those wounds: that he was trying only to stop his wife hitting him. She was beside herself and out of control. Somehow he had to make her realize what she was doing and stop her. As he has told you, while he was restraining her with his left hand, he felt around the worktops with his right for something he could use as a shield against the burningly hot, heavy saucepan with which she had threatened to maim and kill him. He could not take his eyes off her, because there was no knowing what she might do to him. Tragically, all his hand could find was the knife.

'At first, as the photographs show, he hardly grazed her skin with the point of the knife as he told her to stop hitting him. You all heard his unhappy little daughter testify that she heard him shout that again and again. But Penelope Beechen continued to hit his face and try to prise his fingers from her wrist so that she could belabour him with that ferociously hot pan, shouting that she would kill him. She had threatened to disfigure him, members of the jury, and now she was threatening to kill him. From his experience of her violent moods, he believed her.'

Georgina Mayford stopped to drink from the glass of water on the bench in front of her. She swallowed and then smiled at the jurors once more.

'For the prosecution to suggest to you that my client invented his evidence of these assaults is absurd.

It is true, as he has testified, that he reported them to the police only after the first of the articles and radio programmes had been made at the end of last year. As he has told you, that was because he did not think he would have been believed before independent evidence had been published that men, considerable numbers of men, do suffer in this way.'

Georgina Mayford paused there to look once more at the jurors. For the first time there was a hint of mischief as well as courtesy in her expression.

'And you will probably not be surprised about Michael Beechen's reluctance when you remember the evidence of Constable Radstock and the attitude he displayed to the fact that Michael Beechen had been assaulted by his wife. Some of you might have been tempted to share that attitude – and that amusement – if you had not heard the expert testimony of Dr Abel-Fowler. We have all heard jokes, have we not, about henpecked husbands. Some of you may even know the old music-hall song that includes the lines: "Naggin' at a feller as is six-feet-four/And 'er only four-feet-two".'

There were several smiles from older members of the jury then and David Davis mouthed the next line of the song, wagging his head to the rhythm.

'But what my client suffered was no joke; nor was it nagging. It was systematic assault with offensive weapons. Had he felt confident of being believed, he might have reported the worst of the assaults to the police much earlier and it is possible that a concealed video camera could have been installed, as has happened with some reported incidents of wife battering and child abuse. Then, ladies and gentlemen, there would have been no argument. As it is, you will have to rely on the evidence of Dr Abel-Fowler that husbands in Great Britain are assaulted with far greater frequency and violence than most of us could ever have imagined.

'You will remember that he testified that probably one person in every six couples is at risk of domestic violence. And more men than women have been admitted to some hospitals as a result of domestic assaults.

'The prosecution has made much of the fact that Michael Beechen is so much taller, heavier and stronger than his wife was, and they have suggested that he could have hit her with his fists and cowed her into submission. Isn't that an extraordinary criticism to make? My client did not beat up his wife, because he is not a violent man and because it has been deeply inculcated into him since he could first understand words that no man should ever strike a woman.

'He did once slap her, it is true. But that was a simple, open-handed smack to shock her out of dangerous hysteria when one of her children was lost. Most reasonable men would do that, would they not?'

Georgina Mayford dropped her clasped hands on to the bench in front of her and leaned on them, turning her head to look once more at the jury. Her long hair had been neatly pinned into a bun at the back of her head and her wig was perched on top. She looked utterly confident and completely sincere.

'You have heard and seen how deeply he regrets the death of his wife. You have heard and seen how much he loved the person that she really was when she was not in the grip of the irrational violence that sometimes took hold of her when she was suffering from pre-menstrual syndrome.'

Several of the women jurors looked at her with sympathy. She nodded several times.

'It is a tragedy, ladies and gentlemen, that Penelope Beechen suffered from that tendency to violence: a tragedy for her, and for her children. But most of all, ladies and gentlemen, it is a tragedy for Michael Beechen, from which he will probably never recover. His

269

married life was not the anchor and sustaining warmth that most of us hope and expect marriage will provide, but a terrifying rollercoaster of pain and fear and an unhappiness that is difficult for those who are luckier than he to contemplate. But he stuck with it, trying to keep it going, trying to improve it, because he loved his wife and children. And now his wife is dead.'

Checking on Melissa, Michael saw that she was sitting with her head bowed. He could not see much of her face, but her whole posture suggested shame. She was not an actress, of course, and might be unaware of what she was expressing, but she definitely looked ashamed. He could not imagine why she should feel guilty unless it was a kind of global remorse on behalf of all women for what Penelope had done. His eyebrows twitched as he frowned.

'As I told you in my opening remarks, we are not here to try Penelope Beechen,' Gina Mayford went on. 'Even if we were, no-one could say that the pre-menstrual syndrome from which she suffered was her fault. But still less, ladies and gentlemen is it the fault of the man who married her, had children with her, and did his best to protect those children.

'For eight years he held his family together in the most difficult of circumstances. For eight years he suffered and struggled and at the end, in the terror of what she said she would do to him, he struck out. Penelope Beechen died, but her husband will have to live with the knowledge of what happened for the rest of his life. He has suffered from the deepest sorrow and regret, and he will continue to do so. But he is not guilty of murder.

'The prosecution has suggested that the whole story of Penelope Beechen's assaults was invented by my client to disguise his wish to kill his wife. Apart from the fact that it would have been almost impossible to damage himself in all the ways that his wife wounded him, that suggestion would mean that he had been planning her death for nearly eight years. It was seven and a half years ago that he first attended an accident and emergency department after one of her assaults. Do you not think, ladies and gentlemen, that a man who wanted to give himself a reason for killing his wife would have done so more quickly?'

Seeing several smiling faces in the jury benches, Michael began to feel nearly as confident as he looked.

'When you consider all the evidence you have heard, members of the jury, you will realize that Michael Beechen never intended to kill his wife and was doing no more than defending himself.'

Georgina Mayford bowed to the bench and sat down. The judge sat in silence, contemplating the two senior barristers in front of him, before looking at the jury over the top of his tortoiseshell-framed spectacles. Then he began to speak. As she had warned them, he first explained the law as it relates to murder.

'If you are satisfied, members of the jury,' he said at the end of his explanation, 'that the defendant intended his wife to die as he stabbed her, or that he intended his actions to cause her serious bodily harm, then, subject to what I shall say in a moment about provocation, you must bring in a verdict of guilty of murder. If, however, you are not satisfied that he intended to cause her serious bodily harm then you will acquit him.

'Provocation is some act or series of acts done and/or words spoken, which causes in the defendant a sudden and temporary loss of self-control and which would cause a reasonable person to lose his self-control and to behave as the defendant did. Therefore you have to consider two questions: did the allegedly provoking conduct cause the defendant to lose his self-control, and might that conduct have caused a reasonable person to lose his self-control and to behave as the defendant did? Because the prosecution must prove the defendant's guilt, it is not for the defendant to prove that he was provoked. The prosecution must make you sure that the defendant was not so provoked, before you can convict him of murder. If you are satisfied that he was provoked, or if you think that he may have been provoked, then you can only convict him of manslaughter.

'I must also explain to you that a killing in lawful self-defence is no offence. Self-defence is lawful when it is necessary to use force to resist or defend yourself against an attack and when the amount of force used is reasonable.'

Several of the jurors were writing notes by then, clearly not confident of being able to remember exactly what they were being told.

'What is reasonable force depends on all the facts, for example, the nature of the attack,' said the judge, slowing down his words so that the jurors could keep up with him. 'But a person defending himself cannot be expected to weigh precisely the exact amount of defensive action which is necessary. If, therefore, the defendant did no more than what he instinctively thought was necessary, that is very strong evidence that the amount of force was reasonable and necessary.

'Because the prosecution must prove the defendant's guilt, it is for it to make you sure that the defendant was not acting reasonably in necessary self-defence. If you conclude that he was, or that he may have been, acting reasonably in necessary self-defence then you must acquit him.'

The judge waited for all the jurors to stop writing before he added, 'If you have any questions on matters of law, or if you need to refresh your minds as to any of the evidence, you must tell the jury bailiff and she will pass your request on to me. I shall do my best to help you.

'Now, I shall run through the evidence we have all

heard so that it is freshly in your minds as you retire to decide on your verdict.'

He then picked the facts from the speeches and inferences that the two barristers had made and the answers witnesses had given to their questions.

'There you have it, ladies and gentlemen,' he said when he reached the end of his explanation. 'You must reach, if you can, a unanimous verdict. However, as you may know, the law allows me in certain circumstances to accept a verdict which is not the verdict of you all. Those circumstances have not yet arisen. I must therefore ask you to reach a verdict on which each one of you is agreed. Should the time come when I can accept a majority verdict, I shall give you a further direction.'

Watching Melissa turn towards the dark-haired man sitting next to her and smile at him, Michael felt a sudden ferocious sense of betrayal. He also felt a terrible fear.

Several of the other jurors were looking at him, and were shocked by the hostility in his handsome face.

The judge nodded to the black-robed usher who was to act as jury bailiff. She opened the door into the jury room and one by one the twelve of them filed out of the court into the stale, smoky atmosphere of the dingy room. The usher switched on the lights, demonstrated the working of the extractor fan, took their orders for lunchtime sandwiches, locked the door that led out into the passage, removed the key, and left them to their deliberations.

Chapter 18

'As the oldest man present, I propose that we elect a foreman,' said the tall, sixtyish juror called David Davis, breaking into the uncertain silence.

'Good idea,' said Melissa at once.

When she had woken that morning, her mind had been full of Martin and her dead father, but she had managed to keep them out for most of the morning and she was determined to play her full part in the jury's verdict. She saw that Susan Beere was beginning to look agitated. Remembering how sensible and funny Minty had been whenever the four of them had lunched together, Melissa quickly added, 'I propose Araminta Collins.'

'Seconded,' said Adam just as Susan Beere began to nod.

'Those in favour?' said Melissa.

She, Adam, Susan and Mrs Crosscombe put up their hands. So did the young black man with the intelligent eyes and brilliant smile, whose name Melissa had forgotten. Jack Brown, who had had such trouble reading the oath at the beginning of the trial, timidly put up his hand, looking anxiously over his shoulder at Davis, and slowly three of the others joined them.

'All right,' said Davis reluctantly. 'That's a clear majority. It's settled then.'

Melissa smiled at him, knowing perfectly well that he thought he should have been foreman. She pulled out the nearest chair and sat down. Adam sat on her left and the balding, nondescript man dressed in a sagging grey-flannel suit, who had never spoken in her hearing, took the chair on her right. Minty sat at the head of the table with Adam on her right and Susan on her left. The others arranged themselves down the sides of the table.

'Good,' said Minty. 'Thank you all for that vote of confidence in me. It seems strange after we've sat in that box together for five days now, but I don't know everyone's name yet. I suggest that we start by introducing ourselves. I am Minty Collins. I have a business making children's clothes here in Bristol. Adam?'

'I'm Adam Blake. I teach at the university.'

Melissa explained who she was and then turned to the man on her right, who said his name was John Dent. His accent suggested that he had moved to Bristol from somewhere in the South-East.

'I'm in the building trade,' he said ambiguously.

Next to him was the young black man, who reminded them that his name was Nat Turner, adding: 'I'm a plumber.'

'Er. I'm Brown. Jack Brown,' said the man with the wispy beard, looking afraid, as though someone might tell him he had got his name wrong or ought not to have spoken so loudly.

'And I'm David Davis. Dai. I'm retired.'

On his right was the fat young man, dressed that day in vast grey trousers and a red-and-grey checked shirt. His face descended into his neck in a series of swaying chins and his blue eyes looked tiny between the puffy lids. 'Richard Smith,' he said in a voice that seemed far too high to come out of such a large body. 'Unemployed.'

'Mrs Rogers,' said the quiet, tired-looking black woman who had always left the building without stopping to speak to any of the others as soon as the jury were released each day. She was wearing a neatly pressed green dress and a black jersey turban hat. 'Office cleaner.'

Next to her was a thin white woman who had also avoided the rest of them. In her early fifties, she was dressed in a grey-and-blue printed woollen dress with a blue blazer over it and had a blue and pink patterned silk scarf tucked into the neckline. She looked almost as worried as Jack Brown. Clutching her handbag on her knee, she coughed and licked her lips and told them that her name was Diana Jenkins. She made no mention of any work. Mrs Crosscombe came next and Susan Beere last.

'Good,' said Minty, smiling impersonally down the table. 'Now we know where we are. Has anyone made up their mind yet?'

No-one said anything until Dai Davis announced in a deep, rasping voice that Penelope Beechen sounded like a vindictive, aggressive slut, that the defence case made sense to him, and he thought Michael Beechen was probably innocent.

'The difficulty is,' said Adam, nodding to him, 'that we've no proof either way. All we've got to go on is Beechen's claim that he thought she was going to kill him and the prosecution's suggestion that he invented all the evidence of her assaults to provide an excuse, which . . .'

'That's just silly,' said Melissa as both Susan and Nat started talking loudly. After a moment, Minty persuaded them all to take turns.

'I've made the experiment with an iron,' said Susan earnestly when it was her turn, 'and it is perfectly possible to hold a heavy iron in the small of one's own back, despite what the FIS volunteer said.'

'Maybe,' said Melissa, 'but can you imagine anyone actually going to those lengths over so many years? Even if Beechen had had the imagination to do that, and the masochism necessary to put up with the pain, he'd have to have been planning the murder for eight years if the prosecution's theory is correct, and that's ridiculous, surely?' She was looking at Susan as she spoke and was surprised to hear Richard Smith's high voice.

'It's like in *Brighton Rock*, i'n't it? Pinky knew he'd not get done for murder if they thought it was a suicide pact for love. This bloke could've done the same. Stands to reason.'

That set them all off and at least four people were explaining to him exactly why it did not stand to reason at all before Araminta could make herself heard.

'Wait,' she said at last very loudly. There was a sullen silence. 'That's better. Now, I don't want to be bossy,' she went on politely, 'but we really will get on better if only one person speaks at a time.'

Gradually she managed to persuade them of that, but they made very little progress, arguing round and round the subject of Penelope Beechen's assaults. It became clear that Diana Jenkins, Mrs Rogers, John Dent and Jack Brown were going to take almost no part in the discussion, either from lack of interest or because they felt intimidated by the others' readiness to argue. Diana Jenkins followed every shift in the discussion, her eyes moving anxiously from one speaker to the next. Once or twice it looked as though she might join in, but someone else always started to speak before she could open her mouth and she relapsed again into her nervous watching.

At one moment after a long argument with Minty and Dai Davis, during which several jurors had tried to intervene, Susan admitted that she found it enormously difficult to believe that any woman could do the things of which Michael Beechen had accused his wife. Davis snorted at that, and Adam, who had been listening in silence for nearly twenty minutes, said gently, 'I think we have to accept that such things happen. Didn't you read all those articles last year, the ones the prosecution talked about? I did.'

'But it's all too pat and convenient for Beechen, isn't it? His wife can't give her side of the story,' Susan said just as there was a knock at the door. Minty got up to open it. The jury bailiff stood there with a haversack in her hand.

'Your sandwiches,' she said. Araminta let her in to the room, and she unpacked the bag and took out a receipt, telling each of them how much they owed. There was a scramble for the correct change and Jack Brown dropped his money and banged his head on the table leg as he picked up the coins. He dropped them again. His usually pale face was violently flushed and the inadequacy of his beard was even more noticeable than usual.

'Don't worry, lad,' said Dai Davis. 'Let it be for the moment; I'll pay and you can pay me back later.'

When the usher had gone, there was a sense of relaxation as the jurors unwrapped their sandwiches and stuck straws in their boxes of juice or ripped the ring-pulls from cans of carbonated drinks. Melissa, having swallowed a mouthful of her cheese-and-pickle-on-brown, looked across the table at Susan. She was delicately picking pieces of lettuce out of a tuna and salad sandwich and eating them.

'You were saying that it was all too pat, Susan,' Melissa said.

'That's right. The timing is too convenient. I hear what you say about the absurdity of Beechen's planning all this for eight years, but don't you think it's possible that he only decided to kill her quite recently and seized on the battered husband reports to provide an excuse as the prosecution suggested? She might have hit him in the past, lots of people do slap their spouses, but it's quite likely that he's exaggerated what she did to him. Doesn't that make more sense?'

Before Melissa could answer, Davis put down his half-eaten ham sandwich and said aggressively, 'You're sure he must be guilty, aren't you? Whatever the evidence. It's not right.'

Susan, whose dislike of him was obvious, shook her head. 'No, I'm not sure, but look at the size of him. And remember those awful photographs of her body. Whatever she was doing, or threatening to do, he didn't need to stab her like that to disarm her. You can't just ignore that. Remember what the judge said about reasonable force. There was nothing reasonable about what Beechen did. He must have meant to kill her – or at least harm her seriously, which comes to much the same thing.'

'That's my problem, too,' said Melissa, remembering not only the photographs of Penelope Beechen's body, but also Martin lying at her feet with the bees crawling all over his face. 'I think Adam's right and we must accept the evidence of the assaults, but Beechen's reaction to the last one was surely much more violent than it need have been. I know the judge told us that someone being attacked may not be able to weigh up exactly how much force is needed to defend himself, but this was vastly much more than he needed.'

'So you do think he's guilty,' said Minty, licking her fingers and then wiping them on the paper napkin that had come with her sandwich. She took the lid off a polystyrene cup of coffee.

'Yes, but I'm not sure whether it should be murder or manslaughter,' said Melissa, finding it hard to finish her own sandwich. The bread seemed to turn to sweet pappy dough in her mouth. She decided to leave the second half, stuffing it back into the paper bag.

'You can't think him guilty of deliberate, premeditated murder,' said Davis in angry protest. 'It's obvious.'

Melissa stiffened. He had every right to disagree with her, but not to to tell her what she thought. That was one of the things Martin did, and it always infuriated her.

'There was all that provocation, just as the judge said. You can't ignore that.'

'I am not ignoring it, Mr Davis,' she said coldly.

Minty must have heard the suppressed impatience in Melissa's voice, for she intervened then, asking the jurors to vote on each of the three verdicts. Although they had already been talking for well over an hour, it was too soon for most of them to have made up their minds, but Davis voted for self-defence and Jack Brown timidly joined him. Susan and Mrs Crosscombe voted for murder; Melissa and Adam for manslaughter, and the rest refused to commit themselves.

'What about you, Minty?' said Melissa as private conversations broke out all down the table as neighbours tried to persuade each other to change their minds. 'What do you think?'

'I'm inclined to join you and Adam in your compromise,' she said, opening her mouth to add something else.

'That's a cop out,' said Susan irritably before Minty could complete her sentence.

'No, it isn't,' said Melissa, hoping that she did not sound too angry. 'It's a perfectly legitimate verdict, and it seems to me to fit the facts. I do not believe that Beechen set out to kill his wife; therefore he's not guilty of murder. But he used far more force than necessary to defend himself, and so he's not innocent of her death either. QED.'

'Well, you two obviously differ,' said Minty with a smile that was meant to cool the simmering fury she could feel all around her. 'Mrs Crosscombe, why do you think he's guilty?'

The elderly woman, who had finished her lunch, picked up her large brown canvas and plastic holdall and put it on the table in front of her. 'Oh, he's guilty all right,' she said, with both hands on the zip. The others looked curiously at her as she took out her knitting, replaced the bag at her feet and unrolled the complicated, multi-coloured, patterned sweater front that had been wrapped, half-completed, around the needles.

'Can you explain why?' asked Melissa. Mrs Crosscombe began to knit, without even looking at what she was doing, picking up the different wools that ran along the back of the half-made sweater as though she could tell which colour was which simply by feel.

'Have you got children?' she asked Melissa.

'No. Not yet. Why?'

'Because no-one who hasn't had to look after three small children in a little flat like that could possibly understand Mrs Beechen.' She looked around the table and smiled sweetly, adding in her gentle voice, 'Mr Davis, you really cannot write her off as a violent slut who deserved killing. That's most unfair, and quite unreasonable.'

Dai Davis frowned and lit a cigarette, but he did not answer.

'Must you smoke in here?' said Susan Beere in a tone of exhausted patience.

'Oh pardon me for breathing,' said Davis. 'Smoking's not a crime yet, you know.'

Susan shrugged and then smiled on Mrs Crosscombe with more friendliness than she yet had shown to anyone except Minty.

'Listen, Mrs Wraxall,' said Mrs Crosscombe, perhaps emboldened by Susan's encouragement. She leaned forward over her knitting needles. 'Penelope loved him when they first married. You heard her friend tell us that. And then she changed. Can't you guess why? The first of her children was born. And then by the time he killed her, she had three under eight and no help in too little space. Until you've been with three small children day in, day out, night in, night out, you can't imagine how it drives you mad.'

The sweetness of her voice was overtaken by something harder and several of the jurors turned to look at her curiously. Richard Smith forgot the last bit of his second triple-decker sandwich and held it with a piece of mayonnaise-covered tomato hanging out of the triangle of bread. Nat Turner watched fascinated as it slipped slowly down to fall onto Richard's trousers. Still he ignored it.

'You have to make them eat, and dress, and clean their teeth, and keep quiet, and go to bed and stay there,' said Mrs Crosscombe, apparently concentrating on her knitting. 'Every day is a struggle from beginning to end. They whine and complain and disobey and make a mess. They're bored and they want you to play with them, but they don't want to do anything you suggest. They won't eat what you've cooked. Then an hour later they're hungry. When you've finally got to sleep, exhausted, they come and wake you up with a tummy ache or a bad dream. You get so tired and so bitterly angry that you could strangle them.'

Mrs Crosscombe looked up for a moment to smile at Melissa, who was looking nearly as shocked as she felt.

'You don't need to look so horrified, dear. Most mothers dislike their children at times.' Mrs Crosscombe smiled as she pulled a violet thread away from the cerise and the pink and knitted it into the complicated pattern. 'They do love them, of course, but they detest them too, some of the time. It's only natural.'

Richard Smith's eye was caught by the blob of mayonnaise and tomato on his trousers. He fingered it up, licking his finger between each wipe.

'Not all children are disliked,' Adam said deliberately. 'They truly are not. Not all mothers hate their children.'

'No,' agreed Mrs Crosscombe, staring at him through

her kind-looking myopic eyes. 'But lots do. After all, children change a woman's life entirely. It's not natural to be with a difficult, whining child for twenty-four hours every day and not hate her sometimes.'

She saw that he did not believe her and so she sighed and tried to explain more fully.

'Most men – and women who haven't had children – seem to think that as soon as you've given birth – which is the most painful and disgusting process you can imagine – you suddenly know all there is to know about caring for the creature, and that you'll love it. But why should you? It changes your whole life; and when it gets to the stage where it has stopped whining and being sick in the night and might be a friend, it turns on you and then—'

Seeing that Adam was looking sick, Melissa intervened. 'I'm sure you're right, Mrs Crosscombe, but we're getting off the point a bit, aren't we?'

'Perhaps we are. I only said it because I think Mrs Beechen probably hit her husband because she knew she must not hit her children. He was a man, stronger and much bigger than her. She was desperate and he couldn't understand that, and he wouldn't do anything for her. It was safer to hit him than one of the children. He ought to have been able to deal with it. If he was half as competent and superior as he pretends, he would have been able to. He shouldn't have killed her. You asked why I think he was guilty of murder. That's why; it's quite simple. He killed her and he didn't need to.'

'But you're suggesting she had every right to hit him,' said Davis explosively from the far end of the table. 'Hundreds of women have little children and no-one to help, and they don't go round hitting their husbands. My wife never did anything like that. And I was far too busy in the early days, working nights and overtime, to help her at all.'

That set them off again and Nat, Susan, Melissa, Adam, Dai and Mrs Crosscombe argued to and fro about the duties of wives, the tyranny of husbands, the degree of fear that Michael Beechen might have felt as his wife held a heavy, red-hot saucepan by his face, the likelihood that he could have controlled her in some other way, and the precise meaning of the law. Minty joined in sometimes, but the other five jurors did not speak at all.

At one moment Diana Jenkins gasped and opened her handbag, rootling around in it for something. Frustrated, she clicked her bag shut again and sat looking as though she were about to burst into tears. There were large drops of sweat on her forehead and upper lip and her face was bright red.

Mrs Crosscombe, who had been listening politely to Dai Davis, noticed that Nat was staring across the table and turned left to see what had aroused his interest. Seeing the state of Diana Jenkins, she leaned down once more into her big shopping bag and emerged above the table with a new packet of tissues in her hand. She passed them to Diana Jenkins, saying quietly, 'Don't worry about it, dear. Take these.'

'Oh, thank you,' said Diana Jenkins in a faint voice, pulling open the packet and taking out a paper handkerchief so that she could wipe her face.

'Now, Mr Davis,' said Mrs Crosscombe, picking up her knitting again with enough fuss to divert the attention of most of them. 'What was that you were saying?'

There was another knock at the door before he could answer. Once again it was the jury bailiff, telling Minty that the judge wanted to speak to them.

When they had shuffled back into their seats in the jury box, Melissa looked at the clock on the wall opposite the judge's throne. She was amazed to see that they had been in the jury room for more than two hours.

The jury bailiff stood in front of them and asked, 'Members of the jury, have you reached a verdict on which all of you are agreed?'

'No, we have not,' replied Minty, letting herself sound exasperated.

Melissa saw Michael Beechen looking at her again intently, as though he were trying to send her a message, and she closed her eyes.

The judge leaned forward, his robes and white wig making him look unreal, almost like a puppet whose strings were manipulated by some hands above the roof of the court. 'Is there any assistance that I can give you in reaching your verdict?'

Minty looked along the line of jurors, some of them clearly angry and others nervous. Then she looked back at the judge.

'No, I don't think so.'

'In that case I must ask you once more to retire and to continue to try to reach a unanimous verdict; but if you cannot, I will accept a majority verdict, which is a verdict with which at least ten of you agree,' he said, moderating the commanding edge his voice had whenever he was speaking to the lawyers in the court. 'If I can give you any help at any time, please write a note and give it to the jury bailiff.'

'Thank you, my lord,' said Minty with impressive dignity. She managed to look and sound like someone who had just been offered a service rather than like a subordinate who had been urged to greater efforts.

Once more the jurors retreated to their room.

Chapter 19

'There we have it,' said Minty ten minutes later, when several of them had taken turns to use the small lavatory in an annexe to the jury room and settled at last round the table again. 'We have somehow to reach a verdict that ten of us can agree on. Mr Davis, do I take it that you are adamant in believing Beechen to be innocent of murder or even manslaughter?'

'Yes,' he said, stubbing out his cigarette and grinding the filter down into the full ashtray. The force of his action as much as the look of dislike he sent Susan gave a clue to the depths of his anger. 'He thought she was going to kill him. He knew she was violent enough to do it and he had to defend himself. Self-defence. Innocent.'

'I see. Susan?'

'Guilty of murder. He didn't need to do anything nearly so violent to remove the saucepan from her hand,' she said staring first at the cigarette stubs and then at Davis. Her pale face seemed like a mask designed to express contempt.

As they argued with each other, they could have been cast as examples of two worlds that could never meet. Davis was a big, raw-boned, noisy man whose class, generation, education, work and longing memories of his recently dead wife had all taught him that decent women make good wives and mothers. To him someone like Penelope Beechen, who was dissatisfied, angry, challenged her husband, demanded things he could not offer, and kept a filthy house, was a slut, a bad wife and therefore a bad woman.

To Susan, who was physically small, better educated and infinitely more sophisticated, Davis's ingrained beliefs were anathema. She had reported over the years for several newspapers on female victims of rape, of sexual abuse, of domestic violence, harassment, prejudice, poverty, low self-esteem and low expectations. To her, women, bad or good, were nearly always victims. They needed fighting for and defending by anyone with any weapons. When they turned on their tormentors, or broke the law in any other way, they needed understanding and help, not punishment. She might not have put it in so many words, but she believed absolutely that women could never be judged by the same laws as men because women had no power.

'As you know, I think the verdict should be guilty, too, dear,' said Mrs Crosscombe as soon as both Davis and Susan paused at the same time. Mrs Crosscombe had been knitting steadily ever since they sat down at the table again and seemed quite untroubled by the things the others had said. 'He's guilty of murder.'

Minty sighed. 'Then it's down to the other eight of us to work out what we really think and see if we can't agree with one side or other.' She took the cap off her pen and drew a large, floppy flower on the pad in front of her. Then she looked up at her committee. 'I feel rather inadequate to chair the discussion, because I truly do not know what I believe, and I'm not sure how I'm going to be able to decide.'

'Listen, Minty,' said Susan before anyone else could speak. Several of the others sighed. 'Even if you accept that what Dr Abel-Fowler said about battered husbands is true—'

'I think we must accept that,' said Adam suddenly,

sounding more decisive than usual. They all looked at him, some of them obviously surprised by his air of authority. 'We were instructed to try the case on the evidence we've heard,' he said, moderating the commanding edge to his voice. 'Dr Abel-Fowler was presented to us as an expert witness, and the prosecution did not challenge his knowledge or his authority. Therefore we have to accept his expertise. We can't simply ignore it or decide that we know better than he.'

'Very well,' said Susan with what one or two of the jurors clearly thought was unlikely meekness. Richard Smith even smiled, his pendulous chins swaying and his little eyes twinkling.

'Reluctantly I will accept that,' said Susan. 'But it doesn't actually alter what I was going to say.'

'Then I apologize for my intervention,' said Adam formally.

'Consider the apology accepted,' said Susan. They smiled at each other. 'Now, Michael Beechen does not fit the profile of the typical victim of husband-battering. You must accept that, too. After all, the prosecution did raise this point and Abel-Fowler admitted it.'

Adam nodded slowly.

'Beechen slapped his wife when she was hysterical,' Susan said. 'He was not the kind of victim who cannot stand up to his wife.'

'In a way that sounds fair,' said Araminta, still sounding helpless. 'But he couldn't stop her burning him or breaking his arm, could he?'

'Twice she broke his arm,' said Nat Turner, grinning at Susan. 'That's not normal. Could you take a hammer and deliberately break your old man's arm?'

'That's not relevant,' said Susan sharply.

'Perhaps it is,' said Melissa, staring down at her notes in order to avoid looking as though she were issuing a challenge to Susan. 'And the principle *is* the same.

Penelope may not have – sorry, that's not coming out quite right. She certainly did not deserve to die, but she was not a normal victim. She really wasn't. She did play a part in her own death.'

'I don't think the principle is the same.' Susan looked dogged in her determination not to lose her temper. 'I think that the prosecution may well be right. Beechen's an actor and however much he tried to persuade us that he loved his wife and regrets her death, I believe he may be quite as devious as his wretched daughter. I do think that he killed his wife deliberately. I'm sorry that you don't, but I do.'

Melissa's head jerked upwards until she was staring across the table at Susan.

'What do you mean "devious as his daughter"?'

'Isn't it obvious?' asked Susan, surprised by the abruptness of the question. She pulled strands of her deliberately ragged fringe down over her white forehead. 'She's a sly little party with an agenda of her own.'

'I thought she seemed perfectly truthful,' said Davis, frowning as he lit up another cigarette and leaned back, blowing out a cloud of smoke. Melissa could not decide whether he was trying to provoke Susan or merely stating what he believed.

'There's truth and truth. We're all old enough here to know that,' said Susan pleasantly enough, ignoring both his cigarette and his aggressive tone to the obvious relief of Diana Jenkins, who was turning from one speaker to the other as though silently pleading with them to be kind to each other. Richard Smith, on the other hand, looked almost disappointed.

'Maybe,' said Melissa, 'but I still don't understand what you meant. What's Marianna's agenda?'

'Can you really not have seen what she was doing? She spent her time displaying to all and sundry how much better she was at tidying up the flat and organizing the two boys than her mother. Her memories of the night her mother died will naturally be coloured by that.'

There was silence until Mrs Crosscombe changed from pink to mauve wool and said, 'I think that makes sense. Children, especially little girls, can be very manipulative, you know.'

'No, I don't,' said Melissa.

'Don't you?' said Susan, letting one eyebrow fly upwards in mockery. 'Surely you can see that all Marianna ever wanted was to prove to darling Daddy how very much better and nicer she was than horrid Mummy. In fact I wouldn't be surprised if the tension she produced with her antics wasn't what pushed her mother over into violence in the first place – and it probably psyched up her father, too. Without that, he might never have—'

'That's an absolutely monstrous thing to say,' said Melissa loudly, so angry that she was suddenly terrified that she might lose her temper. She took hold of her lower lip between her teeth and the small pain helped her control herself. Letting it go, she went on, 'Whatever Charles Harcombe suggested about both parties to a relationship causing the trouble, you simply cannot blame the child for—'

Before she could say anything else, she felt Adam's hand tightly gripping her wrist. She turned to stare furiously at him, but he ignored her, saying steadily, 'I think we really need to sort out how many of us could vote for a manslaughter verdict. Minty, don't you think we should take a vote? Now.'

Outraged at his attempt to silence her, and painfully disappointed by it, Melissa pulled her arm away. Adam let go at once. But Minty took up his suggestion and called another vote. Melissa sat with her wrist cradled in her other hand.

There were still two votes for murder and two votes for an acquittal, but by then only John Dent, Minty and Richard Smith could not make up their minds. Diana Jenkins, Nat and Mrs Rogers had joined Adam and Melissa in voting for manslaughter.

Minty tried to nudge them all closer to a viable verdict by asking each of her fellow abstainers in turn why they had not voted one way or the other. Neither had anything very useful to say and Minty could only repeat her earlier reservations when Dai Davis threw her own question back at her.

His ashtray soon filled up and the air became fuggier and fuggier. Diana Jenkins still looked hot and several of the others were clenching their foreheads as though they were suffering from headaches.

'Listen, all of you,' said Susan eventually, looking from one to other, noticing which faces were resistant, which angry, which bored and which sympathetic. 'It's been clear all along – from the evidence, Adam – what sort of a marriage the Beechens had. He was a cleanliness-freak, who specifically chose a wife who was the very opposite of himself. Why did he do that? Don't you think that makes him pretty odd even before we think about the violence and which of the two Beechens was the more provocative and dangerous?'

'I do see what you mean,' said Melissa, opening her eyes again and thinking about what Dr Edbury had said to her. 'It's something I've been puzzling over since nearly the beginning of the case.'

'I think', said Susan actually smiling at Melissa for once, 'that he's one of those men who feel such doubt about themselves that the only way they can operate is to surround themselves with people weaker than they are. That makes them feel strong and successful. I think it must be why Beechen chose such an unsuitable woman in the first place.'

There was an obstructive silence. Diana Jenkins looked tearfully unhappy again.

'There's no need to look so upset, Mrs Jenkins,' Susan said in a tone of patronizing patience. I'm not suggesting that he set out in a cold-blooded way to choose an unsuitable woman. I don't suppose for a moment that he had any idea of what was driving him. He probably believed that he had fallen in love with her. But I'm sure his subconscious selected her for the very things that later made him want her dead.'

Diana Jenkins flinched. 'I don't think that's fair,' she managed to say. Susan sighed.

Most of the other jurors stared at Diana Jenkins, but Melissa nodded slowly to Susan, thinking about Martin's need to trample on people whenever he was anxious or humiliated and admitting to herself that she, too, might have had subconscious needs. She had never even acknowledged the possibility until her mother's revelation gave some weight to Dr Edbury's peculiar theories. The thought of what those needs might have done to affect her conscious mind was beginning to worry her. She looked at her watch, wondering how much longer they were going to have to argue with each other. They had been at it for more than an hour since the judge had sent them back to try again and it did not look to her as though they were any nearer reaching a verdict.

'That could be true,' said Nat suddenly, pushing his fingers through his close-cropped hair. He leaned back in his chair so that the two front legs lifted off the floor.

'Thanks, Nat,' said Susan, beginning to look more relaxed. She started to play with one of her long amber earrings as she talked. 'Can't you imagine that for a woman like Penelope – probably unstable, probably lonely, certainly frustrated – perhaps the only way of fighting back against her husband's perpetual belittling was to hit him? If that's so, then I really don't think anyone could think him innocent, even if she did threaten to kill him that night.'

292

'On the other hand,' said Adam reluctantly, 'she might have done it because she was disappointed in him.'

'Wha?' said Richard Smith suddenly rejoining the discussion.

Adam nodded to him. 'Perhaps like a lot of women she had been brought up to believe that men are strong, invulnerable providers of all that a woman needs,' he explained. 'If that's so, it could have been the shock of her discovery that men are just as vulnerable as women that made her turn on him.'

He looked down at his fingernails and added quietly, 'I think some women feel so . . . so swizzed when they discover we're not demi-gods that they would do anything to punish us for our failings.'

'And who made anyone expect demi-gods in the first place?' Susan demanded, completely distracted from the specific argument about the Beechens' guilt. 'Men, of course. They expect to be treated as superior beings when they're nothing of the kind, and they're hardly ever prepared to admit their weaknesses. It's they who pretend they haven't got any; not women. Most men grow up expecting to be protected, cared for and positively served, first by their mothers and then by substitute-mothers, for ever *and* still to be looked up to as though they're better than women. Well, no-one can look up to the sort of man Michael Beechen is.'

'Unfortunately,' said Melissa drily in an attempt to calm the increasingly emotional nature of the argument, 'Penelope Beechen's motives for hitting her husband aren't our concern. As Georgina Mayford said, we're not here to try Penelope. All we've got to decide is whether her husband genuinely believed she'd kill him and whether he was reckless with the force he used to try to stop her.'

Before anyone could answer, Mrs Crosscombe laid down her knitting with a groan and they all looked at her. 'I'm sorry,' she said, panting slightly. 'It's my arthritis. Sitting in one position for so long . . .' She broke off and leaned forward against the scarred table.

Nat Turner and Adam got to their feet and went round to stand behind her.

'Can we help?' asked Nat. 'Lift you or anything?'

'Oh, thank you. If I just walk about a bit, it might help.'

Carefully, not knowing quite in which direction to urge her limbs, the two men lifted Mrs Crosscombe from her chair. She waited, balancing herself against them until she was sure of her footing and then, with one hand on Nat's arm, she walked painfully up and down the small room until she had gained some kind of relief.

The others took advantage of the interruption to rearrange themselves and Mrs Jenkins bolted for the lavatory. Everyone heard the sound of rushing water. She came back with a damp hairline, clearly having washed her face. Mrs Crosscombe let Nat lower her into her chair again, thanked him and picked up her knitting.

As though the clicking of her needles had been a signal to the others, they picked up the argument again and proceeded as fruitlessly as before.

Dai Davis continued to argue passionately in favour of Beechen's innocence until he was seized with a fit of coughing. 'D'you think they'll bring us tea?' he growled when the spasm was over. 'It's long after four. I think we damn well deserve it.'

'I suspect they'll give us as little as possible so that we come to some kind of decision,' said Minty helplessly. 'Look, can we vote again? We must sort something out or this'll go on for ever.'

'I quite agree,' said Melissa.

'I don't see the point,' said Susan. 'No-one's been persuaded to change their mind yet.'

Minty looked round at the tired, irritable faces of her team.

'Has anyone changed their mind or made it up?'

No-one said anything.

'Then we've just to go on. Mr Davis, are . . .'

She got no further because they all heard the familiar knock at the door. A moment later the usher called them back in front of the judge. Melissa found that all her joints were stiff when she pushed herself up from her chair. She tipped her head back and felt the tendons in her neck crack with a noise like a pistol shot. Adam heard it, although he was standing several feet away.

'Are you all right?' he asked, coming quickly to her side.

'Yes, I'm fine,' she said unconvincingly. 'Just stiff-necked. Come on, Adam, we'd better go in.'

Michael watched the jurors coming back and searched Melissa's face for clues to what was happening. She looked rather upset and very tired. He thought she might have a headache too; there was something about her eyes and the way she was carrying her head that made her look as though she were in pain. The others were obviously being difficult, but she had clearly managed to stand firm so far. He glared at the dark-haired man at her side, hating him for looking at her so possessively. What business was she of his? Michael wanted to show her all his sympathy and then stiffen her courage, but she would not look at him.

When all the jurors were sitting down the jury bailiff addressed them:

'Have you reached a verdict on which you are all agreed?'

'No,' said Minty, looking apologetically at the judge.

'Have you reached a verdict on which at least ten of you are agreed?'

'No.'

The judge leaned forward and addressed Araminta. 'Is there any way that I can assist you in reaching that verdict?'

'I am not sure, my lord,' Araminta said readily. 'But there may be.'

'Is there anything in the law on which some of you are confused?'

'Not exactly, although . . . May we retire again so that I can consult the other members of the jury, my lord?'

The judge looked at his watch and then, as though he doubted its accuracy, at the clock on the wall. 'I think the best course of action is for the jury to be escorted to an hotel for the night and court to reconvene tomorrow morning at half past ten.' He paused, as though waiting for one or other counsel to comment but neither did.

Michael's face hardened, thinking that if Melissa were to be subjected to much more her resolution might waver. The dark man would get to her and ruin everything. Gina Mayford ought to understand that and object to what the judge was doing.

'Very well,' the judge continued. 'Members of the jury, the bailiff will escort you to your hotel and stay with you. I must remind you that you may not speak to anyone except your fellow jurors. You will be taken to the hotel and brought back to court tomorrow morning. The jury bailiff will arrange for your families to be informed as to your whereabouts and explain the various arrangements to you.'

He rose. As the clerk ordered everyone to stand, Michael got to his feet yet again. He knew that he could not take much more, but he also knew that he was trapped. He had no option but to endure anything the judge chose to do to him. Penelope had punished him even more effectively in dying than she had done at any moment of their miserable life together.

When the judge had gone, the jury bailiff escorted her charges back into the jury room and explained that there would be a slight delay while a minibus was procured and a police escort summoned to take them to the hotel. She asked them to use the time to write a list of everyone who needed to be told what was happening.

Melissa wrote the telephone number of the hospital beside Dr Edbury's name on the list that Araminta prepared. Adam, who had no-one to warn, watched her. He was still dismayed by the hostility he had aroused in her by interrupting her protest to Susan.

When they were following the jury bailiff and two of her colleagues out to the minibus, he took the opportunity to hang back a little with Melissa so that he could say, 'I was clumsy earlier on in there. I never meant to upset you.'

'We all got a bit emotional.'

'I know. I'm sorry. It . . . Damn! I can't explain here. We must get an opportunity to talk without all these other people.'

He held her wrist again, but more gently than before, and urged her towards the door. They reached the front steps some two minutes after everyone else to find the bailiff impatiently beckoning. Four burly police motor-cyclists straddled their wide white machines, two in front of the minibus and two behind it. As soon as the doors had been shut behind Adam and Melissa, sirens wailed and blue lights flashed and the short convoy set off.

When the jurors reached the hotel, an anonymous modern one on the outskirts of the city, they were taken in and allocated single rooms.

'A meal will be served to you in the dining room in half an hour's time,' said the jury bailiff. 'You will find toothbrushes and so on in your rooms. I will take you up and collect you in time for dinner. Please do not

leave your rooms without my escort. Do you understand?'

'Yes,' said Araminta, speaking for them all.

When the dwindling crocodile reached the room that
Melissa had been allotted, she shut the door and looked
around. It was not a bad little room, simply furnished
with a single bed under a striped cover, a highly varnished
mahogany-veneered wardrobe, chest of drawers and
dressing table, and orange and green striped curtains to
match the bedcover. There was no telephone or television
or radio.

She took off the jacket of her suit, washed, combed her
hair and replaited it and then made up her face again as
well as she could with the few cosmetics she had in her
handbag. There seemed to be nothing else to do but try
out the bed.

To her later astonishment she fell asleep, to be woken
by loud knocking on the door. Stumbling, only partly
aware of who she was and what was happening, with the
heaviness of her sleep making her sluggish and hazy-eyed,
she opened the door. Memory returned with the obvious
anxiety in the jury bailiff's face.

Melissa smiled at her. 'Sorry. I was asleep. I didn't
realize I was so tired.' She collected her jacket and
handbag and went downstairs with the rest of the jurors.

Several tables had been ranged together to make one
long enough to seat all twelve of them. The three court
officials had a small one to themselves, positioned so that
they could watch, but not overhear, the jurors. They all
sat down to soup, roast chicken and apple crumble and
custard.

'I could do with a proper drink,' said Melissa,
looking with disfavour at the jugs of tap water on the
table.

'Me too,' agreed Dai Davis, who was sitting at her left
as far away from Susan Beere as possible. 'That's the

most sensible thing I've heard you say all day. I can't see why we shouldn't have something. I'll fix it.' He pushed back his chair and walked over to the bailiff's table. After a short discussion he returned to say that she would take orders for drinks, which would, of course, be at each individual juror's expense.

'Would you like something, Adam?' Melissa said. 'I want some wine. How about sharing a bottle?'

'That sounds like a good idea. It should help us sleep, too.' In amongst the flurry of orders being given, he added softly, 'But we need to talk first. My room's next door to yours. May I come in later? Just to talk.'

'Yes,' she said simply. 'I'd like that.'

He waited until half past eleven, when the only sounds that could be heard were from the traffic outside the hotel. Melissa got back into the narrow bed when she had let him in. The only light was from a parchment-shaded reading lamp perched on the small bedside table.

'Are you all right?' he asked, sitting down on the bed, facing her. She pulled the sheet higher round her shoulders and looked at him. Her eyes seemed huge in the half-light. Adam had to grip his hands together to stop himself from reaching out to her.

'Mostly,' she said, smiling to make herself seem less pathetic.

Adam brushed some of the loose blonde hair away from her face. He had not expected to make love to her that night, but he made himself admit that somewhere in his mind had been the thought that she might want him. Reminding himself that her husband had nearly killed himself in front of her only two days earlier, he controlled his childish disappointment at her obvious distance.

'Can I help?' he asked after a moment.

'I don't think so. Among other things, it's just that I

don't feel wholly suitable to be trying this case and . . .'

'Why?' he asked, his voice sharp with shock.

Melissa looked at him, momentarily surprised that he did not know what she was talking about. Then she understood. He had always seemed to be aware of so much that she had idiotically assumed he must have known what she felt as she injected the adrenaline into her husband's arm. She told him all of it, half expecting him to turn away from her in horror.

'Don't even think that you have anything in common with Michael Beechen, Melissa,' Adam said, articulating each syllable with great clarity. 'Everyone has horrible impulses sometimes. We all have the capacity for great evil.'

She waited in silence, thinking that for the first time since she had met him he sounded like a priest.

'But only a very few people ever exercise that capacity. The rest do as you did and keep it under control. Melissa, listen to me. This is immensely important.' He gripped her shoulders through the sheet. There was nothing at all lover-like in his touch. 'You had the thought and you put it away from you. You saved your husband's life. Civilization held. Because of that you are precisely the right sort of person to be trying Michael Beechen. You felt the impulse and you got rid of it. Do you understand what I'm saying?'

'Yes,' she said and then added, 'I feel unbearably weedy. I'm not usually like this at all. I don't know what's come over me. Sorry.'

Adam took his hands away and looked down at them, turning them over so that the light caught the lines on the palms. He longed to comfort her, make love to her, tell her that he would do anything he could to ensure that she was never hurt again. But he knew that in the muddle of feelings into which her husband had thrown her, the last thing she could cope with was anyone else's emotion, or any more demands from anyone. He did his best to give her what she needed.

'I could tell you that you hadn't really felt the impulse; that you're entirely sweet and gentle; that you could never harm anyone, whatever they'd done to you. But what would be the point? You'd hate it, because you'd know it wasn't real, wouldn't you? And you'd hate me for lying to you.'

'Perhaps,' she said, sliding further down the bed and trying to rationalize her conviction that Adam did have the answers she needed if he would only give them to her. 'It's true that I've got myself into a terrible tangle about lies and deceit and kind pretences. But, Adam, I don't understand anything any more. I don't know what's right or wrong. I don't know whose fault anything is; I don't know what I ought to do.'

'About the trial or about your life?' he asked, still trying to keep his own feelings out of the way. She was in real need. He had to ignore the rest. Whatever might come to them in the future, she had to have time to get over the shock of what had happened on Saturday.

'Both. My life I suppose.' She looked away, admitting that she had been letting her imagination play with a thoroughly comforting, self-indulgent, impossible fantasy.

If Martin were to recover and decide to leave her, the dream suggested, she would be free to love Adam and make him happy. She would discover that the gift of herself was not only acceptable but actually wanted, instead of the apparently unbearable burden it had become to Martin. With Adam she would be able to be herself as she was meant to be and make no more pretence about anything. Dr Edbury's warning sounded in her mind like a fire alarm and she came to herself with a shock.

'Why did you stop me speaking earlier?' she asked

abruptly, sounding more aggressive than she had planned. 'In the jury room?'

'I'm sorry,' he said warily. 'I knew that I'd upset you, but I never meant to.'

Melissa did not deny it. She was not going to lie to Adam about anything she felt, ever.

'It was when Susan was saying that the whole thing was Marianna's fault,' she went on. 'I know I was in danger of losing my temper, I know I shouted at her, but you can't have thought I'd have screamed obscenities or done anything embarrassing. Why did you stop me?'

When Adam said nothing, she tried again.

'It was an important point that had to be made – that the child really couldn't have been responsible for anything her parents felt or did to each other. She's eight years old, for goodness' sake. It was a quite appalling thing for that woman to suggest. Appalling, Adam.'

Melissa felt her voice rising and her eyes were hot again.

'I wasn't afraid of embarrassment,' Adam said with difficulty. His body tensed as though he were about to have to do battle with a person or an idea. 'It's just that children being responsible for . . . for adult distress is something I find very hard to talk about.' He paused, and looked down at her. His face was far more open than usual and Melissa flinched from the pain in it.

'I knew it was actually you doing the talking, not me, but I . . .' He stopped again, waited a moment, and then went on more quickly. 'Sometimes you and I seem so alike that I was afraid that what you said might set off all my internal alarms and make me do or say things I couldn't control.'

'Adam, I'm sorry,' Melissa said, apologizing more for the anger she had felt in the jury room than for anything she had said. He put one hand out to touch her cheek.

'Don't look so worried. It never occurred to me that you might see it as my trying to censor you. I can't think why it didn't and I'm sorry.'

'It was just that the idea of not being able to talk about something so important really got to me,' she said, trying to explain. 'I felt a mixture of rage and panic. I don't know why there should have been panic but there was. I was terrified.'

'You showed no sign of it,' said Adam, smiling. 'In fact you just seemed furious.' He looked away, thinking that it might be fair to let her see a little of what he was feeling. 'It rather upset me actually, which made me even less able to understand what was going on.'

'You seemed angry, too,' said Melissa, 'and that made it all the worse.'

'I wasn't angry,'

'Then what was it all about? Can't you tell me?'

He frowned. 'It's hard to talk about.' When he saw how anxious she looked he did his best to explain. 'It's simply that for years . . . No: I'll have to go further back to explain. Stop me if you get bored.'

Melissa nodded.

'My mother was a disappointed woman. She made it clear to me – or I thought she did – that it was my responsibility to make up for that. I was to bring her all the excitement, pride, success, even happiness, that she'd never had.'

Adam broke off, smiling crookedly at Melissa's horrified expression.

'I didn't think it all out until quite recently. What I did was run from the weight of her expectations as soon and as fast as I could. It's been humiliating to get to grips with it, but I'm coming to realize that what I thought was my vocation may have been no more than a flight from my poor unhappy mother.'

In her sudden longing to comfort him, to assuage

303

his misery, Melissa reached for his hands. Adam put them into hers and gripped tight.

'You see, we've all got things to make us feel guilty, things that make us feel destructive,' he said at last.

Melissa pushed away the thought of Dr Edbury.

'What is it?' Adam said quickly. She shook her head. 'I know. I shouldn't have asked; and I shouldn't have loaded my past miseries onto you. You're in the middle of an appalling time, and I'm just making it worse.'

'You're not,' she said and kissed him.

Chapter 20

The next morning there was a heavy, unfriendly atmosphere at the long breakfast table, as though no-one had slept very well or wanted to talk. Most of the jurors had chosen to sit in camps with others who had voted for the same verdicts, but even they were not talking. Once more Susan Beere and Dai Davis were sitting as far apart as possible.

Melissa, who had spent most of the night thinking fruitlessly about Adam, the trial, her father, Martin, her mother, Cecily and herself, and trying to see where her feelings for Adam fitted in with what she might or might not have done to Martin, took a place beside Minty. Both women declined the waitress's offer of bacon and eggs and breakfasted on thin coffee and toast. Adam, Melissa was amused – and rather relieved – to see, ate and drank everything he was offered.

At ten o'clock the jurors were taken back to court, chaperoned by the three officials, in the minibus with its police outriders and escorted back into the jury room. As the door to the outer passage was locked behind them, Melissa felt as though she were being slowly stifled. It was not just the stale airlessness of the jury room, but the knowledge that she was trapped there until at least ten of them could agree on the verdict.

They were called into court. Michael Beechen was in the dock, looking far fresher and better rested than many of the jurors. The barristers were sitting at their tables, the juniors looking curiously towards the jury benches as though trying to assess who was holding up the decision and how it might end. Some of the journalists on the press benches were scribbling in their notebooks. One seemed to be sketching.

'Members of the jury,' said the judge, leaning towards them, 'each of you has taken an oath to return a true verdict according to the evidence. No-one must be false to that oath, but you have a duty not only as individuals but collectively. That is the strength of the jury system. Each of you takes into the jury box with you your individual experience and wisdom. Your task is to pool that experience and wisdom. You do that by giving your views and listening to the views of others. There must necessarily be discussion, argument and give and take within the scope of your oath. That is the way in which agreement is reached. If, unhappily, ten of you cannot reach agreement, you must say so.'

The twelve jurors then trooped back into their stuffy little room and sat down at the scarred table.

'We have got to decide whether we're going to be able to reach a verdict at all,' said Minty firmly enough to give Melissa some hope that they might eventually be released, 'and to do that we need to get to grips with what it is that's been stopping us agreeing. At yesterday's last vote, seven of us wanted to convict Beechen of something and three of us didn't know what to do. I think that's where we've got to start this morning, not with the two who are convinced he's innocent.'

She smiled down the table at Dai Davis, asking, 'Is that all right with you?'

He shrugged. 'I can see it's going to be easier for you to persuade three don't-knows than for me to persuade ten of you he's innocent,' he said. 'Despite what the judge just said, I'm not prepared to give in. I've listened to you all as I had to, but I know what I know.' He folded his arms and swung his legs round so that they were not under the table any more. Crossing them and leaning back in his hard chair, he clearly signalled that he was planning to take no further part in their discussion.

'Right,' said Minty pleasantly, not even bothering to ask Jack Brown what he thought. 'I've been worrying half the night about how we can convince each other, and I think part of the trouble is to do with the amount of proof. I want to ask the judge how much weight we need to put on the prosecution's need to really prove that Michael Beechen intended to kill his wife.'

'A lot, I'd say,' answered Melissa. 'He's innocent until they prove him guilty. That's a basic fact of law. The judge repeated it several times when he was summing up.'

'I know,' answered Minty patiently, 'but I want some ruling on how anyone could actually prove a man's intention of something as straightforward as a kitchen stabbing, unless he'd written a diary or told someone what he was planning to do.'

'That's a fair point,' said Adam.

'Then if everyone agrees, I'll send a note in. Has anyone got a problem with it? Or anything else they want to ask the judge?'

Several heads were shaken. Mrs Crosscombe took the knitting out of her bag and set to work. The others all watched her. Dai Davis lit a cigarette. Susan glanced at him and then turned away.

Eventually, after several minutes' writing, Minty raised her head and said, 'How about this? "How much actual proof would the prosecution have to give of the defendant's state of mind before he killed his wife before a verdict of self-defence became impossible?"'

'Wait a minute,' said Adam. 'I don't think the question is quite clear. Beechen's state of mind isn't relevant. It's his intention. Couldn't you change the words to: "How much proof does the prosecution have to offer of the defendant's intention when he picked up the knife and stabbed his wife"?'

'Yes. That is better. I've got no problem with it. Does anyone?'

'Sounds OK to me,' said Nat, who had taken a squash ball from one of his many pockets and was squeezing it in the palm of his left hand. All the others nodded. Minty rose from the table and went to knock on the door that led into court. When it was opened Minty handed her note to the usher, who then shut the door again.

A few minutes later the jurors were invited back into court yet again.

'Members of the jury,' said the judge, 'you have asked me how much evidence the prosecution must offer about the defendant's intentions when he stabbed his wife. The law is quite clear that the burden of proof is on the prosecution. When you retire to your room again you must use your knowledge and experience of life to assess the evidence you have heard in order to judge whether the prosecution has proved its case. If you are not satisfied that the prosecution has done so, then you must acquit the defendant.' He looked at Minty, who nodded to show that she understood.

'When you are considering your verdict, you must not leave your experience and intelligence at the door of the court. Subject to what I have already said about provocation, you must consider what a reasonable man might have intended when he did as the evidence has shown Michael Beechen did on the night his wife died.' The judge paused for a moment, smiled slightly, and added kindly, 'Does that answer your question?'

Minty frowned and then looked along the bench towards the other jurors. There were several encouraging nods. She looked back at the judge.

'Yes, my lord.'

'Very well.'

The judge rose from his chair and the jurors retired to their stuffy room once again.

'I don't know that it does help much,' said Susan as they all sat down. 'We're left having to guess.'

'Yeah,' said Nat, retrieving the squash ball from his pocket. He started to exercise his right hand.

'No, we don't have to guess,' said Adam. 'I think the judge made it pretty clear. Surely if we use our combined intelligence and knowledge of life to decide what a reasonable man thought would happen if he pushed a four-inch knife into a woman's chest, we have our answer. He must have known that it would do her pretty serious damage, even if he did not expect it to kill her.'

'Although,' said Melissa reluctantly, 'the defence explanation that he started merely trying to shock her into dropping the pan so that she couldn't beat him to death with it still makes sense to me. The photographs did show that most of the wounds were pretty shallow. Georgina Mayford's right about that. It is a credible story, you know, much more so than the prosecution's theory of an eight-year murder plan.'

'And Beechen loved his wife,' said Dai Davis loudly. 'However despicable she was, he still loved her. You can't ignore that, even if you do think he's guilty. There were no witnesses who contradicted what he said.'

'Oh, yes there were,' said Susan, laughing at him in a way that made him glare furiously at her and then shrug as he turned away. 'It's perfectly clear from the evidence we heard from the GP and from Mrs Cawleigh that, whatever he said, Beechen disliked his wife as well as despising her, and that he tried to turn her into something she was not.'

'Rubbish.' Dai Davis took out another of his cigarettes and tapped the filter tip rhythmically on the table, setting Melissa's teeth on edge. She said nothing.

'It only proves that he tried to keep his household in

order,' Davis went on, still tapping. 'He told us he did that – for the children's sake. Give the man credit where it's due. He could well have loved her and yet still have wanted her to behave more like a proper wife.'

'But it wasn't his household,' said Susan, raising her eyes to the ceiling. 'They were married. It should have been a partnership between the two of them, not a battle. You can't understand that, can you?'

'Yes it was his household,' said Davis. 'He paid for it all. She brought no money into the household budget. That was his responsibility.'

Melissa did not hear him as she shut her eyes and turned her mind inwards on itself. Looking back, she could see that her partnership with Martin had never been equal, but she could not in justice put all the blame for that on him. Adam's analysis of the disappointment some women feel when they discover the truth about the men in their lives had not been entirely irrelevant to her. She forced herself to stop her chaotic ideas breeding claims and counter-claims.

Opening her eyes, she saw that Adam was looking at her with concern. Smiling slightly, she felt an extraordinarily powerful need to start her life again, to put things right.

'Melissa?'

'Sorry,' she said, starting at the sound of Adam's voice. 'What is it?'

'You were dreaming,' he said gently. 'Araminta is taking another vote. Everyone else has voted. Innocent. Guilty of murder. Guilty of manslaughter.'

'The last,' said Melissa. 'Manslaughter.'

'Sure?' asked Araminta. Melissa nodded.

'Then we are nearly there.' Minty turned to her left. Ignoring Susan, who was sitting next to her, she said: 'Mrs Crosscombe, couldn't you bear to switch from murder to manslaughter?'

For once Mrs Crosscombe stopped knitting. With the puddle of multi-coloured wool lying on her knee, she sat in silence, staring at the ugly, scratched, dark-oak tabletop. After a tense few minutes, she nodded.

'If it's the only way to have him put him away, I'd agree, reluctantly.'

'He might not be put away,' said Susan sharply. 'If we bring in manslaughter, the judge is perfectly entitled to give him a suspended sentence, or no sentence at all. At least I think so; I can't quite remember.'

'Oh dear,' said Mrs Crosscombe.

'On the other hand,' said Adam, watching her carefully, 'a suspended sentence might be the best thing of all. At least Beechen would know that if he ever did anything else violent, he would go straight to prison. It would be a deterrent.'

'The sentence ain't our problem,' said Nat reasonably, changing hands and squeezing the squash ball with his left. 'We just have to make a verdict. The judge—'

'Just a minute,' said Melissa, who had suddenly remembered something from the evidence they had listened to day after day. She took her notes out of the shoulder bag that was swinging from the back of her chair. 'Susan, do you remember what the expert said?'

'Abel-Fowler? Yes, all too clearly. Which bit?'

'It was when the prosecution asked what might make a battered husband snap and start hitting back,' said Melissa, who was breathing faster than usual.

'Yes,' said Diana Jenkins. Her voice was firmer than it had ever been before and her eyes were brighter. Everyone looked at her in astonishment. It was almost as though one of the chairs had spoken. Even Jack Brown reacted. Diana flushed, but she held her ground for once. 'He said that it could be any particular humiliation or something that reminded him of his childhood. He did, didn't he, Mrs Wraxall?'

'Yes, he did,' said Melissa, smiling at her with real warmth. 'And you probably remember the rest, too. What Marianna said about her parents' quarrel that night?'

'Yes,' said Diana, sounding eager. She was sitting straighter in her chair and she no longer looked afraid. 'She told us what her mother had said about having to wash her father's clothes.'

'That's right,' agreed Melissa. She turned back to Susan. 'You know much more about the subconscious and psychiatry than I do. But wouldn't this make sense?' She paused.

'What?'

'I'm about to explain. Listen. We were endlessly told in court about how clean Beechen is, and also that one of the places where the children had to be specially clean and tidy was his mother's house. He used the word "clean" twice in a short sentence when he was explaining that. The prosecution brought it out, but they didn't make much of it.'

'I don't quite see what they could have made,' said Susan, not aggressively but apparently reluctant to be convinced by anything Melissa might say.

She persevered. 'What if it had always been his mother who was so fanatically clean, and not him at all? What if he had learned as a child that he could never satisfy her standards?' Melissa's voice strengthened as she became more convinced of her own ideas. How many of them had been born from her own muddled thoughts and Dr Edbury's analyses of romantic love, and how many from the evidence itself, she did not know.

'What if that was why he chose Penelope, rather as you said, Susan? Specifically because she was such a slut. He could always be certain that he would be cleaner than she. You did say that he's probably one of those men who's actually so unsure that he needs to have even weaker people around him to make him feel strong and good about himself.'

'Yes,' Susan agreed warily.

'Well then, in tormenting her about her filthiness, he could have been reassuring himself that he was actually perfectly clean himself, despite his memories – subconscious no doubt – of his mother's criticisms. And then when the despised Penelope made that crack about his underpants – wouldn't that have been enough to make him snap?'

Everyone else in the room was silent. Susan's face, which had been stubborn, began to soften as she considered the proposition.

'I do see what you mean,' she said eventually. 'Although it's back to blaming women again, isn't it? We're not pinning all the guilt on Penelope now for his violence, and so we've got to find another woman to blame. His mother's the obvious target.'

'Well, I don't see what you mean, either of you,' said Davis from the head of the table. 'It sounds like a load of cobblers to me. Psychological claptrap. Sort of thing you read in magazines.'

Adam turned his head to look at Melissa, who was finding it difficult to suppress the angry comment that Susan had been quite ready to blame the child for her parents' cruelties to each other.

'It's not blaming but explaining,' Melissa said with deliberate calm. 'After all, Susan, his mother's obsession (if she really had one) will presumably have come from her upbringing, and *her* parents' obsessions from theirs. I think that as an explanation it begins to make sense of everything we've heard. And if we don't explain enough to understand what goes wrong between people, we can't get any further towards getting it right and stopping ourselves hurting each other.'

'Possibly,' said Susan, 'but I'm not a romantic. I don't

believe in human perfectibility. Besides I don't think your analysis goes far enough as an explanation of what happened to the Beechens.'

'Why not? After all, we've been puzzled as to why Beechen should ever have married a woman like Penelope; and we've all been unable to see why he needed to use such force to stop her hitting him with the boiling saucepan. This makes sense. If he lost control because of what she said to him, then he might really not have thought about what the stabbing could do. He might genuinely have panicked and been trying to stop her; not stop her hitting him, but saying those things.'

Melissa, who had been feeling as though the words were spurting out of some part of her mind that was not fully within her control, fell silent, surprised at her own certainty.

No-one else spoke until Araminta said softly, 'Melissa, I think you may have found the key. Those things really do begin to fall into place. And if you're right, that makes manslaughter the obvious verdict, doesn't it? No intent to kill, but not strictly self-defence at all.'

'Well, that is what I think,' said Melissa, who was calming down. 'I detest him, and I hate the fact that he used such violence, but it makes sense to me. He was provoked and so the verdict has to be manslaughter.'

'I agree with you.' Diana Jenkins's voice was firm and her smile looked almost happy for the first time since the trial began.

Mrs Rogers on her left nodded. 'So do I,' she said softly.

'Susan?' said Araminta.

She hissed as she breathed in and then sat with pursed lips, running all the evidence through her mind, checking Melissa's ideas against it.

'It does make sense of a sort,' she said after a while, playing with her long earring again. 'It's all quite neat and it's perfectly possible, but I don't know that we could honestly say that it was proven. Unless we'd heard a psychiatrist examining Beechen and discovering whether he really did have that kind of obsession, we'd never know for certain.'

'Maybe,' said Nat, who had wedged one knee on the edge of the table as he pushed his chair on to its back legs again. His chin was tucked into his neck, which had made his voice come out even deeper than usual. 'But it's the nearest we going to get. Manslaughter makes sense, like Melissa says. We done our job; now it's up the judge.'

'Mr Dent, you haven't said anything at all. What do you think?' asked Minty, looking at the man from the building trade.

He shrugged and adjusted his cuffs again. 'I don't know,' he said. 'It sounds likely enough.' He nodded his head in Nat's direction. 'Like he says, the judge can deal with it now. I don't really care. We've spent enough time in here. I'll go with manslaughter and then we can all go home.'

'OK, good,' said Minty. 'Sue?'

Susan Beere sat with her chin up, refusing to be browbeaten. She said nothing. Mrs Crosscombe looked as though she were about to speak, but Araminta shook her head. It seemed to her that it would be best to let Susan come to her decision alone. Any pressure might make her stubborn.

Eventually she nodded. 'I don't know that it's good enough, but it's clearly all we're going to get. I'll vote with you.'

'Sure?' said Minty. 'You mustn't let us put any pressure on you. We can always say that we're sure we're never going to agree.'

Melissa saw Dai Davis rolling his eyes in frustration.

'Yes, I'm sure,' Susan said, sighing. 'I just hope it's not a suspended sentence.'

There was a ripple of relaxation among many of the jurors as they started to collect their belongings. Melissa thought of the end of a long holiday charter flight when the rumpled, exhausted passengers start collecting their bags of duty-free alcohol and arguing about who has the passports. She stuffed her notes into her own bag. Only Dai Davis and Jack Brown, who had moved his chair closer to his protector's, did not get up.

'Mr Davis, d'you want to say something?' asked Minty, looking at him over her shoulder.

'No,' said Davis angrily. 'There's no point.' Jack Brown nodded his head several times.

'Don't worry, man,' said Nat, watching Davis's face. 'We've given the judge all he needs. He can let him out or bang him up for years. And Beechen can appeal anyway. It's not our problem any more.'

Davis nodded. 'True enough. Well, aren't we going? We've been here long enough getting on each other's nerves.'

Minty smiled. 'You're absolutely right. We need to get it over with. Come on, everyone.'

Once more they walked back into court. Remembering a novel in which a character announced that jurors who have decided to condemn a murderer never look at the defendant, Melissa deliberately faced Michael Beechen as he stood in the dock.

His lips relaxed a little as he saw her looking at him and he nodded to her. She looked dreadfully tired, poor thing, but it was almost over for both of them.

'Members of the jury, have you reached a verdict on which at least ten of you are agreed?' asked the jury bailiff as soon as the court was seated.

'Yes, we have,' said Minty with satisfaction. Georgina Mayford could not quite hide a smile at the sound.

There was a distinct relaxation from people in other parts of the court. Michael stood as easily as possible, remembering all the exercises he had done at drama school. He let his lips curve into his most attractive smile as he looked at the judge.

'Is your verdict guilty or not guilty as charged?

'Not guilty as charged,' said Minty. Michael's smile widened and he looked at Melissa in satisfied gratitude. 'But guilty of manslaughter.'

Michael's smile died as he stared into Melissa's face, squinting slightly in an effort to overcome the distance between them. She can't have tried hard enough, he thought. She knew what happened. I know she did. I could see it in her face. That man got to her. He must have. He probably seduced her last night in the hotel and made her change her mind. He has forced her to destroy me.

Adam, feeling Melissa flinch, looked at her face and then across at the dock. He touched her wrist and whispered, 'Don't worry. You've done your job. Don't look at him.' Melissa bowed her head.

'Is that the verdict of you all or by a majority?' asked the bailiff.

'It is the verdict of ten of us,' answered Minty gravely.

The judge smiled at the jurors with what looked like approval, announced that the court would be adjourned until pre-sentence reports could be produced, and that Michael Beechen would be remanded in custody until then.

Michael despaired as he watched the jurors begin to leave the court. The thought of the fourteen dark steps down from the dock to the cells filled him with horror. He willed Melissa to look at him before she left the jury box so that she could see what she had done to him. It was her duty to share what he was being made to feel. It was her responsibility. Her fault.

She refused to look at him. Michael watched her edge along the row of seats and step down to the floor, deliberately keeping her back to him. He stared at her neat, blond plait, silently begging her to turn. He felt sick and furious. As she reached the door and he realized she was not going to turn back, his self-control snapped.

'Melissa,' he shouted. His two warders began to move towards him and he rushed on, 'Don't turn away from me. Look at me. Melissa. You're killing me. Look at me. For Christ's sake, Melissa, look at me.'

With her hand on the double doors, Melissa stopped. She knew she ought not to look back. She heard him wail her name again and turned.

The warders on either side of him had gripped his arms. They were dragging him down towards the stairs. His face was turned painfully towards Melissa and tears were pouring down his cheeks in what looked like sheets of water.

The double doors seemed to give way under her hands as she leaned forwards. She found herself outside the court, gasping: 'How did he know my name?'

Michael Beechen's pain and rage seemed far more real than the voices she could hear around her. She looked around for Adam, but she could not see him. A deep voice said, 'He heard all our names when we were called in court at the beginning. Don't you remember? He probably remembered yours because you're a pretty girl.'

Melissa took a grip on herself and saw that it was Dai Davis who had been talking. He was looking at her much more kindly than usual.

'Don't let him get to you, love. You've done your best.' He turned to Sue Beere. 'So that's it, is it?'

'That's right,' said Susan. 'It's over now. We've done our job and finished annoying each other. You and I could never agree, Mr Davis, but can we part pleasantly at least?'

Davis hesitated for only a moment before he shook her hand.

'Don't we get to hear what the sentence is?' he asked.

'Only if it's reported in the media,' said Susan, accepting his acknowledgement of her greater experience with a smile.

'What happens next?' asked Melissa with difficulty.

'The judge will ask for pre-sentence reports on Beechen's character, any police record, on his family, his prospects of supporting them, that sort of thing. Prosecuting counsel will say why a long sentence is necessary and Georgina Mayford will argue for a suspended one. She'll tell the judge how cooperative Beechen was during police interviews—'

'But he refused to confess,' protested Nat, who was also listening with interest. 'They told us that.'

'Yes, but they said he answered all their questions quite politely, and no-one can deny that he called the doctor immediately after the killing. He didn't even wash the blood off his hands, let alone cut up or try to conceal the body. That always goes down very badly with judges and police.'

'What do you think he'll get?'

'I haven't a clue,' said Susan. 'I wish that we could listen.'

'Can't we?' said Nat. 'We're members of the public. We can go straight in to the public benches if we want.'

'I'm not sure that we can, actually,' said Susan less bossily than usual. 'I think the rules are that no-one can enter the court after the judge's summing-up.'

'Pity,' said Nat, pulling the hood of his sweatshirt up over his neat head. 'I'd like to know.'

'I think I just want to get out of here,' said Melissa, walking towards the door that led out to the street. When she reached the front steps, she breathed deeply and received a lungful of exhaust from a lorry that had just driven by. Choking, she turned away and saw Adam at last.

'I don't think I can go straight home after that,' she said. 'I need some proper air. Would you come for a walk with me? Somewhere we can breathe properly.'

'Yes, all right,' he said. 'What about Clifton Down? It's wonderfully open up there. I'll be with you in a moment.'

Melissa watched while he meticulously thanked and said goodbye to all the other jurors, spending longest with Minty Collins. Melissa contented herself with a smile or a nod or a brief word with any of them who bothered to approach her.

The last was Susan, who said, 'There were times in there when you drove me nearly mad, but I think you probably were right in the end.'

'Thank you,' said Melissa. 'I knew I was making you angry, but it seemed important to keep the line I thought was the right one.'

'It was. I was angry because I didn't realize you were thinking about any of it. You look and sound so confident, so secure in your class and prejudices, that I assumed you were anti-Penelope because of the type of woman she was. My own prejudice coming out no doubt.'

Melissa shook her head. 'I felt desperately sorry for her all along,' she said, adding quietly, 'and for the child.'

'Well, there we always will differ,' said Susan with some of the old tartness. 'I must be off. I don't suppose we'll ever meet again.'

'No, probably not,' said Melissa, shaking her hand. 'But I'll look out for your articles with interest.'

Susan smiled for the last time, turned away and raised her hand in a backwards wave.

'Are you all right?' asked Adam from just behind Melissa.

'Yes. But I want to get out of here. I feel as though I've got the smell of that horrid little room right down in my lungs.'

In a few minutes they were in the car, heading out of Bristol. Adam efficiently directed her to a steep wooded hill that led eventually to the openness of the down, which was a pleasant mixture of neatly mown grass and wild clumps of coppice-like trees and bushes. There, Melissa parked and they got out of the car to walk, facing towards the sea, breathing in the cold, fresh air.

There were a few other people braving the wind, walking their dogs or their children, but no-one was near enough to hear anything they said to each other. Alone with Adam, feeling the strong, clean-tasting wind pushing into her mouth, Melissa began to feel better.

'There's a seat over there,' she said at last, pointing to a bench that was sheltered from the wind by a large clump of brambles. 'Shall we?'

Adam walked beside her in silence and they sat down.

'D'you think we got it right?' she said at last, trying to exorcise the memory of Beechen struggling in the dock, yelling her name. 'His panic and his motives, I mean?'

'God knows. But I thought your intervention was masterly. It made sense of all the things that were otherwise absurd – and it got us a majority for the verdict both you and I wanted from the beginning. And it squared with all the evidence we'd heard. I think we did as well as we could. We'll know whether the judge agreed with us when we find out what the sentence is going to be.'

'I suppose so,' said Melissa, staring into the wind.

'What's the matter?' asked Adam after a while. 'I mean, particularly at this moment.'

She turned and smiled quickly at him, wishing that they could have met in some ordinary, neutral way and been friends.

'I was just thinking about that marriage and the hell it must have been for them. Both of them, I mean. If we were right, just think of the mixed signals Beechen was sending his wife: telling her that she was disgusting and yet at the same time actually needing her to be like that; provoking her into fury, perhaps wanting her to be wild so that he could be sure she was out of control, and then turning away in his superior fashion so that all she could do was hit him. Think how lonely she must have been.'

'I don't suppose it was deliberate,' said Adam. 'If your idea of him is right, then none of it can have been conscious behaviour at all. It sounded as though he understood himself as little as he understood her. He was probably lonely, too.'

'I know,' said Melissa, turning to look at him. Her eyes were wet, but the wind that had been blowing into them was cold enough to make anyone's eyes water. 'That's what's making me feel so awful.'

'Oh?' After a moment he added: 'Yes, I see. Melissa, I wish I could help.'

'You do,' she said at once. 'I can't tell you how much having you as a friend is helping me deal with all this. I . . . I just hope it's not wicked exploitation. You see, you were there; you saw; and you understand so much.'

'I'm glad,' he said after a long silence. He suddenly brushed the back of his neck and then laughed. 'I couldn't think what it is, but I've been leaning against a bramble.'

Seeing the blood on his fingers, Melissa took a clean handkerchief out of her bag and gave it to him.

'I've been maundering on and you've been putting up with thorns digging holes in your neck. Come on, Adam. I'll drive you home and let you get on with your life.'

Drawing up outside his house half an hour later, Melissa put the car in neutral and pulled up the hand-brake. Adam unlatched his safety belt.

'Melissa, in case we don't meet again . . .'

'Adam, don't say that,' she said before she could stop herself.

'But we must be realistic.' His voice was very deep. 'If it happens, I want to say now that having known you for even so short a time has meant a great deal to me.'

'And to me,' she said, hardly able to bear the thought that she might never see him again.

'You've given me something that I don't think I shall ever lose. Goodbye.'

Before she could say anything he had shut the door and walked up the slippery path to his small dark-grey house. Melissa sat trying to understand what he had been talking about.

A little later she felt for her handkerchief to blow her nose again and realized that he had kept it. Shrugging, she sniffed disgustingly, put the car back in gear and drove across the city to the Circus.

Chapter 21

Melissa wanted to get back to work and normality as soon as she reached the Circus, but she felt as though she would be in limbo until she knew not only what Martin wanted of her but also what was going to be done to Michael Beechen.

She telephoned the hospital as soon as she got home, and Dr Edbury gave her a fairly encouraging report of Martin's progress. Physically he was recovering well, if rather weak still, and mentally he would probably be ready to leave the hospital in a few days' time. Until then, Melissa knew she could do nothing but wait.

Having gone downstairs to the offices, she spoke to Bel and the two designers, thanked them for their sympathy over Martin's 'illness' and for all the extra work that her absence had landed on them. They seemed wonderfully normal, and she began to hope that she would be able to submerge herself in work again.

She went through the day's post and answered some urgent questions from Annabel, but she could not settle to all the less immediate things that needed doing. The zest with which she had once worked seemed impossible to recreate. Eventually, having shifted piles of paper from one end of her desk to the other and made several unnecessary and unproductive telephone calls, she decided to take the rest of the day off. One thing she thought she could usefully do was talk to her mother and repair whatever damage her clumsiness had done on Sunday.

There was no sign of Abigail in her house, although

the doors were unlocked and the evidence in the kitchen suggested that she had been in the middle of preparing a meal. Checking the gravelled parking space between the house and the old stables, Melissa saw that her mother's car was lined up beside a blue Mercedes which she had never seen before. Assuming that Abigail had been hijacked by an important visitor, Melissa walked over to the shop to talk to Ann until the strangers left.

When she reached the shop, she saw Ann sitting on her high stool beside the till talking to a tall fair woman who was dressed in jeans and an old blue Barbour and looked vaguely familiar. Melissa waved to Ann when she looked up, and, in order to demonstrate her unwillingness to interrupt, turned aside to examine a shelf full of antique honey jars.

She heard footsteps approaching her and turned to see the visitor standing about a foot away with an accusing expression in her blue eyes.

'Why have you followed us here?' she demanded. 'You're worse than the damned journalists.'

'I don't understand,' said Melissa stiffly. She felt that she had no obligation to give an explanation but did so out of an instinctive politeness and a desire to protect her mother's business interests. 'I'm here because Abigail Hansford is my mother. Who are you?'

'Oh, don't play games. I recognize you from court. Are you really her daughter?'

'Yes. Ann can vouch for me,' said Melissa slowly as she began to understand why the woman had seemed familiar. Her smooth fair hair and blue eyes, let alone the shape of her fine-boned face, made it clear enough. 'You must be a relation of Michael Beechen. What a strange coincidence that you should be here.'

Too late Melissa remembered that on the day when Martin had nearly died her mother had said that she knew Marianna Beechen. The memory had been completely submerged by everything that had happened since.

'I'm Jane Beechen – his sister – and the only reason I'm here is that his daughter insisted on coming before we leave the area.' Her voice was clipped and angry. 'There's nothing else to keep us here. I don't want her hanging about in a hotel until the judge decides he's ready to pass sentence.'

'There isn't really anything to say, is there?' Melissa said after a long pause. She was deeply embarrassed. 'To beg you not to be angry would be absurdly childish. We did what we had to do. And you must hate us for it. I can understand that.'

'Well, that's something.'

Jane Beechen paused and looked around the long, low, light room with its pale beechwood tables and shelves filled with brightly jacketed books, gleaming jars of honey, candles, beeswax polish and cosmetics. Then she looked back at Melissa. A little of the hostility had gone.

'Your mother seems to have given Marianna the knowledge that there are some dispassionately kind and completely trustworthy adults in the world, which is why I was prepared to bring her here this morning.'

'I'm glad that Marianna has found some reassurance,' said Melissa as neutrally as possible. 'She must have needed it.'

'Clearly,' said Jane, her lips straightening into a tight line. She turned away and was looking out of the window to where Abigail could be seen lifting the roof off one of the hives. There was a small figure at her side, dressed like her in a white boiler-suit and veiled hat.

'She said that there was something she had to ask your mother,' said Jane, still not looking at Melissa, 'but she wouldn't tell me what it was.'

Melissa did not comment. There seemed to be no

point. But she could not just leave without saying anything else.

'It wasn't lightly done, you know,' she said at last.

Jane Beechen turned away from the window. Melissa saw that there was anger and a frightening coldness in her eyes again. They stood in silence. Melissa looked round for help, but Ann was checking the money in the till. Turning back, Melissa opened her mouth to ask some anodyne question, but she was forestalled when Jane Beechen said suddenly, 'You know she's started to scream in the night.'

'Has she? I mean, I'm not surprised. The whole experience of the trial and giving evidence, quite apart from anything that happened before, must have shaken her dreadfully.'

'Yes, but . . .' The older woman broke off whatever she had been going to say and looked at Melissa with a pleading expression, which she did not understand at all, but which reminded her vividly of the way Michael had stared at her from the dock. She found it hard not to shudder.

'What's the matter?' she asked at last when the silence had become too uncomfortable to be borne.

Jane frowned and twisted her fingers together.

'She's screaming that she wants her mother. Night after night, she cries out for Penelope. Oh God!' Her voice cracked and then steadied. 'I don't know why I'm telling you, of all people.'

Melissa could not help. The feelings that showed in the other woman's face made her feel like a peeping tom and she looked away.

'I think,' she said eventually, dredging the words up from some unconsidered part of her mind, 'that perhaps she couldn't let herself admit how much she missed her mother until now. She's very young after all. Whatever the truth about that night, Marianna is only eight and she must have loved her mother whatever she was like. She's probably lonely and frightened.'

'Yes; no doubt,' said Ms Beechen, the mask of competence sliding back over her emotions. The two of them looked out of the mesh-covered windows to watch Abigail leaning down to catch something Marianna said to her as they approached the stable block. 'Here they come.'

Marianna was chatting and smiling as she led Abigail back towards the building. She seemed so different from the silent, anxious child she had been in the witness box that Melissa could not help looking to see what effect her apparent happiness was having on her aunt. There was a wistfulness in her chilly eyes.

'I can't do that yet,' she said. 'But with care and patience – and probably luck – I may.' She raised her voice. 'Mrs Hansford, you've been very kind.'

Melissa moved away so that Marianna would have no opportunity of recognizing her. She took a large book down from the shelf and pretended to read it, but she could not resist watching the little group from behind the book.

'It's a real pleasure', said Abigail, looking down at the child, 'to discuss bees with someone as interested and intelligent as Marianna.'

The child looked up at Abigail and smiled shyly but with complete trust.

'I hope I'll see you again soon, Marianna.'

'You can be sure of that,' answered Jane Beechen. 'Can't she?'

'Yes, Aunt Jane,' whispered the child, looking at the floor once again.

'We had better go. Thank you very much indeed, Mrs Hansford.'

'Until the next time we meet, Ms Beechen. I'll see you to your car.' As they left, Abigail looked over her shoulder at Melissa and smiled, adding: 'I won't be long.'

'Poor little thing,' she said a few minutes later as she rejoined Melissa. 'Come on over to the house. We can have some lunch and talk.'

'Thanks. The aunt seems sensible and quite kind,' said Melissa. 'I had no idea they'd be here today or I'd never have come.'

'I was surprised, too. Once I read about the trial I assumed that I'd never see her again. I'm glad the aunt was prepared to bring her. Did you two talk?'

'A bit.' Melissa took her mother's arm for a moment and was glad when Abigail pressed closer to her before releasing herself. 'Thank goodness you and I can talk about it all now. Do you think we got the verdict right?'

'I can't possibly tell you that,' said Abigail. 'I've no idea. But Marianna was undoubtedly afraid of her father, so you may well have done.'

'And of her mother, surely?'

'Good heavens, yes. That part of the evidence squared with the hints she gave me.'

'Before the murder?' asked Melissa curiously.

'No, today,' said Abigail. 'If she'd told me while her mother was still alive, I'd presumably have had to do something, although . . .'

'Wouldn't your philosophy of non-interference have held?'

Abigail frowned. 'I don't know,' she said eventually. 'Luckily I didn't have to decide.'

As they walked into the big, welcoming kitchen, which smelled of coffee, proving bread dough, honey and spices, fried onions, seared meat and wine, Melissa asked, 'What was the question?'

'What question?'

'Jane Beechen said that Marianna had to come to see you before they left the area because she had a question to ask you.'

'Oh, I see. She wanted to be certain that what I had told her about the queens was true,' said Abigail.

'Which was?'

'That no-one knows whether they are the rulers or the slaves of the workers, whether they are endlessly fed and groomed to please them or to keep them imprisoned while they produce eggs for the hive.'

Melissa shuddered. It was not a new idea for her, but it seemed sinister in a way it never had before.

'Was she satisfied?'

Once more Abigail smiled, but she no longer looked amused.

'No. She said: "But if you don't know whether she's their ruler or their prisoner, how do you know whether they hate her or love her?"'

'And what did you say to that?' asked Melissa after a pause.

'I told her that no-one has to decide, that it doesn't matter. All the bees in the hive behave in the way that maximizes the colony's chances of survival. And, for bees, it is only survival that matters.'

'But that wasn't really what she wanted to know, was it?' said Melissa slowly, trying to hold back a thought so bitter that she could not believe it had come out of her own mind. The disloyalty of it appalled her. She looked at her mother and tried to hold down the thought. Like the jack-in-the-box, it kept screaming up at her. She turned aside and closed her eyes, letting the words say themselves inside her mind.

So, Marianna has got to pretend that nothing's happened too, has she? She's got to save you from the pain of knowing that it does matter and she is hurting. Horrible, frightening, emotion-laden pictures appeared in her mind.

'Presumably not,' Abigail was saying, sounding a

330

little worried, 'but the answer must be the same. No child should have to choose between her parents. No child should be put in the position of having to judge one against the other, side with one against the other.'

Melissa opened her eyes and turned back. 'No,' she said with an effort. 'I think you're right about that.'

'Sit down,' said Abigail, laying two places at the big pine table. 'Is bread and cheese all right for you? The casserole is for tonight; it won't be ready for hours.'

'Bread and cheese's fine. I don't really need anything. Please don't be hurt.'

'I'm not, Melissa.' Abigail came to stand beside her daughter and stroked her hair. It was obvious that she had understood. 'But I'm beginning to feel as though I've hobbled you. I thought I was doing the best thing by keeping all the horrors away from you, but Joan says—'

'What?' asked Melissa angrily. 'What business is it of hers?'

'Don't be cross, darling. She's very fond of you, and she's been trying for ages to make me see that our closeness might not be the good thing I've always thought it.'

'That's nonsense,' said Melissa, burying her memories of Martin's angry resentment. 'How could any kind of affection be bad?'

Abigail shrugged, shook her head, tried to speak, and then smiled sadly. At last she said, 'She also thinks that because I never let you understand your feelings about your father, you couldn't know why you felt this compulsion to look after damaged people. She believes that it's come from the same thing as your obsession with the house – so that you could placate your father's ghost.'

'It all sounds rather like Hamlet, doesn't it?' said Melissa with grim humour. 'Or what one of my fellow jurors called "psychological claptrap; kind of thing you read in magazines".'

'Perhaps,' said Abigail a little more lightly. 'But if she's right, I have damaged you and that was the last thing I ever wanted.'

'I know,' answered Melissa. 'I once told Adam that you have the most tremendous guts and that he'd never be able to understand how much I admired you. I still feel that – and more. You do know that, don't you, in amongst all the rest?'

As Melissa watched, her apparently invulnerable mother looked at her and let her see something that had always been hidden before. Strong Abigail might be, Melissa realized for the first time, but she was not inviolable. The loneliness that Melissa had only just begun to acknowledge in her own life had been part of Abigail's, too. Perhaps that, she thought, has been the real price of all the well-meant lies we've told each other, and other people.

'I'm glad,' said Abigail. 'But if there's anything else you want to know about it all, do ask. Now that we've started talking, I'll try to tell you whatever I can.'

Touched, hurting, but aware at last that unhappiness was not necessarily a shameful weakness that ought to be denied even to herself, Melissa shook her head.

'Let's have some of that cheese,' she said with deliberate cheerfulness. Abigail's face lightened at once. She patted Melissa's hand briefly and went to fetch a half-Stilton and a fresh goat's cheese from the larder.

Chapter 22

Martin came home two days later. Melissa was at her desk calculating the final quotation for the furniture and accessories that Dick Walston was planning to order. The designers were hard at work in the studio and Annabel was on the telephone in Melissa's office, arranging for her to see her glassblower the following afternoon. They both heard the front door slam.

'That must be Martin,' said Melissa after a moment.

Annabel said goodbye to the glassblower and put down the telephone receiver. 'Can I do anything?'

Melissa shook her head. 'Just hold the fort here – as you've been doing these last two weeks. Bel, I don't know what I'd have done without you. You've . . . well, you know what you've done for me.'

'It's been a pleasure. I just wish I could help with some of the more important stuff.'

'You're an angel. But I'll cope. I'd better go up and see what's what. I'll see you later.'

Annabel watched her go, amazed as so often before by the apparently unending patience Melissa showed with her dreadful husband's constant bullying and sullenness. How she put up with it all, Annabel would never know. She started to tidy Melissa's desk, which was all she could think of to do to express her solidarity.

Upstairs Melissa found her husband in their bedroom, packing. She stood for a while in the doorway watching him and then said, 'You should have rung, Martin. I'd have collected you from the hospital.'

He turned and glared at her. She walked over to the window and sat down in the soft grey-silk chair, looking out at the perfect circle of houses and the leafless, leaning plane trees in the centre of the Circus.

'What are you waiting for?' he asked aggressively.

She turned to smile at him. 'Just to find out what you want from me.'

He threw a pile of shirts down on the Irish linen and lace coverlet and turned back to wrench open the drawer where he kept his underclothes.

'Why should it matter what I want? It never has before.'

'Martin, we have to talk without playing any more games with each other. I need to know what it is you want from me. I may not be able to provide it, but if I don't know what it is then there's certainly nothing I can do to get it right.'

There was a long pause.

'I want you to be as you were when we married,' he said gruffly. 'When we were happy.'

Melissa looked back out of the window, trying to think of the right thing to say.

'You were happy then, too,' Martin burst out, banging a pair of shoes on to the lid of the second suitcase. 'Until you started to put us through this hell.'

'You talk', she said slowly, still looking at the plane trees, 'as though it's all been my choice and my doing.'

'Well, hasn't it?'

At that she turned back to look at him. 'No, I don't think it has, Martin. Obviously I've played my part, although it's never been deliberate and I'm still not completely sure what it's been; but don't you think you've had a hand in it, too?'

'No,' he said, snapping down the locks of the first suitcase and flinging back the lid of the next. The shoes fell on to the fragile lace, tearing it. He picked them

334

up and threw them into the case with several pairs of heavy brogues from the bottom of his wardrobe and then proceeded to stuff neatly rolled socks into the corners. 'We'd have been perfectly happy if you'd stayed as you were. But you changed and changed until you grew so selfish that . . .' He broke off but the message seemed unmistakable: you wouldn't give me what I needed and so I turned to Cecily for it. It's your fault.

'Martin,' Melissa said, breathing carefully to contain her distress, 'do you really think that you haven't changed at all in the last ten years? Do you think that I haven't longed for those days when we could still be happy together?'

'You've shown no signs of it,' he said, laying corduroy trousers on top of his shoes and socks. 'If you'd wanted that, we would have been happy all the time. I've never understood why you wanted to throw it all away, but I can't forgive it. Sorry. But there it is.'

Remembering what Dr Edbury had said about her refusal to argue with Martin, Melissa ignored her inclination to leave him alone to pack, and for once she tried to explain herself.

'I have never wanted to throw away any of the good things we had, as you must know if you'd stop blaming me for a minute. I suspect what you haven't been able to forgive is what has happened to us both – both, Martin. Haven't we both discovered as we grew up that the person we thought we married is quite different from our imaginings?'

'There was nothing imaginary about the girl you were.'

'What was I, then?'

'You were sweet, gentle, feminine, loving. But you decided to despise me years ago, didn't you, Lissa? That's when the trouble started. All your contempt for me, my work and my ambitions. You flouted everything I told you to do. You went out of your way to show me that you don't respect me any more. You—'

Angry then, as well as hurt, Melissa said quietly, 'If I've despised anything about you, Martin, it's been your inability to share. You can't share either the good things or the bad, can you? It took me a long time to understand that, but you have to have all of the good and nothing of the bad. Always. You have to be the winner, and you can never be wrong, can you?'

She stopped for a moment and then added more quietly, 'That's partly my fault, because in the beginning I accepted it. I let you put all your failures on to me, and I felt guilty for being so miserable about it. Yes, to that extent I have changed; I won't any longer let you make me a scapegoat. If that's what's upset you so much, then I'm sorry too, but there's nothing I can do about it.'

Martin banged down the lid of his suitcase. At the sight of his face, Melissa felt physically frightened, but he did not move away from the bed and eventually she relaxed.

'I really hate you, you know,' he said quietly.

'Yes, I know you do.'

'I'm going now.'

'Fine,' she said, wondering what she ought to say next. If he were really leaving, then there were things they needed to discuss. 'Will you be at Cecily's?'

'I don't think that's any of your business any more.' Martin hoisted his two heavy suitcases off the bed and then dumped them down on the floor. Dragging his keys from his pocket, he pulled three off the ring, flung them on the bed and picked up his cases again.

Melissa stayed in her chair, looking out over the Circus and hearing speeches for the prosecution and for the defence echoing through her mind. She saw Martin's car leave the Circus by Bennet Street and knew that he must be going to Cecily's flat.

Looking round her bedroom, which she had loved for its austere, pale-grey and cream elegance, she tried to think what she ought to do next. The house, once her refuge, her plaything and her insurance, was like an albatross around her neck. She felt completely alone, cut off from the rest of the human race by the things she had done. However much the rational part of her mind might tell her that it had not all been her fault, she could not get rid of the feeling that the responsibility at least was hers.

The door of her bedroom opened twenty minutes later and Annabel looked round it.

'I heard him go, Lissa. Is there anything I can get you?'

Melissa turned to look at her secretary and shook her head.

'Lissa, don't,' said Annabel. 'Don't. He's not worth that much anguish.'

Melissa covered her eyes for a moment. 'I'll be all right. You go on home. I can't . . . talk about it now.'

'Can't I stay? Make you some supper or something? Lissa, I don't think you should be on your own just now. I won't talk or get in your way.'

Melissa managed to laugh. 'I'll be fine. It's just signing off after ten years and knowing quite how badly I've failed. I need to be on my own, Bel. I've always been better at dealing with things alone. Don't worry about it. I'll be down in the office at nine tomorrow.'

'Sure?'

'Yes. I won't be late. No, it's all right, I know that's not what you meant. You're a good friend, but there's nothing you can do here, now. Good night. Go on: go.'

'Bye. Call me if you change your mind. You've got my number.' Annabel paused in the doorway and then added in a rush just before she turned to go, 'You know all three of us are firmly on your side. If anyone failed it was Martin. He was awful to you; he really was.'

Melissa watched the door close. Bel's affectionate partisanship was kind, but at that moment it did not help. After a time the pain would stop and real life would go on, but for the moment Melissa did not know quite how to bear it. All her usual remedies seemed silly. She did not want a hot bath, or anything to eat or drink; she knew that she could not work or read. Hating her own company for the first time in her life, she could not bear the thought of having to talk to anyone else.

Eventually she looked at her watch and saw that it was six o'clock. Getting out of her chair, she left the bedroom, which still seemed to be full of Martin's anger, and went downstairs to watch the news on television. She sat through a series of international horrors, hardly registering what she saw and heard of the wars, the famines, and the imminent economic collapse of nations. The weather forecast was almost over before she realized that the news had stopped and she vaguely heard that there were to be more thunderstorms. Inertia held her in the chair as the local news started and her mind did not begin to focus until she heard the newsreader say:

'In the case of Michael Beechen, found guilty of the manslaughter of his wife on Tuesday of this week, the judge passed sentence earlier today. Our reporter was in court.'

The picture changed from the smartly dressed and jewelled woman in the studio to a shot of a man in a dark overcoat and red scarf standing outside the Old Guildhall in Bristol.

'The judge told Michael Beechen that, even though he had not been found guilty of murder, his offence was extremely serious. He accepted that Beechen's wife had offered considerable provocation during their marriage and on the night in question, but the action her husband took when he stabbed her to death was not, said the judge, the action of a reasonable man. It showed a severe lack of self-control and demonstrated that Beechen has an ability to resort to violence that made it imperative

338

for the court to impose a custodial sentence on him.'

The news reporter moved a few steps nearer to the camera.

'Beechen's counsel had argued that a custodial sentence would separate him from his children, but the judge decided that a separation would not be to their detriment. "Society," he said, "and particularly its younger members, must be protected from the violence that has become all too rife these days. The savagery with which you attacked your wife and the wholly unwarrantable force that you used to prevent her hitting you mean that I have no option but to sentence you to ten years in prison."'

The telephone began to ring. Melissa got up to switch off the television and then picked up the receiver.

'Hello?' she said, forgetting to give her name or number as she usually did.

'Melissa? It's Adam. Did you hear the sentence?'

'Yes.'

'It's about as much as he would have served if we'd convicted him of murder and he'd got life.'

'So it is,' she said, finding it quite hard to talk. 'So the judge didn't think him innocent either.'

'Melissa.' Adam's voice had changed, become more urgent. 'Are you all right?'

'Yes, I'm fine,' she said, remembering the way he had said goodbye to her outside his house. She could not impose yet another burst of marital misery all over him.

'May I come and see you?'

'Do you want to?'

'You must know that I do. Melissa, what is it?'

'Nothing.' She made an effort and smiled to make her voice sound more lively. 'I'd like to see you. When were you thinking of? We could have a meal some time next week in your nice restaurant.'

'I'm thinking of now. May I come? Would it be

inconvenient? Would you rather I didn't see you?' After a pause he added: 'Melissa, are you still there?'

'Yes.'

'Well, what about now? May I come? Is Martin there? Back from hospital?'

'No. Um. I'm on my own. All right.'

'Good. Stay there. I'll be with you as soon as I can.'

She shivered as she heard him put his receiver down. Only then did she remember that he had no car and might have difficulty getting down from Bear Flat. She dialled his number, but there was no answer. Rubbing her aching forehead, she wished that she could think properly. The thought of seeing Adam was like balm, but she knew that she ought to have put him off until she could be certain of herself again.

The front-door bell rang ten minutes later and she almost ignored it. She did not want to be tied up with someone else when Adam came. It was going to be hard enough pretending to be normal with one person, let alone two. But eventually the bell rang again and she went downstairs to see who it was.

'Where were you?' she asked as she opened the door and found Adam waiting on the step. 'You can't have crossed the whole of Bath so soon.'

'At a friend's round the corner.' He put an arm around her shoulders and urged her back inside the house. 'Melissa, tell me what's happened.'

'Come on up to the drawing room,' she said, leading the way to the first floor.

Adam almost sighed as he saw the perfection of the room again with its subtle colours, silk curtains, gleaming eighteenth-century furniture, paintings and china. It was an infinitely more luxurious room than any of her mother's, let alone anything in his tiny white-walled house. He wondered whether he was making a stupid mistake. Then he looked at Melissa's face again and

340

knew that he was right. He made her sit down on a pale-yellow sofa. Sitting beside her, holding her hands, he said again, 'Melissa, tell me.'

She blinked. 'Martin's out of hospital,' she said. 'He's been here to pack and . . . well, to go.'

'I am sorry.'

She clung to his hands, wishing that she could let him know all the things she was thinking without the clumsiness of words getting between them. It seemed terribly important that he should really know what had happened and what it meant.

'It's silly,' she said at last, 'because I've been wanting to know for ages what he really thinks – and to be free of him, too. In fact, I've wanted that terribly.'

'I know. You told me.'

'But when he said . . .' She broke off, trying to hang on to control of her voice and her eyes. 'When he said he hated me, I . . .' She could not go on and pulled her hands out of his so that she could wipe her eyes.

'Adam, you don't want to hear all this,' she said a moment later, smiling vaguely in a way that made him shiver. 'How about some tea? No; wrong time of day. A drink? You'd like a drink, wouldn't you? I'll get a tray.'

'No, thank you. Melissa, I didn't come here for anything but to see you, and help if I could. Don't worry about me.'

'How can I not?'

'What do mean?'

'I like you,' she said, looking at him with no defences at all. 'I did from the beginning. And now I know that it's more than that, much more. I feel all kinds of things for you that make me afraid.'

His severe face had relaxed as he heard the first part of her declaration. 'Why afraid?'

'Because', she said, looking down at her hands, 'I have made such a mess of things with Martin, and . . .' She thought of her mother and Cecily and her father. 'I seem to hurt everyone I care about. I couldn't bear to do it to you, too. I feel as though I ought not even to have let you come here, but I so much wanted to see you again.'

'Well, that makes two of us,' he said more lightly. 'Melissa, I can understand why you feel a bit tragic at the moment, but you must not blame yourself for what happened to Martin. Please, don't do that. You are . . . Listen.'

'I'm listening.'

'He's wrong about you. He may have lived with you for ten years, but he doesn't know you. Something got in the way of that. You mustn't believe that he knew you as you are. You're not the woman he believed caused all his miseries. You're really not.'

'Are you sure you know me?' she said, sounding a little more like herself.

'Yes. I am. Almost since the first day I met you, I've known who you are and what you're like. And everything you've said and been and done since then has shown me that I was right. Ever since then I've been hearing this voice in my mind telling me that I've run away for long enough, that if love is ever going to mean anything for me, it means you.'

'Adam,' she said, letting him take her hands again.

'I've not said anything because I knew you couldn't deal with any more emotion at the moment. I wouldn't have said anything now, except that I couldn't bear you to think anything so . . . so loopy. Melissa, you're the most beautiful, most astonishing woman I've ever met. I wish that there were words to tell you how you make me feel, how I'd risk anything to be allowed to love you.'

He held her hands against his face.

'I know that this is too soon and you can't possibly know what you feel, whether you will come to feel anything like this, but I—'

'But I do, Adam,' she said. 'And that's why I'm afraid.
I've made such a mess, such an appalling mess of it all,
before. I long to get it right, to connect properly, to love
and not . . . harm you. But I don't think I know how.'

'Perhaps it's something we can learn together,' he said,
holding on to her. 'I told you that day by the river in
Bristol that we all have things in ourselves and our past
that make us feel destructive. Melissa, you and I are
tremendously alike, you know.'

At that she laughed, with real pleasure and amusement.

'Alas, I wish that were true. I'd love to be like you,
Adam.'

'I think you are. We have the same fears, and the same
longings. I think it's possible that we've played the
same games with people we wanted to love. I want to
learn to love you now without playing games. And from
the things you've said, I think you do too. Together we
might be able to learn. Can't we try?'

'Do you think it's ever possible to stop games that one
didn't even know one's been playing?'

'Yes,' he said and something in her responded to the
confidence in his voice. 'If we want to enough, we could
do it. I'm sure of that. Melissa, will you try with me?'

She leaned forwards and let herself rest, just for a
minute, against his shoulder.

Epilogue

A series of letters was written the following year.

Place des Vosges, Paris, May 5

My dear Joan,

This is by way of an apology, rather an Oxford Groupish thing to do, I'm afraid, but it seems necessary. You probably felt my hostility at all those Saturday lunches. Can I explain it? If you'd rather I didn't, then just throw this out without reading.

You seemed to be telling me then that I was mad and bad and ought to do something about it. That made me cross. When I started to look back, after all the débâcles last year, I began to see that you'd been warning me about the dragons that lurked in the terra incognita *of my subconscious. Since then I've seen and understood a bit more.*

Adam's been telling me for ages that if I can let myself really look at the dragons, get to know them, they won't be so frightening. They were dangerous once, *but what can they do to me now? I was petrified of them (and therefore angry when you referred to their existence, however obliquely) and so I pretended they didn't exist. Batty!*

Life is difficult as one gets to grips with this business of knowing – and, infinitely more difficult, being known – but we're working on it and it's beginning to look pretty good. I suppose you could say that Adam, like a true romantic hero, has been slaying dragons for me!

I hope all's well with you. My mother sends your news

with almost every letter and it sounds excellent. I'm glad the Directory *has had such success.*

Love, Melissa

Bradford-on-Avon

My dear Melissa

The hostility wasn't yours alone. Some of what you felt was mine. A lot of jealousy in there somewhere, and envy too. I know that you sometimes felt Abigail didn't let you in, but she let you a lot further than she's ever let anyone else. All I can ever do is guess and sometimes I guess very wrong and hurt her. Detestable!

I am glad that the dragons are not so fearsome as they were. I never thought they would be. Abigail seems well, though I think she misses you badly. I'm glad you write. Are you planning to come home? I know she would never ask and so I ask for her.

Love, Joan

Paris, May 10

Dearest Mum,

We're on our way back. After a lot of discussion, Adam has accepted a new job from the beginning of the next academic year – at York. I'm still not certain what I'm going to do and whether I'll live with him up there or just visit. If the latter, they'll be pretty frequent visits. He is extraordinary, and we really do seem to have found a way to live that works for us both.

Long-range negotiations over the business have finally crystallized and I've sold it pretty well. Subject to your agreement, I'm probably going to sell the house, too. I still feel wobbly at the thought, but I think it's the right thing to do. Perhaps we could talk about it when I get back.

Thank you for everything; all your letters, of course, but everything before that as well. I can't wait to see you.

M

Melissa

It's all been too ghastly. Poor old Martin has buggered off at last and I'm terminally relieved – if deeply apologetic for the misery I caused you last year. I can't honestly imagine what had got into me (that sounds a bit ambiguous, but I expect you know what I mean), but it seemed frightfully important at the time. I'm glad you and Adam are OK. He sounds like a good friend as well as the kind of lover we all dream of. What a find! But you always were luckier than me. Can we meet some time?

All love, Cecily

Barnes, London

Dearest Daddy,

I hope you like the socks. Aunt Jane helped nit them, but they are still a bit holey. I'm not very good at niting. My new school's alright. I've got to write a report about what I did in the Easter holidays. I'm going to write about the bee lady. I wish we could come and see you. When will you let us?

Lots of love, Marianna

Wandsworth

My darling Marianna,

The socks are lovely. The other men in my room are all very envious. I think the colour is smashing. I'd love to see you and I miss you very much but it's not comfortable here and I don't want you to have to see it. Like your new school, it's not really too bad, and like you, I expect, I'm learning all sorts of things. We're putting on a play with a visiting director and so I'm keeping my hand in for later.

Will you give my love to the boys? And don't stop writing. Your letters are the best thing that happens to me. I'm glad Aunt Jane helps you. Try not to be frightened of her or your teachers or anyone.

Lots of love, Daddy

Place des Vosges, Paris, May 10

Dearest Abigail,

*As Melissa has probably told you, we're coming home.
Paris has been wonderful and this year at the Sorbonne very
instructive, but it'll be good to be back. I can't wait to see you.
I hope this year's honey harvest is going to be good. I'd love
to come and help if you need anyone. I saw your new article
in* The Beekeeper *and was very impressed.*

*Melissa is well. You can actually see the changes in her
(skin, eyes, the way she breathes, the way she stands), let
alone feel them. It's been a pretty hairy journey for both of us
one way and another, but – as I said – we're coming home.
I truly think we've both made it. I doubt if I could have got
there without her – or you. You've shown me how to make
peace with the past.*

Adam

Darling Melissa

*I'm so glad: glad that everything's looking better; and
glad that you're coming home.*

*I think you're right about the house in the Circus. It's
time to get rid of it and move on. You've had a rough time,
but the luck seems to be running your way again. Thank
goodness!*

I can't wait to see you. I've always loved you.

Abigail

THE END